Also by Peter Behrens

Night Driving
The Law of Dreams

THE
O'BRIENS

PETER BEHRENS

THE

O'BRIENS

A NOVEL

PANTHEON BOOKS
NEW YORK

Copyright © 2011 by Peter Behrens

All rights reserved. Published in the United States by Pantheon
Books, a division of Random House, Inc., New York. Originally
published in hardcover in Canada by House of Anansi Press,
Toronto, in 2011.

Pantheon Books and colophon are registered trademarks of
Random House, Inc.

Library of Congress Cataloging-in-Publication Data
Behrens, Peter, [date]
The O'Briens / Peter Behrens.
p.   cm.
ISBN 978-0-307-37993-1
1. Families—Canada—Fiction.   I. Title.
PR9199.3.B3769027 2012   813'54—dc23   2011029594

www.pantheonbooks.com

Jacket photograph © Superstock
Jacket design by Gray318

Printed in the United States of America
First United States Edition
2   4   6   8   9   7   5   3   1

for Basha and Henry

ACKNOWLEDGEMENTS

~

Jenny Mayher of Newcastle, Maine, was this story's earliest reader. Her viewpoint and suggestions were invaluable.

James Holland's interview with Geoffrey Wellum at http://www .secondworldwarforum.com/my-oral-history-archive/pilots-aircrew/ geoffrey-wellum/ was an inspiring resource for some of the letters in this book.

Thanks to the Canada Council and to the Lannan Foundation for their generous support.

Tháinig an gála,
shéid sé go láidir,
chuala do ghuth
ag glaoch orm sa toirneach.

The storm came,
blew with force,
I heard your voice
calling me through thunder.

— Nuala Ní Dhomhnaill,
from *"Cnámh* (Bone),"
translated by Michael Hartnett

Pontiac County and New York City,
1887–1904

Ashling

THE OLD PRIEST WALTZED with each of the O'Brien children while his pretty housekeeper, Mme Painchaud, operated the Victrola. She was a widow whose husband had been killed at the sawmill. Sliding the disc from its paper sleeve, she carefully placed it on the turntable and started turning the crank. As the needle settled onto the disc, a Strauss waltz began bleating from the machine's horn, which resembled, Joe O'Brien thought, some gigantic dark flower that bees would enter to sip nectar and rub fertile dust from their legs.

This was in Pontiac County, Quebec, in the early 1900s. The Pontiac. Most of the people up there were farmers, though it really was a fur country, a timber country, and perhaps never should have been farmed. People from the longhouse nations had skimmed through in birchbark canoes, taking game, taking beaver, never so much as scratching the meagre soil. Lumbermen had come for the white pine and moved on as soon as they had taken the choicest timber. The early settlers were Famine Irish, and French Canadians moving up from overcrowded parishes along the St. Lawrence: people hungry for land, with nowhere else to go.

The children dancing with the old priest were two sisters and three brothers, of whom Joe O'Brien was the oldest. There were stories that their grandfather had been a horse trader in New Mexico and a buffalo hunter in Rupert's Land before taking up a farm in Sheen Township and piloting log rafts on the Ottawa. Every few years he left his wife and children and went venturing, sometimes as far as California, once back to Ireland. One spring he did not return, and he was never seen again. One story said he had drowned at Cape Horn, another that he'd been robbed and murdered in Texas.

There was a restless instinct in the family, an appetite for geography and change. On St. Patrick's Day 1900, Joe's father, Michael O'Brien, left his wife and children and joined a regiment of cavalry being raised at Montreal to fight the Boers.

Joe O'Brien had inherited from his father the Black Irish colouring: pale skin, blue eyes, and jet black hair. The others—Grattan and Tom, Hope and Kate—were mostly fair (Hope was a redhead), with pale blue eyes and skin that was pink in winter, tawny in summer. They all had good teeth and long legs and rarely were ill. Their mother, Ellenora, had lived all her life in the clearings and knew the herbs growing wild, which mushrooms were safe to eat and which weren't, and by which streams the choicest fiddleheads could be found. She made sea pie, using every kind of wild meat. If a child took sick she brewed maroon tea with treebark and dried gooseberries. She made poultices from leaves, herbs, and scraps of cloth, and if someone had a fever she burned dried grass and brushed smoke over their heads, muttering spells using Algonquin and Irish words that no one, not even herself, really understood.

In the old priest's house the children were learning table manners and geometry as well as the waltz. And absorbing a way of seeing the world as a mystery—layered, rich. The old priest, Father Jeremiah Lillis, SJ, was a New York Irishman, short, barrel-chested, and nearly seventy when he came into the Pontiac. The remote parish was his first pastoral appointment. Before banishment to Canada he had been a scholar, a teacher, a dreamer. He had been sent into exile after it came to the attention of his superiors that certain funds belonging to the New York house were missing. In fact the old man had given away the order's money, as well as his own, to various men and women whom he loved. For these sins, and a few others, he had been dispatched to the Pontiac.

The stout little priest shaved infrequently, so the rasp of his cheek was always rough and sharp, and his breath smelled of cigars and sweet wine. Leading his partner, he would hum the melody, his shoes bussing the Tabriz carpet, building small static charges that sparkled at his fingertips.

On the train north, leafing through the *Relations* of Brébeuf and the other Jesuit martyrs, he had read of the seventeenth-century black robes sent as missionaries into the same country only to have their hearts eaten by Indians. By the time the train halted at the Canadian border he was in tears, and very tempted to disembark, but he had nowhere else to go. He had his trunks and crates and what remained of his collections of oil paintings and china, his table silver and beloved Persian carpets, but the Monsignor had sent him off without enough cash in his purse even for a return ticket to New York. So he remained aboard the train and came eventually to his remote and lonely parish, St. Jerome the Hermit, at Sheen, where he met Joe O'Brien during that first, awful northern summer of mosquitoes and forest fires, of air limned with smoke and smutted with cinders.

The black-haired boy had come by the rectory, selling firewood. "You'll want nine cords, Father. What I have is mostly beech, with some maple and birch and some pine. No spruce, guaranteed. Four dollars a cord, bucked into two-foot lengths, split, delivered, and stacked. You'll not get a better price."

Later the priest would decide that the young O'Briens, and even their haggard mother, had a strange, rough beauty. What was it about young Joe especially? The blackness, the pallor? The clear blue eyes? Was it the boy's gift for silence? On his own part, it wasn't lust. He had many times burned with lust, and he was done with it. At least, he would never again confuse it with love.

The priest was unpacking and shelving his books in the room he had decided to use for his study when Joe returned with a wagon and the first two cords. He began toting load after load of firewood up the rocky little path and into the woodshed, using a canvas sling and a tumpline around his forehead. Father Lillis had thought himself the loneliest person in the world, but watching Joe at work, he decided that the black-haired boy—in his silence, in the ferocious way he drove himself—might be even lonelier.

On the second day Joe got his two younger brothers at work on the stacking, but he did most of the carrying himself, the tumpline taut on his brow, neck muscles supporting the weight, body bent and braced. As if he were struggling down Broadway, the old priest thought, in the maw of a wicked wind. He brought out a jug of lemonade and insisted that Joe pause long enough to take a glass.

"Why so fast, lad? Now, what's the rush? You're killing yourself."

"It's easier to run than walk, Father."

The old priest believed in the accessibility of the spirit world, though the dogma of his own religion was against it. In Paris, in New York, and once in Worcester, Massachusetts, he had visited the sage-scented, candlelit parlours of table-rapping mediums. It was wicked and he risked burning in hell for his apostasy, but for much of his life he had been attending séances, wearing a cheap business suit as a disguise.

Perhaps the old priest was a fool for love. Or perhaps, as he hoped, exile and loss had clarified his vision. In any case, there it was: a black-haired boy; brackish, smoky air with shafts of nearly purple light falling between the shadows of big pines; and an old, disgraced priest feeling all of a sudden powerfully, mystically, spiritually needed. He gave himself permission to become the boy's father in spirit. Whether Joe ever recip-rocated, ever felt himself to be his son, was never clear to the old priest, who tried telling himself that it didn't matter.

~

Joe O'Brien was thirteen years old when his mother, Ellenora, received a letter from South Africa saying that her husband had been killed in a skirmish at a place called Geluk's Farm. She brooded all day without revealing anything to her children. Then, in the middle of the night, she woke Joe. "Your father is dead," she said. "Michael O'Brien is dead, and I'm alone with all of you, aren't I?"

Joe understood that his father had left his power behind, and that he, as eldest son, had inherited it. He believed this without having to think about it. The power was nothing supernatural or even extraordinary; it was just a sense of his own inner strength. It gave him self-confidence and boldness. And he wouldn't squander his power the way his father had; he would use it to protect them all.

Six months after her husband's death, Ellenora received a marriage proposal from Mick Heaney, who spoke a Pontiac dialect so warped and tangled with Irish and French-Canadian lingo that people in Ottawa, fifty miles downriver, had trouble understanding him. He was canny enough at trapping foxes and the rare beaver, and on summer evenings when the farmers' sons raced their traps and buggies on the good road between Campbell's Bay and Shawville—the only stretch of graded road in the county—he might earn a few dollars setting odds and holding wagers. But Mick Heaney was best known as a fiddler; he played at weddings and wakes on both sides of the river, unreeling tunes faster than the wind rushed through the pines in breakup season. "Angel Death No Mercy" was the name of one famous jig he played. "The Cheticamp Jig" and "Road to Boston" were others.

When facing a decision, Ellenora always consulted a wise woman who lived on the other side of the river and owned a blue bottle she claimed to see the future in. The woman told Ellenora that for a widow with five children any man was better than no man at all. So she married Mick Heaney, but she never asked the children to think of him as their father or show him any more respect than he was worth—which was, as far as Joe was concerned, very little.

At weddings and wakes Mick would start things by drawing two or three scrapes as piercing and bitter as the scream of a bucksaw pinched in a green log. Then he would pause, wet his fingers in his mouth, and demand another cup of whisky-blanc before launching into the reel. Once he got going he'd play tune after tune, pausing only to gulp liquor or sip cold water from a ladle. For years he had fiddled at nearly every wedding and funeral in the Pontiac, whether people wanted him to or not. There was a restless spirit in Mick Heaney, a dark spirit; the tunes came in hot, ferocious spurts and would not be denied. At wakes he played so fiercely that his fingertips bled, crusted, and bled again. After fiddling all night he would follow the coffin to church in the morning, then stroll up and down the rows of pine slabs and crosses, sawing away while the priest inside was saying the funeral Mass. When the coffin was carried out and lowered into its grave, Mick always played at his quickest tempo, the frenzy of the music jabbing at priests and mourners, at grief, at death itself.

No one could tell Mick Heaney to stop playing. At one early summer wedding at Fort William, he struck up as the bride and her elderly groom were leaving the chapel. He fiddled through the wedding breakfast, the afternoon sleep, and the evening refreshments, and was still playing at midnight when the shivaree bachelors arrived. After dragging the nuptial couple from their marriage bed, the bachelors—accompanied by neighbours gripping pine-tar torches, wives beating pans, children howling, and Mick Heaney—led them out to witness the bull put to the cow, the stallion put to the mare. The mare rejected the stallion and turned to bite the forearm of the bachelor holding her. She shouldered him, nearly knocked him down, and then nipped him again. Both horses broke free and began screaming and flaring their lips, kicking their heels and intimidating the bachelors—mostly town men from Shawville, Campbell's Bay, and Pembroke, whose gamy banter could not conceal their fear. The young bride was sobbing while her elderly groom, dazed and bloody-nosed, puffed a cigar, and everyone recognized that the shivaree was finished, spent. Weary neighbours began climbing into wagons and traps.

The thing was over, except that Mick Heaney—who never could or would recognize any limit to anything—was still playing. He seemed to need to live unbound by custom, habit, expectation: a life perfectly organized to cause trouble for everyone it touched. All that night he wandered the farm, playing one tune after another. Whenever a bowstring broke, he replaced it from a spool of horsehair in his pocket and kept on fiddling. At dawn, with relatives of the bride threatening to drown him in the Ottawa River, he walked away from Fort William still playing. For days he was heard and occasionally seen wandering the range roads, fiddling for audiences of white pine and eagles, moose, bear, and lynx. Bush loggers heard jigs wafting over their timber slash, across burnt-over ground, through stands of birch and spruce, alder and pine. Farmers milking caught traces of "The Road to Fort Coulonge" drifting across their hay meadows and over bottomlands planted in corn. When a Portuguese section gang encountered Mick along the Pontiac and Pacific Junction right-of-way, he was playing a jig. The labourers dropped tools and began crossing themselves, and the ganger threatened Mick with a beating, but he just strolled off into the bush, still fiddling.

He returned home after ten days of wandering, playing "Banish Misfortune" as he sauntered into the yard. After setting his fiddle down on the porch, he went into the shed, milked the cow, and washed his face and hands in the warm milk. Entering the house, he slapped Ellenora's face for a greeting, then took to his bed for a month. He did not touch the bow again until the Christmas Eve *réveillon*.

~

The old priest was the first person to recognize that Joe O'Brien needed to escape that world up there. Watching the boy sling loads of firewood with the tumpline was like watching an animal that would gnaw its way out of a trap or destroy itself trying. But it was no use trying to educate Joe apart from his younger brothers and sisters; their bond of family loyalty was too strong. If he would help Joe, the old priest knew he had to help them all, so he began inviting the whole bunch to stop at his house after school for lessons in geometry, table manners, and German. He had them memorize and recite poetry to each other so they would learn to speak clearly and forcefully. And he taught them the waltz.

It wasn't that he loved the dance. He did, but that wasn't the point. To waltz in the backwoods, and do it well, broke every notion of what was useful or possible. What he was trying to teach was courage.

Apart from their studies at the priest's house, the children were taught catechism, arithmetic, British history, and penmanship at the Catholic school. Joe knew they could not afford to look as poor as they were, so he spent firewood money buying decent clothes from the Eaton's catalogue. He had one good white shirt and two celluloid collars that his father had left behind, and his father's horse boots, which had been returned from South Africa courtesy of the regiment, along with a belt, a knife, and an empty billfold.

The capitalists who leased the Pontiac's magnificent white pine forests from the Crown lived in Montreal, New York, and London, but there was also a local hierarchy, with Father Jeremiah Lillis, SJ, near the top and the O'Briens near the bottom. Joe understood how much better it was near the top than the bottom each time Mme Painchaud served them crumpets and blueberry jam while they worked at geometry proofs in the priest's cozy study or recited the poems of Alfred Lord Tennyson and Henry Wadsworth Longfellow.

There was life in layers in the priest's house, an atmosphere of incipient surprise. Persian carpets covered pine boards in a voluptuous mottle of red, purple, and gold. Small, dark oil paintings bought in Cologne, Louvain, and Rome hung on the walls. Father Lillis had sent a few paintings to auction at Montreal and spent the money on stained glass windows for his study and dining room. Rich shards of colour broke through those exuberant windows, and exotic scents—silver polish, English tobacco, China tea—drifted though the chiaroscuro rooms. The air was denser there, more laden than the pellucid, astringent atmosphere of the spruce clearings; in that light, even young children could pronounce German poetry and leaf through New York and London magazines.

They were encouraged to tell stories and make jokes. They learned to laugh in a way impossible at home, with the ghost of their father and their mother's stricken demeanour. Their own language became a supple, bending thing for them. It was in the priest's house that Joe began awarding nicknames. Grattan became "Sojer Boy" because he liked to wear their father's belt buckle with its regimental crest. Tom loved to serve at Mass, so he became "Priesteen" or, more often, "the Little Priest." Both girls said they wanted to become nuns, and Joe nicknamed rambunctious Hope "Sister Merry Precious Aloysius," while dainty little Kate was "Sister Peevish Sacred Sublime." The little girls loved organizing rituals in the woods, draping a tablecloth over a tree stump for an altar where the Little Priest could say Mass. Pouring spring water from a birchbark cup, the Little Priest baptized dolls Joe had made for the girls out of straw, moss, and scraps of moose hide.

No one ever called Joe anything but Joe, except their mother, who, when distracted or ill, sometimes called him Michael.

From the start, the priest ordered them to imagine lives elsewhere. "Plan on getting out of here," he kept telling them. Learning the waltz was learning to live outside what they knew, a rehearsal, practice. Waltzing had always been the old priest's exercise of defiance, of his own grace and strength, as well as his assuage of loneliness, and to Joe it became a suggestion that life might hold more than one room—even a gorgeous room in a priest's house—could possibly contain. The lush strangeness of the music stimulated his ambition and determination, qualities that sometimes tasted like steel in his mouth.

There were perch and shad in the Ottawa, trout in some of the streams. In winter Joe and his brothers sometimes chipped through eighteen grey inches of ice before they could drop their fishhooks. There were ducks in the autumn, and woodcock and partridge. Beaver had been trapped out. As for game, there were few deer left in the Pontiac. In spring, moose tormented by blackflies went splashing into the river and sometimes were carried off by the current and drowned.

Joe raised a beef every year and cut and sold firewood. Sojer Boy ran sheep, the Little Priest kept pigs. The girls tended the milk cow and dug a potato garden every summer. They gathered wild strawberries in June and blueberries in July, raspberries and blackberries later in the summer. They sowed wheat or rye and had meadows good for one cut of hay.

Their stepfather was just another mouth to feed, and when he drank he was brutal, but he was absent for weeks at a time. The only other good thing about Mick Heaney was that his seed was infertile, so Ellenora did not bear any more children to share in what little they had.

~

When he was fifteen, Joe knew his mother was exhausted. There were days she hadn't the strength to get out of bed. That winter, using firewood money, he leased timber rights for fifty cents an acre on forty acres controlled by the parish, and he contracted to supply logs at such-and-such a price to a pulp mill downriver. The mill buyer told Joe he was too young to sign a contract, so he had Ellenora sign, with the priest adding his name as guarantor. Joe and his brothers spent the next four months felling and limbing leftover spruce into logs that they skidded over ice trails to the banks of the Ottawa. They saw no money until breakup season, when the logs were rafted downstream in big booms that undulated like something alive, like the skin of the river.

When Joe finally received a cheque, he was able to pay himself and his brothers wages for their winter's work and show a net profit of nearly one hundred dollars. The winter after that, he obtained timber leases on 320 acres that had been stripped of their valuable white pine, hiring neighbours with horse teams to harvest pulp logs from the tangled second growth of alders, birch, and spruce. He opened a savings account at the Imperial Bank of Commerce branch in Shawville and became the

Township of Sheen's first newspaper subscriber, after taking out a mail subscription to the *Ottawa Citizen*. Whenever he went to Ottawa to see the pulp buyers, he brought back crates of oranges for his brothers and sisters, an unheard-of luxury in the clearings.

The next year he arranged to lease 1,280 acres. He rode the P&PJ to Ottawa City, bought himself a new pair of caulk boots, and hired thirty French-Canadian and Austrian lumberjacks from taverns in By Ward. When he returned, he was kept so busy dealing with his jacks, provisioners, and pulp buyers, not to mention temperamental camp cooks, that he did no sawing himself and never wore the new caulks. Instead he cleared out a log hut to use for an office, installing a window, stove, lanterns, table, and stool, ordered himself three white cotton shirts from Eaton's catalogue, and took to wearing neckties and even, sometimes, a green eyeshade. He found he enjoyed the scratch of pen on paper, the scent of ink, the columns of figures in his own clear hand adding up to a profit.

He was seventeen. The business had developed from nothing, nourished by his talent for organization and desire to provide for his mother and his siblings, and by the fury he felt whenever he thought of his stepfather, which made him restless and meticulous.

It was a harsh world in the bush. Because he was considered a boy when he started, he could not afford to stand disrespect. He hired rough, crude men and had to rule his camps. More than once he had to use his fists or a stick of wood, or whatever was handy. He prevailed because he was lithe and quick, and because he had to. He still went to the priest's house whenever he could, but there was no more time for jokes, for nicknames, for little girls' doll parties.

Two or three times a week he snowshoed into the bush, following trails used by wolves more than people. From a quarter-mile away he could hear axes ringing and the bite of the saws, and the noise gave him a sense of his own worth, as nothing else ever had in the years since his father had left them.

The old priest's house had stimulated Joe, allowing him to imagine riches, style, a singing depth of life. Now he had a business of his own and felt its spirit like a half-broke horse between his legs. He loved being alone in his hut, perched on a stool: ledger spread open, a fire snapping in the Quebec heater, the light of the frozen woods gleaming outside. Marking and turning pages in the ledgers gave him a beautiful sense of control. He knew that the stronger he was, the stronger they all would be.

That winter his mother's strength was tearing in a dozen places all at once. Dry in the hips, weak in the limbs, Ellenora was letting go of her life. Sitting on her bed, her daughters fed her spoonfuls of water with apple juice, buttered bread, and mutton cut up into small pink cubes she could barely swallow.

One evening Ellenora asked Joe to drag out a leather portmanteau from under her bed. After digging into it, she wordlessly handed him a letter from a man in Montreal who claimed to have served in the Transvaal with his father and wanted to be repaid seventeen dollars Michael had borrowed from him.

A dept of honour and I would forgive it of pore Michael but there is a wife my own and children, in circomstances, coud you if possible send it there way please.

There was an address on Sebastopol Street in Montreal, and Joe wrote a cheque that night and walked all the way to Fort Coulonge the next day to put it in the post. Trudging home, he could feel money's heft and flex, what it might do for a man and for those near him.

One afternoon near the end of that winter, he was working on his accounts when Grattan and Tom came out to the log hut and told him that Mick Heaney had been putting his hands up the girls' dresses and feeling their private parts. Apparently it had been going on for months, but Hope, twelve, had been too embarrassed to say anything until she realized that their stepfather was also bothering little Kate, who was so frightened she had been wetting their bed.

They all knew something about the sex urge, at least in animals. They had seen shivaree bachelors waving bloody sheets from newlyweds' windows. At weddings and at wakes they were used to seeing rowdies fighting, usually over a girl, and Joe had felt compulsions of which he was ashamed spilling inside his head like porridge boiling over on a stove.

Joe was hurt that Hope had gone to Grattan instead of coming to him, as eldest brother, but he had already sensed that his sisters were a little afraid of him. As boss of a timber gang, he had grown accustomed to giving sharp orders and being instantly obeyed. He could sound ferocious.

He considered consulting the old priest, then figured that the fewer the people who knew, the less it would harm the girls.

"Have you told Mother?"

"I haven't," Grattan replied.

"Don't. We handle this ourselves, alone."

"How?"

"Not sure. I'll figure out something." The outline of a plan was already taking shape in his mind. "Mother doesn't need more trouble. Anyway, she couldn't make him stop."

"What can we do, then?"

"We'll make him stop."

Tom, the youngest brother, the Little Priest, gazed at Joe. "How?"

Joe shrugged. "There are three of us. Only one of him."

"But he's a man."

Tom looked as if the rolled neck of his sweater, which Ellenora had knitted for their father, could swallow him. It had come back in the box all the way from Cape Town, courtesy of the regiment, the oily wool smelling of sheep and flecked with crumbs of orange sawdust.

"Let me think it over," Joe told them.

At the supper table he watched his sisters. Hope was bright-eyed, freckled, and noisy. Kate, the youngest, was fair, and quieter. They wore new dresses paid for with pulpwood money. He wouldn't have been able to tell that anything was wrong with his sisters just by looking at them. Mick had been gone for days and was probably wandering the district, sleeping in sugar shacks and fiddling in taverns from Fort Coulonge to Shawville.

After supper Kate and Hope washed up while the brothers split and stacked a week's worth of stove wood. Then, kneeling around their mother's bed, they prayed a decade of the rosary while Ellenora lay with her head on a fresh linen pillowcase, reciting Hail Marys in a parched whisper, prayer beads knotted in bony fingers.

In the Pontiac it was common for people who fell sick in winter to die in spring. Once their mother was gone there would be nothing holding them to the country. Father Lillis had spoken to Hope and Kate about their vocations and had written to an old friend who was Mother Superior at the Visitation Convent in Ottawa.

"The Visitations are a very quiet bunch, Joe, unlike some orders I could mention. They'll welcome those girls of yours."

Whenever Joe brought home a crate of oranges, Grattan had always peeled off the colourful labels and pasted them in a scrapbook. When the old priest asked him, Grattan said that, more than anything else, he wanted to go to California.

"I'll write my Franciscan friends at Santa Barbara," the old priest told Joe. "We'll see if we can't find your boy something to land on. He has just enough polish, and he knows how to work, thanks to you."

The priest had already written on Tom's behalf to the Jesuits. When the time came, the Little Priest would start his scholastic training for the priesthood at St. John's College, which had recently started calling itself Fordham, in the Bronx, New York.

"I still have a few strings to pull, Joe, some reaching as far as Rome. A Jesuit in the family polishes the apple you'll hand to God."

The old man must have known he was hurting himself by sending the children away. But perhaps he felt he had no choice, not at his time of life, not after the sins he had committed. The O'Briens were his seeds and he was going to scatter them. They would be his sacrifice, his offering.

The younger children understood that the time was approaching when they would be cast into the world. In the meantime they needed to attend their mother, to hold on to her for as long as they could. When they finished saying the rosary, Hope untangled their mother's beads from her fingers and they each kissed her lips, which were dry and tasted of salts. Later, while the others slept, Joe lay awake, planning how to deal with his stepfather. It would be best for family solidarity if Grattan and Tom took a hand.

For once he was impatient for his stepfather's return, and impatience kept him awake. When he tried to sleep, his thoughts fluttered on wings of their own, like birds caught in a house. It was possible Mick had been beaten up, even killed, in some tavern brawl—there were plenty of people, on both sides of the river, who had a score to settle. Maybe he was lying in a ditch somewhere, drunk or dead.

Restlessness pumped a kind of acid through nerves and muscle, and Joe couldn't keep from thrashing his limbs, from beating his pillow, from twisting and bunching his blankets. When he finally slept, he dreamed of a horse galloping across the river at breakup, ice slabs buckling under the pressure and rearing up in hunks to slash at the animal's legs. He awoke panting and lay in the dark with eyes open, not moving, waiting for the anxiety stirred by the dream to subside before he got out of bed, pulled on his clothes, and awakened his brothers. As he pulled on his boots he remembered watching his father put on his own boots; the memory was just an image of powerful hands and fingers drawing yellow rawhide laces tight. Joe shook his head. Dreams and memories never really added up, and he had always tried to leave them in the bedroom as coldly as he could, not to waste daylight worrying about them.

Before Tom and Grattan left for school, the three of them collected axe handles, staves, and rope and stored them in the cowshed. But Mick did not show that day, and the rest of the week didn't see his shadow either. In the bright, cold March afternoons Joe tied on snowshoes and trudged out to count and mark the pulpwood neatly stacked along the banks of the Ottawa, acres of forest transformed into piles of raw logs. He stood to make a good profit, but that week found him making elementary mistakes in his accounts, strewing pages of his ledger with smudges and blots resembling the spoor of some animal from the deep woods—a wolverine, or a lynx.

Joe was confident that he possessed the qualities needed for business success, and he was determined one day to have a family of his own. He knew the religious life was not for him; nonetheless, he could not stop feeling envious of the careful arrangements Father Lillis had been making for his brothers and sisters.

"What about me? Can you not found an order that would have me, Father?" He kept his tone light, so the old priest would think he was joking. Perhaps it was an eldest brother's instinct to dominate in all realms that made him wish the old priest saw in him too the makings of a Jesuit, or at least a Franciscan.

"Leave vocations for the others, Joe." Father Lillis swallowed a piece of muffin, then used a damask napkin to wipe the buttery crumbs from his lips. "Holy Mother Church ain't what she used to be. How many fellows on your payroll this winter?"

"I got sixty-one."

"Horses?"

"Most days, twenty. You think I ought to stay in the bush? Is that what you're telling me? That this is all I'm good for?"

"I don't say so! A fellow like you, with plenty of go, doesn't require an old Father writing letters on his behalf. Do you more harm than good. Follow your own nose, Joe. Stick with your business way of thinking and you'll do well for yourself."

In fact the old priest had not been able to write any letters of introduction on Joe's behalf. He had tried, but after a few lines he was overcome with tears and a sense of desolation so palpable he could touch it. The priest recognized that this was his own death coming. He was seventy-four by then, short of breath; two or three more Pontiac winters would wear him out and the spring would carry him away.

At seventeen Joe wasn't tall and never would be. He was no longer slender, no longer a beautiful boy. He was stocky and tough. Everything about him, though, was meticulous. The quick blue eyes, the black hair, the pallor—Joe was a piece of energy, and the priest was certain anyone with half a brain could read the aptitude behind those eyes. Joe O'Brien didn't need an old Jesuit of tumultuous repute writing tear-stained testimonials on his behalf.

Joe had, in fact, been following a series of articles in the *Ottawa Citizen* about the latest railway boom out west. General contractors and subs, mostly Scotchmen or up from the States, were laying hundreds of miles of branch and spur lines across newly opened wheat country on the far prairies—"the Last, Best West," the newspaper called it, "Breadbasket of the British Empire"—while a second and third line through the sea of British Columbia mountains to the Pacific were being planned. It seemed clear there was opportunity out there for someone used to organizing gangs of men and working them hard, but he had always had a lurking sense that if he left the Pontiac for good, he would disappear. Not just lose touch with what was left of his family but also lose himself. The world had taken his father and not given him back.

Maybe it was just the shyness of the ill-born. He'd grown up in the backwoods, after all, and felt strong enough there; but his strength might not carry elsewhere. He figured he would stick it out in the Pontiac after his mother died and the others left to take up the lives the priest had designed for them. His brothers and sisters had grown up believing their mother's fairy stories. Believing the future was in a blue bottle. They loved talking about their dreams, the way she did; but dream talk and fairy stories had never made sense to Joe, and he'd shut them out of his mind, like troublesome insects.

There was enough scope for his ambition in the Pontiac. Pulp logging was money to count on until he had sufficient capital to enter the lumber trade, where solid fortunes were still being made. When he made his, he'd build himself a mansion house of stone or brick, like those he'd seen at Bryson, Renfrew, and Ottawa. And yet: it was astonishing to read that some railway contracts through the Rockies were being let out at eighty-five thousand dollars per mile.

Spring filtered slowly into the Pontiac that year. Some days, looking up, Joe saw patterns of geese winging north in a soft blue sky, and the air had a sweetness and smelled of mud. He postponed the future and waited for Mick Heaney to show up, and watched his mother dying.

Ellenora took no food and only a little water. The girls washed her every afternoon with soft yellow sponges and rubbed an ointment made from fat and mashed herbs on her sprouting bedsores. On the first of April it snowed a foot, and the old priest, wrapped in a buffalo robe and complaining bitterly of the cold, rode out from Sheenboro on a sleigh, heard Ellenora's confession, and offered her the sacrament of extreme unction. She refused to see a doctor, and no one knew how much longer she would last. The wise woman with her blue bottle had been dead for years.

The morning after the priest's visit, Hope was hanging laundry on the porch when she caught sight of Mick Heaney coming up the road, and she hurried inside to tell Joe. Their stepfather had set his fiddle down on the porch and was pissing in a snowbank when Joe came up behind him, threw a harness strap over him, and knocked him down.

Kate and Hope, shawls around their heads, breathing steam into the chilly air, watched Tom and Grattan kneel on Mick's chest and Joe wrap his wrists and ankles with the same thick cord they used for tying up hogs and sheep. It had started snowing in large, wet flakes.

Lemme gah, yuh sons a' bitches.

They tried to carry Mick into the barn but he writhed and bucked so frantically they dropped him on the frozen mud, where he lay snapping like a turtle, eyes violet against the skin of fresh snow.

Tear yuh lip to hole, yuh crowd a' skunks.

"Come on, boys, let's pick him up," Joe ordered.

Tom stood back, looking worried. "Do you really think we ought to?"

"Yeah, Joe, are you sure?" asked Grattan.

Ah'll fuckin crack the jaysus outta yuh. Lemme gah.

Joe kicked Mick in the ribs, hard. Mick grunted and sucked breath, too startled to scream.

"Listen," Joe said. Hunkering down, he caught the acrid stink of Mick's breath. Their stepfather was flopping like a fresh-caught trout, sucking and biting air.

"We don't care if you live or die," Joe said softly. "There isn't anyone to hear you, and no one to care if they did. So save your breath."

Mick stopped writhing and lay still. The whites of his eyes were stained yellow, his nose and cheeks strewn with a raw lacework of red and purple veins.

Joe stood up and glanced at his sisters on the porch, wrapped in their shawls, fine faces pale with cold. His sisters' thoughts and desires had always been obscure to him, as unknowable as the mental lives of animals, but he felt packed, latent, charged by his responsibility to protect them.

Tom and Grattan were rubbing their feet on the ground like nervous cattle.

"Boys," Joe said, "this is the first of many."

Using the toe of his boot, he rolled Mick onto his stomach, then kicked as hard as he could. Mick yelped.

"You know what that's for. Stay off those girls."

The snow was changing to a hissing, freezing rain. Powerful spring storms would soon be breaking down the last hunks of old snow, skid roads would be turning to mud, and another season in the woods would be over. Joe could smell open ground somewhere. If his father had not been killed in a skirmish on an African farm none of this would be happening. *This day,* he thought, *might not exist.*

Mick snuffled. Joe pressed his boot firmly between his stepfather's shoulder blades to prevent him rolling over or trying to stand up.

It was the sort of day when a horse might slip on the skid road and break a leg. Rain would lacquer bare branches with drippings of silver, and soon it would be mud season, when nothing moved, when the ice on the river was too soft to bear weight, when everything was an argument for staying put, counting up, waiting. The whole country locked down under a kind of mystery.

"You next, Little Priest. Everyone must take a crack," Joe said.

Tom stopped scratching the ground with his boot and gazed down at their stepfather. On the porch the two girls had clasped hands.

"Go on. Give him one, but hard."

But Tom still hesitated.

Joe squatted, seizing a handful of Mick's hair. "Listen to me. Touch any one of us, and we'll do you worse and worse. We'll cut off your old pecker and put it up your nose."

Tom suppressed a wild giggle as Joe stood up.

"Now."

Tom stepped forward suddenly and booted Mick in his haunches. Mick screamed.

"Not hard enough," Joe said. "Now you, Sojer Boy. Give it to him good."

Grattan's kick was powerful enough to flop Mick over on his back, where he lay groaning and rubbing his face with his bound wrists in what looked like a pantomime of someone waking from a deep sleep.

"Let me try again, Joe," Tom said. "I didn't really get much of a piece of him."

Pig killing began that way. Slowly, almost shyly. Smoke and steam and nippy air. The tang of steel knives being honed. And ended, always, with frenzy, laughter and shouting, and black blood soaking the ground.

"Hold on until we get him in the shed," Joe said.

Mick was snuffling again.

"Cry all you want," Joe told him. "You'll still get what's coming."

Seizing Mick under his scrawny shoulders, Joe and Grattan began dragging him towards the barn while Tom ran ahead to let the cow out. They laid him down on the straw and shit, then picked up their axe handles and hefted them.

Joe struck first, then the others. Each blow made a smacking sound, like water bursting on rocks. Joe could hear his brothers breathing hard and see their breath fluting in the damp, chilly air. Tom was giggling and crying at the same time. Not all that different from a pig killing.

"That's enough," Joe said finally. "Stop."

Mick lay gurgling in the straw, lips split like overripe berries. Pink blood foamed at his nostrils. He had soiled himself, and the air stank of excrement and blood. Reaching down, Joe seized Mick's wet shirt-front. The backs of his hands had green bruises, big as walnuts. He was weeping.

Standing in the muddy shed with the rain hissing outside and his stepfather flopping like a broken bird at his feet, Joe felt a heightened awareness of the world, its patterns of noise, light, and smell, and at the same time he saw his life's path with new clarity and vivacity. He would not stay in this country, this forest, the watershed of the Ottawa. It was dark and restricted. He would head out west and take some position—junior clerk, say, or assistant purchasing agent—with one of the big railway contractors. Studying the business from the inside, he would see how money—eighty-five thousand per mile!—flowed through a big undertaking. Once he had learned the courses and channels money took, identified the dams and floods and leaks, he could assemble his own combination of men, money, machinery, and take on such works himself. Running timber gangs in the bush—sixty rugged fellows, half of them without a word of English—had taught him how to organize men, get the job done, and see a profit, always.

And out there he must find a sort of woman who was a better, finer person than he was, and win her somehow, make himself live up to her beauty and ideals and protect her and the family they would make together. He'd spend his love on her and their children, be profligate with love, and she would teach him all sorts of fine, delicate, harmonious things.

Ashling was his mother's word for a strong vision, the kind that came at you, slightly disordered, at moments when you were living on your feelings because you had nothing else to go by, when you'd stepped outside the rules and the regular tempo of life.

"Hear me now, you old buzzard." Joe slapped him until Mick stopped snuffling. "Come after us, lay a hand on any one in this family, I'll kill you and burn what's left on the trash heap, understand?"

Pulling off the harness strap, Joe threw it over a nail. Then, using his father's knife, he cut the cords binding Mick's hands and feet. They left him lying on the straw. Once they were outside, Joe herded his brothers towards the cabin.

"Do you think the fellow's alive, Joe?"

"Did we kill him?"

"I don't know and don't much care."

Joe sent the girls into their mother's room. Then he put the big kettle on the stove and he and his brothers stripped off their clothes. They were not accustomed to bathing in the morning, but all three stood together in the copper tub and scrubbed each other's backs. Joe and Grattan took turns sluicing the warm water over their heads. When he was clean and dry, Joe went out with a pail of water, a towel, a shirt, and twenty dollars he intended to give Mick, along with a warning to never again show his face. But the fiddle was gone from the porch and Mick was gone from the shed, leaving nothing behind but his blood on the straw.

∼

Ellenora died in late April, hemorrhaging and coughing blood. The girls washed the body and scrubbed the room, and that evening Joe went in to take his turn standing by the bed where the long, narrow frame of their mother lay, rosary beads twined through her fingers. Her face was yellow and lined, and it seemed to him that every part of her had shrunken except the nose and ears.

He had seen men nearly killed in fights and logging accidents, but his mother's was the first corpse he had seen, and apart from its stillness what struck him was how fragile, insubstantial, and temporary her body seemed. Ellenora's struggles and losses, her hard work and suffering, had developed from meagre flesh and sinew, a collection of fragile bones. It seemed extraordinary that a body could house the energy a mind produced, the secret powers to love and hate, forget and remember.

No one was interested in buying the farm in the clearing at any price. Joe sold the livestock and equipment at auction, plus his wall tents, cookstoves, and logging tools. He split the proceeds among his brothers and sisters but kept the profits his pulpwood operation had made, the seed of another business that must eventually stand behind them all.

Hope and Kate were bound for the Visitations in Ottawa. Grattan had a job offer from a wealthy Santa Barbara citrus grower, a benefactor of Father Lillis's Franciscans. Joe would accompany Tom to the Bronx and see him settled at Fordham, then head for Calgary via Chicago, Minneapolis, and Winnipeg.

On the morning they were all due to leave, Joe went out early and set fire to his little shed, then stood watching it burn to the ground with everything—ledgers, eyeshade, snowshoes, ink bottle—inside. He had wanted to burn the house down as well, but the others begged him not to. They were thinking they'd come back some day. Joe thought they wouldn't—who returns willingly to a place of sorrow?—but the place was still standing when they left in a hired wagon, the girls up front with the teamster, the brothers on straw bales, all of them wearing yellow kid gloves Joe had bought for a going-away present.

They stopped at the priest's house for breakfast. After the buckwheat pancakes, gooseberry jam, and hot, sweet coffee, Father Lillis asked Mme Painchaud to crank up the Victrola, and as the waltz poured from the horn—to Joe it sounded like a twitter of birdsong mixed into a rushing, galloping rhythm of panicked horses—they each took a turn flying around the room in the arms of the old priest.

Joe was last.

"God bless you, God bless you," the priest whispered.

"And you, Father."

The old man shuffled a few more steps, then laid his head on Joe's shoulder and began to sob. Holding him, Joe felt the priest's frailty, and in his own throat he felt a metallic soreness, which he reckoned must be love. He kissed the old man, and then they all bowed their heads to receive his blessing; Joe could hear the teamster outside stamping his boots impatiently and the horses whinnying for more hay.

They made one more stop, at the Catholic cemetery. The inscription on the granite slab Joe had ordered and paid for gave the facts of his parents' lives. Facts were all that were suitable for stone; anything else seemed vain and vainglorious. Their father's birth date wasn't mentioned because they didn't know it.

Ellenora Scanlon O'Brien,
Born 1870 Died 29th April 1904
Wife of
Miceál O'Brien,
Died 1900
Buried in S. Africa

The girls placed handfuls of tiny, pale wildflowers on the grave, and then they all climbed back aboard. They were only a couple of miles farther along when Joe heard the caw of a fiddle—and there was Mick Heaney stumbling out of the bush, a rancid grin on his face, plucking and sawing the instrument held in the crook of his arm.

Joe ordered the teamster to pick up the pace, but the man complained of heavy mud and said he wouldn't be winding his horses for the sake of a two-dollar trip. Joe was furious—with the teamster, with Mick Heaney, and most of all with himself for not burning the old place down to a heap of black char, broken glass, and ashes when he'd had the chance, because now he realized that Mick Heaney would saunter back to the clearing and dig himself in, selling timothy hay off their meadow, gathering berries from bushes they had tended and fertilized, shaking apples off their trees, living to a fetid old age pickled in raw whisky, and probably dying in the bed their mother had died in.

Fiddling furiously, Mick stumbled after the wagon. Joe yearned to throw something at him but there was nothing at hand. If he'd kept his rifle he might have issued a warning shot, sent a bullet snapping past his stepfather's ear, but the rifle had been sold along with everything else. He thought of jumping down to deliver another thrashing, but the teamster would spread the story—*Heaney and O'Brien! Battling in the mud like a pair of roosters!*—and Joe hated the thought of people laughing at him after he was gone. He struggled to contain his anger. No use dirtying his boots and staining the turn-ups of his trousers with the mud of the Pontiac, which he meant to escape cleanly, and forever.

Instead of looking back he studied his brothers and sisters. The Little Priest was reading a novel by Joseph Conrad; Sojer Boy had slipped off his kid gloves and was cleaning his fingernails with a bit of straw. Kate and Hope were chatting with the teamster. It was suddenly clear to him that his siblings did not share his sense of deprivation, or the fury that was inside him. The strains of "Bonaparte's Retreat" gripped and taunted him, but to them the bleating, yapping fiddle was just the noise of something they were leaving behind. It had no claim on them. It was already slipping past, like the thin breeze and the stink of muskeg.

When he next looked back Mick had fallen a long way behind. The tune had faded like old snow deep in the woods in April. After another quarter-mile he couldn't hear anything, and when he looked back once more, there was nothing but trees, mud, and sky.

~

On the platform at Union Station in Ottawa they huddled together, sharing for the last time a sense of belonging to each other. He and the Little Priest were ticketed for New York with a change at Montreal, and their train was leaving immediately. Grattan would be escorting Hope and Kate to the Visitations, then catching an evening train for Toronto, Chicago, and California.

Before Joe and Tom boarded, Grattan presented them each with a twenty-five-cent cigar. "There you are, boys. Smoke the best!"

Joe felt his throat narrow once more with that metallic feeling as he shook hands with Sojer Boy. But he knew he had done his best for them. They were safe, and leaving behind the thin, acidic soil of the clearings. They were all on their way to richer ground. Hope and Kate were waving and laughing merrily as the locomotive chuffed steam and sucked air into its brakes and Negro porters hurried the last passengers aboard. The whistle howled, the engine gave a tug, steel couplings clanked up and down the length of the train, and the cars began rolling. Grattan and the girls ran alongside for a while, and Tom and Joe hung out the window and waved for as long as they could see them before falling into their seats.

At Montreal they boarded a Delaware and Hudson train. Later that night along the shore of Lake Champlain, while the Little Priest slept, Joe sat in the smoking car puffing his twenty-five-cent cigar, savouring a sense of majestic loneliness and freedom as the train raced south to New York City. He had done all he could to ensure that his brothers and sisters were safe and settled, but for himself he needed more than safety. He needed risks and danger and lots of room to grow, and that was why he would go out west.

~

Stepping onto the platform at Grand Central Depot at seven o'clock in the morning, Joe and the Little Priest were swept along in a herd of businessmen and handsome, well-dressed girls hurrying through the tunnels, riding up the electric stairs, and pouring out into a street howling with motor cabs and buses. Joe sensed energy and wanton danger. Eager for a glimpse of the ocean, he thought he smelled the tang of salt water on a bright breeze smacking up Lexington Avenue.

They both wanted breakfast. At a diner on Third Avenue they sat guarding their baggage at their feet while a Negro rattled handfuls of silverware on the counter and a waiter sloshed coffee into two mugs.

"Gosh, Joe, it all sure moves fast." The Little Priest spoke so softly Joe could barely hear him over the clatter. They had fed at cookhouses packed elbow to elbow with Frenchmen, but never in such a hectic, steamy place as this. Joe ordered ham and eggs for them both from a greasy menu card. Dozens of strangers were gulping coffee, cramming doughnuts into their mouths, and leaving nickel tips.

"Do you suppose it's like this in the Bronx, Joe?"

Looking at Tom, he noticed for the first time his resemblance to their mother. The Little Priest had always been an anxious child, shy of strangers and especially terrified of the bunkhouse men and hoboes who roamed the Pontiac in logging season. When he admitted he was afraid of being "stolen," Joe had reassured him that boys were never stolen except in the old stories of witches, Whiteboys, and roving spirits, but there was nothing much he could say to adjust the flame of such caustic anxiety. Nonetheless, the Little Priest had slept soundly aboard the train while Joe sat up the whole night, watching the dark country flash by, and the quick, yellow-lit platforms of upstate towns. And the Little Priest was now eating ham and eggs with gusto—Joe had observed that his brother's anxieties rarely interfered with his appetite.

"I guess you'll get used to it," Joe said.

New Yorkers swam in the noise and rush of the diner as naturally as trout in a swift stream. The brazen babble of voices, the clatter of dishes, the florid steam of a dozen steel coffee urns—it was all ordinary and entirely normal as far as these people were concerned, a complex of violent sensualities so commonplace that their faces looked, if anything, bored.

Unfolding a sheet of gilt-edged cream notepaper, Joe checked Father Lillis's instructions, which were written in thick black cursive.

N.Y. to St. John's College, Fordham, The Bronx.
Strongly advise take Harlem North train. Check sched. on G.C.
board. Costs more than 3rd Ave. El but direct to Fordham Sta. without
change. Same route return G.C. Depot.

Penn Central Depot, Hoboken, N.J.
(for Chicago w. connect. for Minneapolis w. connect. for Winnipeg)
From G.C.D. 3rd Avenue El, so. to 14th Street.
14th Ave. car. w. to end of line. Walk so. to 10th St. Pier &
Penn. Central Ferry crossing Hudson R.

If overnight in N.Y.
Society of Jesus, 39 E. 83rd St.
Show this note. They will give you a bed.

> *Your Father in Christ,*
> *Jeremiah Lillis, S.J.*

After breakfast they hurried back to Grand Central. The pace of the city forced everyone to speed, and it was impossible for them not to hurry. Clearly, though, some people had dropped out of the race. Vagabonds lay on the sidewalks, smothered in humps of rags. At the corner of 42nd Street and Fifth Avenue a burly woman with a face like a purple pumpkin and slits for eyes held out a tin cup, the crowd streaming around her as if she were a rock in a river,

> *Help Me*
> *I am Blind*

scrawled on cardboard hung around her neck.

At the depot Joe looked up at the board and found a Harlem North train leaving in seven minutes. They raced through the tunnels and boarded it just in time. Their car was nearly empty, and they both claimed window seats just as the train started to roll. Soon it had left the tunnels and was running along elevated tracks. Joe stared down at long avenues hectic with horse cars and omnibuses, with children dodging traffic and boys at every street corner standing on crates, hawking newspapers. Streets flashed by in swords of light, offering glimpses of the shiny East River. Women with bare arms leaned out the windows of tenements, panting in the heat, so near Joe felt he could almost touch them. There was something charged and warm about such relentless, impersonal intimacy. Hundreds of people eating breakfast in tiny kitchens, with no one bothering to look up as the train rumbled past.

There were houses full of whores in Ottawa, women of all nationalities. He had overheard his cooks and bunkhouse men talk of whores who'd do anything for a dollar—and three dollars bought a fellow the whole night. This city was probably full of such women. He could certainly afford the money. But anyone with three dollars could have a whore, and it was purity that attracted him, purity and cleanliness. He must have the sort of clean girl whose family wouldn't let her have anything to do with a fellow from the clearings. Not until he had made something of himself, done something powerful—and even then they'd be wary.

He glanced at his brother across the aisle. The Little Priest was fast asleep, head thrown back, mouth wide open.

The train crossed the black ribbon of the Harlem River, more or less saltwater, Joe figured, and therefore an arm of the sea, which joined everything and separated everything: the rim of the world.

For many months after his father's disappearance Joe had imagined him still alive in their house—living there in secret, hiding out behind the walls. Putting his ear to the plaster when no one was watching, Joe would listen for sounds through the whitewash and lath, through wadded insulation of horsehair and crumpled newspapers. Of course, all he'd ever heard was the scrabbling of mice.

He would be making his own way from now on, teaching himself what he needed to learn. No need of ghosts rattling inside the walls. No need of anyone. He knew how to hold himself within himself. A fellow needed a good hard shell to survive. It was important to be able to see things as they were.

~

The morning had thickened into a blaze of spring heat by the time the Harlem North train deposited them on the sleepy platform of Fordham Station and slid away into the deeper mysteries of Westchester. In the Pontiac on such a warm spring day, the birches would be opening, unfurling bright leaves against the dark mass of fir and spruce. The Ottawa would be thick and sandy with runoff, the first brood of blackflies rising along replete streams.

And where was Mick Heaney now? Hard to imagine he still existed in the world.

"Joe!"

Joe looked around. The Little Priest had set down his grip on the pavement and was pulling out his handkerchief. Dabbing his face, he looked young and frightened. "I guess I don't want to be a priest after all. I want to go home, Joe. Can't we just go home?"

"Where? Where's home?"

The Little Priest gazed at him helplessly.

"Listen," Joe said. "Don't worry about the priesthood. You're not even a scholastic yet. No one's rushing you. You've got three years of novitiate."

"I don't care. I want to go home." His lower lip was trembling, and he stuttered his words.

"Mother's gone. There's not home no more." *And if you're going to cry*, Joe thought, *cry now. Cry in front of me, not in front of them. I won't hold it against you, but they will.*

"W-we can log next winter. I'd help you with the business."

"We're here, Tom. You must give the place a try."

"You'll leave me and I'll never see you again."

"Aw, sure you will. Come on. You're just tired. Here, let me." Joe reached down for his brother's grip. The Little Priest grabbed it and held on for a second, then gave it up, and they continued along the road. Joe saw the campus gates up ahead.

"C'mon, Priesteen." Joe smiled. "You'll probably be pope someday. Pope Priesteen the First—wouldn't that be something?"

~

After helping Tom unpack his things in a stark white cell, Joe said good-bye to his brother out on the Fordham lawn, where a bunch of boys were choosing sides for a game of baseball. In the Pontiac they'd played shinny when the wind blew the frozen bays clear, but never baseball. It was one of the rituals the Little Priest would have to learn.

They shook hands and then Tom turned away quickly, trying to hide his tears. Joe clapped him on the back and tried to say something funny, but his throat had seized up again. He turned and started walking across the dense, springy carpet of lawn. For a long time he could hear the players' shouts and the crack of the bat when someone hit the ball, but he didn't look back. He forced himself to notice the milky scent of clipped grass, the mustiness of elms still damp from a night's rain, the clatter of traffic along the Fordham road. The world operated through a kind of massive carelessness, it seemed. Part of being strong was being able to walk away when you had to. When there was no other choice.

He didn't look back once.

~

New York seethed with buying and selling, a grammar of shouts and argument backed by a chorus of screeching trolleys. From Grand Central Depot Joe walked over to Third Avenue and caught the El to 14th Street, where he bought two hot dogs with mustard from a street vendor and stood on the sidewalk munching, his grip between his feet. The danger was lively, intriguing, and he felt as spirited as a trotting horse.

Instead of catching a car along 14th he began walking west towards the Hudson. Was this how their father had felt after leaving them?

Weightless. Empty. If he threw himself under a streetcar the world would go on making noise.

A peddler was hawking hats from a stack. Joe tried hats on until he located a straw boater that fit. He paid two dollars for it and put it on at a rakish tilt, the way he'd seen other fellows wearing their straws.

It was a long way out to the river. The last blocks were mangy and bleak, with four-horse drays and motor trucks jerking in and out of warehouses, metal wheels clattering over cobblestones. There were slaughterhouses in the neighbourhood. He smelled blood and offal and heard the crying of animals. The city had a killer side.

At last he came out to the Hudson. Steamers with raked funnels, barges, and luggers with dirty sails were moving up, down, and across. The brilliant sheet of New York Bay opened to the south. The pungency of creosote, timbers, and low tide was exotic, exhilarating. A new world it was.

He started walking south past a set of ramshackle wharves. Streetwalkers stood at the corners and waited in bunches outside taverns. Their huge hats had little sprays of flowers attached, and they held Chinese umbrellas against the wild beat of the sun.

At the corner of 12th Street a girl hooked his arm and whispered, "Hey, sojer, fifty cents and we'll have a nice time." But he shook her off and kept walking, startled by the light in her pale green eyes.

He had more or less accepted the obligation to save himself for marriage, but it was stunning to realize that handsome, well-dressed women could be bought for little more than the cost of breakfast. Even stranger to think that the girl he must marry someday, who would bear his children, must be alive now somewhere, thinking and breathing, waiting for him without knowing who he was. As he waited for her.

He thought of the globe the old priest kept in his study. The Pontiac, no bigger than a speck of sawdust, was tucked into a bend of a thin, filigreed line labelled in minuscule letters: "Ottawa R." In those days the size of the world had been a relief to contemplate, however abstractly. Now it was anything but abstract.

Dirty gulls stalked the planking of the 10th Street pier. The ticket seller said he had just missed the Hoboken ferry. He could see it out in the river, thrashing its way across to New Jersey and the Penn Central Depot.

"Where are you headed, sir?" the ticket seller asked.

"Chicago."

"The four thirty-five? You'll still make your train. Next ferry's in an hour. Plenty of time."

Joe looked down at a small excursion steamer berthed on the downstream side of the pier, loading passengers—men in ice-cream suits and spats, women wearing summer dresses. Their chatter sounded gay and excited, as though it were Dominion Day or the Queen's Birthday and they were on a holiday excursion. The deckhands brown as bears.

A boy thrust a bill into Joe's hand—

O'CONNOR'S HOTEL,
W. Brighton Beach
Coney Island
SEASIDE ACCOMMODATIONS,
OCEAN VIEWS BATHING
All meals,
Reasonable.
STEAMERS DEPART & RETURN 10TH ST. PIER
ON THE HOUR

As he watched the last people boarding the little steamer, its whistle spat two impatient shrieks.

No one was waiting for him across the river. No one in Chicago, Minneapolis, Winnipeg, or Calgary. Once he reached the West he would have to start becoming someone, to build something out of nothing. Out of the Pontiac, the backbone of hardship, the memory of rough hands tying bootlaces. These things were all that held him together now.

He wanted to be alone with himself, to block out the world for a few days. He'd come out stronger; he knew he would.

Picking up his grip, he hurried down the steep ramp and boarded the little paddlewheeler. After paying the fifty-cent fare, he went forward to stand in the bow. A moment later her lines were thrown and she backed off the wharf and began slipping downriver, past the black butts of wrecked piers.

The air was active, like steam gushing from a kettle. Joe watched flights of black ducks streaking over the surface of the bay as the little steamer slipped below the palisade of grey buildings that punched into Manhattan's sky like curled fists. Now no one knew him in the world, and he was both frightened and excited by his freedom.

~

On Coney Island he took a room at O'Connor's Hotel: four dollars a day, breakfast included, dinners extra. In flaring sunlight he walked the beach wearing his straw boater, carrying his shoes. Men and girls in bathing costumes hurtled into chilly waves. He bought a suit of bathing flannels, black. At a saloon on Surf Avenue he ate oysters, drank two cold mugs of Milwaukee beer, and thought of the girls whose fathers owned shops in Shawville or were professional men, girls he had never spoken to and never would see again.

He felt like a person without a name. It wasn't such a bad feeling.

Standing at the mahogany bar, foot on a brass rail, he bought a bottle of whisky without knowing exactly why and slipped it into his coat pocket. He had never liked the smell of whisky.

Surf Avenue blazed with thousands of electric lights. Ignoring the hawkers and shills at the arcades and freak shows, he walked back to his hotel, aware of the weight and pressure of the slender, curved bottle in his pocket.

He had left his window open, and the sheer curtains fluttered in the night breeze. Taking a notepad and pencil from a small leather secretary case, he drew up a chair alongside the window and sat down. He could see the Iron Pier, outlined in electric lights, and the black ocean beyond. Uncapping the whisky, he took a swallow. The taste was bitter, but satisfying in a violent way. He made himself take another drink, then opened the pad on his knee and started writing down the names of his ancestors. He didn't know many. Then the names of his parents and his brothers' and sisters' names, and their birth dates. At last he wrote down his own name, and on the next line

wife

then

sons

then

daughters

Then he began listing all the sums of money he had earned in his life, noting when and where he'd earned them, and whether as wages or profits. He listed his savings, and a valuation of every item in his grip, down to the spare collars and darned socks.

The room was a place out of time. Everything had paused, and he felt himself within himself, existing without struggle.

He kept picking up the slim bottle and taking short, sharp swallows. He could see Hope and Kate on the platform at Ottawa, waving, and Sojer Boy, brash and confident, and the Little Priest's pale face at Fordham.

Before he could finish adding up his columns, he had fallen asleep, waking an hour or so later slumped in the chair, the flimsy curtains brushing his face. The breeze through the window was damp with mist. Stumbling to the washstand, he splashed water, urinated into a night jar, undressed, and crashed into bed. His head was whirling, but for a few unclear moments he could nearly see the girl he would find, the one he'd marry—the clear one, the cool one, white hands and graceful neck, calm voice explaining everything. Body like a flower—that beautiful, that secret.

He awoke in the morning to a window painted white with glare he couldn't face; he had to turn away. He put on the bathing flannels and his coat over them, along with his hat and shoes. The mechanical elevator carried him silently down to the lobby and he marched across the broad verandah and down a flight of wooden steps onto the beach.

The sand was loose and walking was difficult until he reached the tide line, where the sand was still packed and moist. Slipping off his coat, he folded it neatly, placed it on top of his shoes, and walked down to confront the surf.

Wading out, he felt the cold biting at his feet, ankles, calves. When the water struck his thighs, he pitched himself into the next wave. The immersion was sharp and stinging. Swimming through the froth was a struggle but he managed to get out beyond the break, where the surface was calmer. He rolled over onto his back and shook his arms and legs, spinning droplets and splashing, tasting the salt on his lips and staring at the cold white moon still hanging in the sky.

If ever he could cut loose the past, this was where it could be done. Floating on his back in a rolling calm, he really didn't feel much of anything. Nothing about his brothers and sisters, anyway. Just the salt and the moon and the ocean swell. And a kind of exhilaration flickering, a small flame inside the curious heat of himself.

~

Each day on Coney Island began with Joe throwing himself into the ocean and ended with him sitting by the window in his hotel room with the Iron Pier and the dark sea before him, and the whisky.

During the day he plunged into waves and trudged up and down the beaches, staring out to sea. His skin darkened and his teeth and eyes glowed. Whenever he thought of the challenges and risks facing him, he felt daunted and afraid to start. The seashore and the hotel room: at certain moments he told himself these might be all and everything he needed from the world. He didn't really believe that, and most of the time he was perfectly aware they never could be, not for him, who wanted so much more—a wife and children, money and power in the world. But still, every day—every night—some shard of instinct, some whispering inner voice was inclined to stay out there forever. To hide. To freeze. To go no farther. To be content with the sea, the room, and silence.

He spoke to no one except waiters serving meals and barmen selling whisky. At the end of the week a mass of cold rain struck the shore. With the change of light and atmosphere he felt fresh resolve. Carrying the empty whisky bottles in a sack, he settled his hotel bill, then dumped the sack in a trash barrel on Surf Avenue, caught the steamer back to 10th Street, and rode the Penn Central ferry across to Hoboken, where he boarded a train for Chicago and the West.

VENICE BEACH, CALIFORNIA,

1912

The Orphan

I SEULT HAD SUFFERED from asthma in New Hampshire and was almost an invalid, but her health had improved when she had come out to California with her widowed mother, who was already ailing herself. In Pasadena Iseult, with her slender hips and full breasts, became almost beautiful—dark and glowing, her chestnut hair lightened by the sun. But after her mother died she thought of selling the Pasadena house and going to live by the seashore, where there were even fewer noxious weeds, where she could breathe cool ocean air.

She had read about Venice, California, in *The Examiner*. Mr. Abbot Kinney, an impresario, had drained marshes south of Santa Monica by digging a network of canals, and he was building houses where people could live in the style of the Venetian Renaissance. He'd also built a concrete boardwalk and amusement pier and convinced the Pacific Electric Railway to open a new route from Hill Street Station all the way out to the new community. Seaside Venice had already acquired a raffish, bohemian reputation, all by itself out there on the rim of the world where the white fog—the *marine layer*—was often bitter and deep.

On a bright winter Sunday six weeks after her mother's death, Iseult rode the electric cars into Los Angeles, then out to Venice. Thousands of people had come for the day, and with them she wandered the ocean-front promenade past a barn that billed itself the world's largest dance-hall, and another that called itself the world's largest roller-skating rink. On the pier a seafood restaurant was built to look like a ship. The vulgar, boisterous atmosphere was as far from Pasadena as she could imagine. She bought a hot dog and ate it while she watched grown men compete in a sandcastle-building contest.

Strolling out onto Fraser's Pier, past the Mystic Maze and the Panama Canal exhibit, she came to the Incubatorium. She had read about it in *The Examiner*: infants prematurely born were cared for there—and exhibited. A gaudy sign insisted

ONCE SEEN NEVER FORGOTTEN

while another declared

ALL THE WORLD LOVES A BABY!

Babies had been fascinating her lately. She was alone now; she was no one's daughter and sick to death of her supposedly delicate health. And she was not fooled by her own good manners and niceness, though others might be. She knew just what a raging, self-conscious, desirous little beast she really was.

When Iseult was twenty, her beloved father—a scholar by temperament, a mill owner by inheritance, a New England gentleman of the old school—had killed himself. He'd never had to struggle with anything other than his own disposition and native sorrow, but it had been too much for him all the same.

In Pasadena in the weeks following her mother's death, she had felt like a worn-out flag snapping in the wind, a forgotten banner signifying nothing. She wanted something and didn't know what, something bigger than herself that was also in some way latent. She had often—more so since her remaining parent had died—imagined having a strong, coarse man in her bed, holding him there. Roughness seemed a kind of strength to her.

Desire was like that: frightening and promising, though the most she had been able to do so far was stare at the ceiling and touch herself in a way that thrilled, embarrassed, and frustrated her.

She paid her quarter to the ticket seller, who wore a starched white cap and apron like a nurse. Once inside, Iseult found herself peering through a window into a large, bright white room where a dozen incubator machines were arranged in two rows. The numbered incubators looked like iceboxes or small kitchen ranges of shiny white enamel, with steel fittings and glass doors. As she watched, a nurse opened one machine—number thirteen—and extracted a baby no bigger than a loaf of bread, with morsels of red hair on its head.

Iseult watched, fascinated, as the nurse unwrapped the baby from its swaddling, then tried to feed it by spilling liquid into its nose with a narrow spoon. Most of the liquid, whatever it was, seemed to run off down its chin.

She was standing so close to the observation window she could smell her breath clouding the glass. The smallness of the life she was looking at frightened her. The baby writhed and kicked feebly. Maybe it was famished. Couldn't the nurse do a better job? Where was its mother? Didn't incubator babies have parents?

On her father's side of the family there was a pack of Boston aunts, uncles, and cousins. They had always seemed stiff and cold. Her mother's people were warmer and kinder, but they were textile manufacturers in Lille, so she rarely saw them.

How could something as small and defenceless as Number Thirteen ever survive? The nurse had given up trying to feed it and was brusquely changing its tiny diaper. Showing all the maternal tenderness of a baker sliding a loaf into the oven, she bundled the baby and slid it back into its incubating machine.

This was giving Iseult a sharp pain in her chest, and she couldn't stand it. She fled. Short of breath, gasping, she forced herself to walk all the way out to the end of the pier, struggling for calm. Cold, sour marine air opened her bronchial tubes. Elderly Japanese men were fishing; pelicans tried to snatch fish from creels and bait from buckets as the men shooed them off with cries like angry birdcalls. She had never felt so alone in the world.

~

Iseult had never been good at developing sustaining friendships with other young women. At boarding school in New York City, most of her classmates were from large Catholic families and accustomed to layered networks of relationships, easy habits of intimacy. As the only child of older parents, she was not. Almost everyone else in Harrison, New Hampshire, had been poor, and nearly all of them had worked at her family's woollen mill. During much of her time at boarding school she had been ill with one thing or another, isolated in the convent infirmary or recuperating in the White Mountains.

Sometimes she imagined that her body lacked whatever organ it was that sweetened the other girls, pumping into their blood the nectar that gave them self-confidence as well as a profound instinctive need of one another. Her classmates were fixed and defined by their relationships, by secrets shared, by arguments and rituals of forgiveness. Her classmates developed crushes on the prettiest, youngest nuns and paid to have Masses said for their favourites at uptown chapels and churches, even at St. Patrick's. During Iseult's second year at the convent, buying Masses became something of a fad, and Mother Superior had to ban the practice after parents complained about the sums of money their daughters were spending; at St. Patrick's Cathedral even a Low Mass in a side chapel could cost twenty-five dollars. The more daring girls then sought out obscure Italian or German parishes on the Lower East Side, in Yorkville, or even in Brooklyn, secretly paying to have Mass cards printed and Masses said, even if no one from the convent could be there to hear them.

It seemed to Iseult that almost everyone at the convent was besotted. Mother Power, the tall, plainspoken nun who taught mathematics and was in charge of the infirmary, was the exception. Most Sacred Heart nuns were French or Irish, but Power was from San Antonio, Texas. Her manner was aloof. Girls were wary of her. She did not encourage crushes. Anyone coming to her class unprepared was sharply questioned, sometimes reduced to tears. Girls spoke of hating her. Behind her back they called her "Mother Longhorn" or "the Texas Cow."

Mother Power did missionary work every Saturday afternoon in Hell's Kitchen. One Saturday Iseult was alone in study hall with her sketchbook open, trying to draw her own left hand in pencil, when Mother Power came in looking for a satchel. Seeing Iseult, the nun brusquely invited her to come along.

Maybe it was chance, or maybe she recognized that Iseult was the most alone, the wickedest in her thoughts, the hungriest for connection. Or perhaps she had watched Iseult fighting through sickness and decided she was tougher than anyone realized.

"You might as well see how the other half lives. I warn you, I walk there and back. I don't take the 'bus, and certainly not a cab."

"I'd like to come."

"Another thing to get straight is attitude. You're not Lady Bountiful. And they're not beggars. You'll get more from the Kitchen than the Kitchen will ever get from you."

"Yes, Mother. I'd still like to come."

Mother Power walked along 54th Street with bold strides, the skirts of her habit swirling. The leather satchel over her shoulder was stuffed with missals, rosaries in little tin cases, apples, and pieces of hard candy.

"Sickness can give you strength," she told Iseult. "City air isn't as bad for you as everyone seems to think. It's foolish and missish, this fear of life and dirt that's bred into you girls. Study the life of Mother Cabrini, Iseult. Puny little thing she was as a girl in Italy, much sicker than you've ever been. Much smaller too, a shrimp. You've good bones, Iseult; you're going to be rough and tough. Cabrini, bless her, was never nothing more than a holy ghost of a girl, but see what she has accomplished, the orphanages and schools she started in this country for her Italian people. Learn from your weakness, Iseult, and you'll soon be stronger than any of the jewel-box girls."

That afternoon they had visited tenements lining the streets from Eighth Avenue to the river. The nun examined sick children, washed, deloused, and dosed them, and scolded their mothers. Iseult saw children with welts and bruises, children scabby with insect bites, children with broken arms in handkerchief slings. Mother Power had a list of doctors and dentists who would treat them without charge if she wrote a note and pinned it to their clothing. She threw open every window she could reach and shooed healthy children outside to play in the streets, where acacias and other weedy trees were sprouting the first green of summer. She distributed apples and candy to a pack of newsboys living in a livery stable on Ninth Avenue.

At Times Square the Texas nun seemed to know people at every corner and under every marquee. "Variety acts wrecked on drink, burlesque queens in a family way, busted circus people—Broadway and 42nd Street is one of the neediest spots on this earth, Iseult."

North of 42nd Street, Mother Power stopped to talk to a tramp while

the Broadway crowd broke around them. Iseult watched her hand the
tramp a rosary along with a silver dollar extracted from the folds of her
black habit. At a loft on 34th Street, Iseult helped hand around rosaries
to Polish girls sitting at Singer machines, sewing black woollen bathing
costumes. Hundreds of finished costumes were piled in crates on the
workroom floor, the stink of lanolin and sizing recalling New Hampshire, where the power looms rumbled day and night.

Trudging up rancid staircases to factory lofts and tenements was hard
work. The air was musty or worse, and Iseult was shocked at how oblivi-
ous people seemed to illness and mean circumstances. In a third-floor
walk-up on 47th Street, holding a struggling, squealing, urinating infant
as Mother Power dabbed mercurochrome on a rat bite, Iseult felt she was
participating in a great struggle. She had always wanted a great struggle.
When she was sick and despising her illness was also when she had felt
most determined, bravest, most alive.

That night, lying awake in her white iron bed, Iseult told herself she
had found her vocation. She would take vows of poverty, chastity, and
obedience, join the Order of the Sacred Heart, and go into the Kitchen
every week in her own swirling black habit.

She didn't tell anyone about this decision. She was afraid Mother
Power would ridicule her, for one thing. And she knew for certain that
her parents would object. Her father, a New England Congregational-
ist married to a Roman Catholic, feared all nuns, though he tried not
to show it—in his mind they were close to witches. Her parents would
probably want to remove her from the convent and install her in another
sanatorium in the White Mountains.

On Monday Mother Superior, a pink-cheeked little Irishwoman,
quizzed Iseult about her outing. "A girl with your medical condition
missionizing in Hell's Kitchen? I never heard of such a thing. What
was Mother Power thinking of? I don't want you going there ever
again."

But the following Saturday Mother Power came into study hall
again, and Iseult hurried to fetch her gloves and hat before anyone could
stop her.

"Don't think you are different than these people, Iseult, because you
are not," Mother Power called above the din of traffic on Eighth Avenue.

"And don't get sentimental either. Always try to see things up close, and as clear as you can."

It was strangely warm as they went south of the Kitchen into a meatpacking district, where the air stank of blood, railway soot, and cattle crowded into pens. Iseult and the nun handed out prayer beads and recited a decade of Hail Marys with German and Austrian butchers on the loading dock of a slaughterhouse, the men in bloody boots and aprons. Heading north on Ninth Avenue, Mother Power pointed out street corners where Negroes had been tortured and hanged during the Civil War.

"Catholics did this, Iseult. The suffering of the innocent is inflicted a hundred times worse on Him. The Christ feels every lash, every burn, every scar. This was where the martyrs died, and now it's a flesh market."

Young women dressed completely in white, carrying little parasols, occupied most of the street corners along those blocks of Ninth Avenue.

"You know what prostitution is, don't you, Iseult?"

"Yes."

Patrick Dubois, a boy she'd known back in New Hampshire, had insisted that prostitutes—he called them "chippies"—lived in the Thatcher Hotel, between the woollen mill and the railway station. Her parents never said anything about them, just as they never mentioned the scrawny, unkempt children Iseult saw sitting on stoops along Textile Street. Often enough, walking past those ruthless three-deckers, she had overheard men and women inside, screaming at each other.

Ferme ta gueule, tu, putain de cochon!

They had sounded like people losing their minds, and she used to wonder if her father made a practice of hiring crazy people. Or did tending power looms cause people to lose their minds? It was Patrick Dubois, not her parents, who told her of a famous battle between Irish mechanics and foremen and French-Canadian factory hands on the bridge over the falls: one man thrown into the river, another kicked to death in the road. She'd wanted to ask her father what he remembered, but her curiosity would only have annoyed him.

The spry little river was the reason her great-grandfather had come up to New Hampshire in the 1820s, and in the early days the mill machinery was geared directly to the speed of the wild stream. Her grandfather had tamed and scheduled the river, first by damming it, then by install-ing steam turbines. A business doesn't like wild things.

At the precinct house on 35th Street, Iseult and Mother Power prayed decades of the rosary with kneeling policemen, then visited the lock-up. The cells were relatively quiet on Saturday afternoon, awaiting the weekly bacchanal between Times Square and the river, although anything like real silence could not exist in such a place, with drunks and morphine addicts snoring and whimpering, someone muttering crazy nonsense, someone else weeping. Iseult helped Mother Power hand prayer beads, missals, and holy pictures between the bars, and the cutting, violent stink of bodies was almost overpowering.

Iseult knelt beside the nun as she led the inmates in a novena, then stayed close, watching her comfort a German prostitute named Flossie, who had stabbed a man the night before. Clinging to the iron bars, Flossie was pretty in a demolished way. She might have been eighteen or thirty. Her yellow dress was torn at the shoulder, and whatever hap-pened to her, she didn't want her mother finding out.

"In Brooklyn my mother lives. I shall write a letter, say I go to Ger-many, home."

All her life Iseult had been handled like a carefully wrapped package. When the nun touched Flossie's hands, knuckled around the bars, and the girl began sobbing, Iseult, absorbing Flossie's noise and scent and the plainness of her despair, felt an almost sickening awareness of her own privilege.

Prostitutes. Raw rivers. Secrets, drunks. Broken glass, bodily vio-lence, dirt, and various forms of hunger. It was curiosity that drew her to the Kitchen, not religious feeling. She had never been able to feel that God was close. Her notion of having found her vocation had been a delu-sion, a conceit, a fantasy.

Flossie let go the bars and started coughing and wheezing. Mother Power sent the female jailer for a jug of cold water and tried to get Flossie to drink, but it didn't do much good—cold water never did, in Iseult's experience. She could still hear the girl coughing as they left the precinct house.

She would never be a nun like Mother Power, but she would try see-ing herself in others, others in herself. She went to the Kitchen with

Mother Power every Saturday for the rest of the term. Mother Superior must have known but for some reason never again tried to stop her from going. Mother Superior made fun of Mother Power behind her back but, like everyone else, she was also scared of her.

The first Saturday in June was graduation day at the Convent of the Sacred Heart. Iseult and her classmates, all in white and carrying nosegays, entered the chapel where their parents were already seated. Cardinal Farley celebrated the High Mass and afterwards there was a strawberry tea. It was a warm, emotional afternoon. Girls who over three years had barely spoken to Iseult hugged and kissed her.

Mother Power attended High Mass with the other nuns, but sometime during the strawberry tea she disappeared before Iseult had a chance to say goodbye to her. It was a Saturday, after all.

That evening Iseult's parents took her to dinner at Delmonico's, where she drank her first glass of champagne. The next morning they boarded a Pullman and travelled up to Maine, where her father had taken a big, breezy cottage at Kennebunkport for the summer. With her mother she joined a ladies' art club and spent many afternoons trying to paint seascapes that were no worse and no better than anyone else's. That fall she started at Smith, but a wicked bout of asthma weakened her and her parents would not allow her to return to college after Christmas; she was confined to bed for most of the winter. The next year her father died, and a few months later she and her mother left New Hampshire for good and moved to Pasadena.

Iseult never saw Mother Power again but often thought of her. Bold, awkward, lit up by something inside herself, the nun was the first woman Iseult had met who possessed a powerful vision of herself operating in the world.

~

She felt the California sun hot on her bare neck. She was wearing one of her day dresses, cotton poplin in crisp blue and white stripes. Her New England relations would have been annoyed that she wasn't in mourning.

No one she knew would ever have thought of settling in Venice, California. The Boston relations somehow had the idea that now her mother was dead she would go back and live with them in their narrow, dark Back Bay houses. She wasn't going to, not in a million years.

Colonnades—surely a Venetian touch—shaded the sidewalks along Windward Avenue, though the columns were plaster, not Italian stone, and sounded hollow when she tapped them. There were half a dozen raucous saloons. In Pasadena and L.A., saloons and pretty much everything else had to close on Sundays, but Venice had its own laws.

She found the real estate office a block back from the beach, in a storefront between a seafood restaurant and a shop that sold Indian moccasins, ships in glass bottles, and striped beach towels. Peering into the office through the plate-glass window, she saw empty desks and a potted plant of gigantic proportions. She wondered if the office was closed, then noticed a man with his feet up on a desk in the back of the room, reading a newspaper. A bell jingled as she opened the door. The man lowered his newspaper. Seeing her, he took his feet off the desk and stood up.

"May I help you?"

"I'd like to see some properties."

"Oh. Well. I can certainly help you with that."

He was maybe a year or two younger than she was. His skin was tanned, eyes blue, and teeth very white.

"Perhaps you'd like to finish your lunch first." There was half a chicken sandwich on his desk.

"Oh, no. Wasn't all that good anyhow." He came forward, picking up his hat. "I'd be happy to show you what's on the market. Not a lot of houses, but there are some choice lots. I'm Grattan O'Brien."

Some men seized Iseult's hand and squeezed as if it were a bird they wanted to crush before it could escape. Her mother had disapproved of men and women shaking hands, considering it a vulgar Americanism. Grattan's handshake was firm and quick, but she felt something intimate in his touch. As though he had rubbed some bone of herself. She felt her cheeks flushing with thoughts that weren't words, just burrs of feelings, inchoate, startling.

But one could ignore feelings; one didn't need to let them show.

～

On Windward Avenue, in the shadows of the colonnade, voices were keyed up and the air smelled of fried food. People spooned ice cream from paper cups. A man in front of a store had watch chains draped over his arm. "Real gold!" he called. "Come along, gents, don't put a fine watch on a cheap chain! Real gold watch chains, only one dollar!"

As they walked, Grattan O'Brien told her that Mr. Abbot Kinney planned to make Venice the most extraordinary residential community in America, a garden city with shining waterways instead of dusty streets. She was doing her best to pay attention while constantly feeling death, the presence of death behind everything.

"We'll go by the Lagoon and see if we might catch a gondola. There are only a couple of houses to see. The lots have been selling, but the fact is not many people have built yet."

I am an orphan, Iseult thought to herself. *An orphan led westward, windward, by a young man whose wrists and hands are brown and glossy smooth as the branches of a manzanita tree.*

The Lagoon was a stagnant green pond flanked by what he called the Amphitheatre.

"They held swimming races here this morning. The Amphitheatre seats 2,500. This was all wasteland when Mr. Kinney first saw it. Nothing but mud and birds."

White plaster columns, plaster statues everywhere, and banks of rickety seats: she thought it looked a bit like a Roman ruin and a bit like the Dartmouth College swim tank. On the far side of the Lagoon, three black Venetian gondolas were tied up at a float where the boatmen, in striped jerseys, were smoking and playing cards. Mist was blowing inland, giving some texture to plain, brutal sunshine. She could feel surf thumping on the beach.

"Luigi, *per piacere,* let's take the *signora* down to the Linnie."

The gondoliers looked up from their card game. One of them shrugged, tossed down his cards, and stood up. "Sure thing, Mr. Grattan."

"How's business?" Grattan asked.

"Ah, not so good."

The man stepped into one of the gondolas, then held out his hand for Iseult as she stepped down. It was pleasant to be on the water, to sense something soft beneath the hull, liquid depth, a mystery.

Grattan sat down next to her and the gondolier slipped his line and pushed off.

With its toothed stern rising like a wicked tail, the gondola resembled a dragon. It had something of a canoe's narrowness and fragility. The gondolier hummed a tune as he worked the scull.

"It's a nice way to go, don't you think?" Grattan said.

It was wonderful: the scent of tarry wood and the black hull sliding noiselessly across the Lagoon, headed for the Grand Canal. A flock of ducks paddled in the sluggish water.

"What's the difference between a canal and a ditch?"

He smiled. "Good question. You dig a ditch to drain a swamp or to bring water to crops. The canals are so people can enjoy living by water. That was Abbot's idea, anyway. In summer it's often fifteen degrees cooler out here than in Los Angeles. You can sleep under a blanket all summer. You're from back east?"

"Yes."

"I'm out of Canada myself. Don't let me get started on the ocean air out here, or you'll think I'm huckstering you."

They glided along. To the north she could see the olive green Santa Monica Mountains, and the purple San Gabriels to the east, beyond Pasadena. Something dreamy, sleepy, about moving on water. Her mother would have called this day a whim. Was that what it was? How weightless and unencumbered she felt.

The gondola slipped beneath a couple of footbridges. There were only a few people strolling along the canals. She saw survey sticks and sand piles but few houses.

"We haven't actually sold that many lots, to tell you the truth. People don't appreciate the canals; they want real streets so they can park automobiles in front of their houses. They might not own an automobile yet, but they hope to."

"You're not being a very good salesman. You shouldn't be giving me reasons not to buy."

"Well, we do have the electric cars. It's only fifty-two minutes to Los Angeles. I want to give you the whole picture. Venice hasn't worked the way Mr. Kinney had in mind. I shouldn't say so, but I believe he's tired of the whole thing. People just aren't interested in beauty—not his idea of beauty, anyway—so he has to give them fun parks and crazy rides and the Pier. A person like you might be happier living in Ocean Park or Santa Monica."

"A person like me? What sort of person is that?"

"Well, Santa Monica's more civilized, that's all I mean. There's not a lot going on at the office—you may have noticed. All the other salesmen have quit, and I'm thinking about it. Nothing to do all day gets kind of lonely."

"How can you be lonely with the biggest dancehall in the world?" she teased. "And a roller-skating rink!"

"You ought to meet my wife," he said. "She could tell you what it's like out here."

Iseult turned away, let her fingers dabble in the water. Her throat felt tight and dry.

"You'll hear coyotes at night," he was saying.

Wild sun, hard blue sky, the slip of the hull through green water. Not a very sensible place to live.

The gondolier was humming and every now and then burst out with a stanza in Italian. Was he singing for her, she wondered, was it part of his job? Did it matter? No. Shutting her eyes, she let the music float by as the sun stroked her face.

What she was most conscious of was animal will: a jump of desire. Grattan, slender and crisp. She longed to bite him, taste his skin.

~

He showed her through a pair of bungalows on the Howland Canal, then one on the Linnie, all three built to the same pattern. Inside they smelled of raw wood, sawdust, grout, and stale new paint. Squirrels or raccoons had gotten inside one of the Howlands and made a nest of rags, dry grass, and twigs on the kitchen floor.

Big white New England houses could be iron chains around the necks of their inhabitants, and she had watched her father being dragged to his death by the gloom and weight of such a house, until he had climbed up to the attic one Sunday afternoon and blown out his brains with a Colt Navy pistol his own father had carried through the Civil War.

She liked the Linnie Canal cottage best. Maybe it was just the name. *Linnie* sounded like a pretty girl, *Howland* bleak and masculine. It was strange to stand in an empty house alone with a young man, a stranger. She felt vulnerable and open, without edges.

Grattan said, "I guess I don't understand why people are so keen for houses in the first place."

"Everyone needs a home, Mr. O'Brien."

"Do they? I think I carry my home inside my head."

"What does your wife think?"

"Oh, she wants us to buy a house," he said gloomily. "We live in her studio right on Windward. Above the Chink laundry. She says it won't be good for the baby. She's due in a couple of months."

"Congratulations."

"I'd like to feel I can up stakes whenever I choose. All rooms are boring, sooner or later. I like the outside."

Mr. Grattan O'Brien was restless. She wondered if it worried his wife.

It took only a minute to see everything. Dirty windows, plaster dust, stale air. She tried to ignore her lewd feelings and pay heed to the space, the way the light worked within the small rooms. The kitchen sink, brightly tiled counters, yellow and black. Icebox. Bathtub, porcelain toilet, sink, white tiles on the floor. Windows in the sitting room looked out to the green glint of the canal. Could she make a home for herself?

"I guess you like it or you don't," he said. "It's a nice time of day out here, though, isn't it? The way the light cuts in. These houses are very bright most of the time. Look, why don't you nose around a bit by yourself, get a feel for the place. You don't want me looking over your shoulder. I'll wait outside."

She thought about his wife: busy, pretty, young. More ambitious than Grattan, perhaps, and getting a little impatient.

"Thank you. I won't be long," she said.

"Take your time, Miss Wilkins."

He went out, closing the door behind him. She stood still and heard him strike a match. And the gondolier was still crooning, singing for no one but himself.

Alone this time, Iseult took herself once more through the bright, bare rooms. The layout was very simple. It was a nothing little house, the bedroom half the size of her bedroom in Pasadena. Still, it was bright. Hard to imagine someone dying in these rooms. The spare room that could be her library, studio, thinking room.

What sort of passion might spill in this house? The houses she'd known had all spoken her family's dark language. Venice, California, was awfully far from everyone and everything, but did that matter? She had enough income to live modestly. She was prepared to be lonely for a while. In a bare little house of her own she might find clarity and calm, she might find her own purpose.

~

As they were gliding back along the Grand Canal, Grattan didn't ask what she thought of the Linnie cottage. He didn't say anything. Something in him seemed to have turned off, or turned inward.

They disembarked and he insisted on walking her to the electric car stop, where a three-car train was boarding passengers.

"I hope it hasn't been an utter waste of your time," he said.

"I hope it hasn't been an utter waste of yours."

"Certainly not." He smiled and they shook hands, then she boarded the last car. The floor was gritty with beach sand. She found a window seat and looked out. Grattan O'Brien was still standing there, hat in hand. There was something unfinished about him; some protective carapace was missing. She would want someone tougher. Stubborn, forceful. A man to take her places she couldn't get to on her own.

The train started with a jolt and she turned away from the window. The car was packed with sunburnt mothers and infants, beach umbrellas and picnic baskets, fathers and uncles already nodding asleep, older children fussing. She seemed to be the only person travelling alone.

The day before her mother's death, the son of one of her mother's friends, home from his junior year at Yale, had telephoned Iseult and invited her to a tennis and tea party at the Pasadena Club. "Tomorrow afternoon at, say, three o'clock?"

That was when she broke for the first, the only time. Holding the telephone receiver to her ear, feeling the oxygen being squeezed from her lungs and not having the strength to pull it back in.

The telephone was on a wall in a dark panelled hallway that reeked of cleaning fluid. For weeks her mother's housekeeper, Cordelia, displaced by shifts of hired nurses, had had little to do but dust the barren rooms of that mostly unlived-in house. She was a tall, stringy coloured woman from Oklahoma and it was hard to guess her age. She was slender and long-waisted and there was something mannish about her, a sense of power and fluid strength. Determined to earn her keep, she had been scouring, buffing, and waxing so ferociously that the Pasadena house shone with a kind of cruelty, everything glossy, ugly, and perfectly arranged, so that the house itself seemed like a kind of funeral.

Hearing the Yale boy's treble over the telephone wires, Iseult felt her lungs deflate, withering as grief closed in. Unable to withstand the pressure, she dropped the receiver. As it dangled on its wire, she got slowly down on hands and knees, touched her forehead to the Tabriz carpet, then rolled over and lay on her side on the mottled wool, gasping and wheezing, until Cordelia, hurrying through with a tray, tripped over her and let out a startled yell.

Cordelia telephoned the doctor, who arrived in an automobile and gave Iseult an injection that allowed her to breathe normally; within a few moments she was in a deep stupor. Cordelia summoned the Japanese gardeners to carry her upstairs, then undressed her and got her under the sheets.

Iseult had woken up the next morning with a sour taste in her mouth and a cracking headache. She dressed and went downstairs without first going to check on her mother as she usually did. She was drinking coffee in the breakfast room when Cordelia walked in, placed a brown hand on her shoulder, and said, "I tell you, girl, your mama is gone."

She had, in fact, died during the night. The sitting nurse had awakened Cordelia, then packed up and left at dawn.

Cordelia poured herself a cup of coffee and Iseult went upstairs alone.

The room had been scoured and the windows opened wide, and much of the smell was gone. Cordelia had gathered flowers from the garden and set them on a table at the foot of the bed. Iseult's mother lay with peculiar stillness under a fresh white sheet drawn up under her arms and crisply smoothed. Her hands had been placed one on top of the other. The pillow was fresh and plump.

First her father, then her mother—each death had hardened her a little. She was alone now, and more boldness was going to be required. Life had to be engaged, life had to be started.

No, she would not stay in Pasadena.

Even with the windows open, the atmosphere in the trolley car stank of hot metal, rubber flooring, and sweet, stale food. Steel wheels made a steady, flatulent grinding underneath. Every seat was taken. Across the aisle a sunburnt girl had fallen asleep with her head on the shoulder of the young man holding her hand.

Animal appetites were embarrassing because they would not be denied, and only with difficulty could they be controlled. Before her parents sent her to Sacred Heart Convent, while she was still taking her lessons at the schoolhouse in their town in New Hampshire, there had been that one rough, wool-smelling boy, Patrick Dubois. One bright afternoon in April, Patrick had forced her, step by step, down the wooden stairs that led to the school's cellar. It was supposed to be a game: she was supposed to be his helpless prisoner.

Confident that she was the one really in charge of this exciting little contest, she had lingered on each step, challenging him. "You can't make me."

"Aw, yes, I can."

"Try it, then."

That was the signal for Patrick to place big, meaty paws on her shoulders and apply pressure until she took another step down. Thirteen steps in all, then they were standing on the dirt floor of the cellar. It must have taken ten minutes to get down there. Patrick was just tall enough that he had to crouch a little below the floor joists.

Patrick Dubois lived with his parents and sisters in one of the tenements her grandfather had put up during the Civil War. He was a pupil at her school but he also had a paid job. Three or four times a day, all winter long, he left the classroom and disappeared into the cellar, where he shovelled and spread coals in the furnace. He kept a towel and a bucket of water warm down there, and a scrap of yellow soap to clean himself with, but it did no good. When he resumed his seat in the back of the classroom, there was always a gash of wet soot somewhere on his face, neck, or forearm. She could smell coal on him; anthracite had a scent like an old, dead fire, the scent of underground.

At the bottom of the cellar stairs they stood facing each other. There was just enough daylight coming down that she could see his expression, and what frightened her was that he looked so nervous.

"Aren't you going to give me a kiss?" he said. Licking his lips. His eyes shiny and wandering. He had probably dared himself into that moment in that place, and now nothing was going to stop him from carrying out his dare. He would hate himself if he did not, and whatever she said or did wouldn't matter. She really didn't have anything to do with it anymore. Neither did he, in a way. Not anymore.

April days were long in New Hampshire. Not like, say, November. Still plenty of light after the school day ended, light falling down the cellar stairs. According to her mother, the town school was well and good for town children, but Iseult's horizons extended beyond the town, which was why her parents would be sending her off to Sacred Heart Convent in New York City, where there were girls from all over the country, from Mexico and South America, and she would learn important things.

"Like what?" she'd asked.

Her mother had smiled. "Such as not to say 'Like what?'"

"Why not?"

"It sounds common." Her mother, born in New York City of French parents, had grown up mostly in Europe and had a slight timbre of accent, delicate and French.

"Why?"

"Because it's ugly. And brusque. It sounds rude."

So in five months Iseult would be going off to boarding school, but at that moment she was still down the cellar with Patrick Dubois and the game that had run out of words after that question of his.

She finally said, "No, thank you."

Whenever she recalled that afternoon, what came back first was the April light. Had it been November she never would have gone down there with him.

"Aw, come on."

"I believe I'll go upstairs now."

"Don't be a minx. One little kiss."

"I believe I'll go upstairs."

"Aw, come on. It's not going to hurt, Iseult."

"I must go home now. Please let me go."

"Not until I get a kiss," Patrick Dubois said. "Come on now, Iseult, I don't want to get your clothes dirty. You're so clean, Iseult. The cleanest person in the world, you are."

He hadn't moved, or touched her. He was just looking at her, and she sensed that, if she acted wisely, the situation might be brought back under her control.

"All right," she said.

"On the lips. Has to be on the lips, now. A real kiss."

Crouching under the floor joists, arms by his sides: a big boy, clumsy. If she was quick she could dodge him and probably beat him up the stairs. She didn't move. She wasn't afraid of him anymore.

"Sheesh," he said. "Are you going to or not?"

She took a step closer and, standing on the tips of her toes, brushed his lips very quickly with her own. "There." She stepped back. "Now you're going to tell everyone I kissed you. You're going to say it was my idea, aren't you."

His lips rough, dry, tasting of carriage drives on dusty roads.

He shook his head. "I won't, Iseult."

"Promise."

"I promise I won't."

"If you don't tell anyone, maybe we'll come down here again sometime."

She left him standing at the schoolhouse door, a broom in his hands, while she went out into the lucid light. Sweeping up was another of his duties, also washing blackboards, straightening desks, locking up. How much did the town pay him for all those chores—twenty dollars a year? His father would have kept all the money.

Silver bare trees lined her walk home.

How often after that had she gone down the cellar with Patrick Dubois? She never let him put his arms around her or touch her, but their kisses ripened. She learned the taste of his mouth and tongue. And she wrapped her arms around his powerful neck, folded her knees, and felt his erection scuffle through their clothes as she lifted her feet off the ground, so that he was taking her weight on his neck and shoulders, so that she was hanging from him—he the trunk, she the branch.

Everyone who had ever been close to her had tried to insist on their right to control her. She knew her own body only slightly. The sexual feeling was like turning her face to the sun.

Another person could seem as clear as a glass of water, but water was still a mystery, wasn't it? Springing from depths as it did. Drenching from the sky.

∼

Her mother's Pasadena lawyer, a Spaulding of the Massachusetts Spauldings, said, "There'll be no trouble selling the house, but Venice? Really, Iseult. Those beach towns are tawdry."

Spaulding was a stern Yankee gentleman and a founding member of the Pasadena Theosophical Society. He had persuaded Iseult's mother to join when she became ill with the stomach cancer that would kill her. Iseult had been to a few theosophy meetings; it sounded like nonsense to her. Something happened to stern New England Congregationalists—and devout Roman Catholics—in California. Maybe it was the sunlight, or the orange juice, or the sweet desert dust in the air. Iseult couldn't imagine the same people back in New Hampshire earnestly discussing reincarnation, astral bodies, and oneness with the universe.

"Have you ever been to Venice?" she asked Spaulding.

The lawyer shuddered. "No, but I read in *The Times* that the red cars carried twenty thousand out there last weekend. Quite a horde! Not the place for me, thank you very much."

"I own Pacific Electric stock, don't I?"

He nodded. "You do. A little."

"Do you?"

"I believe I do."

"Then shouldn't we be happy that all those people are riding out there?"

"It doesn't mean we have to go with them. You ought to consider Santa Barbara, if you must live by the sea."

Two weeks later Mr. Spaulding, radiating Puritan disapproval the whole way, drove her in his automobile out to Venice to sign the sale agreement. His peevishness intensified when they found Mr. Grattan O'Brien in the shabby real estate office with his feet up on the desk, this time reading a book. Another man, dark and stocky and almost too well dressed, was sitting at another desk reading a newspaper.

"My brother Joe O'Brien, Miss Wilkins. Joe's on his way to Mexico. He has been building a railway in Canada all summer."

"Which line?" the lawyer asked.

"Canadian Northern," Joe O'Brien replied politely. "A mountain section, through the Selkirks in British Columbia."

"You're an engineer?"

"I've one or two on my payroll. I have the construction contract, you see."

He wasn't exactly handsome, not like his brother, but his black hair was thick. He was perfectly shaved, his stiff collar was snowy and perfect, but something about him was dark and hard, gleaming.

Spaulding looked at the young man more closely. "I've always said that the only people who make money from railroads are the men who build them. No one sees a profit running them, shareholders least of all."

"My piece is frozen up and snowed under at the moment, so I'll be finishing in the spring. I intend to look into some work down in Mexico. They've been planning a line from Chihuahua to the Pacific. It's mountain country."

"How old are you, sir, if you don't mind my asking?"

"I'm twenty-five. But I've been in the business a while."

"The Mexicans are in the throes of revolution."

"They're going to want to build that line someday. So I'd like to have a look."

Picking up his newspaper, Joe O'Brien moved to a desk at the front of the office while Grattan started handing over documents to the lawyer, who settled gold-framed spectacles on the end of his nose and scanned each page.

Something made Iseult look around and catch Mr. Joe O'Brien looking straight at her. He held her gaze boldly for a few moments before turning back to his newspaper. If she never saw him again she'd not forget him. Not exactly a rough, but not smooth either. It was confidence, not his looks, that made him seem older than twenty-five.

The lawyer said something but she missed it.

"Excuse me, what did you say?" she asked, irritated with Joe O'Brien for looking at her so appraisingly.

"You won't be allowed to sell to Jews, Mexicans, or coloured." The lawyer spoke without looking up from the document in his hand.

"Mr. Kinney was instructed by his lawyers to put that in," Grattan said. "It's the standard thing, here along the coast, anyway."

"Of course it is, and a good thing too," the lawyer said. "Protects everyone."

"Are Catholics all right?" she said, just to prick Spaulding, though he had come all the way from Pasadena as a favour to her.

The lawyer, who had been devoted to Iseult's Catholic mother, ignored her question.

"Of course, of course," said Grattan.

"Well," said Spaulding, shuffling the papers together, "this is all in order, but are you certain it's what you want, Iseult? Can you really find happiness so far from your friends?"

People always wanted her to be safe, maybe more for their sakes than her own.

"I can afford it, can't I?"

"That's not the issue."

"Thank you for your advice. And thank you for coming out here. I'm very grateful. But this is what I want."

"If you're ready to sign, I'll call in the notary," said Grattan. "He's just across the street."

The lawyer checked his watch. "I've a lunch engagement at the Jonathan Club in exactly one hour, Iseult. I can take you as far as Hill Street."

"No, thank you. After we're finished here I think I will visit my little house."

As soon as the papers were signed and notarized, Spaulding shook hands with Iseult, nodded briskly at the young men, and left, giving her the impression that he was washing his hands of the whole business. Grattan was searching in his desk drawer for her keys when Joe O'Brien spoke up.

"Congratulations, Miss Wilkins. I wish you the joy of it."

"Why, thank you, Mr. O'Brien."

Maybe he expected her to look away first, maybe that was what he was used to, but she wouldn't, and was satisfied when, after a few more moments, he looked down again at his newspaper. A little test of wills, and she'd won.

Grattan, meanwhile, was still rummaging for keys. She picked up the slender volume on his desk.

Poems of the Past and Present
by
Thomas Hardy

"I never understand poetry," she announced, a little proudly.

"Yes, well, maybe that's the point," Grattan said. "Ah, here they are." He offered her the keys on a little metal ring.

"But why read something you can't understand?"

"To participate in the mystery!"

From his chair across the room, Joe O'Brien snorted.

Grattan smiled. "Joe claims he doesn't have an ounce of artistic sensibility in his body. He says he's the one of the family that does not. A hard man through and through, aren't you, Joe."

"Artistic sensibility never bought you a pair of boots," his brother said.

"That's true. Joe, how about going out to the Linnie with Miss Wilkins? The place hasn't been opened or aired since you were there last, Miss Wilkins. Joe can check if the water's turned on and see that you have no trouble with the front door sticking and such."

"Thank you, that won't be necessary. I can manage perfectly well."

"Oh, let old Joe accompany you, Miss Wilkins. He's a gentleman of leisure these days."

Joe O'Brien got to his feet. "It is no trouble," he said. "I should like to see the property."

Grattan was graceful, amiable, and unformed, but some essence of Joe O'Brien was implacable. He stood waiting by the door, hat in his hand.

She nodded. "Very well." But as soon as they were outside she said, "You really needn't take the trouble, Mr. O'Brien. I can find my way by myself."

"Well, I need the exercise."

They were the same height exactly. His dark suit, stiff collar, and homburg seemed out of place on Windward Avenue, where dapper fellows wore ice-cream suits, white shoes, yellow straw hats.

They headed out to Linnie, walking the path along the Grand Canal.

"I've never been to Venice, Italy," he said. "Does it look much like this?"

"Hardly."

"You seem like someone who has seen a lot of different places."

"I was in Venice when I was twelve. I'd like to go back someday."

"I aim to see all those European places."

"I'm sure you will."

"Why would you want to live alone?" he asked.

She glanced at him.

"I guess you don't have to answer," he said. "It's none of my business but I'd like to know. I've lived alone, and I liked it well enough for a while."

"I want room to breathe," she said.

The fact was that she had been following some instinct she barely understood. Her mother would have called it a whim. It was more than that, but it wasn't a carefully thought-out plan. They walked in silence for a while and he seemed lost in thought. Was he mulling over her response? Maybe he was thinking of railroads in Mexico.

"Yes," he said finally. "I guess I understand. Everyone needs that."

"Does it make sense, Mr. O'Brien, do you think?"

He hardly knew her, but he would speak the truth.

"You'll know in a while."

They continued walking in silence. The silence somehow felt engaging, not awkward. Perhaps because she could sense he was thinking about her.

"You can rely on my brother," he said after a while. "If you have any trouble out here, you can rely on Grattan. Elise too. You ought to meet her."

"Perhaps I shall. You're building a railroad, Mr. O'Brien. I suppose you're never alone."

"Just a piece of a railway," he corrected. "I have thirty-five miles and hope to get more. There's seven hundred miles, more or less, to be built."

"How many men work for you?"

"My outfit? Just before the freeze-up, fifteen hundred. Give or take. They're scattered now."

"Where are they?"

He laughed for the first time. "That's a question. I'll round up another bunch in the spring. Some can't talk a word of English. A lot of them are foreigners, or Chinese."

He showed little warmth on the surface but there was something inside, fiery. He was strange and hard but he was interested in her; he listened.

"You're not a poet," he said. "Are you an artist?"

"I daub, I sketch. I play the piano, unhappily."

"Unhappily?"

"Because I'm not very good."

"'Room to breathe'—that makes sense to me. Of course, I want to do more than breathe."

It was such an odd thing to say. When she looked at him, he smiled. Then she had to smile too.

"My manners need work," he admitted. "It comes of living in the muck and the mountains. I've a little book of manners I study from time to time. I even practise fine phrases in the mirror—you'd laugh to see me."

"Would I?"

"I think you would. Does this look familiar, Miss Wilkins?"

They had arrived at the Linnie Canal.

"Yes. And there's my cottage." Smaller than she remembered.

"I guess you might rather go in alone," he said. "Call me if you want a hand with anything. I'll wait outside."

He waited on the canal path while she fitted the key into the door and let herself in. She went quickly around the small, bare rooms. They delighted her. Everything white and empty and sunlit. The place needed a good dusting and cleaning and some furniture, but that was all. The space felt light, generous, open. This would be the real beginning of her life.

She went back to the door. "Everything's quite all right, Mr. O'Brien. Would you care to inspect the place?"

She held the door open as he came in, removing his hat. "You are my first visitor, Mr. O'Brien, the first I've ever invited into a place of my own."

"That is an honour."

She led him through the little house. There really wasn't much to show. "It's the light I love," she said. "Just as it is right now."

"You'll want furniture."

"But not too much. I'm not keen on furniture. People fill their houses with big, dark blocks of—I don't know what—upholstery, and stuffing, and smelly wood. Furniture steals the light, that's what it does."

"Gives you something to sit on, though."

She laughed. "Yes, you're right."

"The Chinese don't have much use for chairs, even a camp stool. On the works you'll see the Chinamen squatting on their haunches, eating and talking a mile a minute. Sound like birds. Clever birds. They are good workers."

"This will be my bedroom, I think."

He hardly glanced at it. The room had no trace of anything female or personal, but she sensed his discomfort. Instead he peered into the spare room on the other side of the hall. "You could keep a maid in here."

"I don't want a servant, won't have one. We'd be on top of each other. I'll find a woman to come in by the day and clean. I can take care of myself. I'll want to leave this room empty, I think."

"Empty? You ought to get some use of it."

"I don't mean I won't use it. I'll leave it empty and let it fill up with ideas."

He was looking at her oddly.

"I might do some painting in here. Or drawing. Or reading, or just thinking."

"You've an artistic sensibility."

"Perhaps. And it's never bought me a pair of boots either."

~

The week after Iseult took possession of the Linnie cottage, she sold most of the furniture in the Pasadena house to a dealer. She gave all her mother's clothes, except one shawl, to Cordelia. The table silver she kept, most of the china, and all her books. Also two trunks of linens and a cedar chest packed with blankets woven in the New Hampshire mill.

Moving day was a Sunday. Cordelia's husband, Floyd, owned a half-share of a motor truck. They arrived with their thirteen-year-old nephew Chisholm for a helper, Cordelia wearing an enormous blue hat and a starched apron over her satin going-to-church dress.

Floyd and Chisholm loaded up the truck and they set off, with Iseult squeezed into the front seat between Floyd and Cordelia, the nephew riding in back with the chests and trunks. At a filling station at Palms Junction they ate a picnic lunch of fried chicken while Floyd and Chisholm repaired a flat tire.

When Iseult opened the front door of the cottage, the first thing she saw was a dozen white roses in a bucket on the floor. There was a note:

~~Venice Land Company~~
~~Windward Avenue~~
~~Venice, Calif.~~

Tues., Feb. the 2nd

Dear Miss Wilkins,

Good luck in your new home, I will call around to see if anything is needed.

Regards,
J. O'Brien

So he had not left for Mexico yet.

Cordelia glanced at the card, then at her, but said nothing.

Floyd and Chisholm carried in the trunks and chests, then took a nap outside while Cordelia swept, mopped, and dusted and Iseult stored her china and silverware in cupboards and kitchen drawers. She hung some of her clothes in the closets but there was no sense unpacking everything else until she had furniture of her own. It might have been wise to have held on to a few more pieces, but she could not forget the way her parents' tables, cabinets, and chests absorbed light and gave nothing back except sombre shininess and the stale scent of a hundred years of waxing.

Cordelia helped make up a temporary bed on the bedroom floor, using the stack of woollen blankets. Cordelia disapproved of her arrangements, she could tell. Maybe selling her parents' bed had been hardhearted, but she didn't want to sleep where her mother had died. And all the other beds in the Pasadena house were much too large and dark for the Linnie cottage anyway.

When everything was done, Cordelia folded her apron, tucked the twenty dollars Iseult gave her into her pocketbook, and started putting on her hat. Her dress was yellow gold satin with royal blue checks that matched the hat.

"Now, I am thinking of your mama." Cordelia was carefully adjusting her enormous hat. Suddenly she turned and looked straight at Iseult. "You hear what I am saying, girl?"

"Oh yes," said Iseult.

"Be careful what help you take on. Some gals are rank, thieving hussies."

"Oh, I'm not getting any help," Iseult said. "It's time I learned to do things for myself."

"You? How you gonna tend yourself? Here is what you do: find the coloured church out here and—"

"Millions of people take care of themselves. It can't be that difficult."

"You ask the coloured pastor and he'll set you a good girl. Don't go forgetting yourself out here on the ocean. Find yourself good help. Be wary of strangers. People see a girl alone, next thing they want something from you. Watch yourself. Don't follow no awkward religions, but say your prayers. Wear your hat and cover your arms. Bathe every day and be a good girl, for Cordelia's sake."

It was the first time since her mother's death that anyone had admonished her, and she felt an emptiness blooming. Cordelia opened her arms and Iseult stepped into the mothering embrace.

"Don't you mind. Gonna be all right, sugar. You gonna be all right."

Cleansed by tears, she felt weaker, also stronger.

"There you are now, plum," Cordelia said. "You on the track of feeling now."

~

The next morning was foggy. Wearing a nightdress and a silk robe one of her great-uncles had brought from China, Iseult roamed from room to room, relishing her solitude. At noon she was still not dressed. There was nothing to eat in the house. She sat down in a corner of the spare room with a novel, *Howards End*, but found herself unable to concentrate.

In one of the drawers of the escritoire she found a sheaf of her mother's stationery and envelopes, scratched a line through the letterhead, and wrote Joe O'Brien what she hoped was a calm, cool, polite little note.

~~Marie de C. Wilkins~~

Weds. 3rd February
Linnie Cottage,
Venice, Calif.

Dear Mr. O'Brien,

   Many thanks for the welcome of the roses. Linnie Cottage would have been quite barren otherwise. I am settling in.
   Everything is a little strange, but I am getting used to it.

Yours truly,
Iseult Wilkins

Even as she signed it she felt dissatisfied with it—a dead piece, no roots or branches—but she folded it and slid it into an envelope that she addressed to

Mr. Joseph O'Brien
c/o The Venice Land Co.
Windward Avenue
Venice, Calif.

She went to the window. The fog was dissolving in a breeze. The light was sparkling now. Wild blue sky.

Feeling almost angry with herself, she pulled her note out of its envelope, picked up her pen and added

p.s. Would you care to stop for tea any day this week about
4 o'clock. —I.W.

She washed her face, dressed, and walked to Windward Avenue, where she placed an order at the Italian grocery. Ice was sold at the feed and grain store and she ordered a block delivered. The man at the telephone company office said she certainly could have a 'phone: lines were up along all the canals. She bought soap at the drugstore and stamps at the post office and mailed her note. The post office was only a short way from the real estate office. She could have stopped in under some pretext and might have seen Joe O'Brien, but she wanted him to come to her.

When she reached home her groceries were waiting in two crates on the kitchen floor. A block of ice feathered with sawdust had been settled in the icebox. It took her most of an hour to put away her groceries, deciding just where things ought to go. It was satisfying, managing by herself.

For the rest of the day she roamed from room to room. It wasn't restlessness exactly. She felt happy, almost too satisfied to be still. The empty house and the calm space was exactly what she needed. For dinner she heated a can of tomato soup and crumbled a cracker into it. For dessert she ate half of a big, tasteless California pear.

She slept in her blanket nest on the floor and woke late. There was no fog. She made coffee and walked through the rooms holding a steaming cup, still pleased with the emptiness and the morning light in each room. She did not leave the house or even dress. Late in the afternoon she filled the bathtub and lay in it with light and air wafting in the open window. Feeling sleepy, she touched her floating breasts and tried to imagine carrying and delivering a baby. It seemed impossible, but plenty of people had done it, even in her family.

She didn't know yet what she was going to do. She wanted to just *be* for a while. To collect herself. Much of her life had just been a refraction of her parents' desires and needs. She wanted light, and time to think— if that was what one called the business of living in one's mind and instincts, with nothing else for company. More an animal than a person: that was what she wanted to be for a while.

But animals need heat. She started to wonder why Joe O'Brien had not called on her as promised. After all, his brother had described him as "a gentleman of leisure." She felt a cut of anxiety. Perhaps he had left already for Mexico.

She had no claim on him, only that he'd promised to call.

She stepped out of her bath, dressed quickly, and began straightening her empty rooms again. That she might never see him again was troubling. How sensitive and intelligent he had seemed, with his blackness and those quick blue eyes. He had listened so carefully, but after mulling over what she said maybe he'd dismissed it as girlish and silly and decided to have no more to do with her.

But he had probed her thoughts. Listened to her. And she'd felt her body exercising some radiant power over his—she hadn't admitted that to herself until now, but it was true. She'd felt it. She made up her blanket bed and began cleaning her kitchen, scouring the sink, washing down countertops, throwing out orange peel, coffee grounds, and empty soup tins. She couldn't stop. She went from room to room, dusting every window ledge, breathing sharp, shallow breaths, her heart pounding. After an hour the house was perfectly orderly and clean, but still it did not satisfy, and she did not know what more she could do. Then she remembered Cordelia in Pasadena, washing windows every couple of weeks.

Lifting Joe O'Brien's white roses from their bucket, she breathed in their fragrance. Then she put them in the bathroom sink and filled the bucket with a solution of vinegar and water and began cleaning windows, starting in the kitchen and working her way through every room. They didn't seem very dirty at first, but the slanting afternoon sunlight began detailing every smear. No matter how much she polished she could see swirls on each pane.

When she ran out of rags, she went through her clothes until she found a dress, grey silk, made by the Chinese dressmaker on Fifth Street who made frocks and gowns for the matrons and daughters at the Pasadena Club. It was the dress Iseult had worn to her mother's funeral. She began tearing it up and using the scraps of silk on her windows. She cleaned every piece of glass in the house, including the mirror above the bathroom sink. And still they weren't clean—they were murkier than ever.

Suddenly she was exhausted. She dumped the bucket into the kitchen sink and refilled it with cold water, then gathered the roses from the bathroom. Stepping over the dress lying in tatters on the floor, she felt ashamed of what she'd done. Without eating or undressing, she lay down on her blankets and almost immediately fell asleep.

Awakening in darkness in what she knew must be the heart of the night, she could not get back to sleep. She had lost all her composure and clarity. Her mind was sore from exhaustion.

She could hear coyotes yipping. In Pasadena there'd been coyotes; she was used to their hysterical noises. Dogs of death, her mother once called them, the only time she had heard her mother use that word.

A house was just a house. He had a railroad, mountains. He was making something of himself. She was trying to but not getting very far. Sunlight, space, setting—they were aspects of existence but weren't in themselves reasons for living. They were like the wind blowing across the land, not the land itself. She had to find her purpose; she needed her own ground.

Alone was no good. Someday she would need children and a sense of life widening, not narrowing.

Patrick Dubois on the stairs; her father in his upstairs library all alone; Joe struggling with his little book of manners—men might seem harder, more forceful, but really they were as unsure of themselves as women.

Desire was the most interesting thing.

She grew even more restless. Her legs thrashed and kicked under the blankets. She heard noises rising outside, rustlings and scrapings. Coyotes? She fought panic. Finally she went out to the living room, wearing a blanket around her shoulders. It was three o'clock by the Leavenworth clock. From her front window she could see hundreds, thousands of electric lights sparkling on Venice Pier. Was the Incubatorium closed; were the newborns asleep? Were the nurses? Perhaps they had visitors through the night. Perhaps she ought to dress and go out there, she thought; there was nowhere else she felt so alive.

No.

I have to get this under control, she told herself, *or I am going to lose my mind.*

She dragged her nest of blankets into the living room. As she lay on the floor, the electric glow falling through the windows resembled moonlight. All the energy she had been using in the past few days to bolster her sense of self was spent. Wrapped in the old blankets, she felt drained and spiritless, but she lay awake for a long time before she could sleep.

~

The morning fog was white and wet. She made herself take a bath before getting dressed. She measured and boiled coffee and buttered and ate a slice of bread, trying in each small sequence of actions to recover her poise. Lightness, joy, freedom seemed very far away. Everything tasted like nothing. These bare rooms were nothing, and so was she.

She was afraid to leave her house; afraid that if she did, she'd never return to it.

The fog had not cleared by noon. It seemed to curdle more thickly than ever.

That was the afternoon Mr. J. O'Brien came to tea.

~

The knock on the front door startled her. "Miss Wilkins? Are you at home?"

She considered not answering the door, hiding in her bedroom. She wasn't strong enough to entertain a visitor, especially him. But if she hid from him she'd despise herself even more. She was bathed and dressed at least.

She opened the door, smiling. "Mr. O'Brien, what a nice surprise! Won't you come in?"

In one hand he held a bunch of irises wrapped in a sheet of newspaper, in his other hand a wrapped parcel. He thrust the flowers at her.

"How kind! I've so enjoyed your roses. Please come in." She took the flowers into the kitchen and started clipping the stems. She didn't have a vase so she filled a glass with water and brought the flowers out.

He wore his blue suit, a striped shirt, another stiff white collar, and a maroon necktie, and he looked handsome, dark, and strong.

"A present for the house." He held out the parcel.

"Really, this is too much, Mr. O'Brien."

"Hardly. Open it."

She pulled away the wrapping. It was a big quarto-sized volume: *Interior Arrangement and Furnishing of the California Bungalow.* Kneeling on the floor, she opened the book and slowly turned pages. There were photographs and floor plans, drawings of chairs, lamps, and furnishings.

"Oh, this is quite thrilling! How thoughtful of you."

"I thought you might find something in it."

She saw him glance at her nest of blankets on the floor. "I don't have a real bed yet," she said quickly. "Or chairs or a table. So your book will be my guide."

"There may be one or two ideas there you can use. Maybe I'd better come back some other time, when you've had a chance to settle in?"

"I have tea and sugar and milk. I think we'll manage."

He followed her into the narrow little kitchen and she felt him watching her while she lit the stove and got out her mother's tea things.

"Are you finding room to breathe?" he asked.

She looked around at him and smiled. "Will this white fog ever lift, Mr. O'Brien?"

"Oh, it won't last. By the way, you can order firewood at the feed and grain on Washington Boulevard. A fire would cheer things up."

He carried the tea tray to the living room. She had failed herself so far, but having another body in the cottage was reassuring. His masculine voice and scent relieved the pressure of the emptiness.

"We'll sit on the floor," she said, "if that's all right."

"Of course it is."

His body gave the room dimension. The emptiness no longer seemed monstrous. He poured tea while she opened the book and examined the photographs, elevations, and room plans. Each house, each room, every piece of furniture had clean horizontal lines.

"Some of our friends in Pasadena lived in these sorts of cottages. They were called cottages, but they were quite grand houses." She slowly turned pages. "My mother didn't like them but I thought they were beautiful."

"That is the sort I would want to build, with plenty of space. Room to breathe. Is your furniture being shipped from the East?"

"No, no. I will have new things."

"There's a fellow in Santa Monica, a furniture maker—he will build anything you like so long as it's modern. He carved a propeller for Grattan."

"A propeller?"

"Grattan owns a share of a flying machine. He's always trying something new. The propeller represents most of his equity, I believe. She originally had a four-blade metal propeller, but when they were replacing the engine, they decided that a two-blade wooden propeller was the best match. It's lighter than the metal one."

"Are you an aviator?"

"No. I've been up a few times with my brother. I used to fly in my dreams, but it isn't really much like it is in dreams. The motor's noisy, and the wind. They have to watch the rudder and the trim. She takes a fair bit of muscle to fly."

"Aren't you afraid of crashing?"

"They've had a couple of crack-ups, nothing they haven't been able to fix. Takeoffs and landings are the trickiest."

"But weren't you afraid of being killed?"

"I didn't think about it. I wouldn't be much of a loss to anyone at present. I don't approve of my brother flying, though. He's married, and they've a child on the way. What business does he have floating around the sky? He spends too much time in the clouds—"

"And ought to keep his feet on the ground?"

"That's it. I could use him on the contract. Elise is for it, but he won't agree. He isn't practical. None of my family are. My mother believed she could see the future in a blue bottle. Grattan and I are the only ones out in this world. The others have vocations; they needn't worry about their next meal. I hope Elise can knock some sense into him. The world doesn't owe anyone a living. Maybe it should, because no one asked to be born, but it doesn't."

His hands holding the teacup were nicked with scars and older than the rest of him.

"You ought to meet Elise. They live at her studio. She makes a living with postcards and studio portraits, but every Sunday she goes out on the boardwalk and takes snaps of strangers—I don't know why, because there's no money in it. Just the film must cost a lot. She is a Jew, Elise. The priest at St. Monica's refused to marry them even though she agreed the children would be baptized Catholic. I wrote him to see if I could change his mind; my brother Tom did as well, but he never replied, so Grattan and Elise were married at Santa Monica City Hall."

He wanted her to see him as connected, rooted, responsible. He might be all that. And part of him was darker, stronger, and more fluid.

She had no family of her own within two thousand miles.

"When do you leave for Mexico, Mr. O'Brien?"

"Soon enough. Shall I help with cleaning up? I know you don't approve of servants."

He helped carry the tea things to the narrow little kitchen. He was a fastidious person, polished, nothing at all like Patrick Dubois—but there was that roughness. Was there any kindness in him as well? Maybe he just wanted things.

She handed him his hat and held open the front door. White fog still battened the cottage. "Thank you again for the flowers, Mr. O'Brien."

"Miss Wilkins, you are like no one else I've ever met."

She felt excitement rising in her chest. The cold marine layer slinking inland from the beach tasted pungent, almost sour.

"I'll call again if I may."

"Of course."

"Goodbye."

"Goodbye, Mr. O'Brien."

~

His presence lingered. Houses required presence—ghosts, men, tea leaves, conversation. Otherwise any house was a trap, and a bungalow on a canal in Venice, California, was a box shrouded in white fog, the heaviness and stillness of atmosphere signifying nothing.

~

Even in a Sunday crowd Elise O'Brien wasn't difficult to spot: a small person, hatless, unmistakably pregnant, a camera slung around her neck. She was heading north on the boardwalk, but slowly; she looked to be about the same age as Iseult. She kept stepping out into the stream of people heading south, standing still and letting the crowd break around her while she peered into her viewfinder.

Iseult could not imagine what she was making pictures of. The teeming throng recalled Broadway and warm afternoons on the West Side, from the slaughterhouses to the Kitchen. There was no composition that Iseult could recognize as such, no one remarkable or colourful, just the drifting, shifting, sunburnt, ice-cream-eating crowd. A few people stopped and spoke to Elise, but not many. Most of her subjects didn't seem to notice her. And Elise kept moving on.

Iseult tried stepping into the oncoming crowd. People became blurred bits of motion. Details registered discordantly: straw hats, prams with squeaky wheels. Tongues licking ice cream.

It made her dizzy.

She followed Elise O'Brien for nearly an hour, entranced by her boldness and the mystery of what she was doing. On their afternoons in the Kitchen, Mother Power had opened Iseult's eyes to the city, and she wondered if Elise too possessed keys to a wider world.

~

Late that afternoon she found herself climbing three flights of stairs above the Chinese laundry. The staircase smelled of steam and hot linen. On the third-floor landing a sign on a door said:

E C PHOTOGRAPHIC PARLOR

Iseult knocked.

"Who the hell is it?" a woman's voice demanded.

"My name is Iseult Wilkins."

"Yeah? What do you want?"

"I'm a friend of Joe O'Brien."

"Hang on a sec."

A moment later the door was flung open and Elise stood there. She wore a blue smock and seemed even smaller than she had on the boardwalk, and more pregnant. "So you're Miss Wilkins. Grattan told me about you."

Iseult extended a white-gloved hand. "How do you do?"

Elise O'Brien wiped her hand on her smock; they shook. "That was you tracking me on the boardwalk this morning."

"I'm sorry. I should have introduced myself."

"Nah. When I get going, I can't stop to be polite. Especially when I'm shooting for myself, like I was today. Did you feel the energy out there? Isn't it something? Lately I've been letting the postcards go to hell. Grattan doesn't mind but Joe thinks I'm nuts, and I guess he's right, because we sure could use the dough.

"So, Iseult Wilkins, you want to come in? I was just going over today's haul."

The studio was one large room. There was a chemical odour. Photographic prints were pegged out on a laundry line and tacked up along the walls. One end of the room was set up as living space, with a kitchen table and an icebox and books stacked on the floor on both sides of an unmade bed.

Elise picked up a camera. "This is the camera that's for sale, an FPK—stands for 'Folding Pocket Kodak.' It's a 3¼ by 5½ image on 122 film. Zeiss Kodak anastigmatic lens. It's a nice piece of equipment if you like the panorama format. Most of the body's aluminum, but the sides are wood, so it has a bit of weight. If a camera's too light you get the shakes. Here—see how it feels. Did Joe tell you a price?"

Iseult accepted the camera. "He didn't tell me you were selling anything."

"Then why are you here?"

"Why are you selling it?" In its complexity and polish, the camera had an unexpected beauty.

"We need the dough. I'm keeping my five-by-eight for studio work and I have my Wilkin-Welsh for the boardwalk. Studio work pays the bills, but I like getting outside, like today. The boardwalk is tough—all that light, all that chance and change—but if I'm paying attention something always reveals itself, just for a split second, and then I'll get a crazy, cockeyed picture. It gets so the camera's part of me out there, not something I'm holding. I'm actually a very shy person. Where I'm from—Brooklyn—I count as shy."

Elise was sitting on a broken-down sofa. A grey cat rubbed against her leg and she reached to stroke it but couldn't bend over enough. She laughed. "I'm as big as a house. This big Irish baby."

The leather-wrapped camera was cool and weighty in Iseult's hands. She admired the polished steel and brass. The lens slid out on bellows of red leather. A rubber bulb snapped the shutter. She could remember walking along Textile Street in New Hampshire and hearing—feeling—the restless beat of the power looms. Her family's wealth had been founded on that mill, but she'd been brought up to fear and despise machinery.

"I met Grattan out on the boardwalk. See, over there." Elise pointed to a wall where dozens of photographic prints were tacked up haphazardly. The photographs had all been taken on the boardwalk. None were posed, and all of the subjects seemed preoccupied with other things. It took Iseult a while to find Grattan. He was wearing a straw hat, a blazer, and white trousers. His pale eyes showed wildly against his sunburnt face.

"Sometimes I walk up and down that goddamn boardwalk all morning and don't see a thing. Then there's a certain person comes along. Maybe on a bicycle. Maybe eating ice cream. Maybe happy, maybe not. But something about them gets me and then I'm all nerves, shaking. Sometimes when things are really moving I get so anxious I just have to fire the camera, let fly a picture, just to release the energy. I like your dress, Miss Wilkins. It's nice. *Très chic.*"

Iseult looked over her shoulder. Elise was peering down into the viewfinder of a large box camera pointed at her.

"Thank you."

"Maybe I'm only out on the boardwalk on account of it suits my personality. Have you been to see the Incubatorium babies, Miss Wilkins?"

"Yes."

"I used to feel like one of them before Grattan came along. It's awful. I'd pay my quarter and sometimes the kid I was watching the day before wouldn't be there anymore, and not because it suddenly got better. You want the FPK, Miss Wilkins? It's yours for seven dollars. Including a glass back and a bunch of 122 film stock."

"Will you teach me how to use it?"

~

The 122 film came out of its box rolled up on a little wooden spool, and over the next few days Iseult shot roll after roll. Lessons had to be on the boardwalk because Elise was uninterested in any other venue. In the afternoons Elise began teaching her to use the techniques and chemicals of the darkroom. Iseult wrinkled her nose at the flat, putrid smells, but watching her first images swim up out of their chemical bath was thrilling.

On Friday afternoon her head was full of fumes after hours of developing and printing. It was time to go home, but she decided she would walk out to the pier to watch the sunset first and let the ocean air blow the chemical smell out of her nostrils. She asked Elise if she wanted to come along but Elise shook her head.

"Nah, I'm gonna keep working. After this kid is born I'm not going to be able to do this, am I. I got to shoot, I got to print. If you go by the office, tell Grattan to bring something home for supper."

She met Grattan and Joe O'Brien outside the real estate office just as Grattan was locking up for the day. She hadn't seen them all week. Joe O'Brien looked grumpy, and she sensed some tension between the brothers. She delivered Elise's message.

"I'll pick up some chowder and crackers," Grattan said. "Do you want to join us, Joe?"

"No thanks. If you are heading for the pier, I'll go with you, if I may," Joe O'Brien said to Iseult.

He offered her his arm and they walked out on the pier. The sun was a red ball and the air smelled briny, as sharp as ammonia. It was chilly, and the Japanese fishermen had bundled themselves up in blankets. Joe O'Brien was silent and seemed preoccupied.

"A penny for your thoughts, Mr. O'Brien."

"Oh, I'm worrying about my brother. Nothing new."

"Why must you worry about him?"

"He's my brother, Miss Wilkins; it comes with the territory. Anyway, he's got nobody else to worry about him. Elise doesn't worry nearly enough, if you ask me, not for a woman with a baby on the way and a husband who hasn't made ten dollars all month."

They watched the red sun sink below the horizon. When it was gone, the air immediately seemed colder. She shivered.

"I'll walk you home," Joe O'Brien said.

"What about Mexico, Mr. O'Brien? When do you leave?"

"You don't see it, do you?" He sounded impatient, almost angry.

"See what?"

"You are the reason I'm still here, Miss Wilkins."

They walked in silence, her arm in his. She was thrilled by what he'd said. Up Windward, past the Chinese laundry and the photographic parlour where Elise and Grattan were probably eating dinner, if Grattan had brought home chowder. Elise hated to cook, and they had only one little gas ring.

It was dark and cold along the Grand Canal and the Linnie. They finally arrived at the cottage and stopped on the path. She hesitated, then gently withdrew her arm from his.

"Good night, Miss Wilkins."

"Thank you for bringing me home."

"I'll wait here until you're inside."

"Will I see you again?"

He waited a moment before answering. "If you'd like to."

"I would. Yes."

"Then you shall."

He waited out on the canal path while she unlocked her front door. She wasn't going to ask him in. The cottage was a mess and she still had no furniture except a gorgeous new bed, and she could hardly show him her bed. Besides, she needed to be alone with what he'd said. She didn't want him saying anything more for now.

"Miss Wilkins?"

She turned to look at him.

"All this business is pretty damned awkward, isn't it."

"Yes, it is. Good night, Mr. O'Brien."

Acrid scent of the sea, of rank grasses and cold sand.

"Good night, Miss Wilkins."

~

Elise said that the best thing about coming to California was everything you could leave behind. "Everyone should move to California once in their life. Think if you'd stayed in Cow Hampshire, Iseult. Think how tied down you'd feel."

"It was sometimes hard to breathe there," Iseult admitted. She had not told Elise what Joe said on the pier.

"I got no use for people myself," Elise said. "People make such a big fuss about their families, and I just don't get it. Me, I come from a family of rats. Papa Rat, Momma Rat, Bubbie Rat, and all the baby Rats of Williamsburg, Brooklyn. I'm done with all that clawing and nibbling. Myself alone feels nice to me."

"What about your husband? And the baby?"

Elise did not respond.

"You care about Grattan, don't you?"

"Sure I do." Elise's small face suddenly looked older. "I've put myself in a cage, Iseult. You think I don't see it? The world is not set up for a woman to stay free. Maybe I should've held on to the life I had, not let go so easy."

Iseult glanced at her.

"Aw, sheesh," Elise said. "Poor little me, huh? Let's get out there and shoot some film."

~

~~Venice Land Company~~
~~Windward Avenue~~
~~Venice, Calif.~~

20th February

Dear Miss Wilkins,

    There will be a surf riding demonstration Sunday afternoon next, between the piers. Would you care to see it from the beach? I shall call for you at one o'clock, unless I hear otherwise.

Best regards.
J. O'Brien

P.S. Bring a bathing costume, if you care to, and we might try the Plunge.

Searching for her bathing costume, Iseult finally found it in one of the trunks she hadn't bothered to unpack yet. She had trouble getting to sleep and woke early on Sunday morning, made coffee, loaded film, and polished the lens of her camera. She kept looking at the Leavenworth clock. It was quite possible he would forget his invitation, she decided. He might have left for Mexico already. Was it possible? Could he have? He was deep in his life already and she was stopped on the surface of her own.

She started cleaning her house, unnecessarily and somewhat frantically. By noon she was exhausted. When she opened the windows in the bedroom, the air outside was warm and pleasant and smelled of the sea. Falling down upon her bed, she drifted into a dream that she was riding a train. Not in one of the coaches but on the black locomotive, boilers seething, drive wheels pounding. She woke with a pillow clenched between her legs and caught a glimpse of something outside her window. Racing to look, she saw Joe O'Brien circling her house on a snarling, sputtering red motorcycle with a sidecar, bouncing over dirt and dry yellow grass, raising a tail of dust. Seeing her, he braked to a stop. He wore goggles and a big grin. He reached down and cut the motor; there was abrupt silence and the sweet tang of gasoline.

"What do you think?" he cried. "Isn't she a beauty?"

~

He parked the motorcycle in front of the big red-brick bathhouse on Rose Avenue. "We'll watch the surf riders first, then come back here for a plunge. The tank is heated salt water."

She pulled off the goggles he'd made her wear and retrieved her straw hat. Climbing out of a sidecar was nearly as difficult as climbing in. She felt tight and uneasy. It wasn't her clothes—the blue skirt and fresh white blouse would do, though she was uneasy about her bathing costume. Maybe it was the wild sun and the hot, strumming wind. She was unattached, weightless, dizzy.

"All set?" He wore a bathing costume under his seersucker jacket and cotton trousers. All his clothes were new. He picked up the picnic basket, offered his arm, and they started down Windward towards the hard blue line of the sea. On the beach between Fraser and Ocean Park hundreds of people had gathered to watch the surf riding. Joe O'Brien rented a striped umbrella and a couple of beach chairs and they watched the riders—three Hawaiians and three white boys—start out, kneeling on big polished planks and paddling ferociously. With their black costumes, dark skin, and sleek hair, they looked like seals. One board was caught by an incoming wave and flipped, but the others kept paddling, dashing their boards over the waves. Out beyond the surf break the riders straddled their boards and floated up and down on the swells, facing out to sea, waiting.

There was no point in breaking out her little camera. The lens would make nothing of the scene: the distance too great, the figures too small. A good pair of binoculars would have been useful.

A rider stood up on his board. Shading his eyes, he stared out to sea. Then he knelt and quickly swung his board around until it aimed at the beach.

"Here it is," said Joe. "What they're waiting for."

She could see the swell rising, green and blue, behind the riders. The hump of water was moving fast. They were paddling furiously to keep ahead of it. One, two, three riders were pulled up over the crest, but the two others had caught the wave and were riding on the edge of it, standing on their boards, balanced and calm. She'd never seen anyone capture the force of nature so neatly. She felt a tremble of excitement and suddenly knew she had to transpose her life into another key—harsher, riskier. It wasn't enough to be alone. Watching the surf riders moving in perfect equipoise through tumult and complex disorder, she felt space opening up within her chest, lungs expanding, the power to breathe deeply and well.

~

In the ladies' dressing room she gave a dime to an attendant with peach-coloured hair and was handed a key to a stall. She entered one and started to undress, hanging her clothes on the hooks provided. Standing naked in her small cube of space, she looked down at her white flesh and nipples prickling in the cold—or maybe it was excitement, fear. She could hear showers hissing somewhere, women's laughter, a baby screeching.

Her costume was black flannel in two pieces: drawers that reached her knees, with a skirt attached, and an unbecoming blouse. Her breasts felt exposed and heavy. Her mother had always said that her legs were good. Long and strong.

As a girl she'd been a dipper, not a swimmer. Secluded female dips at Squam Lake just after dawn, with aunts and female cousins.

What would he see? She was afraid, but she knew she had to go out there.

She found him sitting at the edge of the giant swimming tank, waiting for her. Hundreds of people were dousing and plunging, and the enormous room echoed with splashing, screams, and laughter. He was wearing his costume.

Man's body like a tree trunk, she thought. Solid. Humming. Energy within.

"Shall we take the plunge?" he said.

"I suppose we'd better."

They descended the tiled steps together. She slipped into the warm, briny water first and started swimming, nipples prickling again, wet wool pulling at her skin. He caught up and they swam the length of the tank side by side, only their heads above water. Men with droopy moustaches and girls with ringlets plastered wet splashed and shouted. Her silent swim with Joe O'Brien through that uproar felt as intimate as she had ever been with anyone. She felt naked and warm, without fear.

~

When he brought her home on the motorcycle, her hair was still damp and she could taste salt on her lips. It was late afternoon and the light was cooling. She hadn't changed because she hadn't wanted to shower with strangers, so she wore his seersucker jacket over her bathing costume, the rest of her clothes and her shoes in a bundle. He wore his bathing costume with trousers and tennis shoes. She thought of asking him in for tea, but she knew she needed to be alone after the wild scattering the beach and the surf and their swim had given her. Still, she didn't want to let him go.

"May I take your photograph?" She hadn't opened the camera all afternoon but she wanted to capture him before he left. Something important was at stake. The last time she had felt so alone with a man was in the schoolhouse cellar with Patrick Dubois. "On your machine, I think. That would make a splendid photograph."

"Let me get dressed first. I'll go around back, put on the rest of my clothes."

"No, really," she said. "Just as you are. Please."

He looked at her with such a serious expression she wondered if she had offended him somehow. Maybe he thought she was making fun of him.

"Please."

He shrugged. As she opened the camera he walked back to the machine, threw his leg over, and sat in the saddle. For a moment she was afraid he might grab the handlebars and try to pose as though riding. Instead he leaned back slightly, crossing his arms on his chest.

As she peered into the viewfinder he looked straight at her, with more force and determination than she'd felt in any other man's gaze. A hardened loneliness in him, matching and filling something in herself. He was almost beautiful. Maybe she was too.

She made six exposures from different angles.

"I like to smell the sea," he said. "I'll miss it. Miss you as well."

"When do you leave for Mexico, Mr. O'Brien?"

"Damn Mexico. I like it here."

If you want to kiss me, she thought, *you might as well do it now. I want to be open, not closed.* What if she slipped off the seersucker jacket, pulled the black woollen blouse over her head, and offered herself to him? A woman shaking with desire and loneliness, like a door left banging in the wind.

He kick-started the engine and ran it up a couple of times. The noise was too much, and before she could say anything more he had started off down the canal path, kicking up dust, not looking back once.

Was he annoyed with her for taking his picture on the motorcycle? Maybe it wasn't how he saw himself. She had his jacket anyway. He'd have to come back for that.

~

She developed the negatives and laid out the first set of prints for Elise to look at.

"Hmmm, these are good," Elise said. "These are rather wicked."

"What do you mean?"

His bare arms were crossed, the goggles were pushed back on his head. Clear eyes, burnished face. His black hair was stiff and coarse with salt.

"Maybe you've caught a little bit of Mr. Joe O'Brien that he didn't want you to see."

Iseult reconsidered the images. *He looks like the future*, she thought. Lucid, gleaming, and something withheld.

She went home to bed, slept deeply, and the next morning walked all the way to Santa Monica to buy expensive German paper at the camera shop on Third Street. Then she went to the studio, chose the strongest image, and printed it over and over again until she was satisfied.

~

~~Venice Land Company~~
~~Windward Avenue~~
~~Venice, Calif.~~

1st March, 1912

Dear Miss Wilkins,

   Would you care to see some flying? My brother and his partners will be at the aerodrome at Griffith Park, Sunday next. I could call for you at say 9 a.m. and make a day of it. But let me know. I think you must have my jacket, by the way.

                    Yours truly,
                    J. O'Brien

~

Linnie Cottage
2nd March

Dear Mr. O'Brien,

   If you come by at 9 o'clock I shall be ready.

                    Regards,
                    Iseult Wilkins

~

The motorcycle roared up through the canyon and down into the San Fernando Valley, which sprawled like an exhausted animal in the heat. Their tail of dust caught up with them as Joe turned off the main road at a sign:

LOS ANGELES AERONAUTICAL CLUB

It was supposed to be an airfield, but as they were driving in, the place looked like any ramshackle California farm. She saw a barn. Then she saw a big, luxurious Pierce-Arrow automobile parked next to a pair of flying machines tethered to the ground. The barn doors were open and Grattan and two other men were inside, working on a flying machine. As Joe helped her from the sidecar they came out, all three wearing blue coveralls.

"What do you say, Grattan?" Joe asked. "Will you be going up?"

"Good flying weather, isn't it." Grattan introduced Iseult to the two Frenchmen. M. Levasseur was tall, thin, and gawky in his movements, like a heron. M. Tourbot was stocky and dark, and he shook her hand with some impatience.

"We have installed the new propeller," Grattan said. "If you and Miss Wilkins will lend us a hand, we can roll her out. I'm taking the first hop."

They trundled the machine out of the barn, Iseult and Joe at one wing, Tourbot and Levasseur at the other, Grattan pushing the tail. The aircraft seemed delicate and fragile, like an enormous dragonfly, she thought.

While Grattan strapped on a leather helmet and pulled on leather gauntlets, the Frenchmen adjusted wires and struts. She watched the cloth-covered wings warp and flex when little M. Tourbot manipulated a pair of wooden pedals in front of the pilot's wicker seat.

"Now, Miss Wilkins, would you like to go up?" Grattan said.

A quick panic so deep she felt like laughing. And a sense of everything being unreal, colours changing, sparks of light flying off M. Levasseur's spectacles.

"Of course," she heard herself saying. "I'd love to." She couldn't bear to show any fear in front of Joe O'Brien.

"No, Grattan, don't be ridiculous. Of course she won't," Joe said. "That's not why I brought her out."

"But I want to," she insisted.

"No," Joe said. "I won't allow it."

"I tell you, I want to go."

"No. It's too dangerous."

"Joe's right," Grattan said. "It is too dangerous."

"Miss Wilkins, there was never any question of your going up in the machine. It never occurred to me."

"Why did you bring me out here, then? And who are you to tell me what I can't do?" She turned to Grattan. "Grattan O'Brien, if you're a gentleman, you won't be bullied by your brother. Does your offer stand, sir?"

"Well, I guess it does, Miss Wilkins. If you put it that way."

"I will not stand here and allow you to break your neck," Joe said. "If you think that's the kind of man I am, Miss Wilkins, you don't know me." There was a kind of fury, a passion, in him she'd not seen before; his eyes shone with it.

Iseult touched his arm. It felt hard. "Come on, Joe O'Brien," she said softly, "let's talk. I must talk to you."

It surprised her that he allowed her to lead him away while Grattan and the others went back to fussing over the machine. She and Joe walked out onto the crisp stubble that had once been grass. Locusts were sputtering and flicking themselves at the sun.

She held his arm. "I want to be closer to you," she said. "Do you understand? This is what matters now. This is what is interesting. Don't you feel it?"

He stopped. Standing in the forceful sunlight, eyes narrowed, he gazed at her.

"Don't you?" she repeated.

"All right. Go up, if that's what you want. I won't stop you. Only you ought to marry me, Miss Wilkins. I think it would be better if you did. I want to marry you right now."

"You do?"

"I strongly do."

She could hear the wind whining through struts and steel wires. She looked over her shoulder at Grattan and the two Frenchmen, who were busy, or pretending to be. No telling if they'd overheard.

Meanwhile, Joe O'Brien had somehow regained all his composure. "There it is, Miss Wilkins," he said wryly. "Fine piece of an offer, wasn't it? Pretty smooth."

"Do you wish to withdraw your offer, Mr. O'Brien?" she said.

"No. Not in a million years."

~

Fear wasn't bad unless you let it show. She hadn't eaten since breakfast: maybe that was why she felt weak. Or was it just pure fear stirring her intestines? Her mouth tasted dry. *I really don't want to be mangled*, she told herself. *Don't want to be burnt. But if we get up and down again, everything will taste better. I'll know myself better.*

"We shall want to shift the machine about again, I suggest," the tall, skinny Frenchman, M. Levasseur, said. "The wind is turning."

M. Tourbot and Joe each took a wingtip and she helped M. Levasseur and Grattan lift the tail. The undercarriage was an assembly of varnished wooden struts supporting a pair of spoked bicycle wheels. The wings and the forward part of the body were covered in yellow cloth; the rest of the framework had been left bare and looked like a skeleton.

They swung it around until it nosed into the wind. Tourbot and Joe supported the wings while Grattan climbed gingerly into the pilot's seat, then signalled for Iseult to scramble up into the observer's seat. She tried to hold her skirt about her, sensing that if she put a foot in the wrong place she would break the taut fabric of the wing. Her seat had a leather belt attached and M. Levasseur demonstrated how to cinch and buckle it. Then he ran around and gave the propeller a spin, then another, and on the second spin the motor began to spit and snarl.

Iseult felt the machine trembling. It seemed as frail as a paper lantern, except for the dirty stink of exhaust spurting from the motor and the manic whipping noise from the propeller. The machine began to move forward in a series of awkward jerks, with the three men walking along supporting the wings and the tail, the motor raging, frame creaking, wires and struts groaning and squeaking as the wings sagged and flexed.

They began picking up speed. Now Joe and M. Tourbot were running to keep up, barely holding on to the wingtips. Looking down at the rushing ground, she saw a rabbit leap into a hole, and then they were lifting off, white rubber wheels skimming the grass and rising, spinning free as the machine bucked into the air. They kept climbing at a shallow angle. She could feel the propeller dragging them up, the engine screaming. Invisible airflow punched the machine and she felt it skip and shuffle, but still she felt the motive pull upward. She stared at Grattan's bare neck, the back of his head wrapped in brown kid leather. He began tramping hard on one of the foot pedals, warping the starboard wing, which dipped. They were turning. She clutched his seat back, terrified of falling out. They were still climbing as they turned. Dry pasture below, tawny squares of wheat fields, a streak of grey road, cows, blue buildings on the edge of Glendale, the San Gabriel peaks.

Flying level now. Grattan twisted around and grinned at her.

Exhilaration.

~

The landing was fast and alarming, fear climbing in her throat as the plane dropped suddenly. A side wind buffeted the machine and made it skip, but Grattan straightened it out and lifted the nose at the last moment. Iseult felt the bicycle wheels bump, skip, then bump again and start running over the rough ground.

The Frenchmen and Joe were waiting by the Pierce-Arrow, M. Tourbot gripping a green champagne bottle by its neck, and five fluted glasses. M. Levasseur came forward and helped her climb down. She heard him telling Grattan they had been in the air twenty-seven minutes. M. Tourbot filled their glasses and, standing beside the plane, made a toast. "All honour to yourself, *mademoiselle. Félicitations!*"

The wine tasted sweet and good. She touched the yellow cloth covering the wing. Everything lit with sun, the crisp wine and the fierce engine smell and the toasted scent of dry grass. Even the dust kicked up by the desert wind had fragrance. She coughed and felt the first minute ache in her chest. She looked around for her silk scarf, thinking to hold it over her nose and mouth, but she couldn't see it anywhere.

Tourbot and Levasseur were drawing straws to see who would pilot the next flight. Grattan was kneeling on the ground and greasing the wheel hubs.

"Are you going to fly?" she asked Joe.

He shook his head. "No, not me. There's enough excitement here on the ground for me. Have you had a chance to think over what I said?"

A spell of coughing shook her.

"Joe! Miss Wilkins! Come give us a hand!" Grattan shouted.

M. Levasseur had won the draw and was climbing into the pilot's chair. He sat pulling on his gloves and helmet while Iseult and the others picked up the machine and started turning it into the wind.

The coughing fit had passed but she could feel her lungs itching. All her life, high excitement and stimulated feelings had been followed by disastrous spells of bronchial inflammation. Sore lungs and weak, whispery breathing. She'd learned to seek solitude and emptiness for a kind of peace.

M. Tourbot ran forward to spin the prop, and as soon as the motor fired he scrambled up into the observer's chair. He was still buckling himself in as the plane began moving. Joe supported one wing, Iseult held the other. Grattan was supporting the tail. She could feel the machine quivering and flexing as the undercarriage trundled over the rough ground. It began picking up speed. She had to walk faster and then run to keep up. The wing surged from her grasp and the plane stumbled over grass for a few more yards, then the wheels lifted off. She stopped running and stood shielding her eyes against the sun, trying to ignore the ache in her chest, watching the frail machine staggering up into the blue sky.

There was more champagne in an ice chest underneath the Pierce-Arrow. "It's great having Frenchmen for partners," Grattan said. Joe would not take any more wine but Grattan refilled her glass and his own. Keeping to the narrow strip of shade beside the automobile, they ate hardboiled eggs, cucumber sandwiches, and peaches from a wicker basket.

She was sitting on the running board and Joe and Grattan were lying on the grass when she felt Joe's thumb and forefinger wrap around her ankle and hold on. She felt electrified and calm all at once. Nothing seemed impossible. Her lungs ached, but if she was lucky and stayed calm the inflammation might subside. Perhaps more cold champagne would help. She refilled her glass.

The O'Brien brothers lay on their backs and passed a pair of binoculars back and forth. The distant buzz of the airplane engine was no louder than the insect hum. She sipped her wine. She had taken off her little jacket, but even in the shade she could feel the dry heat licking her, like sitting too close to a stove. Every now and then he touched her ankle.

"It *is* dangerous, you know," Grattan said. "Joe's right about that. I'll tell you the honest truth, Iseult—I would not let Elise come out today, not in her condition."

The ground was warm, storing heat. She sensed the attack coming. It was the dust, the golden dust. The dry wind and the running and the fear. With each breath she could feel tiny switches of pain in the bottom of her lungs.

Joe had removed his hat, jacket, celluloid collar, and necktie. His white shirt was open at the neck and rolled up at the sleeves. His eyes were shut; his face was bathed in sun. He was only a year older than she was. A few years ago he had been a boy.

What would it be like to lie on top of him? How would it feel to have his hands on her? The clarity of the thought startled and embarrassed her. Picking up the champagne bottle, still cool and wet, she rolled the dark green glass over her lips.

"He is rolling her a little stiff," Grattan said.

Looking up, she watched the machine on its jerky, buzzing circuit high above the field. The wings dipped as it continued banking into a turn. Grattan stood up and held the binoculars pressed to his eyes. Joe arose and stood beside him.

"Something wrong?" Joe said.

"Too much rudder."

She took a mouthful of champagne, hoping to stop the next fit of coughing, but it couldn't be stopped and the spasms racked through her. Joe glanced over at her, then went back to staring upwards.

"Ease up a little!" Grattan was saying. "Come on, *mon vieux!* Pull it out."

She took a sip, hiccupped, choked, spat out wine, and scrambled to her feet. Clutching the champagne bottle and an instinct to escape, run, hide, she started walking blindly past tethered flying machines smelling of varnish, cloth, and grease, crisp grass crunching under her shoes. She was coughing, spilling wine and tears.

"Oh hell," she heard Grattan say.

When she heard the screaming engine, she looked up and saw the machine in a plummet, gathering itself to itself, spinning on its own axis. She heard Grattan coming up behind her. He ran past, heading for the place where it—they—would hit. Joe ran past her as well.

The flying machine hit the earth with a sound like a branch snapping. Insignificant. It hardly registered. The engine scream cut off at the moment of impact.

Silence. No smoke, no shock, no resonance. Just the play of the wind.

After her father's suicide she had smelled gunpowder in every room in the house, an acrid, salty tang that lingered for weeks. Her mother had insisted it was all in her imagination, and perhaps it was. On a warm day in March, three weeks after the suicide, their furnace man had lit every stove and grate in the house and furiously shovelled coal into the furnace. Two Irish housemaids, with the help of three French-Canadian operatives borrowed from the mill, threw open every window in the house and scrubbed it from top to bottom. It hadn't done any good. She'd still smelled gunpowder.

It was after that ferocious, useless housecleaning that her mother began talking of selling everything and going out to Pasadena.

Grattan and Joe were racing across the grey pasture towards the tiny, livid heap of wreckage. She started running too. It was instinctive. A sense of wildness and panic to mark the profundity of death. Breathing askew, eyes blurred with tears and champagne, she ran, her lungs sore and straining. When she tripped over a cable tethered to one of the flying machines, the taut steel wire slashed her shin and she went down hard. The side of her head whacked the grey ground, and then she was out of that place.

~

They were wed at one of the side altars in St. Monica's. She had known Joe O'Brien five weeks. Mr. Spaulding, Cordelia, Grattan, and a hugely pregnant Elise made up the wedding party. The wedding breakfast was at the Ship Restaurant on Abbot Kinney Pier. Grattan, as best man, read telegrams of congratulation from the seminarian brother, Tom, followed by terse best wishes from Iseult's Boston aunts and uncles and fulsome French congratulations from her relations in Lille. There was no word from the O'Brien sisters, cloistered in their convent at Ottawa. Joe kept reaching for her hand under the table. After the breakfast Grattan drove them to the Los Angeles train station in the Pierce-Arrow. He was trying to sell the car on behalf of the French consul, who was handling the affairs of the two dead flyers. Joe's red motorcycle had already been delivered to the station and loaded into the baggage car. They intended to explore the Sierra Madre mountains in Mexico and the route of the proposed railway.

The Pierce's buttoned leather seats smelled rich in the sun, and Iseult felt fresh and eager. For a wedding present Joe had given her all the equipment she needed to set up her own darkroom and process her own film, everything packed into steel boxes that were being shipped to his agents in Edmonton, Alberta. Grattan and Elise had given her a brand-new Vest Pocket Kodak that made images $1^5/8$ inches by $2\frac{1}{2}$ inches on 127 film; it was compact enough to fit in the palm of her hand.

The Linnie cottage was closed up. They planned to return to Venice when construction season ended in the mountains. Nonetheless, it had saddened her to lock that door. Had she failed the cottage somehow? Perhaps. But she needed risk, and she needed connection. Herself alone would never be enough.

Los Angeles was nearly beautiful under a shining spring sun, though the grey buildings downtown, banks and offices, did not seem quite real in such a clear, hard light. Joe wore a silk hat and morning coat and held her hand tightly. His silence did not surprise or upset her. They were both operating on instinct; there would always be times when language was not useful or needed, when voices would only tangle things up and get in the way. She sensed that they were both awestruck by what they'd just done, the union they'd committed themselves to.

He had booked a drawing-room suite on the Sunset Limited. At El Paso they would disembark, cross the Mexican border with the motorcycle, and board a train for Chihuahua City.

A smiling Negro porter showed them to their Pullman suite. They had a bedroom, bathroom, and drawing room, where meals would be served if they chose not to visit the dining car. The drawing room was full of flowers, and they sat on the sofa holding hands while the train bumped and shuttled through the endless sprawl of Los Angeles train yards. Sunlight cut and flashed at the windows.

"I want you," he said.

He was looking out the window when he said it.

"Yes, I know."

"What you told me, about room to breathe. You're always going to have that."

"Yes."

"I won't try to put you in some little-woman box," he said. "I'm not interested in that. Happiness means freedom. The shape of the marriage, we must build it together. A house for both of us. Plenty of room."

"And children," she said.

"Yes, I suppose."

The train had passed the dry purple hills of Covina and was picking up speed when Iseult stood up, unpinned her hat, and slipped off her short silk jacket. She undid a couple of buttons on her silk blouse, then looked at her husband.

Wordlessly Joe leaned over and began taking off his boots. Then he too arose and began undressing.

"I've been with women before. I should have told you before."

"You don't have to tell me now."

"There's not much to tell."

"Good."

Bright daylight hopped and bounced in the compartment. The train was so long that she could barely hear the engine as they cleared San Bernardino and began picking up even more speed on the level grade, running past orange and pecan groves. The window was a sheet of blue California sky. He shrugged out of his morning coat and removed his gold watch from his waistcoat pocket. He took off the waistcoat, slipped off his grey silk necktie, and removed his gold cuff links, an extravagant wedding present from Grattan. Finally he pulled out his pearl collar stud, a present from Iseult, and removed his collar.

"I think of your body," he said. "Your scent. There's nothing more powerful to me."

Her shyness was becoming a kind of excitement as she unbuttoned the waistband of her narrow grey skirt.

"You're the flower," he said. "Your body's the flower. That's how it seems to me."

Intensifying alertness, curiosity unleashed. Hunger. She had on a linen slip, a chemise, black silk stockings, and buttoned shoes. He placed his hands on her hips. He was wearing only a pair of cotton drawers. Powerful chest and powerful arms. Until then she had felt as if everything were happening in a dream, but now it was coming into better focus. It was becoming clear.

People never got quite what they expected. The world was various and changeable, and maybe they were bound to disappoint each other. Maybe their marriage would be bleak and lonely, resembling her parents', but she really did not believe so. She was on fire, and Joe O'Brien was hard and solid. Everything about him addressed the future, not the past. Marriage was going to be a road, not the place where the road stopped.

He reached up under her linen slip to the tops of her stockings. His fingers brushed the skin on her thighs and she shivered with . . . what? Expectation. Savage joy. Unlike anything else. He touched her softly, gently, right *there*, and she was so startled and thrilled that she almost howled.

He was unrolling her stockings and speaking softly. "Where I come from, if the neighbours don't like a match, they come after the couple on the wedding night, banging pots, lighting fires, sometimes worse."

"Do you suppose they're coming after us?"

"That's why I booked us aboard the Sunset, Iseult. Fastest train in the West. They'll never catch us."

Iseult. It was the first time he'd used her name. His hands feeling her calves and moving higher.

The parts of her body already exposed—arms, calves—were shivery and thrilled; her skin was hungry to be touched. She felt jubilant. What kind of history awaited her? Within the next hour they'd know each other completely. They were looming together now, pleasure and pain; only death could separate them. One day she'd have to watch Joe O'Brien die, or he'd watch her.

He touched her again, exactly *there*, and she was aware of the train adding another notch of speed. He pulled off her shoes, her silk stockings, and through the soles of her feet she felt steel wheels clacking over joints. He stood up, and she lifted her arms and let him pull off the linen slip and chemise. Her breasts were free. He dropped the clothes on the floor and kissed her throat, then between her breasts, her nipples. He gently pushed her into the bedroom and onto the white soft bed and they did not leave their compartment for eight hundred miles.

At El Paso she watched the red motorcycle being unloaded from the baggage car. She climbed into the sidecar and they drove across the Rio Grande bridge to the depot at Juarez, where the machine was put aboard a train for Chihuahua City.

Rebels attacked before the train had even left the station, firing pistols and galloping horses up and down the platform. Joe pulled her down to the floor and lay on top of her, and it was there, on the dirty floor of a Mexican day coach with his weight holding her down, that she had the first inkling that she was pregnant.

Mexican dust, cracking glass, voices screaming in Spanish. Bullets slugging into varnished wood. A man's body holding her down. Slight nausea, exhilaration, and a sense of her life coming open, sudden and entire.

The Contract

November 1912

WINNIPEG WAS FRUSTRATING. Joe hated wasting time in the city, arguing points that should have been obvious, when he needed to be in the mountains, driving work forward. The season was rushing to a close. At most there were only two or three weeks left before mountain weather shut him down for the year.

After two days of meetings and ridiculous, penny-pinching arguments, the generals grudgingly approved every single one of the variances his engineers wanted. Joe hurried back to his hotel, sent off a couple of quick telegrams, ate a hasty, greasy supper in the restaurant, and headed for the train station, carrying his grip.

The station was crowded with footloose men, harvest hands clutching carpet bags and beat-up satchels, blanket rolls slung over their shoulders. All of them heading somewhere, getting clear of Winnipeg before winter locked in. He felt blessed to not be one of them, to have a wife, and a baby on the way, and an important piece of work to get through.

His responsibilities grounded him. Before his marriage he had sometimes been overwhelmed by sadness while hurrying through important train stations. Struck by a drowning sorrow that made it impossible to keep going, to reach the platform, to board the train. He could only stagger to the waiting room and collapse on one of the benches. It was as if his spirit—the soul of himself—had evaporated, leaving him empty and stranded. Sometimes he'd recover in time to board the train. Other times he missed his connection entirely.

But marriage to Iseult had given him direction and purpose. A bright, challenging woman made it clear: life was worth living. No more

stranding in great depots. No more feelings numbed in the midst of rushing, purposeful crowds.

Around dawn, as his train was approaching Edmonton, he raised the
shade in his berth, saw the snow, and knew there would be more of it
in the mountains. At the Edmonton telegraph office he was told that the
wires west of Tête Jaune Cache had been down for twenty-four hours.
Towards noon he boarded a supply train. At Tête Jaune the track was
blocked with snow, the telegraph lines were still down, and he had to
spend the night in the guest house at the big Canadian Northern construction camp, nearly sick with impatience to get back to Iseult.

The next morning he left a fifty-cent tip for the Chinese steward who
served him breakfast, then caught a ride on a 4-8-4 locomotive headed
west with a snow blade attached. The storm had passed through and the
sun was shining. Standing up in the cab with the engine driver and fire-
man, sipping strong, sweet tea, he felt refreshed. At such times when he
was heading home, or where he thought of as home, the substance of his
life felt as dense and real as a chunk of coal.

If the good weather held there might be a couple more weeks before
freeze-up, when the camp would shut down and the men would scatter
and he'd take Iseult to California to have the baby. He would probably
need to make a business trip back east sometime during the winter, and
probably to Winnipeg as well, but their child was going to be born into
the sunlight and salt air of the coast.

West of Yellowhead Pass a series of avalanches had slumped over
the right-of-way, but the engineman was able to power up and drive
through. Three hours out of Tête Jaune the locomotive slunk, hissing, up
to a pair of timber stops at Head-of-Steel.

Jumping down, he made his way along a snowy, icy rut to the shed
that served as the contract's central office. It had been put up in a hurry,
the way such buildings always were, using logs harvested on the site,
and it would be abandoned at the end of the season. Next year's Head-
of-Steel camp would be twenty miles west, along the North Thompson
River, on a site his crews had already surveyed and logged clear.

A pair of Quebec heaters were hissing and groaning in the main room
when he came in. Stoves had always smelled of power to him—hot iron
somehow the scent of leadership, chiefdom, magnanimity—but their

heat never spread very far, and most of the clerks and purchasers had on scarves and mufflers, and some were wearing overcoats or mackinaws, with derby hats or knit caps pulled down over their ears. Many of his clerks were young Englishmen, though not much younger than he was. He enjoyed their odd, yawpy accents, and there was always one or two with an appetite for administration, for studying and interpreting the flow of numbers through a contract.

Exchanging quick greetings with a dozen men, he headed for his private office. He liked having a scrap of Persian or Turkish carpet on the floor of his room even though the walls were just logs chinked with a mortar of clay, lime, and straw. Whenever he bought an expensive rug at auction or from a dealer, he usually acquired a few old remnants at the same time, which he would use in his office. The purple, scarlet, and gold intricacy of an antique Tabriz or a silk Isfahan, no matter how threadbare, had a meaning he couldn't quite put his finger on. The patterns were gorgeous and bewitching. When he was tired, he sometimes sat contemplating an intricate scrap of carpet on his floor, obtaining a kind of satisfaction available nowhere else. He hadn't tried explaining it, even to Iseult. A good piece of carpet gave him spirit somehow, and he didn't give a damn if his men trod their muddy boots on it; they could not obliterate its magic.

Otherwise his room's furnishings were plain: a rolltop desk, a chair, and a green metal file cabinet. Snowshoes hanging on the wall. Back in August Iseult had sometimes left a handful of wildflowers in a glass of water on his desk, and he'd appreciated the femininity, the generosity of the gesture, and the peppery scent of the little alpine flowers.

Survey maps covered every inch of wall space, with the route marked in with a blue grease pencil. An army cot, South African War surplus, was set up on one side of the room, with a Hudson's Bay blanket neatly folded. He had started taking naps in the afternoon because he hardly ever slept through the night. At two or three in the morning he would rise without waking Iseult, throw on his clothes, and make his way through camp to the main office. After lighting a lamp and starting a fire in one of the stoves, he would start working through the stacks of documents always on his desk.

Like any big operation, a railway construction contract had a tendency towards turmoil and inefficiency, but with good organization, painstaking administration, and rigorous accounting even the most complicated undertaking could be successfully managed and controlled. Any man who despised paperwork—who thought it beneath him—was abdicating power over his own affairs, leaving his fate in the hands of those who had grasped and mastered the arts of administration.

He quickly riffled through the stack of letters, reports, and telegrams that had accumulated in the four days he had been away. There was nothing that couldn't wait until he'd seen Iseult. He ought to have brought her some sort of present, but it had slipped his mind, and there had never been any time for shopping anyway.

He was getting ready to leave his room when his chief clerk, a Belfast Irishman, appeared in the doorway. "I must have a word, sir."

"Sure, what is it?"

"Sad news, sir."

Joe looked up. "What the hell are you talking about?"

~

That year Head-of-Steel was in a valley in the Selkirks, beside a green river flowing off a glacier. Another railway contractor had gone bankrupt over the winter, the news reaching Joe on their wedding trip as they came out of the Mexican mountains. He'd immediately booked a first-class cabin on a steamer from Vera Cruz to New Orleans. From New Orleans they'd gone by train to Chicago and on to Montreal, where Joe had met with the Canadian Northern Construction Company's chief engineer and undertaken a new subcontract for another eighty miles of grade through the British Columbia mountains, in addition to his original thirty-five-mile piece.

Subcontractors had to buy every tool, spike, and length of timber from the general contractors, paying cash at prices the general contractors set; Joe explained to Iseult that the generals skimmed most of their profits that way. The generals were in fact the same promoters who had persuaded the Dominion government to back bonds they had sold in London and New York to finance their railway.

Joe had calculated it would take three years to complete their whole piece, figuring eight good months each year, April to freeze-up. Penalties were written into the contracts, and if he didn't finish on time they stood a good chance of losing everything. "Either we make our fortune on this job, Iseult, or it'll bust us."

She had offered to sell the house at Venice Beach so he could have that money, along with the balance of her inheritance to use as working capital, but he'd refused. "I want you keeping all that's yours. I aim to give you more of everything, not subtract from what you have. I'll shake it out of the bankers, you'll see. Those fellows know we're a going concern, and they'll want a piece of us."

He had met with bankers in Montreal and New York, and she had been startled, and a little frightened, by the enormous sums of money they were prepared to loan him. He hadn't seemed at all surprised. "They've certainly given us enough rope to hang ourselves." He smiled when he said it; it was clear he had no intention of "busting," and she realized that nothing was going to stop him from carrying through what he intended.

There were bunkhouses at Head-of-Steel, but most of the four thousand men he employed lived in small, remote camps called stations, strung out for a hundred miles along the projected route. Supply dumps and repair shops were at Head-of-Steel, along with horse pens and feed barns. Joe's clerks, timekeepers, telegraph operators, and purchasing agents worked in the log building that served as the main office. Iseult and Joe lived in a white canvas-walled tent set in a private compound with its own cook shed, outhouse, and kitchen garden. They were at some remove from the bunkhouses, sheds, and equipment shops clustered at the railhead.

His men had built her a small hut she used for a darkroom. Iseult had been taking photographs of the men and horses at work—shyly and hesitantly at first, but as the men became accustomed to her, she became accustomed to herself with the camera and started carrying it all the time. They had given her rolls of oilcloth but it was impossible to strain out every chink of light from her darkroom. When Joe worked late, she stayed up too; night was best for developing. She got used to moving and touching in the dark and trusting her hands.

Most of her prints weren't nearly as interesting as the world around her, but every now and then an image swam up out of the developing medium and surprised her, and that was enough to keep her going. Making photographs, she felt a kind of magic in her hands, something she'd never experienced holding a pencil or a paintbrush.

The plank floor of their tent was covered with Persian rugs Joe had bought at auction in Montreal. He'd ordered their camp beds from Abercrombie and Fitch. Their bed linen was a wedding present from Mr. Spaulding; the Hudson's Bay blankets were from Grattan and Elise, and Joe's Montreal bankers had sent a pair of prime buffalo robes, very heavy and almost suffocatingly warm. His two sisters, cloistered in their convent in Ottawa, had sent a holy picture, an image of the Sacred Heart. Early in the summer Joe had raced the two thousand miles to Ottawa to try to see them before they took final vows. He wanted to persuade them to leave their cloistered convent.

"I should never have put them in there, Iseult. They're asking them to take vows and give up the world—how can you give up what you've never had?"

The Mother Superior agreed to speak to Joe through an iron grille, and she told him that his sisters refused to see him. He threatened to return to the convent with a policeman, but he knew no police would dare bust into the Visitations. He was staying at the Chateau Laurier; that night he received a telegram from Head-of-Steel saying that men had been killed in a tunnel blast gone awry, and the next morning he caught a train back to the mountains.

All summer Iseult and Joe had been dining off her mother's china and using her father's table silver and candelabra. Oil lamps at night gave their white tent a cozy glow, and a little woodstove kept them warm. Mail came from Tête Jaune and Edmonton on the weekly supply train, and Iseult usually got a letter from Elise, who had delivered her baby in June, a red-haired girl named Virginia.

I'll spare you gruesome details Iseult but when you go into labor don't think something's wrong just because it hurts so much because it does.

There was always plenty of mud at Head-of-Steel. Wolves scavenged the camp's perimeter. Iseult had seen grizzly bears stalking across avalanche slopes like irritable men, and herds of elk feeding on young aspen, stripping the bark with their tongues. The mountains were no idyll and the risks were momentous, but Iseult, pregnant, shared her husband's sense of great endeavour. And intimacy with a man like Joe was exhilarating and strange. His legs were powerful. He had rough hands but could be shockingly tender. When the tunnel collapsed in late May and those men were killed on the job, lovemaking gave each of them sustenance through the horribly black mood of that week.

She had slept in her husband's camp bed every night until her body got too big and she had to sleep in her own. She had nursed injured men and held the hands of men who were dying. She had dug, planted, and passionately defended the kitchen garden, and though most of her beans and onions had been lost to rampaging elk, she was still harvesting beets and potatoes even with frost in the ground. Joe's men had built a chicken house, and she kept eleven hens, all of them good layers. Early in the season she had paid the camp tailor, an elderly Chinese, Mr. Bee, to make her two pairs of trousers out of honey-coloured canvas duck, she'd knitted her own thick woollen socks, and she had ordered a pair of caulk boots from Eaton's catalogue in a boy's size that fit her perfectly. She greased the leather herself with a compound of bear grease and ashes, first warming the leather by the fire, then rubbing in the grease with her hands.

She had made hundreds of photographs. She was learning to see through her cameras, to trust what she couldn't see, and to trust her powers of touch and feeling in the dark. She had photographed every stage of the work so far. At Joe's suggestion she had sent to the *Star Weekly* in Toronto her photographs of men building a trestle bridge, and the magazine had published one of them with the caption "Hard Work Builds an Empire." Though her canvas trousers no longer fit, she had kept in resolutely good health through her pregnancy by working ferociously in her garden and riding her little mare right up to her eighth month. She had hiked up and down the grade with her cameras and helped Joe pump their handcar along temporary rails to remote stations, where he checked that the drinking water was clean and she delivered her garden produce and eggs to the cookshacks, collected letters for the post, and dosed any men who were sick. It was nothing like the sort of life she had been afraid of settling for in New England or Pasadena. All her loneliness had burned off like a coastal fog.

It had been close to the end of the season when Joe left for Winnipeg on business. Their payroll had to be met each month but the generals paid them according to a fixed schedule: so much per yard of finished grade. When his surveyors and engineers insisted on last-minute variances costing thousands of dollars, Joe knew he would never get accommodation out of the generals without a twelve-hundred-mile round trip to Winnipeg and days of negotiating. He had offered to take Iseult with him, but her instinct was to stay put.

The morning after he left, the first blizzard of the season blew in from the west coast, shutting off the camp from the world and Iseult from the rest of the camp. For the first couple of hours she stayed in bed, carefully disassembling, cleaning, and polishing her FPK camera, using a set of brushes and small, beautiful tools one of the machinists had made for her, and listening to hard rain, then ice, then wet snow rattling on the canvas walls of the tent. By the time she had replaced the last brass screws in the camera body she was starting to feel restless. She closed up the camera and got out of bed. Peering out of the tent, she saw her favourite little saddle mare standing forlorn in the corral amid the driving sleet.

A young Chinese man, Lee Peng, did all their laundry and most of the housekeeping and cooking. Iseult had been trying to get Lee Peng to teach her to cook, but he seemed shy and uncomfortable when she was in the cook shed, even if she was just chopping vegetables or helping wash up. Lee Peng was supposed to feed their horses when Joe wasn't around, but the little mare looked awfully bleak and rangy, she thought. A feed of hay might help her withstand the bitter storm. She pulled Joe's mackinaw over her nightgown and stepped into her caulk boots.

Outside the tent she was nearly bowled over by the force and appetite of the wind. Snow had drifted around the chicken house and she could hear the birds clucking softly inside. The snow was falling so thickly now that it was hard to see the corral, and she could not see the little mare at all.

The blizzard had stripped all the lazy autumn air out of the valley, replacing it with air that smelled active and smoky. The wind was grunting. In New Hampshire, blizzards never came on so fast, with such a smothering of snow.

She figured her chickens were all right. Their water pan might skim over with ice, but that could be dealt with in the morning. She ought to have gone back inside the tent, but the mare had caught her scent and now came ambling up to the corral fence, looking like a grey ghost, ice slabbed on her back.

Iseult struggled through the drifts to the hayrick. Seizing a pitchfork and hoisting a load of hay, she was about to pitch it over the rail when she felt a small, dirty stab of pain in her belly. She tossed the hay, then replaced the pitchfork. With one hand supporting her cramping belly, she staggered back to the tent, closed the flap, and lay down on her bed without taking off the wet mackinaw or the caulk boots. She felt dizzy and nauseated, and furious with Joe for going off and leaving her with the animals. Wind shook the canvas walls.

When the contractions started, she tried to absorb the blows and keep breathing. She had been born at home—most people were—but Joe was in favour of the hospital in Santa Monica. He wanted a clean white place, he said, with the best scientific care.

After the turmoil of the contractions she lay panting and confused. She was struggling to get back to sensible thinking when she heard Lee Peng whispering, "Missus, Missus," in his soft, beckoning voice. She looked up and saw his head poking through the tent flap. His brown eyes regarded her.

"Sick, Missus?"

She was still wearing the woollen mackinaw and boots. Her sheets were damp from melted snow.

"I'll get up," she told him. "You change the sheets, please."

"You want tea, missus?"

"First help me get these boots off."

He stepped into the tent and approached the bed hesitantly. Standing at the foot, he started tugging at her caulks.

She didn't know how old Lee Peng was. She had asked him but he didn't seem to know, or perhaps it was just unlucky to say. He might have been seventeen, or twenty-five. Joe's foremen told her the Chinese practised all sorts of mumbo-jumbo having to do with the power of numbers, and were ferocious gamblers. The gangers said it was impossible for a white person to tell if a Chinaman was sick or well, contented or furious—the Chinese were an inscrutable race. When Chinamen butchered an elk, they ate every part of the animal, even the liver, which they steamed; the antlers, which they ground to a powder; and the hooves, which they boiled in a broth. They were hard workers, the foremen allowed, but unpredictable. They seemed content to live without women.

All the men killed or injured in the tunnel blast, back in May, had been Chinese. The survivors has been loaded into carts and brought to Head-of-Steel, where Iseult tried her best to nurse them. Two more men died before the supply train arrived, and their frightened faces had stayed with her.

The survivors had built a bone-house for their dead, because no Chinaman wished his bones to be buried in a strange country, according to the foremen. Friends or relatives were expected to retrieve the bones after a couple of years, clean them, and carry or send them back to the home village in China.

The first time she noticed Lee Peng he had been standing alone outside the bone-house, weeping, both hands wrapped in bloody bandages. She learned his older brother had been one of the men killed in the blast.

With his tender hands, Lee Peng was no longer much use for station work, but instead of letting him go, Joe had sent him to help Iseult with the kitchen garden. After Lee Peng had been working alongside her in the garden for a few days, Joe said they might as well hire him to do the housekeeping. "The boys up there say he is a pretty fair cook."

She had replied that she didn't need a servant, she could manage by herself. She was already worried that Joe didn't think much of her cooking. She'd not spent time in any sort of kitchen before coming into the mountains; Joe was a more experienced cook, since it had so often been his responsibility to feed his brothers and sisters. But when he came back to the compound after a long day in the office or up on the grade, she liked to have something ready for him, even if it was just bacon and eggs—though she often burned the bacon.

"In a few more weeks you might not feel like doing quite so much," Joe had argued. "And I don't like to send him back to the tunnel. I think his head got shaken up. Some men are never the same after a blast."

Iseult had gradually grown fond of Lee Peng, despite his impermeable silences. When the wildflowers appeared in late summer, he went with her to the high alpine meadows and they gathered flowers in bunches, which they left at the bone-house or brought back to the camp. They scattered mothballs around the garden perimeter in a vain attempt to keep away the ravaging elk, porcupine, and skunks, and were constantly mending and patching the wire fences. By August they were harvesting more beans, spinach, parsley, and carrots than they could consume, and every few days she was delivering baskets of produce and fresh eggs to men at one or another of the remote stations.

Every Saturday night Lee Peng took a basket of greens and a couple of dozen eggs up to the station where he and his brother had worked, and where the other men were all from the same village back in China. On Sunday he returned to Head-of-Steel and another week of cooking, cleaning, gardening, and laundry.

Lee Peng was helping her stand up when a sharp pain tore her insides. She grunted and clung onto his arm. Looking down, she saw that her nightgown was soaking wet. Her head suddenly felt light and she would have fallen down, but Lee Peng supported her, got the heavy mackinaw off her shoulders, and helped her into Joe's bed.

The blizzard was growling outside the tent and she could hear Douglas firs creaking. The odour of birth fluid on her soaked nightgown was sweet, dark, and strange.

Lee Peng found a fresh nightgown in her trunk but she was too weak to even sit up. He found scissors in her sewing basket and began cutting away the wet nightgown, then pulled it off her. Underneath she wore a flannel chemise and a pair of Joe's drawers stretched over her pregnant belly. The drawers were soaked with water and blood. Scowling, Lee Peng cut them away too. Using a towel, he began cleaning the mess from her thighs. He helped her to sit up, got the fresh nightgown over her head, and fitted her arms into the sleeves. The sheets on Joe's bed were a mess; the young man quickly stripped Iseult's bed, made it up again with clean linen and helped her back into it, where she lay feeling like a package with something smashed and broken inside.

She watched Lee Peng jab wood into the stove. She wasn't thinking of her baby in any distinct way. Mostly she was conscious of the low, determined snarl of the wind. The storm and the sight of her own bloody trace had put Iseult into a kind of trance, but she was aware enough to feel abandoned when Lee Peng left the tent abruptly without saying a word to her, carrying dirty sheets and towels in a bundle under his arm.

A second flurry of contractions arrived some time later, much less violent than the first. Lee Peng had deserted her, and where was Joe? She could hear the fire crackling in the airtight and smell the oil burning in the lamps. Her thoughts resisted coherence. She wanted her mother. She had also lost control of her bowels and made another, worse mess in the bed.

She did not know how much time had passed when she became aware of a girl in the tent, watching her. The girl was stocky, with a red, plump face and a man's body, or maybe it was just the thick clothes she wore: padded jacket, woollen muffler, weather-beaten hat.

The girl's nose wrinkled at the stench and she turned and spoke sharply in Chinese to Lee Peng, who had mysteriously reappeared. How long had he been standing there? Iseult watched him hand the scissors to the girl, who sat down on the bed and began cutting away her second filthy nightgown. The girl's fingers were almost unbearably cold to the touch. Iseult wept.

Taking off her padded jacket and pushing up the sleeves of her sweater, the Chinese girl started bathing Iseult's legs, using a pan of water heated on the stove. The girl's face softened and the harsh red burn of cold on her plump cheeks softened too. She helped Iseult across to Joe's bed once more. Lee Peng bundled the ruined sheets and threw them out into the storm.

Pain came in staccato chops. Iseult heard herself whimper, "Don't leave me, please don't leave me."

The girl stayed sitting on the bed and Lee Peng stood near the doorway, both of them watching her as though they were expecting her to do something more, say something more. What more did they want of her? Why couldn't they help her? Couldn't they see she was dying?

The birth was not particularly painful, perhaps because the infant, a girl, was so undersized, as small as the smallest red baby in the Incubatorium on the pier at Venice. Smaller. The Chinese girl washed and bundled her and kept putting her on Iseult to nurse, but the little thing would not take the breast. Lying on her mother's stomach, she died after a little while.

~

Joe's chief clerk said that from what he'd been able to understand, the child, a girl, had not lived two hours. The Chinese girl was now looking after Mrs. O'Brien.

"A girl? Where did she come from?"

"One of the coolies must have brought her in. She was down on the timesheets as a man, apparently."

"The little girl . . . Where is she?"

"I set the carpenters to make a wee coffin, sir, and had one of the storerooms cleaned out. We've put the bairn there, awaiting your instructions."

He would keep hold of himself. There were things to be done and he would do them. "I want to send a wire to New York the moment the line is up."

The chief clerk quickly took a notebook and gold pencil from his waistcoat pocket. Joe dictated the telegram, then left the room and strode out through the office quickly, daring anyone to offer condolence, daring anyone to meet his eye.

```
CNCPYELLOWHEAD WU BALTIMORE
4085813-13332 CNCP
9 NOVEMBER 1912
TO: T O'BRIEN
WOODSTOCK COLLEGE
WOODSTOCK MD

REGRET TO INFORM DEATH OF INFANT. CAN YOU ADVISE FUNERAL
RITES. WILL ARRANGE TRAIN PASS. PLEASE INFORM. JOE
```

~

Lee Peng said the girl was the widow of his brother. She had been working alongside her husband when he was killed in the tunnel blast.

"Offer her our condolences, if you please," Joe said. "If her husband had any wages coming, she's due whatever it was plus fifty dollars widow's benefit. Ask her if she will stay here and take care of my wife. I'll pay her two dollars a day."

He found Iseult in bed, staring at a book. Bending over, he kissed her cool forehead. "How are you feeling?"

Holding the book open, she looked at him but didn't speak. Someone had brushed her hair, differently than her way of brushing it. The tent was warm, dry, clean, with a fire knocking in the airtight stove and an aroma he recognized, of roasted herbs—his mother had also burned herbs when there was sickness or trouble in the house. A tray beside the bed was untouched: milk, honey, tea, slices of lemon in a little dish, and a biscuit.

"We'll have another baby," he told her.

She shook her head. Tears started down her cheeks. He reached for her hand and she pulled it away. She stared fixedly at her book. It wasn't possible that she was reading, but she stared at the book with tears shining on her cheeks, and even turned a page.

"Iseult, I'm so sorry I wasn't here."

He wanted to take away the book and comfort her, but she wouldn't look at him and he didn't know how to proceed. She was only protecting herself, he figured. Grief was a rough blade. While he searched the tent for the prayer beads and Catholic missal the Little Priest had sent him for his twenty-first birthday, the girl held a steaming cup to Iseult's lips and, cooing in Chinese, tried to persuade her to drink. Iseult had carried their child in her womb; her pain must be even sharper, deeper than what he was feeling.

~

The storeroom was hardly a room. Just space and shadows. Kneeling, he clutched his rosary beads, each one the size of a sunflower seed. Strung together in tens—decades, so called. He hadn't prayed a novena since quitting the Pontiac, but he figured the ritual was due their child. He had no belief whatsoever that he or anyone else would ever touch the hand of a god. He didn't need a god. After the death of his mother he had left his Catholicism in the Pontiac, but he believed instinctively in the continuum of the dead, the living, and the unborn: a sleepy, barely cognizant community of souls. Saying the old prayers was acknowledging his own connection to the dead generations that had preceded him and the ones that would follow after.

The earth floor was cold and hard on his knees. The oil lamps weren't trimmed properly. They smoked. Candles would have been better. There ought to be a box of tapers somewhere in their stores.

> *Hail Mary, full of grace, the Lord is with thee.*
> *Blessed art thou amongst women and*
> *Blessed is the fruit of thy womb, Jesus.*
> *Holy Mary, Mother of God, pray for us sinners*
> *Now and at the hour of our death.*

The harsh drone of his voice reciting the rosary in the cold, empty room might have frightened his daughter. He would have picked her up and held her, sung to her, done anything in his power to console.

~

WU BALTIMORE CNCPYELLOWHEAD-EDMONTON CANADA
3075833-13762 WU 11 NOVEMBER 1912
TO: J O'BRIEN
O'BRIEN CAPITAL CONST LTD
MILE 84 TETE JAUNE BRITISH COLUMBIA CANADA

PERMISSION TRAVEL DENIED RECTOR FATHER MAAS QUOTE NO
FUNERAL RITES FOR UNBAPTIZED AND SACRED CANONS DECREE NO
COMMUNION WITH DEAD IF NO COMMUNION WHILST ALIVE ENTRUST
CHILD TO MERCY OF GOD END QUOTE. BEG YR FORGIVENESS TOM

~

At the head of the funeral procession, Joe walked along the gravel grade wearing his best blue suit and carrying the white coffin in his arms. The chief clerk had suggested they put it on a handcar, but that hadn't seemed right. Iseult came next, Lee Peng and the Chinese girl helping her along, then the clerks in derby hats, tweed suits, and celluloid collars, their polished boots getting muddy. Then the engineers, surveyors, and gangers.

Then a couple of hundred navvies, teamsters, and mechanics walking two and three abreast along the grade. Their clothes were in rough shape so late in the season: overalls crudely patched, moth-eaten pullovers. Boots mended with wads of tar.

He had told the timers that wages would be paid but no work was to be done. The funeral procession was as long as any train that would howl through those mountains, but the only noise was hundreds of pairs of boots scuffling on gravel, wind moving through firs and cedars, and cawing ravens flapping from treetop to treetop.

The Chinese bone-house was on a hillside, probably an avalanche slope, west of the camp. There was hardly any soil; the open ground was bare rock or scree. Squat, solid, built of stone, the bone-house almost concealed itself on the bare slope. It was unlikely that anyone would ever notice it from a passing train. The rough stonework was meticulous; they had used no mortar. He had allowed them some sheets of galvanized iron for the roof.

Leaving the grade, jumping the ditchwork, he started up the slope with the coffin in his arms. Two warm days and a night of heavy rain had dissolved nearly all the snow in the valley, but the peaks were gleaming white, and now he could feel the weather changing again, pressure dropping, wind picking up. It wouldn't be long before snow was flying again. Their season was just about over.

Glancing back, he saw Iseult leave the grade and start up the scree slope with the Chinese widow helping her. Most of it was limestone debris, with a few gnarled firs. His biceps were sore from carrying the coffin all the way from the main camp. His fingers were stiff. He set it down on shaggy silver grass outside the bone-house and looked around. Men were leaving the grade and coming up the slope but keeping respectfully behind Iseult. He felt the first drops of rain: sharp, needle-like. Soon it would be sleeting.

When she reached the bone-house, she shook off the Chinese girl's hand and stood gazing at the white coffin.

"Iseult."

He ought to have made her ride in a handcar or insisted she stay in bed. Underneath her enormous hat, her face was white. Purple pans below her eyes. The rain was coming down harder. "Iseult, none of this is the end, not for us. We'll see her in all the other children. I promise you we will."

She glanced up. She didn't believe him; he saw that in her quick eyes. He'd make it his life to prove it to her. He hadn't married her and brought her all the way into these mountains to give her an ending—to finish her life, perish her. No, goddamn it, no. There would be more. There'd be more of everything.

The men were now gathering around. One of the Chinese station men tried the timber door with his shoulder, nudged it open a few inches, then nodded at Joe and left it slightly ajar. Joe had holy water in a silver flask borrowed from one of the gangers. Holy water was supposed to be blessed by a bishop or a priest but he had done it himself, following directions from his missal, and it would have to serve.

As soon as he took the missal from his coat pocket the wind ruffled its flimsy pages and he lost the place he'd marked. He was still trying to locate it when he felt Iseult grasp his arm. The men stood six or seven deep in front of the little stone hut, a crowd smelling of dirty hair, wet wool, and leather. She held on to his arm so tightly—was it possible she hadn't given up on him entirely? Maybe it was just that he was all she had at that particular moment. Squeezing hard. Fingers like furious bones through the cloth.

Whether she trusted him or not, he swore to himself he would do his best to deserve her. He found his place and began reading aloud the Rite of Burial for Unbaptized Infants, the sound of his voice amounting to very little on that wind-battered slope.

~

Tools, machinery, and material were stored in sheds and supply dumps. Buildings not needed for storage were demolished or burned. What was useful was put aside, the rest thrown into the giant bonfires. Men straggling in from remote stations were paid off in Bank of Montreal scrip exchangeable at Edmonton. A couple of hundred of the best horses were collected in pens near the railhead for shipping out; the others were being turned loose and left to forage through the mountain winter.

On their last morning in camp she asked him to burn down the tent

instead of packing it up and storing it away for next season. It was a good
tent, but he took a can of coal oil and doused the floorboards and canvas
walls. Then he dipped a pine bough in coal oil, lit it, and walked around
the outside of the tent, touching flame to canvas. As they watched the fire
consume the tent, consume the first eight months of their marriage, the
scream of a train whistle came floating up the valley. A few hours later
they were aboard and gone.

~

In Venice that winter he took over the spare room for his study but still
spent hours each day in his brother's real estate office on Windward
Avenue, where he had commandeered a desk and a telephone and spent
the days writing and receiving letters and telegrams to and from Canada,
London, and New York.

There was a lot of white fog. Iseult didn't know what to do with herself. Elise O'Brien was absorbed with her daughter, Virginia, and it was
hard to go for afternoon walks on the boardwalk with Elise pushing the
baby in her beautiful white pram.

Iseult decided the only thing she could do to help herself was to find
other women who needed help. The next day she went to Santa Monica
Police Department, then to the sheriff's station at Ocean Park, and asked
to visit the women in the lock-ups. The policemen and deputies were
surprised, and amused, by her determination. In both places she was
denied, but when she returned the next day and repeated her request,
she was admitted.

She began visiting women prisoners every afternoon, writing letters
for them and listening to their stories. One Portuguese girl had been
sentenced to forty days for smashing a shop window and stealing a hat.
Another girl had stolen an automobile parked in front of the baths and
driven it onto the beach, where it got stuck in the sand. Another girl had
stabbed a man with a penny knife. They were mostly prostitutes. She
brought them newspapers and magazines and soap and hairbrushes and
cigarettes and underclothes and small presents. When the women were
released from jail, she gave them small sums of money.

She felt he was unwilling to share her grief, to take up any share of the burden of it. She had to carry it all alone for both of them. When he came home late one night from the office, she was in her bed. He was bending over her, trying to kiss her, but she couldn't contain her anger anymore. She pushed him away and sat up.

"I've never felt an ounce of love from you," she said. "You don't know what it is. You're afraid of it."

"Maybe that's true," he said. "You've been through a lot. I've asked a lot of you."

"And never given anything back," she said. "Nothing but mud and cold and pain. I wish I'd never met you."

"Things are hard now. They will get better."

"Maybe they will for you. That's all you care about anyway. If you cared about me the baby wouldn't have died."

He had taken off his tie and collar and slipped off his suspenders, but now he pulled the suspenders back on.

"What are you going to do, run away?" she taunted.

He picked up his coat and hat. She knew she'd hurt him. He looked tired and there was something broken in his face. She'd not been able to hurt him before, and it gave her a satisfaction almost delirious, and a taste like salt on her lips.

"Go away then, run away," she said triumphantly. "You can't face it, can you. You're not so tough as you think. Go away! I wish you'd never come in here. I should never have let you in. Go away and leave me alone."

He left the room, and a few moments later she heard him leaving the house.

She was sitting up in bed. She felt more awake and more aware than she had in weeks. There was a glow from her anger. She listened carefully, thinking he might come back at any moment. She had no idea where he'd gone, and after a while fell back on the pillow. She was beginning to feel bruised by her own outburst.

He wasn't going to abandon her, was he? He was certainly going to come back. Their marriage was a shallow thing, not really grounded, but she knew that much about him, or hoped she did.

After half an hour, unable to sleep, she got up, picked up her little Kodak from a shelf, and took it back to bed along with some tools and brushes wrapped in a soft cloth. The shutter had been sticking; she made herself concentrate on cleaning and adjusting the camera. She was worried but she still felt better than she had in weeks—cleaner.

Then she heard him come into the house. She switched off her bedside light and didn't say anything. She waited for him to enter their bedroom, but he didn't. She heard him go instead into the room across the hall, which was crowded with metal file cabinets and boxes of paperwork. He shut the door.

At least he was home. In the morning they'd be able to sort things out. He was essentially kind, essentially passionate. They needed to have another baby. He felt things the same way she did; he just didn't want to admit feeling them. He was guarding himself. That was understandable; it was what men did. In a few moments she would go and fetch him and bring him back to her bed. She felt confident that all was going to go better between them from now on.

She fell asleep without quite meaning to, feeling raw and guilty and satisfied. A few hours later she awoke with moonlight streaking across their twin beds and a strong, almost visceral awareness of her husband's animal loneliness. His bed was untouched, empty. What was left of her anger had washed away while she was asleep, like snow under spring rain.

She put on a wrapper and went and knocked on the door of his study. He didn't respond. She called his name. He didn't answer. When she tried it, the door was locked from the inside. Remembering her father and the Colt Navy pistol, she panicked. She pounded on the door and called his name, then ran outside and peered in the window, but the shade had been drawn and the window closed tight and bolted. She looked around for something to break the glass but there was nothing, just clods of sandy earth. She hurled one against the window and it made a thud, then a gritty, trickling sound, but the glass wouldn't shatter. She ran back into the house, telephoned the operator and asked her to ring the fire department, then ran back outside and pounded her fist on the study window. It would not break. Maybe she didn't want it to. Maybe she was afraid of what she'd find.

She went to the canal path and paced up and down in her nightdress alongside the still, dark water. It was just a ditch, not a real canal. Venice was a fraud. The cottage had never been a home for her; she hadn't wanted to live alone in white fog. To breathe well wasn't enough. Books and pictures weren't enough; peace, order, and repose would never be enough. She wanted to build a life with a man, a hectic life, a messy life—mud and mountains, risks and riches. And children. She kept seeing the two young Chinese station men who'd died in her arms the summer before. Joe wasn't going to die in her arms, was he?

A hook-and-ladder truck came grumbling along the dirt track behind the cottage, and three volunteer firemen—she recognized one, the delivery boy from the Italian market—clumped inside. One of them put his shoulder to the study door and broke it open easily. They found Joe lying on his side on his favourite maroon, gold, and purple Isfahan rug, an empty whisky bottle beside him.

The firemen revived him a little and carried him to bed. They seemed amused. One of them helped her undress him and get him into his nightshirt and between the sheets, where they left him snoring.

She'd never seen him helpless before, and maybe that was what she'd needed from him all along—a thorough, reckless commitment of self. Abandonment of coolness and all dignity. Passionate proof of his solidarity.

She made herself a nest of blankets on the living-room floor, but sometime before dawn she awoke, went back to their bedroom, and lay down beside her husband on his bed. When he stirred, she began to stroke him, then rolled herself on top of him, and they made love for the first time since she—since they—had lost the baby. Without saying a word, and afterwards they fell asleep in each other's arms.

She did not wake up until almost noon. He was in the kitchen, brewing coffee, baking bannock, squeezing orange juice, and scrambling eggs, all of which he carried in on a tray along with the *Los Angeles Times*.

"We ought to sleep together, Iseult, from now on, don't you say?"

She nodded vigorously, and after he had pushed their beds together they lay in bed most of the afternoon, eating, sharing the newspaper, and making love again, in bright warm yellow daylight.

He didn't refer to what had happened the night before, and she didn't say anything either. What mattered the most—what had saved the marriage, as far as she was concerned—was that she had broken through to him, however savagely, and they could be close again. She thought she understood the meaning of his behaviour the night before. It was a weird language he was speaking to her, but at least he'd spoken. And she might never see another bottle of liquor in the house. He was, she figured, abstemious by nature.

The beds stayed adjoined. She ordered gorgeous new sheets: one set of Belfast linen and two sets of crisp cotton percale. Everything had to be white. She kept up her visits to the women in the lock-ups. They both wanted another child, and that spring she carried her second pregnancy into the Canadian mountains.

August 1913

THAT YEAR MEN CAME UP from the Coeur d'Alene mining district to hire on as blasters. It turned out they were IWWs—Wobblies—with plans to organize the contract. Iseult had seen the conditions the station men endured in the remote camps along the line. It didn't surprise her that they wanted a union.

A negotiating committee presented themselves but Joe refused to see them. Bullets were fired through some of the gangers' tents. Then one morning Iseult found a death threat scrawled on a scrap of paper in one of her husband's shirts.

Neither of them wanted to take chances with this pregnancy, and he had already been urging her to start for California, though it was only August. Grattan had found a buyer for the Venice bungalow after she decided it would be too small for them with a baby. Joe wanted to find a house on a beach. Through her mother's old theosophist friend Mr. Spaulding they had leased a house on Butterfly Beach at Santa Barbara, with an option to buy. The baby would be born at the Cottage Hospital in Santa Barbara.

She was reluctant to leave her husband and her garden, now teeming with cabbages and kale, beans and onions, strawberries and spinach. The garden provided half the men at Head-of-Steel camp with fresh vegetables, and her hens were laying tens of dozens of eggs each week. But for the baby's sake she had been prepared to quit the mountains, until she discovered the note in Joe's shirt pocket. Then everything changed.

O'Brien, you must give the men their needs you damned bastard or the big Bomb will kill you.

As soon as she read it she knew Joe would be harmed if she left him. It was just a feeling, but she was sure of it. She went back to packing, even adding a few more items to her trunk, but a vision of fire, of conflagration, kept returning. Finally she sat down on the bed. The vision was as real as a taste on her tongue, and it would not go away. When she stood up, she started unpacking. When he came in that evening, he was surprised to see all her things still in the tent and her trunks nowhere in sight.

"I thought we agreed you were going out on the supply train, Iseult."

"I read the note."

He scowled. "What note?"

"The one that said they'll kill you with a bomb. Why? Were there others?"

"Don't be silly. It doesn't mean a thing, Iseult. It's just the way these IWWs talk. I think they're all reading Russian novels."

"They've killed people before, haven't they. When they blew up the *Los Angeles Times*, they killed plenty of people."

"I don't want you worrying. It's not good for your condition."

"I'd worry more if I weren't here. I'm not going."

So she stayed, and Joe pretended to be annoyed but was also gruffly grateful, which he demonstrated in small ways: working in the garden under her direction in the evenings; bringing her buttered toast and hot, sweet coffee before he went off to work; rubbing her aching feet at night while composing nonsense names for their baby. Lady Lancelot Goldilocks O'Brien. Strenuous Happenstance O'Brien. Loitering-Magnificently-in-the-Mountains O'Brien.

Then three cases of dynamite disappeared from a shed. One of the clerks happened to write to his brother, a Vancouver newspaperman, saying that foreign anarchists were plotting to blow up the railway. The story ran in newspapers across the Dominion, questions were asked in Parliament, and twenty Royal Northwest Mounted Police under an inspector were dispatched aboard a special train, with horses, a machine gun, and orders to arrest the IWWs. By the time the police arrived the Wobblies had disappeared, probably across the border into Idaho, but work was shut down all along the grade and a meeting was called. The police pitched their camp at one end of the valley and groomed and exercised their black horses while men poured in from the remote stations and held their union meeting in a meadow on the other side of the river.

Iseult had spent the morning working in the garden and repairing fences. Elk had broken in again during the night, eaten all the radish tops, and unearthed a row of carrots. They were a constant problem. She had tried everything to keep them out but nothing seemed to work. A few nights earlier Joe had offered to sit up with a rifle and take care of the elk when they appeared.

"You mean, kill them?"

"That would be the general idea. One or two, anyway."

"Not while I'm with a baby!"

"What does that have to do with it?"

"Everything!"

"But they're stealing our food, aren't they? The baby needs those vegetables too—you're feeding the both of you. You kill chickens, don't you? What's the difference? You fix that fence and they'll knock it down again. Nothing will stop an elk from feeding up, not this late in the summer, except a bullet."

"They do make me mad—they're so clumsy. But I won't have you shooting them. We're the intruders here. It would not be good for the baby."

Instead she nailed up extra slats on her fence. He hadn't noticed, but she had not actually, personally slaughtered a chicken in weeks. Mr. Bee, the Chinese tailor who was helping her in the kitchen, did the killing and plucking now. Earlier in the summer she had steeled herself to the task because it was necessary, someone had to do it, and squeamishness was no excuse. She was happy enough to eat chicken, so death had to be faced, and faced directly. She'd killed, plucked, and dressed half a dozen. An awful, bloody business, but it also made her aware of a new kind of strength, grounded in awareness of her own courage and determination.

But in the past four weeks she hadn't killed a single bird. Probably the unborn baby was making decisions for her. It was the same in the darkroom: over the summer she had shot rolls of film, but the smell of developing fluid had become repugnant to her and, she presumed, the baby. She couldn't go in there anymore. Pregnancy sometimes made her feel like a tenant in her own body.

Using a steel bar, she pounded more rocks around the postholes to firm them up, then strung more wire, knowing none of it would do much good. Elk roamed the whole valley floor in late summer, females, with one or two bulls bossing each herd. They were feeding up for the winter and looking for salt licks. The bulls made a strange call—Joe called it "bugling"—a whistle more than a cry. She liked hearing it. It was resonant and intriguing, like the whoop of the barred owl circling the main camp every night, marking his route with hunting cries.

But she did resent their ravaging her crops, and if she weren't pregnant she might have let Joe shoot one or two. Or done it herself— she had more direct and legitimate cause than he did. The garden was hers.

She worked on the fence until she was tired, then went and lay down in the tent. Neither Lee Peng nor his sister-in-law had returned to the mountains. The elderly Mr. Bee helped with domestic chores. He wasn't much good at taking care of stock and was too frail to be of use in the garden, but he did allow her into the cook shed, where she had learned a lot from him.

She and Joe had visited the bone-house early in the season, pumping a handcar twenty miles back along the grade over flimsy temporary rails. There were no mountain flowers that early in the year; instead she'd brought along a chenille scarf that had belonged to her mother— from France, a brilliant orange. She'd left it there, wedged between some rocks. They had both cried. Her palms were covered with milky blisters; Joe had had to pump the whole way back to Head-of-Steel without any help from her.

After a short nap in her camp bed, she arose hungry. She fixed herself some bread and butter and jam and a mug of tea. Then she slung her little Kodak around her neck and headed out for the meadow where Joe had said the police would be exercising their magnificent horses. No workers were to be seen as she walked through the main camp and out along the grade. The desolation and silence were unnerving. All the telegraph wires had been cut a few hours after the train arrived at Head-of-Steel with the policemen.

The grade smelled of dusty, ancient river gravel. And oozing tar in the sleepers. Everything was perfectly quiet except for the wind hissing through the tops of the Douglas firs.

She found Joe in the meadow by the river, with the policemen and their black horses. The workers were holding their union meeting in a meadow on the other side of the green, galloping North Thompson River. Not much sound came across the garble of the fast water. The speakers were standing up on a platform the men had built using lumber and sleepers removed—"stolen," Joe had growled—from the dumps of stores scattered along the grade.

The men across the river could talk all they wanted, call him a capitalist and a bloodsucker; words didn't count for a lot with him somehow. Not the same as for other people. Her husband handled language reluctantly, as if it were an unfamiliar table setting. He probably used fewer words in a year than many people did in a week. Actions were what he cared about, what he understood—actions, and things he could touch, feel, and grasp.

She opened up her camera and began photographing the policemen, all expert riders, dashing their mounts around the little gymkhana course. They had set up the jumps using aspens they'd chopped down and limbed. She knew that her Kodak's shutter was too slow to capture the atmosphere of strain and competitive tension, and that her lens wasn't fine enough for detail that would make the scene worthwhile. Usually the camera helped her see the world, but sometimes it felt extraneous, pushing her out of the moment instead of bringing her closer.

She put the camera away. She was wearing a skirt with a short jacket she hoped disguised her pregnancy, and a hat that she'd bought at I. Magnin in San Francisco on their way north that spring. The hat was very much the latest Paris mode and she'd paid far too much for it, but she had just saved six dollars by buying her summer's supply of photographic paper at a discount supply shop Elise had heard about on Third Street in downtown Los Angeles. She had been sensing the first twinges of pregnancy in San Francisco, and, feeling a need to indulge herself, she'd bought the ridiculous, beautiful hat and wore it whenever she plausibly could. Of course she hadn't used much of the photo paper, hadn't printed in weeks.

A constant, faint hubbub floated from across the river as speaker after speaker addressed the men—in at least half a dozen languages so far, according to Joe. "I don't care what language they're talking. It's all anarchy."

"They want a show of force," the inspector said. "We can't have a crowd of foreigners thinking they rule the mountains."

Joe shook his head. "You've got twenty men and they're a couple of thousand. I don't like it any more than you do, but if you interfere with their meeting you'll get more trouble than you bargained for. Best let things cool off. Anyway, I'll need these fellows back at work. I'm going to go back to the office and study the numbers and see what I can offer that'll get things moving. First snow'll be soon enough, then freeze-up, and we'd all be stuck here. If they're willing to talk sensibly, I can talk sensibly. Anything to get the work on its legs again. Walk with me, Iseult?"

"I think I'll stay out here a little while," she said. The deserted camp had felt lonely and bleak; the daylight was better, more cheerful, away from the penumbra of firs. The policemen's scarlet jackets and yellow stripes were enjoyable daubs of colour. There wasn't a lot of colour at Head-of-Steel, especially after a while. It all started looking like mud.

She sat on a blanket spread on the grass, watching policemen jumping the big black horses over the aspen fences. Faint noises from the union meeting mixed with the dash of the river and the clattering of insects. The meadow grasses were dabbed with devil's paintbrush and coneflowers.

The police had a little campfire going, with tea brewing and biscuits baking in a Dutch oven. After a while the inspector, holding two enamel cups and a plate of biscuits, approached and asked if he might join her.

"Of course."

He offered her one of the cups and held out the plate of buttered biscuits. They were delicious and the tea was hot, strong, and sweet. She hadn't realized how hungry she was.

The inspector took off his Stetson. His hair was thin and sandy. He was a handsome man, though not interesting to look at.

"I see you're in a happy state, Mrs. O'Brien."

She didn't immediately grasp his meaning. Then she did. She felt her face flush. "Yes . . . well. Thank you."

"Do you have other children?"

"We don't."

"My wife and I expect our first around about Christmas time."

"We the same. Congratulations."

"Of course, I'm awfully old to be a father for the first time—I am forty."

"That's not very old," she said, thinking that it was.

"How old is your husband, if I may ask?"

"Joe will be twenty-seven next month."

"Very young for such an undertaking."

"He's always had a lot on his shoulders. He's used to it. He likes it."

"Forty years old." The inspector shook his head. "That's awfully late to start a family, but the Force don't make it easy for a man to marry, even an officer. It's a gripe we all have. They make no allowances, really. Of course the men aren't even allowed to marry, not below a sergeant's rank. And an officer's pay isn't much good. My wife finds it hardly sufficient to keep a decent household. I give her everything I can but she says it isn't enough."

It surprised her that anyone would mention such private domestic matters to a stranger.

"She has often implied that I . . . that I . . . " He paused and blinked. "That I falsely represented that particular aspect of my situation. Before we were married, I mean. She has accused me of falsely giving her an impression that my salary was greater than it is. It's ridiculous—I never did anything of the kind. I did talk about my prospects, probably more than I should have. I've always been looking for a promotion. Inspector's rank in the Force is something like between a subaltern and a captain in the army. In the Force they say a man needs to be a superintendent before he can keep a family happy on his pay. I only wish I had listened to them."

She was listening to the noise of the river. Summer weather in the Rockies rarely lasted more than a day or two at a time.

She no longer felt sick in the mornings, but this pregnancy was not so lighthearted as the first; there were undertones. Whenever Joe looked at her changing form, she knew he was thinking of the lost baby. She had found herself also thinking of death as much as birth. This pregnancy was making her moody. Not malcontent, but slow. Content to sit on the grass, listening to insects scraping their legs and twittering.

While the inspector talked about meeting his wife at a garden party

given by an English lord on his ranch south of Calgary, Iseult watched
his face, which was bony and sallow. His clipped moustache was the
colour of old, silvery hay. He kept crossing and uncrossing his long legs.

He said he was going to quit the Force and return to England as soon
as he had some reliable prospects there; he missed England terribly.

After almost eighteen months of marriage, how close were she and
Joe? What did love mean, really? They'd lost a child. They would neither
of them get over that, she was certain. Right now they were both trying
to forget what had happened, and in the excitement of a new pregnancy
that almost seemed possible. But it was a deep scar and it really wouldn't
ever fade, would it?

The inspector was still talking about England. Every year he missed it
more. Really, England was the only country to live in, the only place that
felt like home. The colonies were well enough, but he was an Englishman
through and through.

She half-listened. Joe never bored her. She'd hated him, yes. She'd
blamed him—because someone had to take the blame.

She loved him coming inside her—violence and tenderness, force—
the way he could release himself. His way, determined and gentle, of
touching her. She was thrilled by their lovemaking, and he'd confessed
he hadn't believed women were built that way, to get any pleasure at all.

Six times that summer he'd come into her on a mossy forest floor,
the Douglas firs whispering above their heads and her white firm belly
loaded with mystery. The doctor in Los Angeles who'd examined her last
winter warned that her pregnancies would be difficult from now on and
they oughtn't to count on more than two children, maybe three. Joe had
a plan that they must build a big house somewhere in the East—New
York or Montreal—and build or buy another house in California, by
the sea. When this contract was finished, he'd said, they were going to
Europe, for six months at least. He'd once gone to Havana to negotiate a
contract, but otherwise had not travelled outside the States and Canada
and the remote mountains of Mexico.

The drone of the inspector's voice was making her drowsy, and she
was grateful for the bit of privacy her enormous hat provided. She was
startled when he reached out suddenly and took her hand.

"You're the sort of female I ought to have waited for," he said. "I have been watching you and trying to think where it was I went wrong, what I could have done differently, and I don't know what it was, except I was too eager. My God, I've dashed everything, made such terrible mistakes; my life is an absolute hell. My wife is unhappy. She hates Edmonton. She's from Ontario; her father managed a branch bank in a mining town, and she hated it there. But she won't hear of England; she says it's not home for her. She has never been happy anywhere as far as I can tell. She doesn't know what it is—happiness. A child won't make her happy; she'll just spread her unhappiness to the child. I can't bear her voice sometimes. The only passion I feel these days is the need to get away. The rest of the time I feel dead. Being with her is much worse than being alone. Why? She's the woman I chose to marry. Now it frightens me to think of her with our child. She's near the end of her tether as it is. I've told her I'll get her a maid somehow but she says I don't bring in enough money for it; she says our trouble is all because of that. She accuses me of lying—"

Iseult pulled her hand away and he released it.

"I'm sorry, I'm sorry," he said helplessly.

"I'm sorry to hear of your troubles, Inspector, but do you think it wise to talk of such things? I would be upset if I knew my husband was talking to strangers. Marriage is a mystery between two people, isn't it? You can't let others in. Think of your wife and how she would feel."

He stood up, his leather belt and boots creaking. His face had gone stiff. "You're quite right. My apologies. Good day, madam."

For a moment she was afraid he was going to come to attention and salute, but he turned back to the horses and men, fitting on his broad-brimmed Stetson as he walked away.

She felt depressed and frightened. And ashamed of herself. She ought to have let him talk. Maybe it would have done him some good. Maybe it would have done his wife some good. Mother Power would have recognized the need, the despair. The nun would have listened. But it was too late. Not wishing it to appear that she was running away—even if she was—she finished her tea before standing up. Her belly seemed to be swelling by the hour. She adjusted her hat, folded the blanket and draped it over her arm, and walked self-consciously past the policemen standing around their little fire.

Heading back through the deserted camp, she thought of stopping at
the main office, where Joe and his clerks were at work. But if she told
him about the inspector seizing her hand and pouring out his troubles,
Joe would make some wry joke, and she didn't feel like laughing. The
man's despair had really shaken her.

Mr. Bee had swept out the white tent and smoothed her bed. She put
her camera on a shelf. She decided she ought to go out in the garden and
dig up new potatoes; hard work always made her feel better. But instead
of changing her clothes and going out again, she slowly unpinned her
hat, took off her boots, and lay down on her camp bed. She stared at the
canvas roof gleaming with sunlight and thought again about whether
she loved her husband. She did, but love changed in marriage, became
an element in a compound with a complex chemistry. It was never quite
stable, it seemed.

~

That night the strikers stacked up railway ties like tepees, doused them
with coal oil, and set them alight. Every few hundred yards along the
grade, bonfires were burning. From their tent Iseult could see the orange
flames, but it would be no use trying to shoot the scene on the film stock
she had.

"Burning themselves out of work," Joe grumbled. "Those sleepers
cost a dollar apiece."

She squeezed in next to him in his camp bed, crowded but warm.
What did love consist of, really? Legs and hands and voice. Loyalty. He
was headstrong, passionate, male. Did he love her or just want to own
her, or was it the same?

He slept.

He believed the contract was his alone. He did not see that the
men and the contract and himself—and herself too, for that matter,
and their unborn baby as well—were all part of one thing. He acted as
if everything—the mountains, the weather, even the quick passing of
seasons—belonged to him. The men in their hundreds were *his* men.
Employees or enemies, he could see them only in relation to his own
plans and determination. Perhaps it was how he saw her.

She lay with her cheek pressed on his warm skin, and, yes, it made her feel safe. They were powerfully connected to a shared grief and his seed was inside her, but marriage was a mystery—whether theirs would sustain under the pressure of all that he wanted, whether it would keep breathing, whether it would mean anything at all.

~

In the middle of the night something woke her. She didn't know what it was at first. Her heart flurried. Then she heard men singing and recognized the tune: "John Brown's Body." Sitting up in bed, she tried to make out the words.

Joe grunted and growled and sat up groggily beside her. "What the hell?"

Solidarity forever! Solidarity forever!
Solidarity forever! For the Union makes us strong.

Were they headed for the compound? Were she and Joe and their unborn baby in danger?

"Goddamn them," he grunted.

"Would a union be so terrible?"

"Jesus, Iseult!" He began punching pillows behind his back.

"Well, would it?"

"If I let in a union—especially the IWWs—the generals would cut me out. We'd never get another contract, and there are outfits in Winnipeg and Spokane that'd be more than happy to take over this one."

He reached for his cigarette box on the bedside table, took one out, and struck a match on his thumbnail.

The singing wasn't getting any closer. It was getting farther away.

"I worked it out. I'm going to offer a bonus. Ten-dollar bonus to every man who goes back on the line tomorrow and sticks it out till freeze-up."

"Ten dollars isn't very much. May I have a cigarette, please?"

He was irritated but offered her the box. Her eyes were adjusting to the darkness.

Flaring another match on his thumb, he lit her cigarette. "What's the matter, Iseult, are you going Red on me?"

Maybe he meant to sound amused, but he was angry. He needed to control everything, keep everything in his hands. If he thought people were getting away from him it made him furious.

"They are trying to hustle me, Iseult. I won't be hustled. We could lose everything. If I offered any more it would be like taking bread from our children's mouths."

"What about their children?"

"Any man that works hard and saves his pay will go out with a sum at freeze-up. Anyway, they're bindlestiffs, hoboes, not family men. You see what they do with their money."

"Maybe they have children somewhere."

"Then they ought to go back to work and not listen to a bunch of crazy anarchists." He drew on his cigarette. "Listen, Iseult, let me give you some news. Most things worth having, you have to take from someone else."

What had he taken from her? In bed next to her husband, four and a half months pregnant, smoking one of his cigarettes and aware of his heat between the sheets, his hip against hers, his leg against hers, the smell of his skin and his hair . . . despite all this closeness, this *proximity*, he might as well be a stranger. He really was a stranger.

She thought of the inspector. Were most people walking around with such unhappiness inside? While her parents were alive, the air in their house had seemed dead. They'd never said anything, but she could always taste their disappointment in each other.

Maybe Joe expected her to argue. When she didn't, he said, "I can't be responsible for anyone else's happiness. Only for yours and our children's."

She was remembering one of her sojourns with Mother Power, and a girl encountered in a precinct house in Hell's Kitchen, a German girl who had stabbed a man. How many men had a girl like that slept with? Proximity—skin heat—didn't necessarily mean anything. Women sold it, men bought it. Wives slept with husbands. A woman's body next to a man's didn't mean they were close, didn't mean they had ever really penetrated each other.

He lit another cigarette and kept on talking. Offering a bonus in the middle of a contract came close to betraying his principles, he said, but the important thing was getting enough work completed before freeze-up so they'd be in a good place to start next year.

She was barely listening. All that mattered to him was getting the work completed and on schedule. It didn't matter who survived or who didn't. She'd not felt such fierce loneliness since the baby's birth and death. This man, this Joe O'Brien, her husband, had once stepped through the fog and promised life, connection, children, meaning. But really people were alone. Even in marriage—perhaps most of all in marriage—they were still alone.

Maybe it was the pregnancy; carrying a baby made her conscious of herself and her skin and her body as a series of walls, and him standing outside, harsher and at the same time less powerful than he had once appeared. Maybe she was finally growing up. Maybe that was all.

~

At Santa Barbara, Calif., Jan. 18, 1914.
To Mr. and Mrs. Joseph O'Brien
A son, Michael Fergus.

> —*Santa Barbara Press*
> *Spokesman-Review, Spokane*
> *The Province, Vancouver*
> *Winnipeg Free Press*
> *Toronto Mail and Empire*
> *Montreal Star*

August 1914

O N SUNDAYS when the weather was fine, they would take their
baby and a picnic basket and a camera and go off in a handcar,
zinging along rails freshly spiked to sleepers embedded in mile after mile
of just-finished grade. Iseult loved Sunday picnics in the meadows among
wildflowers, alongside streams. Sometimes she tried to photograph the
flowers but more often she photographed Joe and the baby. After nursing, she and the baby napped in the sunshine while Joe fished for brown
trout and kept an eye out for grizzly bears.

The IWWs had not returned to the Selkirk Mountains. Most of the
railway had been completed, no new lines were planned, and plenty of
men were out of work, tramping up and down the fifteen-hundred-mile
line between Winnipeg and Vancouver.

Near the end of that third season, news came over the telegraph that
war had been declared in Europe. The Britishers immediately began to
celebrate, and dozens of "Austrians"—mostly Ruthenians, Poles, and
Italians from lands claimed by the Austrian emperor—were roughed up
and their tents and lean-tos violently demolished. Chinese station men
were also attacked, even though the Chinese emperor wasn't involved in
the war. Some of the Austrians and Chinese fought off the attacks and
others fled their remote stations, tramped back to Head-of-Steel, and set
up camp as close as they could to the frame house where Iseult and Joe
were living with their baby. The house had been shipped in on a flatcar
and assembled in three days, and as far as Iseult could tell it was the
only frame house for a hundred miles in any direction.

The next morning hundreds of nervous station men were camped

outside in tents and impromptu lean-tos, all wanting their pay, all wanting to quit the mountains before the Britishers attacked them again. Joe
went out and told them they were safer in the bush than in Vancouver or
Edmonton, at least until the war fever had cooled a little. Any man who
wanted to leave could see the timer and pick up his pay, he told them,
though he could not guarantee their safety once they quit the contract.

That day the Britishers were preoccupied with drinking and amass-
ing fuel for a bonfire. They ignored the Austrians and Chinese, and by
afternoon most of the foreigners had gone back to their remote stations.
At dusk a torchlight procession came through the camp, led by a girl
from the Dovecote riding a mule and waving a Union Jack, with hundreds of Britishers marching behind her. Iseult watched from the nursery
window, her son in her arms. She did not understand this war fever. Her
grandfather, wounded in the neck at Cold Harbor, had always spoken
bitterly of his Civil War soldiering.

She could hear Joe and his American gangers and engineers in the
kitchen downstairs. There was feeling in the camp against the States for
not joining the war, and the Americans were wary. Some were carrying
pistols, though Joe had assured them the excitement would blow over
when the whisky was gone.

Iseult sat down in a rocking chair and began nursing Mike. He was
a big, healthy boy with a good appetite, and he settled contentedly into
her arms. She felt his body relax and she relished his warmth. They both
enjoyed nursing, the circle surrounding them, protected and complete.

After he fell asleep on the breast she swiftly changed him and put him
in his bassinet. She didn't feel like going downstairs. With the men so
rowdy in the kitchen, she might not be able to hear the baby. Covering
Mike with a blanket, she pulled the chair over to the window and sat
down.

The men had lit their bonfire out on the grade, and she could see
figures cavorting around the flames. Two days before, no one at Head-
of-Steel had given a moment's thought to the European situation. Now
some were dancing around a big red fire while others—the foreigners—
huddled out in their stations, afraid of being attacked.

Joe had received a telegraph message that dozens of fires were being
lit tonight along the grade, all the way back to Winnipeg: a chain of fire

to celebrate the British Empire's coming into war. Maybe, thought Iseult, they expected soldiering to be more interesting than building railway grade. Perhaps they were excited at the prospect of crossing the ocean.

She and Joe had been planning to sail from Quebec to Liverpool on the twentieth of October, with their baby. She'd been looking forward to their first trip to Europe together. He had business in London and they'd intended to see her relations in France, then visit Italy.

The previous winter, a week or so before Mike was due, Joe had driven from Santa Barbara to Los Angeles in their new Ford touring car to see her mother's old friend Mr. Spaulding about a real estate investment. Joe had been due back the next morning—it was a single day's trip—but he hadn't shown up. In the middle of the afternoon she received a telephone call from the assistant manager of the Huntington Hotel in Pasadena, who told her a Mr. J. O'Brien of Santa Barbara was under the care of the hotel nurse, and could they expect a family member to come and take him home as soon as was convenient?

Her first thought was that he'd come down with malaria. There had been malaria at some of the remote stations along the line.

"I don't like to say, madam; I'm no doctor. But there was an empty whisky bottle in his room when the maids went in."

She had telephoned Grattan in Venice Beach, and he rode the electric cars out to Pasadena, collected Joe, brought him back to Venice, and drove him up to Santa Barbara the next morning. At Butterfly Beach Joe stepped out of the automobile looking spruce, shaved, and healthy. He insisted that he could easily have driven himself home, but Grattan had wanted to try out the new automobile.

"He just about burned the brakes on the Conejo grade. You ought to know you can't treat a machine that way, Grattan."

"You weren't sounding so snappy this morning, brother." Grattan turned to Iseult. "I made him take a plunge in the ocean first thing this morning. He was howling, but I think it did him good. Woke him up, anyway."

"I had a minor headache," Joe insisted. "That was all."

As soon as Grattan left for the train station she made Joe tell her what had happened.

He said that Mr. Spaulding had taken him to dinner at the Jonathan

Club in Los Angeles, to celebrate their real estate deal. "I guess I was more tired than I thought. Been working the numbers pretty hard, you know. And I've been . . . anxious . . . about this fellow." He touched her pregnant belly. "Took a drop more than I ought to have, I suppose. It took me by surprise, I'll tell you."

"More than a drop," she said.

But as soon as he'd admitted his anxiety about the pregnancy, she was ready to forgive him. And five days later Mike was born at Cottage Hospital: a happy, healthy, eight-pound boy.

Tonight at Head-of-Steel, as she watched the Britishers' bonfire funnelling drafts of embers into the cold sky, she tried to imagine what might be happening in France. She could remember watching soldiers in red trousers parading past her uncle's house in Lille. Were her French cousins in uniform? Were they marching now? Were men shooting at each other?

She had left a stew simmering on the stove, and the sweet aroma of carrots and beef broth, thickened with white barley and flavoured with onions, was drifting upstairs. She could hear Joe's gangers laughing and talking. Pretty soon they'd have a poker game going.

She had stolen two of Joe's cigarettes, and now she lit one because she was hungry.

The bonfire was as big as a house. Watching the figures whooping around the flames, she recognized the girl who'd been riding at the head of the parade. She was standing off by herself some distance from the fire and waving a torch back and forth, back and forth, like a child with a Fourth of July sparkler or a little girl with a magic wand, pretending to be a princess.

Joe had never once mentioned the Dovecote. It was Mr. Bee who told her there were women living in tents one mile down the line who would pay twenty-five cents for one bunch of carrots.

"Women? Who are they?"

The old Chinese man looked at her for a moment, then shrugged. "Bad women. Very bad."

She had wanted to go and see for herself, but the grade was too rough for Mike's beautiful English pram, a present from the Pasadena Theosophical Society, and he was too much for her to carry all that way. And there were always gangs at work on the grade, tamping gravel, spiking rails to sleepers. The men were polite but she felt self-conscious near them.

It would have been much easier if there had been other women in the main camp—wives, mothers with children. But there weren't. When she asked Joe if there really were women living in tents one mile down the line, he admitted there were.

"Why didn't you tell me?"

"You didn't ask."

"How was I to ask if I didn't know?"

"Are you going to pay a social call?"

"Are they prostitutes?"

"I suppose they are. They came up from Edmonton last month, and there's not much I can do about it."

The following Saturday night she had noticed that the main camp was almost deserted. Most of the men were at the Dovecote, which had its own supply of liquor. On Sunday morning, as she and Joe pumped their handcar along the temporary rails, she saw men sprawled in the ditches, sleeping it off.

Joe said he couldn't tell them how to spend their money as long as they stayed healthy enough to work. "If they start catching disease, I'll go down there myself, burn down every last tent, and chase the ladies back to Edmonton."

The bonfire's lights and shadows flickered on the wall of the nursery. Iseult felt a little flutter in her stomach. When she had told Joe she thought she was pregnant again, he had been delighted. They could still travel to Europe as planned, though perhaps not for as long. She would have the new baby in California in the spring.

Now war, if it lasted, made Europe unlikely.

She distrusted the night's excitement, those bonfires burning for war along a thousand miles of railway grade. They frightened her more than the IWWs and the bomb threats had. She glanced at the crib, where Mike was making gentle, chirring sighs, then gave her pregnant belly an affectionate rub.

Joe had said this might be their last season in the mountains: the Canadian railway boom was just about finished. There were no more big contracts on the horizon. With Mr. Spaulding and some Pasadena theosophists for partners, he had bought land south of Los Angeles, in Orange County. He planned to build houses and put Grattan in charge of selling them. He was also thinking of establishing a London office, or at least a representative, so he'd be able to bid on construction contracts coming up in the Caribbean, Africa, and India.

The savoury scent of that stew. Why hadn't he brought her up a bowl? Like everyone else he was distracted by the war excitement. He was worried his men would start quitting in droves and heading off for Edmonton to enlist.

It had spooked her, seeing the American gangers with pistols lumped in their coat pockets. They were wary of the Britishers. Or perhaps carrying a pistol was an unconscious gesture of solidarity with the men outside, an acknowledgement that the war changed everything for everyone, even the neutral Yanks. The stakes had been raised. They were living in history now, and history was more satisfying than a railway camp.

Joe was a gentle husband but there was an element in him as hard as a drill bit. Earlier in the month he had buried two men up the line without even mentioning it to her. Two Italians who had borrowed a rifle and shot an elk. The day had been hot, they hadn't butchered fast enough, and the spoiled meat had killed them. She'd learned about it from Mr. Bee a few days afterwards.

Any death upset her, even more so since Mike's birth. She had not been able to bring herself to visit the bone-house all summer. It was sixty miles back along the grade, but that wasn't the real reason. Now that they had a baby, she didn't want to lay any shadow across the little boy's life—that was what she told herself. Once or twice Joe had mentioned going back to the avalanche slope, but maybe he felt the same way, because he certainly had not pressed the matter.

But she was furious at him for not even mentioning the Italians. Maybe he'd been trying to shield her, but to not mention that two men had died seemed horribly callous, as though the deaths were of no consequence.

"You ought to have told me, Joe."

"Why?"

"Because I'm your wife, that's why!"

"Half a dozen fellows got pretty sick. We didn't know what it was at first. They figured shooting an elk might mean trouble for them, so they weren't about to tell us."

"My God. You don't feel a thing about it, do you."

"You can't eat game this time of year. It spoils too quick, even if you know what you're about when you're butchering."

"Death is important, Joe!"

He looked at her quizzically. "Of course it is."

"Where did you bury them?"

"Along the line."

"Where, Joe?"

"I don't recall the mile marker. I could look it up. "

"Is there anything to even mark the place?"

"We buried them decently. They were Italians, so I assumed they were Catholics."

"Your daughter is buried along the line—do you even remember?" she said.

He had turned away without a word, and she knew she'd wounded him. She was being unfair. He hadn't mentioned the deaths only because he knew the news would upset her. But she thought of their lost child every day anyhow—did he really think she didn't? He aimed to keep driving ahead and never think of the past, bury every sorrow under tons of ballast, timber, and steel. He could tell himself he was sparing her feelings, but it was really himself he was protecting. He was the one most frightened; she was only afraid of not feeling. And now she had a baby, a passionate stake in life, and another baby growing inside her. She was strong enough; she could handle just about anything now.

She was also hungrier than ever after nursing; her body needed replenishing, her flame was burning low. He ought to have brought her a bowl of that stew. And some bread and butter. And a cup of tea. From the sound of their laughter the Americans downstairs were drinking whisky. Joe wouldn't touch a drop. There were a few pears left from a box Elise had sent; they were in a bowl on the kitchen table and the gangers would probably finish them off. It wouldn't have occurred to him to put a few away, save them for her and the baby. And his foremen would finish the stew and their boots would make a mess of the floor, which she swept constantly and mopped twice a day because there was nothing but dirt in a construction camp, dust and mud.

She finished the cigarette, pushed open the window, and dropped the end outside. There weren't so many people around the bonfire anymore. It was dying down and the women had disappeared, probably back to the Dovecote. Maybe the war excitement was already turning into just another spree—whisky, card games, and prostitutes; men spending their pay and sleeping it off along the right-of-way. The Austrians and Chinese hunkered out on the stations were probably quite safe, though they might not realize it yet.

She wondered how long the bone-house would stand on that bare scree slope with the dribble of glacial runoff bringing down more rock and gravel every year, and she wondered if either of them would ever see it again.

She and Joe, the men and their war fever, the women of the Dovecote, the girl she'd watched waving her flag at the bonfire all by herself, as if the roistering passion in the camp didn't matter, couldn't possibly touch her—they would all be quitting the mountains in a few weeks. What would become of them? She only knew for certain that the country must lock down, and soon, and that when the completion money came in she and Joe were going to be rich. They were healthy and young and on the way to having a second baby and their future was bright.

She wondered how strong they were really. Head-of-Steel was one thing, the open world another.

In a few weeks snow would blanket the mountains, smother the valleys, and the green river would freeze as hard as steel. They would all leave something behind in the mountains. Only the luckiest were getting out with anything, and even the most fortunate, the most privileged, would be leaving pieces of themselves.

MONTREAL,
1917–1923

Armistice

Brown's Hotel
Albemarle Street, London W1
7th October 1917

My Dear Brother Joe,

The air in France is completely different than the air in England yet no one seems prepared to admit this is so. I don't mean merely that it has a different smell—of course it does. I mean the physical structure of the air on the Continent has been changed—I think by the war.

It is lighter and gummier. It has lost its old consistency. This is an effect I have never heard described, perhaps it's quite new, after the heavy-heavy bombardments of the last 12 weeks all along our Div. front, we have been getting rocked in quite an exceptional manner, the ground sometimes jellifying.

I attribute this change in the atmosphere to the concussive power of steady bombardment, which has after all been banging along the front from Switzerland to the North Sea for over three years now, with rather exceptional heavy spells recently. It is well known that any gas will change its structure, electrically, in response to change in pressure—& air is merely another gas as I tell my lads (gas is on our minds after Arras!). So, my theory: bombardment has shaken the atmosphere & reorganized the structure of the air. The air is lighter in France because concussion has you might say purified it. A cubic yard of French air must weigh less than half the equivalent volume of English air & it's not merely a matter of London's smut & smoke because the difference was noticeable as soon as we disembarked

the Channel steamer—I've been given a theatre ticket, Maid of the
Mountains, & must go now, love to Iseult and children,

ton frère,
Grattan

Joe thought the letter sounded quite mad. His brother had written from London, where he was on his first extended leave after eleven months at the front. At the start of the war Grattan had left his wife and daughter in Los Angeles and travelled to Montreal to join the Canadian Expeditionary Force. He wrote Joe frequently from France and Joe had enjoyed reading the letters aloud to Iseult: they were brisk and salty and gave a humorous picture of life in the trenches.

One week after the mad missive from London, there was another troubling letter, from Scotland.

Kinross House
Perthshire
15th October 1917

Joe my dear,

The night train—Euston to Waverley Station, Edinburgh. Nothing
you would call a berth. At Edinburgh a cup of tea and rock buns
and boarded as per instructions the local train for Perth. Between
Dunfermline and Kinross saw the most remarkable animal. Now I'll
admit I only had my eyes on him for a matter of seconds. If you ask
what breed I wouldn't be able to tell you. Something small & terrier-
like, perhaps not a recognized breed at all.

But the power of connection, Joe! It cannot be denied.

Other people recognize animals are "totems" . . . It's only this
morning—that I've finally been able to accept that what I was seeing
was something more than just a dog in a garden!

The dog was available to deliver a message. I've been working to
break the code & get it straight.

I saw my soul prowling in a garden behind a terrace house
somewhere on the line between Dunfermline and Kinross . . . prowling
& confused. I saw myself.

I know now that I simply can't go on as I have been. I must
remove from that dripping garden, that boxed way of seeing.

I want you as my trusted brother, Joe, to tell me, have you ever had
any similar experience?

*The Montgomery family here have taken in six Canadian officers
as houseguests, we are being treated splendidly, horses to ride birds to
kill,*

*Your brother,
Grattan*

Joe looked up at Iseult. "What the hell is he talking about?"

She shook her head. "He's trying to make sense of his experience. I can't imagine what it would be like arriving in London or the countryside straight from the war."

After Grattan returned to France there were no letters at all for a while, only terse postcards demanding books, chocolate, and cigarettes. Then he wrote to say his application to join the Royal Flying Corps had been accepted and he was in training to be a fighter pilot.

Too much bloody mud down there. Sick of mud. Cleaner in the sky.

By then, the third year of the war, Joe had brought Iseult and their two children out of the West and settled them in a big stone mansion house on Pine Avenue in Montreal. He still owned a house on Butterfly Beach; they would spend summers at Santa Barbara once the war was over. The Western railway boom was finished—the government had been tearing up track and shipping the steel to France for military railways—but O'Brien Capital Construction Co. Ltd. had been winning government contracts and building shell factories, barracks, and military hospitals from one end of the Dominion to the other. Joe was prospering.

Once Grattan started flying, the tone of his letters changed once more.

*. . . the most sullen mamzelle last night in Paris lush sweet thing my
god the right girl tastes like a berry, Joe, bursts in your mouth, we
must have done the jig four or five times . . .*

*. . . sisters, worked in the officers' estaminet tea and fried potatoes papa
is a officier belgique it cost 2 francs well-spent did you ever make two at
one time Joe I'm feeling old this morning believe me . . .*

*. . . has a lovely white belly and black bush and doesn't speak a word
the whole way through . . .*

. . . had another girl on the train, gave her one fr., she screamed bloody murder . . . did you ever notice, Joe, that a cunt is awfully like a wound? You can buy a girl at Amiens for a cup of chocolate, some of them are all right, I used to think they ought to be pretty, though to tell you the truth just about anything will do.

Joe could not bring himself to read such things aloud, but when Iseult insisted on seeing the letters he handed them over, and she read them while sitting in an armchair by the fire.

The Pine Avenue house was magnificent, but cold and old-fashioned. It didn't really suit them. He planned to build them a Montreal house of their own after the war.

"I don't like you reading that filth."

Iseult looked up. "It's all connected, Joe, don't you see? He's trying to stay alive."

"It's filth."

"The war is, but this is more than that. He can't deal with anything not raw. Brutal, even. He has to try to make things very simple."

Iseult was in touch with her sister-in-law, Elise, in Los Angeles. When Grattan began flying, he stopped sending money to his wife and daughter, who were still living in Elise's photography parlour above the Chinese laundry on Windward Avenue. The United States was in the war by then. People in Los Angeles had stopped going to the beach, and Elise could no longer support herself and her daughter with studio portraits and postcards. She had found work in a factory in West L.A., stitching fabric for aircraft wings.

When Iseult asked Joe to do something for Elise, he wired money for a pair of train tickets, and she and six-year-old Virginia arrived in Montreal in January 1918, penniless and without winter clothes. They settled into the Pine Avenue house and Joe loaned his sister-in-law five hundred dollars to set up a photography business in the Queen's Hotel, across the street from Windsor Station. She started making studio portraits for hundreds of young soldiers passing through the city on their way overseas.

They learned that Grattan hadn't written her a letter in months, and the only communications she received from him at Pine Avenue were printed Field Service postcards.

NOTHING is to be written on this side except the date and signature of the sender. Sentences not required may be erased. <u>If anything else is added the postcard may be <u>destroyed.</u></u>

I am quite well

~~I have been admitted to hospital~~

~~{sick} and am going on well.~~

~~(Wounded) and hope to be discharged soon.~~

~~I am being sent down to the base.~~

~~I have received your~~

~~letter dated May 29~~

~~parcel " _____~~

~~telegram " _____~~

~~Letter follows at first opportunity.~~

~~I have received no letter from you~~

~~{lately}~~

~~{for a long time}~~

{Signature only} G. C.

<u>Date July 1st 1918</u>

The cards made Iseult furious, but Elise didn't complain and never asked to see the crazy, lascivious letters Joe was still receiving. He'd filed them all—he could not bring himself to let go of any piece of paper concerning the family. But if Elise asked to see them, he was prepared to say he'd burned them.

"Grattan knows what he knows," Elise told Iseult one day. "When the war's over, then maybe he'll want to tell me."

During the last nine months of the war, Captain Grattan O'Brien of the Royal Flying Corps shot down thirteen enemy planes. One week after the Armistice, the King pinned a DSO on his chest in a ceremony at Buckingham Palace, and six weeks after that, when Grattan stepped off the train at Montreal, a herd of reporters was waiting to interview him. Sojer Boy was a celebrity.

Instead of taking Elise and Virginia back to Los Angeles, Grattan accepted a position with the Canadian branch of a British firm manufacturing aircraft engines. He settled his family into a modest row house on Carthage Avenue in Lower Westmount, with Joe holding the mortgage.

Their sisters, Hope and Kate—who had taken their vows as Soeur Marie-Bernadette and Soeur Marie-Emmanuelle—died of influenza that first winter after the war. They were buried in a vault at the Visitations' convent in Ottawa without Joe's even being aware of their deaths until weeks later, when the Mass cards arrived.

His sisters had trusted him for guidance, and he had broken all their chances by pitching them into that cloister—this was what he felt. In his greed and hurry to escape and seek his own freedom, they were the ones who had paid the price.

The Little Priest, on the other hand, had done well with the Jesuits. In May 1919 Joe, Iseult, their two children and their Irish governess, and Grattan, Elise, and Virginia all took the train to New York for Tom's ordination at Old St. John's in the Bronx and a champagne reception, which Joe paid for, at a Catholic country club in Westchester.

The Montreal spring had been cold, but in Westchester summer was already sweet and heavy. In the middle of the party Joe and Tom left the clubhouse and went for a walk along one of the gorgeous fairways, both of them carrying flutes of golden champagne. Tom was silent, and Joe assumed he was savouring the moment, as he was himself—the evening light slanting across lush grass, the glow of family pride on his brother's behalf.

He was startled when Tom, without the slightest warning, burst into tears and started babbling about how much he had hated the Church for refusing Joe's little girl a funeral Mass; hated his Jesuit rector for not giving him leave to travel to British Columbia; and hated himself for not having had the courage to make the trip on his own.

Joe had never held a grudge—Tom had been a powerless seminarian in those days—but before he could speak, the Little Priest had flung his champagne glass to the grass and collapsed on his brother's shoulder, clinging and sobbing, until Joe could feel the dampness of tears through his coat. They were a couple of hundred yards from the clubhouse, standing under great oaks. The orchestra was still playing and music floated across the grass. It was likely no one had noticed them, which was lucky.

"I'll tell you this." Tom's voice kept breaking and catching, as though the words were too sharp for his throat. "The Church failing—so human—somehow made my faith stronger. Like a piece of steel in the centre of my faith. But you're my brother, Joe. I failed you. Left you alone in the wilderness. Can you forgive me?"

Tom had just taken holy orders, swearing himself to support a burden of faith that Joe had been letting go of all his life, it seemed, piece by piece. It would be disrespectful, Joe knew, to try to persuade his brother of what he himself had come to believe: that chanting, benedictions, and sprinkles of holy water were distractions, that the mystery of life and death could be approached only in fear, in solitude, in silence.

Patting the back of his brother's crisp new black silk cassock, he told Tom he ought to save his sins and imagined sins for the confessional, not dwell on them. He took out his cigarette case and handed Tom one, and they stood under the great oak trees smoking while a lush scent of evening rose from the fairway grass.

The Little Priest was being sent to Europe to pursue studies in advanced mathematics. He had found himself a home and a career with the Jesuits. If the order was imperfect, at least it believed in itself, and that was all that really mattered.

After finishing their cigarettes the brothers walked arm in arm back to the clubhouse, where they found Iseult dancing a foxtrot in the arms of Tom's Father Superior.

～

Back in Montreal, Grattan quit the aircraft company after a few months, complaining that their designs were flawed. Joe put his brother on salary, even though things were in a slump and O'Brien Capital Construction's only active project was the veterans' hospital at Sainte-Anne-de-Bellevue, being developed from temporary sheds put up during the war. Part of the contract involved building a railway siding, reception sheds, and tunnels so that the hundreds of long-term cases still being transferred from military hospitals in England could be disembarked directly on the hospital grounds. Grattan wanted to test the system and insisted on making an experimental trip from Montreal out to Sainte-Anne lying on a stretcher, with a couple of Joe's men carrying him on and off the train. The next morning he came bursting into Joe's office.

"Those reception sheds are fit for cattle, not men! The tunnels are freezing! We're not building a prison out there, Joe. It's supposed to be a hospital."

Grattan was taller than Joe and still wore the suits he'd had tailored in London, where he'd been a celebrity, a fighter ace, a wild colonial boy, petted and fawned over by English aristocrats.

"We're building to the specs we were given," Joe replied. "They're getting exactly what they're paying for."

"Do you know how many men have died out there since the end of the war?"

"They had the influenza."

"Hundreds! Have you seen the cemetery?"

"The cemetery isn't in the contract. We're rebuilding the hospital. It won't be fancy, but it'll be a hell of a lot better than it was. Look here—you're my brother, Grattan, but you can't just storm in here and start yelling at me."

Grattan dropped heavily into a chair. "Oh Jesus, brother. Those boys got so used to being herded like cattle, they don't expect anything better."

"I can't run my business this way."

Grattan sunk his face in his hands. "Two hundred men on the iron lung. And, oh Lord, some of the chlorine gas cases . . . I saw it all in France, Joe, but it seems worse here."

There was nothing for Joe to say.

Finally Grattan looked up. "I guess I'll need to find some other sort of work, brother."

"That is probably not a bad idea."

A few weeks later, at eleven o'clock in the morning on Armistice Day, 1919—exactly one year after the guns had fallen silent in France—workers in a rolling mill watched Grattan's Ford car smash through an iron railing running along the Lachine Canal, just below the Côte-Saint-Paul Bridge. As whistles and bells sounded all over Montreal, heralding the city's first two minutes' silence in honour of the war dead, the Ford plunged nose first into the discoloured waters and sludge of Montreal's industrial artery and sewer.

Grattan, shivering and vomiting, was plucked out of the canal by workmen using a boathook. When Joe went to see him, he claimed he'd been checking his wristwatch when he lost control of the car. He insisted he'd been planning to pull over at eleven o'clock to observe the two minutes' silence.

Grattan developed pneumonia and spent the next four months recuperating in the veterans' hospital at Sainte-Anne, also receiving electroshock treatments for sleeplessness. In the last weeks of his stay, a pretty night nurse read him the letters she was receiving from her brothers in Ireland, and on the Sunday after his release Grattan appeared on the church steps after High Mass, handing out Sinn Fein newspapers to anyone who would take them. At Sunday lunch at Pine Avenue he announced that he had joined the Loyal and Ancient Order of Hibernians, a disreputable organization with a clubhouse on Bridge Street in Griffintown, Montreal's Irish slum.

"You'll be my guest at our next dinner, Joe. We've a speaker coming up from New York. The British swine have been burning people out of their homes—they've broken every inch of glass in the country. They come in motor trucks in the middle of the night, break up cottages, drag fellows from their beds, strip women naked in the street. Pour a scalding cup of tea on a man's testicles to get information."

It was not the sort of talk Joe liked to hear in the presence of small children and servants. Stifling his irritation, he left Grattan to Iseult at her end of the table and began talking business with his sister-in-law, something he enjoyed. Elise had recently photographed Winston Churchill and Georges Clemenceau when they came through the city. Her portraits of the statesmen had been widely published, and now she was booked for weeks in advance. Her smart little advertisements—"Portraits by Elise"—were running in fashionable American magazines, and she had repaid with interest the money Joe had advanced her.

Grattan's voice carried the length of the table. "If the British don't get out of Ireland they'll be shot down and thrown out one by one! It's the plain truth that the best of them were killed in the war. Their occupation army in Ireland is dregs, halfwit boys from the slums of Birmingham, thugs and degenerates—"

"That's enough Irish for today," Joe interrupted. "Unless you happen to know a good Irish joke."

Grattan's fist banged on the tablecloth, rattling silverware. "But it's murder, Joe! They murder women and children!"

The children—Mike, Margo, and Virginia—were listening, faces rapt.

"It's not a war, it's a bloody massacre!"

"Let's drop the subject," Joe said calmly.

"Grattan, shut up," said Elise.

Grattan sulked for the rest of the meal. When he approached Joe afterwards—"Can we have a word between ourselves?"—Joe reluctantly led the way into his study. He had other things on his mind. Ever since coming to Montreal he and Iseult had been looking forward to building a house of their own, and he had just that week made an offer on a piece of land in the garden suburb of Westmount.

Grattan sat on the horsehair sofa and Joe sat at his desk, prepared to be bored. One of the maids brought in tea and departed. The brothers lit cigarettes.

"What's your opinion of the state of affairs in Ireland?" Grattan asked.

Looking at his brother sitting on the sofa, one long leg crossed over the other, Joe decided that Grattan, instead of growing up, was becoming more and more childish. A large, strange, steely-voiced child with a military moustache and an officer's forceful bearing.

Joe could not remember being told, but he had always known that their grandfather had come out of Ireland as a boy and up the St. Lawrence on a coffin ship, crawling ashore at Windmill Point, less than a mile from the spot where Grattan's car had plunged into the Lachine Canal.

"I don't have any opinion, Sojer Boy. I don't give a rat's ass about Ireland."

"Well, Joe, I am sorry to hear you say that. After all, you're an O'Brien and an Irishman by blood, Joe, same as I am."

Joe shrugged. "What does that mean?"

"The fact is, I can't bring myself to stay out of the fight any longer."

"What fight?"

"For the independence of Ireland, Joe! To throw off the British yoke."

"You need to get your feet on the ground, get a job, and start making some money. Elise is getting sick and tired of your muling around."

"Perhaps I'm one of the *fianna*," Grattan said. "Old Irish for the warrior race. You can't put a square peg in a round hole. The fact is, there's a war on and I'm going back across to take up the fight. I've booked my passage from New York to Queenstown, leaving next week."

"Oh, for Christ's sake."

"What I'm asking is that you look out for Elise and Virginia while I'm away."

"You want me to take care of your family while you go off and play soldier again?"

"I've nothing put by, but Ellie is doing pretty well."

Grattan reached inside his jacket, Joe assumed for a handkerchief or a cigarette case. But his brother's large white hand came out holding an automatic pistol.

"I took this from a man I killed," Grattan said softly, "and now it shall go back to war with me." The ugly German weapon gave off a sharp scent, like varnish.

"Put that thing away!" Joe said. "Bringing a gun into my house—are you out of your mind? I've a mind to belt you, you goddamn fool." For some reason seeing the weapon in his study made him think of his step-father staggering up the road, cawing his fiddle.

Grattan uncrossed his legs and leaned forward, holding the pistol loosely, barrel pointing at the floor. It looked small in his hand.

"I'll tell you one thing," Joe warned. "If you go to Ireland now, you're going to lose your wife and your daughter."

A faraway expression shrouded Grattan's face, as though the heft and weight and oily scent of the pistol had him entranced.

"She won't stand for you deserting her a second time. She'll move to New York or back to Los Angeles and take the girl with her. You'll never see them again."

"Elise doesn't understand the situation of Ireland," Grattan said softly.

"She never will, and neither will I. Listen to me, Grattan."

Grattan looked up. He all of a sudden seemed very tired. He held the pistol gingerly, as though it was too dirty and heavy to hold much longer and he was about to drop it.

"You're not going to Ireland. So get that idea out of your head."

Grattan sighed deeply.

"You're going to settle down in Montreal with your wife and your daughter. What you want is a job. Grattan, are you listening? This is the truth now I'm telling you."

He waited.

When Grattan finally spoke, he sounded weary. "Yes, Joe, you're right. Of course you are."

"All right, then. You've had a rough time of it lately—"

"But Joe . . . there was something I was to ask of you . . . something important. What was it?" He seemed dazed.

"I don't know," Joe said mildly.

Grattan struggled to recall, then his face suddenly brightened. "The passage—I'll need a loan for my passage, say two hundred dollars. Second class, New York to Queenstown. Elise won't understand."

He had seemed so much better—stronger—when he first got back from the war.

"Grattan," Joe said gently, "you won't need it. You're not going."

Grattan seemed stunned. He shook his head. "Well, that's right, I suppose," he said slowly. "I'm not."

"You're going to stay here and dig in. What about real estate? That seemed to work at Venice Beach. If you hadn't been selling those bungalows I'd never have met Iseult." He reached over, took the German pistol from Grattan, and dropped it in a desk drawer.

Grattan sighed again, deeply.

"I'll tell you what, Sojer Boy. Some men I knew out west have been buying up farmland north of Outremont. They've laid out streets, parks, sewers—they're putting in a garden city up there. The Town of Mount Royal, they're calling it. With the electrified railway under the mountain it's just twenty minutes to downtown."

"Selling lots isn't my cup of tea, Joe. Even in California I wasn't much good at it."

"You need to get your feet back on the ground. Otherwise you're living on what your wife brings in, and that's no good for either of you. I'll give these men a call on your behalf. All right?"

Grattan nodded.

Joe tapped him on the knee. "We've come through a lot, you and me. I'll set you up with these Mount Royal fellows. And in the meantime, if you need help with expenses, you can always come to me."

～

At certain times, not always predictable, a longing for solitude and silence came over Joe, and that was when he had his secretary book a sleeping room on the Delaware and Hudson overnight train to New York. He'd go directly from his office to Bonaventure Station. He bought his whisky from Pullman porters or cab drivers, from elevator operators and bellmen in the great hotels. He would barricade himself in a room at the Plaza or the Biltmore or the Commodore and slowly drink himself through the feeling of not belonging anywhere. He would awake on the floor more often than not, and with a terrible hangover, but feeling at home in the world once more. After sending his suit out to be pressed he would order himself a good breakfast, take a steam bath and a rubdown, and get a shave, haircut, and shoeshine at the hotel barbershop. He always kept an eye on the clock while picking out presents for Iseult and the children on Fifth Avenue, and if there was enough time he'd choose a couple of shirts and neckties for himself at Brooks Brothers before heading to Grand Central and boarding the next train to Montreal.

At first he tried to conceal these jaunts from Iseult, but she found out easily enough. She wanted him to speak to a doctor, if not his own, then one of her medical students. But he could not imagine what any medical man could say or do that would have the slightest influence on the way he felt during those times, or how he could possibly describe to someone else what he could not explain to himself.

Iseult wrote the Little Priest, now at Georgetown University in Washington, D.C., and he wrote back inviting Joe to a spiritual retreat in the Allegheny Mountains. Joe declined, although he told himself that if Father Jeremiah Lillis, SJ, were still alive, he might have gone into the woods to see him. The old priest had known something of loneliness and disgrace. But Joe had heard from someone out of Shawville that Father Lillis was dead and buried years ago.

He didn't need to consult any medical student and he didn't need a retreat in the Allegheny Mountains. New York City was his retreat.

~

The Armistice had been followed by a slump—three years shrouded in gloom and still tasting of the war—before Joe sensed the Dominion waking up again. Suddenly everyone wanted a car. Everyone needed a radio, and everything worn out by the war—clothes, manners, ports, bridges, governments—suddenly needed replacing. O'Brien Capital Construction Co. Ltd. moved into brilliant new offices in the Canada Cement Building on Phillips Square. Joe's wartime contacts with politicians and businessmen all over North America and the British Empire proved useful, and soon the firm began signing contracts to build hydroelectric dams, ship terminals, and an oil pipeline from the ice-free harbour of Portland, Maine, to Montreal.

Mike was eight years old, Margo six. Iseult was pregnant again. When they had first settled in Montreal, she'd asked him for a cheque for five thousand dollars. She'd used it, along with money of her own and another five thousand from the American Women's Club of Montreal and the Montreal Ladies' Benevolent Society, to establish a clinic in Sainte-Cunégonde for pregnant women and mothers and children. The clinic was staffed by students from the McGill and Laval medical schools, clean milk was sold there for a few pennies a quart, and a free dental clinic was held every Thursday.

At Christmas and on Iseult's, Mike's, and Margo's birthdays, Joe's presents to Iseult were always cheques for the clinic. He had only visited it once or twice himself: the sight of sick children and undernourished mothers distressed him. He'd write a cheque anytime Iseult asked him to, but he didn't want to have to look at those people.

It was time to start building their house in Westmount. Iseult chose the architect and Joe's men began excavating. Iseult's darkroom was in the design from the start; she drew up the detailed plan herself: a medium-sized room, accessible through her bedroom, with a red lamp recessed in the ceiling and windows with steel shutters. She would have a pair of deep sinks, shelves for chemicals and photographic papers, and a long worktable with her enlarger mounted at one end. The room would have mechanical ventilation and a fireproof cabinet for storing lenses and cameras—her old FPK with its red leather bellows, the Nagel, and the Ernemann Miniatur-Klapp Joe had given her for Christmas.

There were twenty or thirty fellows at work on the excavation and rough grading—more than the job required, but Iseult had insisted that the foreman hire a dozen men from Sainte-Cunégonde, fathers and brothers, who came wandering up the hill each morning pale and scrawny and blinking in the light. She photographed every stage of construction: the electrician and his assistant lugging great spools of copper wire on their shoulders; the driver of the cement truck with his pet cat; men laying hardwood floors, wearing leather hockey pads strapped to their knees.

But her children would always be her main subject. She never posed them but took quick snaps, aiming and shooting fast, a technique learned from Elise—though Elise herself now posed all her subjects, charged them a lot of money, and made them look serious, thoughtful, and gravely intelligent.

Joe kept hundreds of Iseult's photographs organized in leather-bound catalogues on shelves in his office on Phillips Square, each print numbered and dated. Sometimes when he looked through them, all he could think was what an extraneous, cruel gift love was in a world where nothing lasted. When he felt that way, he knew he was soon for a hotel room in New York.

Iseult was nearly six months pregnant the day she brought Mike and Margo out to Skye Avenue to watch the foundation being poured. It was sunny and warm, excellent conditions for pouring concrete. They ate a picnic lunch. Joe sipped lemonade and watched the fresh cement slide from the mixer truck and slop into the forms. His son and daughter were laughing, his men were working, his machines were howling, and his pregnant wife was squeezing his arm as they watched the solid footings of their future literally taking shape. If that moment proved to be as near as things ever got to perfection, he told himself, he would be satisfied, because in his heart he'd never expected half as much.

~

It seemed that Grattan's life too might be acquiring a solid foundation at last. On Joe's thirty-fifth birthday his brother invited him to lunch at the Ritz-Carlton. Grattan was selling house lots for the Mount Royal Land Company, he and Elise had just bought a new Buick, and in a few weeks their daughter, Virginia, would be starting fifth grade at the Sacred Heart Convent on Atwater Avenue.

After ordering a bottle of champagne, Grattan began telling Joe about a business proposition he'd received from his old squadron leader, an Englishman now living in Buenos Aires.

"Dicky's getting out of B.A. and taking up ranching on the pampas. They're exporting beef like mad from the Argentine. It sure sounds like a wonderful country, Joe. Dicky's offering to let me in as a partner. I'd help run the ranch. It would mean putting up a bit of operating capital, but not much."

"It's the other side of the world."

"So is the Town of Mount Royal, Joe. Too bloody far. Haven't sold a lot in weeks."

"You bought a new car."

"Elise bought it."

"When things fall apart in South America, what are you going to do next?"

"Drink your champagne, Joe."

"No, I can't. I've got a busy afternoon."

Grattan tossed down his own glassful, then refilled it. "Not bad. Nearly as good as the stuff we drank in France. Used to drink champagne for breakfast, Joe. Good wine was a lot easier to come by than a decent cup of tea."

"You have a family, Grattan. You can't ditch them." Joe wondered if his brother had enough cash in his wallet to pay the check. It would be close to fifteen dollars. If he really hadn't been selling anything, he had no business spending money on lunches at the Ritz when he had a wife and a ten-year-old daughter at home.

"Jesus, Joe, we ran away from real life to get this far, didn't we?"

"You're not making any sense."

"We could have stayed in the bush. That was plenty real, wasn't it." Grattan smiled and sipped champagne. "Think about it, Joe. Here we are, lunching at the Ritz. We're as far from where we started as the Argentine is from here. Mental and spiritual distance. We've come this far, both of us. Don't see why I can't go a little farther."

"Just what have you accomplished so far? Besides killing thirteen men. Probably fellows a lot like yourself."

"Jesus, Joe." Grattan slumped forward, gazing into his champagne glass. He had on one of his beautiful English suits, a fine worsted, better than the suits Joe ordered for himself at Brooks Brothers in New York. Probably Grattan still owed his tailor. Or perhaps someone else, some hero-worshipper, had picked up the tab.

"Do you ever try to add up, Joe, everything you've seen and done in your life?" Grattan's tone had shifted from exuberance to plowing unease. "Christ, adding up everything I've done, places I've been—that used to feel wonderful. Remember saying goodbye on the platform at Ottawa? Hell, I was scared. Dropped the girls off at the Visitations. Went on to Toronto, then Chicago. Met a woman on the train. Got off at Denver and she took me to a hotel—married woman, husband in Colorado Springs—never told you about her, did I? Lost my cherry at Brown's Hotel in Denver. Got back on the train next morning. The orange grove at Santa Barbara . . . I didn't like those Franciscans much, those sandals and brown robes—an eerie bunch. Hired on at a cattle ranch in the Santa Ynez Valley. Awful dusty. Met Elise at Ocean Park, snapping pictures on the boardwalk—that was an adventure, meeting Elise. Selling house lots for Abbot. Elise getting pregnant, us getting married. The priest at St. Monica's refusing to marry us on account of her being a Jew. Virginia's birth. My life handled like a book in those days: I could open it at any page I wanted and go on from there."

The café had been filling with lunch patrons, including men Joe had done business with, most considerably older than his brother, men who would not have served overseas.

"What about you, Joe?" Grattan said, looking up.

"I don't even know what it is you're asking." He had hoped his brother's feet were planted on solid ground at last, but they weren't, and probably never would be.

"Do you feel it all connects, Joe? I can't seem to find the connection from one part of my life to another. Can't hold it in one hand anymore like a book. A lot I seem to have forgotten. The war—I really ought to think more about the war. A lot happened. I ought to think about it, but there's never enough time."

Joe was observing two men whom the maitre d' was obsequiously showing to a banquette. One of them he recognized: Louis-Philippe Taschereau, KC, a courtly lawyer who represented the Archdiocese of

Montreal in civil matters. As one of the parish wardens of the Ascension of Our Lord, the new English-speaking church in Westmount, he had met with Taschereau a couple of times to review deeds and construction contracts. The lawyer had recently built himself a house not far from where Joe and Iseult were building. Taschereau's lunch partner was dressed like an American college man, in a grey flannel suit and a shirt with a button-down collar. His dark hair was sleekly groomed.

"I used to feel life accumulating, page by page," Grattan was saying. "I was learning by experience. I've lost that feeling."

Joe turned to his brother. "South America isn't a plan. It amounts to desertion, if you want to hear the truth. You'll lose everything worth having."

"Captain O'Brien?"

The young collegian, Taschereau's lunch partner, was standing by their table. He made a very slight bow. "Baruch Cohen."

Grattan looked blank.

"Second Lieutenant Cohen. I was with the 199th in France. Buck Cohen."

"Oh Lord, yes," said Grattan, squinting. "When exactly were you with us?"

Joe couldn't tell if his brother remembered Cohen or not.

Cohen seemed perfectly at ease. "Well, I took over a platoon in Major Murphy's company on the night of the seventh of July, 1917. We were in the trenches at Arras. You, Major Murphy, and Captain Grimstead were the company commanders. I was hit a couple of hours later, a blighty. Three months' recovery in England. When I returned to battalion, Murphy and Grimstead were dead. So were all the platoon commanders, and you'd joined the RFC."

Grattan rubbed his jaw and stared blankly at Cohen, who turned to Joe. "If you're Captain O'Brien's brother, I know you by reputation, sir. You're one of the railway men."

"Used to be."

"A pleasure to meet you, Mr. O'Brien."

The Jew had better manners than most ex-officers Joe had met. Buck Cohen was slight and youthful, though tightness around his eyes made him seem a little older.

"You at McGill?" Joe asked.

"Oh no." Buck Cohen smiled. "I pursued studies before the war, but my university days are over."

"Don't you miss it at all?" Grattan said, somewhat hungrily.

"University?"

"The war."

"I can't say I do. I'm keeping busy. Still a lot of catching up to do. The war seems an awfully long time ago."

"I was talking to my brother about South America," Grattan said. "What do you think about South America?"

"Very little, to tell you the truth. Where are you working now, may I ask?"

"I'm selling cow pasture in the Town of Mount Royal. Only no one's buying."

Joe told himself he had never wanted to boss his brother. He'd just wanted Grattan to be safe. Maybe it came down to the same thing. Maybe he didn't really know how to be a good brother, or husband, or father. He'd acquired no wisdom, had nothing deep and learned to go on. All he'd ever had to guide him was raw feelings and instinct, and when he was in a self-justifying mood, he told himself these amounted to love.

"You might come and see me sometime, Captain," Buck Cohen was saying. "My operation is growing. Other things being equal, I prefer working with men who've been overseas."

"What business are you in, Cohen?" Joe asked.

Cohen shrugged. "Import-export."

"What do you handle?"

"Oh, pretty much anything." Taking out a small leather notebook and a gold pencil, Cohen jotted something on a slip of paper and handed it to Grattan. "If you ring my secretary she'll schedule an appointment. Do come round. A pleasure running into you, Captain O'Brien. I enjoy meeting fellows from the old battalion. Doesn't happen that often. They were wicked days, weren't they?"

"Wicked?" Grattan smiled slowly. "That's the word. Wicked they were. Wicked were we. Here's to the dead, boys." He raised his champagne glass in a toast.

Without hesitating, Cohen picked up Joe's water tumbler and clicked glasses with Grattan.

"The dead boys," Buck Cohen said.

~

Joe's office had an abundance of gold leaf on the ceiling and an enormous fireplace where a log fire was cracking and glowing. It was November. A few snowflakes had been swirling among the grey buildings, but now the slots of sky were hard blue, and down in the square the pavement was mostly bare, with only a dusting of snow on the King-Emperor's shoulders.

On Pine Avenue a car and driver were standing by to whisk Iseult to the Royal Victoria Hospital at a moment's notice. After two flawless births at Santa Barbara's Cottage Hospital she had wanted to have this baby at home, but he would not consider it.

He knew when she saw snow flying she would remember the baby they had lost in the mountains. People always would remember what had hurt them. What gave them pleasure they let go of pretty quickly.

His secretary buzzed and said his sister-in-law was on the line. Assuming Elise was calling to ask about Iseult's condition, he picked up his desk phone. "No news yet, Elise."

"Joe, Grattan never came home last night. I'm awful worried."

Grattan had not mentioned ranching on the pampas since their lunch at the Ritz. Early in the fall he had scratched his leg on barbed wire while hopping a fence to show clients a piece of land. The scratch had become infected, and for a while it had looked as if he might lose the leg, but the wound had finally healed.

"Have you tried calling his office?" Joe asked.

"I did, first thing. No one's seen him since before lunch yesterday." Elise sounded calm, but he knew she wouldn't have called unless she was worried.

"How has he seemed lately?" he asked cautiously.

"How do you mean?"

"Since he got out of hospital. Sold any lots?"

"Joe, it's Armistice Day."

He lit a cigarette. "What exactly are you thinking, Elise?"

"You know what I'm thinking." She started to cry.

It was the first time he had heard someone crying over a telephone wire, and he was dismayed by how helpless it made him feel. Holding the receiver to his ear, he spun his desk chair and looked out across the city to the Royal Victoria Hospital, a grim, grey Scottish castle on the silver flank of Mount Royal.

"You think he's had another accident?"

"If you want to call it that."

"What would you call it?"

"I don't want to call it anything, Joe. I just want him home! This time of year he always gets crazy. I want him to be all right. Oh God."

"Ellie, listen, he's probably out on a tear. If you'd been downtown this morning you'd have seen the vets on St. Catherine Street, celebrating. They've been at it since last night. He's probably celebrating too, the fool."

Elise sniffled. "It could be, Joe. Maybe he's tying one on. It could be that."

Joe looked at his wristwatch. "The Governor General's unveiling the new war memorial in Dominion Square in an hour. There'll be a crowd. I'll bet Grattan shows up. I'll walk over and see if I can't find him."

"Joe, what if he went in the river?" Her voice sounded small and far away. "They'll never find him then; they'll never fish him out."

"Don't think that way. He'll turn up."

"He isn't strong, Joe. He isn't. Not like you."

She was weeping again. His sister-in-law was almost as tough as he was but she'd probably been dreading Armistice Day for weeks. She must have had a sleepless night.

"I'm going to the unveiling. I'll call you as soon as I find out anything." He hung up the phone.

The newspapers had been referring to the new war memorial as the "Cenotaph," whatever that meant. When people feared a thing, they dressed it in language to blur its shape. Dead soldiers were now "the fallen." Death in the war was "sacrifice."

Rising from his desk, he walked over to the windows. Bits of snow were swirling again between grey buildings. The sky was pale and looked cold. He ought to get hold of his driver and make sure he had chains ready for mounting on the tires. The streets approaching the Royal Victoria were the steepest in the city.

Intending to check the weather forecast, he picked up a copy of the *Montreal Herald* that lay folded on his desk. The front-page story was yet another gun battle in Vermont between rumrunners and hijackers. Two Italians from Montreal had been found shot to death in a highway ditch outside St. Albans. There had been many similar stories lately in the *Herald*. Every night, trucks loaded with Canadian liquor sped down the back roads of New England, headed for New York City. He'd recently heard that Louis-Philippe Taschereau's young client Buck Cohen was one of New York's major suppliers of contraband liquor, and on his way to becoming one of the richest men in the Dominion of Canada.

A thought struck him. Joe crossed the room and opened his door. His secretary, Miss Esther Dalrymple, looked up from her desk.

"Get Louis-Philippe Taschereau on the line, please."

"Certainly. Oh, Mr. O'Brien?"

"Yes?"

"The girls at the switchboard are holding a line free in case Mrs. O'Brien calls."

"Excellent. Thank you." He respected Protestants like Miss Dalrymple, who lived with her mother in Verdun. She was not beautiful but she was punctual, efficient, and quick. A few moments later, Taschereau's office was on the line.

"I connect you now," a French-Canadian secretarial voice intoned.

"*Oui? Monsieur O'Brien? Comment allez-vous?*"

"*Ça va bien, merci. Et vous?*"

Joe deployed his lumber-camp French for the polite preliminaries before switching to English. "M'sieu, the reason I called is that I've a brother who may be in some trouble down below the border." It was a guess, but his hunches had often proved correct.

"Well, I'm sorry to hear that," said the lawyer. "What sort of trouble?"

"He may have been doing some trucking business down there."

There was a pause.

"Your brother? This would be Captain O'Brien?"

"Yes. The fact is, he never came home last night. One of your clients has trucking interests, and I thought he might have heard something."

There was silence at the other end of the line. Had he annoyed Taschereau by referring to his connection with a rumrunner? He didn't know the lawyer well. On the other hand, it was a fact that Taschereau represented Cohen, who had sold more liquor last year than anyone else in the world, according to a story in the *Toronto Telegram*.

"Well," said Taschereau, "these matters are obscure to me, but I can certainly try to find out."

"If something's happened I wouldn't want his wife to find out from the newspapers."

The lawyer sighed. "These people . . . " He let the sentence trail away.

Your clients, you mean, Joe thought. "Thank you, monsieur. I'm much obliged."

"Not at all. I'll call you by the end of the day."

Joe next placed a call to his home. Iseult's voice came clearly over the wire. "Nothing to report," she said. "This is getting very boring."

"What are you doing?"

"Sitting in the sunroom and looking through *Vanity Fair*."

She usually spent three days a week at the Sainte-Cunégonde clinic, delousing children, keeping records, and paying bills, but she had agreed to stop going there until after the baby was born.

"I feel like a beached whale, Joe. I don't like this house. I can't wait to be in our own home."

"You haven't spoken with Elise this morning, have you?"

"No. Why? Is anything wrong?"

"Grattan didn't come home last night. And it's Armistice Day."

"Oh, Joe."

"I'm going to Dominion Square. They're unveiling the war memorial. Maybe I'll see him there."

~

In Dominion Square, hundreds of people wrapped in overcoats stamped their feet against the bright cold. Women clutched wreaths, sprays of poppies in cellophane, lilies wrapped in newspaper. There were red-cheeked schoolboy cadets and plenty of young men wearing medals, but women outnumbered the men. The sky had cleared, the wind was sharp, and the light snow that had fallen was being tossed around on hard ground.

A flight of pigeons whipped overhead. The Governor General and an array of officers and aides-de-camp were on the reviewing stand in their polished boots, with moustaches and chests of ribbons, clutching leather riding crops. The Anglican bishop of Montreal was addressing the crowd in an elderly Englishman's quaver: "Sacrifice . . . gallant . . . glorious . . . Empire . . . blessed . . . " Joe couldn't tell if he was speechifying or praying, the words were being tossed around so by the wind.

The crowd was dense near the new war memorial but there was plenty of open space in the square: acres of frozen yellow grass and brown flowerbeds. The South African War Memorial—a bronze cavalry trooper holding down a restless bronze horse—was on the other side, opposite the new Sun Life Building. He usually ignored it, but sometimes, on his way to the train station and New York City, he stopped and read the inscription.

TO

COMMEMORATE

THE HEROIC DEVOTION OF THE

CANADIANS WHO FELL IN THE

SOUTH AFRICAN WAR

AND THE VALOUR OF THEIR COMRADES

Heroic, devotion, valour—ten-dollar words. *Abandonment, early sorrow,* and *poverty* were the plain real words, and they ought to have left space on their monument for a few of them.

Looking up, he saw bare branches, wild sky, and restless pigeons. It was warmer within the pack of bodies, sharing heat. The brand-new monument—the Cenotaph—just unsheathed, stood twenty feet tall. No bronze figures, no decoration, just polished granite fitted together almost seamlessly. It was good stone. He wondered where it had been quarried and at what price.

Archbishop Bruchési was speaking in French and Joe felt the mostly English crowd getting restless. War had divided the city, with French Canadians rioting against conscription. All that was supposed to be forgotten now.

The Archbishop shifted to Latin for his benediction, and as Joe scanned for his brother the crowd began singing a Protestant hymn,

"O God, Our Help in Ages Past." A dowdy middle-aged woman clutching a wreath was escorted to the foot of the Cenotaph by a cadet, and Joe felt a narrow slice of pain enter his chest as he watched her lay the tribute. He would kill anyone who threatened his Mike. If they came at his boy waving their flags, he'd kill them.

He glanced at his watch. Just about eleven o'clock. Out on Dorchester Boulevard cars and trucks were pulling over to the curb. Buildings and sidewalk grates still spewed steam and smoke, but the noise of the city had abruptly died away. The silence—a novelty in 1919, dogma now—was being strictly observed.

The railway men hated it, he knew. It played hell with the timetables. People were making a fetish out of remembering the war when most of them would be better off forgetting all about it. Life ran forward, never back.

He gripped his walking stick. This was his city now, a shining collection of death and memory. Opposite the South African War Memorial, the Sun Life Insurance Company was building a new headquarters, the biggest building in the British Empire. Saint-Jacques Cathedral, St. George's Anglican, the battlements of Windsor Station—all grey stone, coldness. There was permanence here, and he liked that. Everything he had done had brought him this far.

A sharp squawk broke the silence and a murmur of disapproval passed through the crowd. Another squawk, a little louder—then some notes scratched the air, a lick of melody, and he suddenly realized that someone, somewhere, was playing a fiddle.

Looking across the square he spotted his brother, the tallest in a group of five or six other men, all wearing trench coats except one fellow in a woollen cap and mackinaw, who was striking away at a fiddle perched at his neck. The tune snarling across the frozen silence was "Cheticamp Jig," one of the bawdy pieces Mick Heaney used to play.

The two minutes ended. Official silence began to loosen and dissolve. People started chatting, stamping their feet, coughing. Out on Dorchester Boulevard the automobiles began moving. Streetcars jangled their bells and resumed their metallic slither, but above everything Joe could still hear the taunting, raucous fiddle.

He started towards his brother.

Grattan saw him coming and saluted. "Hello, Joe! Cold enough for you?"

"What the hell are you doing here?"

"Same as everyone, I guess."

The fiddler had moved a little way off and seemed to be locked in a furious struggle with his instrument, bow flying and music sputtering into the cold air, banging into the brutish surround of stone buildings. With his black hair and chipped face he could be an Indian, a Caughnawaga Mohawk from across the river.

Joe shuddered. The squawking notes were like insects pecking at him, needles jabbing. "Where the hell have you been, Grattan?"

The velvet collar of Grattan's cashmere overcoat was turned up against the cold. Joe had always been secretly proud of his younger brother's distinguished appearance. No one looking at Grattan would ever guess he'd been raised in the clearings.

"You've been running whisky for Buck Cohen, haven't you?"

Grattan nodded. "I sure have, Joe. Delivered a cargo at Stockbridge, Mass., last night and ran straight back. Jesus, it was cold in the truck."

"You got shot, didn't you? Back in September. It wasn't any goddamn barbed wire."

Grattan shrugged. "Bullet just scratched me, but it wasn't clean."

"Let's get out of here," Joe said. "Walk back to the office with me. I've had a telephone call from Elise. You'd better speak to her."

Grattan shook hands with a couple of the men in trench coats, then he and Joe started across the square. The fiddler was still playing but his melody was slower now, not a jig. Mournful. A lament.

"What the hell did he bring that goddamn thing to a wreath-laying for?" Joe said.

"Don't know. There were a few Caughnawagas in the battalion. Joe, I couldn't tell Elise or she would have made a fuss. I make two hundred bucks for a night's work and don't have to do anything but ride along. Buck's always worried about his trucks getting jumped."

"What are you, some sort of gunner for the gangsters? Is that what you've come to, Grattan?"

"Well, I haven't done much gunning, but that's what it comes down to, in a pinch."

"Did you see the paper this morning?"

"That wasn't us. We stay clear of St. Albans."

They were passing brown flowerbeds, bare and lumpy. Feeling overwhelmed, Joe suddenly halted. "I can't stand that music."

"Pay it no mind, brother. Let's go someplace warm. I could use a nice lunch."

A small ache in Joe's chest was radiating into his shoulder and right arm, tingling down to the elbow. His eyelashes were sticky with tears as he stared down at his shoes. He was wearing doeskin spats, buttoned up the sides. When had he started wearing spats? A year ago? Ridiculous things. Grattan didn't wear spats.

"Grattan, do you suppose Mick Heaney is dead?"

"Christ, I sure hope so. I used to dream of running into him in France."

"I wish we'd killed him when we had the chance."

"Well, we damn near did. Where'll we lunch? How about the Piccadilly? My treat."

They resumed walking. Joe had heard of businessmen suffering heart attacks in the middle of the day. At the Montreal Amateur Athletic Association pool, where he swam twice a week, he'd overheard a member compare the pain of his heart attack to being shot in the breast at dawn by a firing squad. Was he going to keel over and die in Dominion Square?

"I'll call Elise from the Pic," Grattan was saying. "Last night was the easiest two hundred bucks I ever made. Drank coffee all the way down, slept all the way home."

Joe's legs were shorter than his brother's and he had to exert himself to keep up. The pain in his chest seemed to be fading.

At the Piccadilly Tea Room on St. Catherine Street, they were shown to a small table near the window. He rarely went out for lunch. When he did it was a business lunch, usually at one of the downtown clubs, the Mount Royal or the St. James, where he was respectable enough to be offered lunch but not membership. Along with a few French Canadians, the Scots had their cold hands on the wealth of the city, which they had been piling up since the days of the fur trade. An Irishman would never be invited to join their clubs until he got so rich they couldn't ignore him.

A pretty waitress in a stained uniform brought their menus and

Grattan headed off to the manager's office to telephone Elise. The café was warm, steamy, and noisy. Conversations were in English and French. Women sat with their furs draped over the backs of their chairs. Most people wore Flanders poppies on their lapels and few men wore war ribbons. Grattan had not worn his decorations.

Thirteen enemy planes. Thirteen dead German flyers equalled one DSO. Maybe all it signified was that Grattan was crazy.

Grattan returned from the manager's office looking sheepish.

"Reach her?" Joe asked.

Grattan nodded.

"Am I supposed to lie for you?" Joe said. "Or did you tell her where you were?"

"She really ran me rough, Joe. Really hauled me over the coals."

"Did you tell her you're finished with the rumrunner business?"

"Well, Joe, you're the boss."

"No, I'm not. Take responsibility for your own life."

"Sure, sure. You are my big brother, though."

It was Friday, and Joe ordered salmon on brown bread. Grattan hesitated and then ordered the same. As soon as the waitress left he slipped out a flask and added a dollop of amber whisky to his water glass, then glanced at Joe.

"No, I don't want any." He had no taste for liquor when he didn't need it.

"I was on my way to grab a bite for lunch yesterday afternoon when Buck pulled over in a great black touring car and offered me the run. The trucks were already loaded when we got to the warehouse. There wasn't time to phone Elise."

"What about the other times?"

"I always told her I was out with the boys."

In many ways Joe felt closer to his sister-in-law than to his brother, respected her more, yet he and Grattan carried the same seed of whatever it was—mud, blood, hardship. He wouldn't anoint his own children with that legacy. They would come of age in safety in Upper Westmount.

After their food arrived the brothers ate in silence. The plate-glass window facing St. Catherine Street was steamed from the cold outside and the moisture and warmth within. Grattan hardly touched his pepped-up water glass—he never had been much of a drinker. There had always been something fastidious about him. Which was why those wartime letters, with their *mamzelles*, *cunts*, and prostitutes fucking on trains, had been so shocking. The war had cut Grattan loose from decent life, like a kite with a broken string.

While Grattan was putting down money to pay the bill, the waitress returned and said there was a call for him on the telephone in the manager's office. He glanced at Joe, shrugged, and left to take the call. Joe wondered if Buck Cohen had somehow tracked down his brother and wanted him for another job. Another whisky run.

Grattan returned a minute later. "That was Ellie. She just had a call from Iseult. Iseult felt something and she's on her way to the hospital."

~

The brothers rode up Peel Street in a taxi. Joe felt unwell. Maybe it was the salmon. Maybe it was anxiety over this pregnancy, a weight he had been carrying in his gut all month and trying to ignore.

The day had grown colder, the streets festooned with white smoke and steam. The cab passed between a pair of gates and ran up a carriage road to deliver them at the front door of the hospital's Ross Pavilion.

Joe reached into his pocket for money to pay the fare, but Grattan said, "I'll take care of it, brother. You go on. I'll find you inside."

The door was held open by a gaunt young commissionaire, a veteran with campaign ribbons on his chest and a scarlet cellophane poppy on his lapel. Taking the elevator to the third floor, Joe hurried to the nursing station, the soles of his English shoes cracking crisply on the linoleum. A little red-headed nurse in starched cap and pinafore led him down the polished corridor and opened a door.

Iseult was barefoot on the floor at the foot of her bed, gripping the white iron bedstead with both hands. Her legs were spread apart, her head was lowered between outstretched arms, her flannel nightgown ballooned over her swollen body, and she was grunting rhythmically.

"Jesus, let's get a doctor in here," Joe said to the little nurse, who disappeared.

Pain, hot breath, and a smell of shit clouded the room, and for a moment he thought of Mick Heaney sprawled on his back on the frozen dirt in the shed. Weak wintry light smeared the room. Curtains halfway open revealed a panorama of grey city and black river. Iseult's face was pale, damp. He pulled off his gloves, dropped them on the bed, then rubbed his hands briskly to warm them and began massaging the small of her back and her hips. Gently at first, then with more firmness.

She stretched, arching like a cat. "We're going to be fine," she told him.

"I know that."

"Has Grattan turned up?"

"Yes."

"He's all right?"

"Yes."

Grattan and Elise must have run into each other in the lobby, for they entered the room together, followed by a baby-faced doctor and a senior nurse who glared at Joe.

"Good afternoon, Mr. O'Brien," the doctor said. "Quite a crowd."

"Good afternoon."

Joe could feel the senior nurse bristling. She clearly wished to order him from his wife's room, but something in his stance must have warned her it would not be wise. She turned and followed the doctor to Iseult's bedside and briskly drew the curtains around the bed.

While they examined her, Joe stood by the window, hands clasped behind his back. The light over the city was grey and white. The river would freeze soon. In a few more weeks the ice would be thick enough to drive trucks and wagons across.

Fear as much as ambition or intelligence had brought him this far. One slip, one moment of weakness, and the river current would have him.

Elise touched his arm. "Thanks for going to look for Grattan. You're a good brother, Joe."

He nodded. Those closest to him knew him the least.

The curtains around the bed were swept back. The senior nurse glared at him and he glared back at her. He wasn't ready to leave Iseult to the care of the medical profession, not just yet.

The door opened and the little red-headed nurse wheeled in a tea trolley.

"Everything's quite normal, Mr. O'Brien," the young doctor said. "Enjoy your tea but don't stay too long. Our patient needs her rest."

The doctor and nurses left the room. Elise plumped Iseult's pillows and smoothed the covers, then kicked off her shoes and hopped up on the bed, where she sat cross-legged and started pouring tea. Everyone except Iseult took a cup with sugar and milk, buttered toast, raspberry jam, shortbread.

Iseult was silent, absorbed in her body's mysterious processes.

Elise was silent too, probably wondering what crazy scheme Grattan might get involved in next. And Grattan was probably planning his next escapade.

Clink of china, greasy scent of butter, smell of heat glowing off the iron radiators.

The doctor had seemed terribly young, but Joe knew Iseult trusted him. She had asked him to lend a few hours of his time to her clinic. Within her body, protected by her tissue, muscle, blood, their third—fourth—child waited to be born.

Slipping off the bed, Elise crossed the room, her stocking feet making a brushing noise on the linoleum. She switched on the electric light, then went to the window and drew the curtains shut. Returning to the bedside, she murmured something to Iseult that Joe didn't catch, then started massaging Iseult's swollen belly and singing what sounded like a lullaby, or a love song, in a language Joe did not understand, possibly Yiddish. It sounded right, anyhow, like sweet air in the room, like warmth, like safety.

No point in thinking how vulnerable they really were, how exposed.

On the Run

I BELIEVE HE'S IN DETROIT," his mother said.

The O'Brien Capital Construction Co. Ltd. was building a bridge from Detroit to Windsor. In Detroit Mike's father usually stayed at the Book Cadillac Hotel; he would bring home bars of soap in the shape of books for Frankie, Mike's younger sister. But Mike had also overheard his mother telling Aunt Elise that his father could be in New York, and by then—Mike was nearly fifteen—he had a pretty good idea what New York was all about.

Later that evening he was in his room doing a delicate bit of soldering on his radio set when his mother entered without knocking.

"That radio's taking too much time from your schoolwork!"

He reminded her that the science master at Lower Canada College had encouraged the boys to build sets, even helping them order parts. The radio wasn't taking time from his schoolwork; it *was* schoolwork.

"Do not speak to me like that, Michael!"

"Like what?"

"As if you know everything and I don't know anything! Don't use that tone of voice."

"What tone of voice?"

"Oh, stop it." She sat down suddenly on his bed. "Oh, stop it, myself. The smell of that awful gunk has gotten to my head. I can't think straight."

"Solder doesn't smell any worse than your fixer."

"I suppose it doesn't." Flopping backwards, she lay staring up at the ceiling.

At least she wasn't holding a camera. She sometimes came into his room and snapped photos of him doing homework or working on his radio or assembling a model plane. Other parents brought out the camera to record birthday parties or Christmases, but she had always taken pictures of them doing ordinary things. Homework. Eating breakfast. Riding their bikes. Mike and his sisters were so accustomed to it they hardly noticed. Their father filed all her photographs in albums. He used to keep the albums in his office downtown but he had brought them home. Now they were in a special bookcase in his study. Mike and his sisters were allowed to take them out and look through them, but they never did.

He suddenly felt sorry for his mother.

"I'll open my window and leave the door ajar. The draft'll suck out the fumes."

She got up, came over to where he was sitting, and rubbed his hair. "Don't stay up too late."

After she left he went back to soldering, most of his consciousness concentrated in his fingers. He was surprised when the notion of leaving home—of running away—came to him all of a sudden, like a flashbulb popping. It wasn't a plan he had been cooking up; it wasn't really even a plan. All of a sudden he just saw himself walking down the Westmount hillside, headed for the train yards.

His parents had been at odds with each other lately, never raising their voices but mostly keeping to separate parts of the house. His sisters had their own lives, their school friends. He'd slip away and they'd hardly notice. He'd be leaving his radio set behind, but he'd come back sooner or later, or maybe he'd build another.

He told himself he'd rather be heating a can of beans over a hobo fire in the Alberta badlands than spending another day on Skye Avenue in Westmount. He'd been born out west; he and Margo were the only real Westerners in the family. Maybe what he felt was a homing instinct, like geese winging north in spring.

∽

He had trouble sleeping that night. Anxiety seemed to exist on its own, like a powerful radio signal, especially when he lay in bed. He had never tried describing the feeling to anyone. It didn't seem to fit into words. It didn't have a cause or a reason that he could put his finger on. Even giving the hum of feelings a name—*anxiety*—had been fairly recent. It had always been the way things inside him were, his tuning for "normal."

Once he left home, he told himself, he'd be too busy looking out for himself to worry. He liked horses, and maybe out in Alberta he'd become a cowboy and there wouldn't be any time to lie in bed feeling anxious about things he couldn't name.

~

The next day, Saturday, his mother was meeting Aunt Elise for lunch, then going to the art museum. Margo was spending the weekend at her pal Lulu Taschereau's and Frankie was at a birthday party on Roslyn Avenue. The maids and the cook always took long naps on Saturday afternoon.

He packed bread, cheese, and apples in an old Royal Flying Corps haversack that his uncle had given him for a get-well present when he was recuperating from pneumonia. Uncle Grattan had recently quit selling real estate and bought an old farm in the Laurentians, which he planned to turn into a ski lodge. Mike's father had called it another hare-brained scheme and said Grattan needed to grow up and probably never would, but Mike had been with his uncle when strangers came up to him in the street wanting to shake hands with him. Sometimes they even saluted. A stranger had come up to Grattan one Saturday morning in the hardware store on Sherbrooke Street, said something Mike didn't catch, then laid his head on Grattan's shoulder and started crying. Everyone in the store was staring, but Grattan had put his arms around the man as if he were a kid who'd fallen off his bike and needed comforting. Afterwards Mike asked who he was.

"Didn't catch the name. Says he was in my company in the 199th. Probably was. So many went through I don't remember all the faces."

"What was wrong with him, Uncle?"

"I guess he's got a little bit of trench fever."

"How do you know?"

"Because I've had it myself."

~

The servants were asleep and the rest of the house was empty when he sat down at the typewriter in his father's study. He didn't want his parents worrying any more than they had to. He didn't want any fuss.

```
May 27th, 1929

Dear Mother,

    I'm not running away only taking a trip by myself.
Shall let you know when I get there. Shall be all
right. Don't worry about me.

                    your son,
                    Michael J. O'Brien
                    P.S. I'll be o.k.
```

Leaving his note beside the telephone, he quit the house and, with Grattan's RFC haversack slung across his shoulder, walked down Murray Hill and across Murray Park.

The park was their natural home. He and his sisters knew every flowerbed and piece of shrubbery, had climbed every tree worth climbing. They knew how water in the different drinking fountains tasted: metallic in some, salty in others. When he was ten, his father had given him a wristwatch and said a man with a good watch had no excuse for being late ever. What he'd meant was that Mike was responsible for bringing his sisters and himself home from the park in time for their evening curfew. June, just before they left for Santa Barbara, was the luminous month, and he always hated leaving friends and games then while the sky was still bright. The girls never wanted to leave either, but the three of them would cross Westmount Avenue together and trudge up Murray Hill under the canopy of elms and maples, on sidewalks strewn with bright green maple seeds. Their mother might be in her darkroom or off at a committee meeting or washing babies at Sainte-Cunégonde, but their father was always waiting outside under the portico, clutching the evening newspaper and wearing a silk smoking jacket, with his reading glasses pushed back on his head. Maybe he figured that if he didn't watch for them something bad would happen. And something *could* have happened. Frankie could have been hit by a truck losing its brakes on Murray Hill. Margo could have been electrocuted by a power line brought down by a sudden thunderstorm. Mike could have fallen out of his favourite apple tree and broken his neck instead of just scraping his elbow. A thousand things could have happened. Only they never did.

Leaving the park, he continued down into Westmount Glen and through the dank tunnel under the Canadian Pacific main line, which debouched into Sainte-Cunégonde, where poor people lived, where children died of tuberculosis caused by bad milk. He caught a streetcar along Notre-Dame Street, then walked through another seeping tunnel under the Lachine Canal. On the other side of the canal St. Patrick Street was hectic with motor trucks. The weeds growing in pavement cracks had a certain sour smell. A stone wall topped with coils of barbed wire ran along Wellington Street, flanking the Grand Trunk train yards. The air smelled of rust and train brakes and he heard yard engines at work on the other side of the wall, shunting cars, making up trains.

Coming to a gate manned by a railway policeman, Mike crossed the street and waited on the opposite side until a truck pulled up and sounded its horn. As soon as the gate swung open, he crossed the street and slipped through without the cop noticing him.

Cuts of boxcars lined dozens of sidings. Crouching beside a track bed, gravel cutting into his palms, he watched brakemen and a yard engine put a train together. Skirting them, he headed for a switching shack and found the destinations board, but the train and track numbers were in a code he wasn't able to decipher.

The sun was warm. Tar oozed from sleepers. Dodging between boxcars, scrambling over couplers, he was wary of being spotted. When he saw a couple of hoboes climbing into a boxcar, he thought about asking them where the train was headed, then decided not to. He didn't want to expose himself to people who knew everything while he knew nothing. He'd be better off figuring out stuff on his own.

He was hiding behind the embankment, peering over the grade and watching brakemen checking automatic couplers and linking up brake hoses, when a man in a blue suit darted out from behind a cut of tanker cars, ran across the tracks in a crouch, and dropped down beside him on the tarry gravel embankment. Putting a hand on Mike's arm, he gasped, "Train? Yes? Where?"

The words were scraps, harshly pronounced. He wasn't a brakeman or a guard. He didn't look like a hobo, wasn't carrying a bedroll or knapsack. There was a blue shadow of beard on his cheeks and chin. His blue suit was too big for him.

"Where?" he repeated, gesturing at the train.

A foreigner.

"Out west," Mike answered. "Alberta."

"Chicago? Toronto, Chicago? My brother, Chicago."

Cha-cago.

Signal bells started banging and a big 4-4-2 locomotive and tender coupled up to the train. A brakeman came along the track waving a green flag, and they both ducked heads below the grade.

"I'm going to jump that train." Mike was suddenly determined.

"Nikos." The man thumped his chest. "Greek!"

"Mike."

"My brother is restaurant. Cha-cago."

With a series of massive clanks and squeals, the couplers pulled snug and the train started moving.

"Cha-cago," the Greek repeated.

Most trains out of the Montreal yards, Mike knew, were westbound, headed for southern Ontario or up around the Lakehead. He hadn't been able to read the board but there was a better than even chance this train was going in the right direction.

The rank smell of weeds along the embankment made him feel sad for some reason. Scrambling to his feet, he started walking alongside the moving train, keeping up with a wooden boxcar. The doors were open and the car smelled of rotten oranges. The wooden floor was higher than he'd expected. He realized he wouldn't be able to hoist himself aboard while the train was moving.

Falling back a little, he noticed an iron footplate and ladder at the end of the car. If he could get a hold on the ladder he could climb up to the roof and ride there. He'd seen men riding on boxcar roofs in California, so there was probably something to hold on to up there.

The train was moving faster. He started running to keep up. It was amazing how such a giant thing could pick up speed so quickly. He heard someone running behind him and without looking around knew it was the Greek.

Mike knew he wouldn't be able to keep up with the train much longer. Reaching out, he grasped the iron bars on either side of the iron ladder, and as soon as he touched the bars he could feel the train's muscle, its momentum. The iron bars seemed to want to surge right out of his hands, but he held on. The trick was to get his feet up onto the footplate. Once he did that it would just be a matter of holding on and climbing to the roof.

The train was starting to pull him off his feet, and he made himself run faster. If he let go he'd be pulled under the steel wheels by his own momentum and the suck of speed. He swung his legs up, scrabbling for the footplate, and felt a dose of panic as his body swung in the gush of air. Then his feet touched and he was able to stand on the footplate, pull himself inboard, and start climbing.

Looking back down, he saw the Greek loping alongside like a wolf. He looked up at Mike and his lips parted in a smile, exposing teeth that were brilliant and white. As he reached for the ladder the Greek made the mistake of seizing it with only one hand instead of grasping it with both. How could he have guessed the sheer power, the rolling pull of that train, until he'd actually touched it? And as soon as he did, it twisted him sideways. He lost his footing, spun around backwards, and was sucked underneath the wheels.

He didn't scream. Or if he did, Mike didn't hear it; the sound was submerged under the enormous bearing of the train.

Mike scrambled to the roof and crouched, holding on to some iron ribs and shivering, while the train ground along, skirting the factories of southwest Montreal. He had never seen anyone killed. He hadn't imagined it could happen so quickly and be over so suddenly and that everything would just go on afterwards.

The string of boxcars squeaked and crackled. His boxcar was so far back in the train that he could barely hear the engine. He clung on and shivered. It was as if his brain had been rubbed by some giant eraser, and it wasn't until the train started across the Victoria Bridge over the

St. Lawrence that he understood they were heading east, not west: to the Eastern Townships and the Maritimes, not Toronto or the Lakehead.

The train picked up even more speed coming off the bridge. It was too late to jump off. His face stung in the wind. He had forgotten to bring water and suddenly he was very thirsty.

Starting off in the wrong direction was a stupid, basic, humiliating mistake. Huddled against the wind, he wondered how long he could keep holding on. He didn't trust that the peeling wind wouldn't blow him right off the top of the car. He tried to shut down his thoughts and just watch the country slipping by: meadows, bean fields, orchards. After a while he started feeling a little more normal. He didn't need to hold on so tightly; the constant breeze wasn't going to blow him off after all.

People were always being killed by trains. If he'd read about an accident like that in the newspaper he probably wouldn't have thought much about it, would have forgotten all about it after turning the page.

Three hours after crossing the St. Lawrence, the train halted on a siding at a pulp mill. By then he'd had enough of going the wrong way. The Greek's bluish jaw and bright smile were coming back to him. He knew the trip was over and he'd have to go home.

What would they find on the tracks? A lump of blood and meat and whatever was left of the blue suit? How did they bury a person after something like that?

The stench of wood pulp was sour. He climbed down from the boxcar and asked a startled yardman if there was a telephone somewhere. The man collared him and dragged him into a shack where a foreman was smoking a cigar. Mike asked in French if he could telephone Montreal and have someone come and fetch him.

The foreman said there was no phone in the shack but there was one in the mill's main office, which was, unfortunately, closed because it was Saturday afternoon. Mike could use that phone, but it would cost money to pay for the call.

"*Combien?*"

"*Puis, un piastre.*"

The foreman tucked the dollar into his pocket, then led Mike through the noisy, steamy mill and up to the office. The room was deserted but there was a phone. He gave the operator Grattan and Elise's number; his aunt answered the phone.

"Are you all right, Mike? What's going on? Where are you?"

"I'm okay. I just need to talk to Uncle Grattan, please."

Grattan agreed to come and fetch him. "I'll be there in a couple of hours. Sit tight."

After he hung up there was little to do but watch the workers tending the giant newsprint machines. In a while the men started shutting everything down. The shift was over.

He went back out to the railway siding, found the boxcar, and inspected the wheels and undercarriage. There was no trace of blood or gore—just grease, flecks of sand and gravel, and the acrid smell of brakes. Across fifty or sixty miles everything else had dissolved or been blown away. He didn't know if he was going to tell someone or not. It would start feeling very different once he began talking about it, he knew. He would keep it to himself a while longer, think it over some more.

He followed a group of workers leaving the mill and crossing the highway. The evening damp smelled of hay from meadows that sprawled towards a river. A few men got into ancient cars but most set off walking down the highway towards the lights of the town.

He went back inside the mill and played barbotte with a night watchman who was missing his right arm. They rolled dice at a nickel a game. The watchman said his wound had been *un petit bleu, vraiment non plus qu'une éraflure*, but instead of healing it had grown very tender, and the next thing he knew he was at a dressing station, then a field hospital, where a surgeon told him he had *septicémie* and was going to lose the arm. "*Je lui ai dis, okay, je vais vous donner mon bras si vous me permettriez de revenir au Canada.*"

After giving Mike a cigarette, which made him dizzy, the watchman stretched out on a cot and fell asleep. Mike wandered across the highway to a brightly lit lunch wagon with a tin Kik Cola sign and a half-dozen trucks parked out front. Behind the lunch wagon the fields were planted in corn and beans.

He sat down at the counter and asked the waitress for a glass of milk. *Un verre du lait, s'il vous plaît.*

Did the Greek's brother really work in a Chicago restaurant? Would he ever learn what had happened?

He felt as though he wasn't really in the café, wasn't really anywhere.

He'd started for the West and this was as far as he had gotten. He knew he hadn't the strength to go farther, not just then, anyway.

He'd finished the milk and was about to ask for a slice of apple pie when Uncle Grattan suddenly sat down on the stool beside him. Grattan wore a tweed jacket and old grey flannels and a gold ring on his left hand that Elise had given him on their fifteenth wedding anniversary.

"Thanks for coming, Uncle."

"I'm glad you called. Your mother was getting worried."

"I left her a note."

"Yes. That's what had her worried."

The waitress came over and Grattan asked for a cup of coffee.

"Tell me what the plan was," he said to Mike after the waitress left. "Did you have a plan? Or were you just hightailing it?"

He needed to hold on to what had happened a little longer. Keep it in his hands awhile and just think it over. "I was going out to Alberta," he said, "but I got on the wrong train."

"Ever hopped a train before?"

"No."

"Not that easy, is it. I used to bum into L.A. on the lemon cars out of Santa Paula. I'm not going to ask why you left. Maybe I have a general idea, and I guess the details don't matter. But I want you to promise me something."

"I was born out west, Uncle. I'm not from here. I don't belong here."

"Nonsense. A person belongs wherever he's willing to stop and dig in. I've experienced a vivid sense of belonging in certain shell holes. I want your word of honour you won't try it again. Too hard on your mother. Train yards aren't the place for a boy. Easy to get hurt. People get killed."

For a moment he considered telling Grattan, but something made him hold back. "I'm not a boy, Uncle."

"No? What are you, then?"

"Well, I guess I am."

"Before you try something like this again, talk it over with your parents. Come to some sort of understanding. *Tu comprends? Donne-moi ta parole.*"

"I swear."

"Don't go boasting about this escapade to your pals: you'll start a train-jumping craze. And don't tell your sisters, or you'll just scare the pants off them. Do you want anything else? Another glass of milk? *Mademoiselle, s'il vous plaît, apportez un verre du lait pour ce gars.*"

They walked out into the fresh-smelling dark. Grattan's car was a brand-new Chevy Capitol, maroon, with a black cabriolet roof. The previous autumn Grattan had taught Mike to drive on a range road up north. He didn't have his licence yet but he knew how to handle a machine.

Grattan had set the choke and was about to push the starter when Mike resolved that he wasn't going to tell anyone, certainly not his father and maybe not even Grattan. Not for a while anyway, maybe never. If he told it would become just a story. Right now it felt like a part of him, a limb, an eye, a pint of his own blood.

"Uncle?"

"Yes?"

"I want to be like you, not like him."

Grattan sat back in his seat. Taking a pack of cigarettes from his coat pocket, he stuck one in his mouth and struck a match.

"I'd like to save you some grief, pass along my manly wisdom. But I don't have any. I've always looked up to Joe. You can learn a lot from successful men like your father. A father's protection and love are rare, rare things. We lost our old man, and things got pretty rough after that, believe me."

"I don't know what I'd learn from him except sneaking off and getting drunk."

"Now you're sounding like a kid again."

Grattan pressed the starter with his foot and the engine caught. As his uncle steered the nimble little Chevrolet out onto the highway, Mike let the acceleration push him back against the seat. Sweet engine noise filled the silence. His uncle spoke from the other side of experience, and that counted for a lot, but the only way he would ever get to that other side was to go there himself someday, and on his own. Maybe he'd already started.

Disorder

MOTHER SUPERIOR STALKED into geography class, interrupting the lesson. She looked angry, and the little nun teaching the class looked scared. Boarders, day girls, teachers—everyone at the convent was scared of Mother Superior. Born a Protestant, she had all the rage and zeal of a convert.

"Margo O'Brien! Gather up your books and come with me."

Margo glanced at her best friend, Lulu Taschereau, who gave a little shrug. Tasch had been teaching Margo, Mary Cohen, and Lulu's cousin Mathilde to play bridge, and they had been playing rubbers in the dormitory by candlelight and flashlight. Had Mother Superior found them out?

Margo wondered if she was being expelled. But why weren't Tasch and the other bridge players being summoned?

In the corridor Mother Superior impatiently clacked the string of black rosary beads she wore around her waist, each bead nearly the size of a walnut.

"A taxi has been called for you and your sister." The nun's cheeks were pink, her blue eyes sparking behind steel-rimmed spectacles. She was angry about something. "It will be at the front door in exactly half an hour. Go upstairs and start packing. You and your sister. There's no time to waste."

"Am I being expelled?"

"Do you deserve to be?"

Maybe it was a set-up so she would rat on the other bridge players. Margo stared at the nun boldly. She wasn't going to play that game.

"You're not being expelled," Mother Superior admitted. "Your mother is taking you all to California tonight."

"California?" Margo was stunned.

"I can't imagine what she's thinking." Mother Superior clacked her prayer beads. "Now get cracking, O'Brien! Help your sister pack her things. Hurry! No time to waste!"

"But I have to say goodbye to Lulu."

"I will not have class disturbed again. Pack your things and see to your sister. I'm sending Monsieur Desjardins up in fifteen minutes to fetch your trunks. I want you and Frances down here waiting for the cab when it arrives. Off with you now!"

Margo had no choice but to head for the stairs, passing the chapel and its sick-sweet scent of old candles and holy water. They went out to Santa Barbara most years, but in summer, after the school year ended. What was her mother thinking of, pulling them out at the very start of winter term, so soon after the Christmas holidays?

She found her nine-year-old sister sitting on her little bed in the junior-school dormitory. All the cubicle curtains were pushed back and Frankie, alone in the long white room, looked small. Her trunk was on the floor at the foot of her bed. There was nothing in it yet.

Seeing Margo, Frankie broke into sobs, shoulders heaving. Sitting down beside her, Margo began rubbing Frankie's back. Sometimes it calmed her, helped her get control of herself. Sometimes nothing worked.

After a minute or so Frankie began to quiet down. Looking up at Margo, exhausted, eyes haunted, she whispered, "Something's wrong with Mummy or Daddy. Are they in hospital, Margo? Are they dead?"

"Of course not. Don't even talk like that. Mother wants us to go to California, that's all. No one is dead. Period."

"Someone is. I know someone is." Frankie started crying again.

"Frankie, will you dry up, please? We have to get packed. We've only got ten minutes."

Your mother's taking you to California. What about their father— wasn't he coming? He loved California, loved the beach.

Frankie had always been the emotional one. Gusts of sadness and fear would break loose and she would fall into crying fits. More than once their mother had had to summon Dr. O'Neill to give her a shot that put her to sleep for the rest of the day and through the night.

Margo wetted a face cloth and began dabbing her sister's face.

"Are Mother and Daddy really okay?" Frankie whispered.

"Yes, of course."

"And Mike too?"

"Of course."

Frankie was trying hard to pull herself out of the crying jag, Margo could see. Once they really got going, the tears were unstoppable.

"We're going to California. It's exciting, Frankie."

But it wasn't. It was awful, depressing, humiliating. Maybe their mother was planning to get divorced in California, the way movie stars did. No one ever got divorced in the province of Quebec. If their parents divorced there was no way she and Frankie would be allowed back at the convent, and their friends would certainly drop them.

And her best friend, Tasch, whose uncle was a bishop and great-uncle an archbishop, had just invited her to spend the weekend on Edgehill Road. It was likely that Tasch's brother Johnny would be home from boarding school as well, though Margo had been careful not to inquire. Tasch said terrible things about any girl who showed interest in her brother.

The weekend before, she and Tasch and Mary Cohen had stopped at Murray's Drugstore on the way home, to try on lipsticks. According to Tasch every girl had one shade of lipstick that was her most flattering colour, but to find it you had to experiment. Margo had not yet found her shade. And applying lipstick was not easy: lipstick smeared on the teeth was disgusting, Tasch said, even worse than your slip showing, and nearly as horrible as farting in a plié.

When the salesgirl finally refused to let them try any more lipstick until they bought some, Tasch said haughtily, "*Nous n'achetons pas nos cosmétiques dans les pharmacies.*" Margo was impressed by her friend's boldness and rudeness, though the salesgirl probably didn't understand a word of French.

"Look, kids, buy something or get lost," she snapped.

They headed for the magazine rack. Tasch and Mary Cohen grabbed movie magazines, then slid into a booth and ordered tea with extra honey and toasted cinnamon buns, which they spread with butter and more honey and devoured while Tasch read aloud a story about Hollywood stars who sunbathed in the nude.

Margo had been facing the door, so she had seen Johnny Taschereau entering with some other Brébeuf boys. Each time she saw him she felt a thrill, though he had no single feature that could be called handsome. He'd had bad skin for a while and his cheeks were lightly scarred. But he laughed readily and his teeth were white and straight and friends always surrounded him.

Hearing her brother's laugh, Tasch turned and stuck out her tongue at him. Johnny waved at them. According to Tasch, her grandmother expected Johnny to become an archbishop and her father expected him to be a Rhodes scholar and lawyer, then prime minister of Canada.

Margo licked honey from the toasted bun. Johnny was saying something that coaxed a smile from the grumpy Scotch waitress and had all his Brébeuf pals laughing. He certainly wasn't handsome, but he seemed to enjoy being alive, every second. Maybe that was it.

And now her projected weekend *chez Taschereau* was not going to happen unless her mother let her stay behind for a few days, which was most unlikely.

The windows in the dorm had been locked and sealed ever since the furnace was lit back in October. Glass lacquered with white frost glowed in the daylight. There'd been a blizzard the day before; sleighs had been the only vehicles moving on Côte-des-Neiges Road. After study hall Margo and Tasch had tobogganed down the hill to the seminary, and after supper twenty nuns and girls had shovelled off the ice rink and gone skating, the tips of their noses red and stinging, breath and laughter exploding in white clouds from their mouths. After lights out she and Tasch and Mary Cohen and Mathilde Rousseau had played three brilliant rubbers of bridge by flashlight.

It was hard to imagine California sunlight and the house on Butterfly Beach. Her parents had never pulled her out of school before. Her father often went away on business, but family routine had followed the same cycle for years: Montreal and school in winter, Butterfly Beach in summer. Frankie had sensed something seriously wrong, and now Margo wondered if her sister was correct. Were they really leaving without their father?

~

After hauling their trunks downstairs, the porter, M. Desjardins, went to tend the furnace. The porter's little room was just inside the main door of the convent and there was a phone on the table. Margo checked up and down the gleaming hallway for Mother Superior and didn't see her.

"Frankie, tell me if you see the witch coming."

Ducking into the little room, Margo quickly dialled her father's office.

"I'd put you through in a jiff," the receptionist said, "but your dad's not here. Might be in Duluth, or New York. Want to leave a message?"

"Margo, she's coming!" Frankie whispered.

Margo heard Mother Superior's prayer beads click-clacking and hung up the phone. A cab was pulling up under the stone portico outside. The blue sky had clouded over. It looked as though more snow was on the way.

As the taxi driver was fitting their trunks into his car, the exhaust pipe fumed white smoke. The cold air smelled harsh and unsettled.

"Tell your mother she'll have to write well in advance if she hopes to have you back here," Mother Superior said. "I make no promises. Tell her I'm surprised and disappointed by this very abrupt withdrawal."

You old witch, Margo thought, *what do you know about her, or us, or anything?*

~

The taxi fishtailed up Côte-des-Neiges, tires churning and slipping while Margo gazed out her window and Frankie sat very close, practically clinging. The city was still buried under snow from yesterday's storm.

"Nothing is wrong," Margo said.

"When people say nothing's wrong, something always is." Frankie started to cry again, quietly.

"Here, use this." Margo fished a handkerchief out of the pocket of her coat. She also had a pack of Sweet Caps cigarettes in there. She and Tasch had shared a few furtive puffs the night before, after skating, and remembering this in a smelly taxi that was taking her away from her friend caused a fresh pang of dislocation and anger. She gazed out at the snowed-in city. Everything important was rooted here.

She wondered if her mother planned to photograph their departure.

Two years before, Frankie had crashed her bike on the steepest part of Murray Hill Avenue, then stood in the middle of the road wailing, skin peeled off her knees. Their mother raced out of the house, but before reaching Frankie she stopped, peered through the viewfinder of the little Leica she wore on a strap around her neck, and snapped a photo of poor Frankie with her bloody knees, wailing.

Iseult snapped them so often and they were all so used to it that Frankie probably hadn't even noticed, but Margo had.

She'd better not be taking any pictures tonight, Margo told herself.

~

On Skye Avenue the front path and steps had been shovelled out and swept clean of snow. Frankie raced for the front door and rang the bell. Margo followed slowly.

Alicette opened the door. "*Ah, bienvenues, mes filles.*"

The maid waited to pay the cab driver, who was bringing in their trunks. In the front hall Mike was pasting labels on a trunk and a couple of suitcases. The grandfather clock on the stair landing started to bong; it was quarter past four, very nearly dark outside.

"We're booked on the International Limited at five thirty," Mike told them. He always knew the names of the trains.

"I don't want to go," said Margo. "Dad isn't even home. He's gone to New York."

"Margo, is that you?" her mother called from upstairs. "Come help me get organized."

"Where's Daddy?" Frankie yelled.

Their mother appeared on the second floor, smiling down at them. "Daddy's away."

"Isn't he coming?" Margo asked.

"Come up and lend a hand, Margo. There isn't much time."

"Where is he?"

"In New York. I want you to sort your and Frankie's summer clothes."

"Mother Superior said if we leave we might not be allowed back."

"Don't be silly."

"How long are we going for?"

"We'll talk about it on the train."

"I have to know how long if you expect me to pack properly."

"The winter. Maybe longer. Come upstairs; I don't have time to argue with you."

"The whole winter? What about Daddy?"

Her mother didn't answer, had already turned away. Margo's legs felt stiff, numb. She didn't think she could climb the stairs. It was horrid leaving everything like this, hurtling away.

"Mother!"

Their mother reappeared at the top of the stairs. "Please, I need your help, Margo."

"Why are we going so all of a sudden?" Frankie said fiercely. "Where is Daddy?"

"Why doesn't he meet us in Chicago?" Margo said.

"We'll be on the beach in a few days. You love California." She disappeared again.

There was nothing to do but go upstairs, drag out the trunks, find the summer clothes, and start packing. Margo had always been organized—Frankie was the scatterbrain—but this time her packing was anything but thorough. She dragged some things from the cedar chests in the attic and tossed them into the trunks—bathing costumes and tennis shoes, polo jerseys, summer frocks and sun hats—but she knew she was leaving many useful things behind. They would be missing all sorts of gear once they got to Santa Barbara. If her mother really believed they could be uprooted so handily, so easily, she'd find out she was wrong.

Mike and the maids dragged the trunks downstairs. Two cab drivers waiting in the front hall began hauling luggage outside. Their cabs were hidden by the heaps of snow in the front garden but Margo could see smoke from the tailpipes curdling and gleaming in the moonlight. The sky had cleared again. It was starry and very cold, and Frankie was fussing over which coat to wear to the station.

"Your Red River, of course," Margo said. "Hurry it up." Red Rivers were navy blue wool coats with scarlet piping and scarlet sashes that tied around the waist.

"It's going to be hot in California," Frankie complained.

"Well, tonight it's cold as a witch's elbow, and it'll be worse in Chicago. Anyway, a warm coat makes a cozy extra blanket on the train."

"C'mon, Frankie, skip the fuss," Mike said.

Frankie began pulling on her Red River and the toque and mittens that matched the scarlet piping. Margo slipped into her Harris tweed overcoat with the velvet collar, a Christmas present from her parents. She liked the silhouette: very sleek and grownup. And her chic velvet cloche hat, picked out at Holt Renfrew with Tasch's help.

They all got into one taxi and their luggage went in the other. Margo and Frankie sat on either side of their mother. As the cab turned onto Westmount Avenue, Mike and the driver were already discussing who had the best team that year, the Maroons or the Canadiens. Margo looked out at hillside streets half buried under snow. Westmount Avenue wasn't much more than a single lane through the drifts. They passed the enormous stone mansion where her pal Mary Cohen lived with her parents. Cars were trapped in driveways by hard furls of frozen slush flipped up by the street plows. Under the moonlight everything had a blue cast. Her mother gave her hand a squeeze.

Margo had been going to California all her life. Changing trains at Chicago always meant changing stations without much time to spare. The frantic taxi rides across town from Dearborn Street to Madison and the Los Angeles Limited had always made her stomach ache with anxiety. When she was little, she would cling to her father's hand, terrified of being left behind, stranded, forgotten. Chicago was where she had first felt the size and recklessness of the world.

"Morenz is the best there is," Mike was telling the cabby. "He'll stop on a dime and leave you nine cents change."

Margo suddenly remembered her set of monogrammed silver hairbrushes, a Christmas present from her parents, which she'd left on her dressing table at school. Who might take them? Who would save them? Who would keep them for her?

"Morenz is a scrambler," the cabby was saying, "but can he take a beating?"

"It was sixty-eight degrees in Los Angeles yesterday," her mother announced, giving Margo's hand another quick conspiratorial squeeze.

Her mother seemed to want her to think that what they were doing was fun. Jolly. An adventure. Her mother could squeeze as much as she liked, say whatever she wanted, but Margo was not going to be persuaded. It was obvious they were running away from him, and therefore from themselves, and nothing good would come of it.

Wild January Thaw

SNOW HAD MELTED. Fields north of the border were black and white under a sky heavy as lead. His head hummed as the train ran up to the St. Lawrence. He worked at the ache with more coffee. His spirits, in general, were all right. The train had pulled out of Grand Central a few minutes after noon and was due at Bonaventure at ten p.m. He'd made himself take lunch in the dining car, then snoozed for a couple of hours.

After a jaunt there was a calm that came along with the lows, and sometimes he could see things more clearly then, or so he imagined. On the other hand, who alone could gauge with accuracy their own powers of seeing or understanding? Who'd be there to point out all they had missed?

He'd started selling off stocks early in 1928, thereby missing what, in the eighteen months before the crash, had looked like some pretty spry returns. But it had been time to get out. Gusts and blows ruled the stock market, which had much in common with the ocean; plenty of men he knew had drowned there. It was certainly never to be trusted. The market had nosedived but Iseult and the children would never know hardship. No tumplines on their foreheads. No bent backs or shoeless autumns. No Ottawa River rising in April thick with snowmelt, raft pilots drowned, fields flooded, animals carried away.

He wore a striped shirt bought at Brooks Brothers that morning, and a new silk tie. His suit had been sponged and pressed by the Pullman porter before they'd passed Poughkeepsie, and he looked all right, considering. His suits would never fit so well as Grattan's, but then he didn't have Grattan's shoulders or long legs.

Back in the first years of Prohibition, buying liquor from cab drivers and bootblacks in New York, he had never been sure what he was getting: raw alcohol with caramel colouring, bathtub gin. It hadn't mattered much to him—he wasn't in it for the taste—but now the stuff was pure and golden. In this twelfth year of Prohibition, excellent Canadian whisky could be had more cheaply in Manhattan than in Montreal, which said something about the efficiency and acumen of a businessman like Buck Cohen.

He had picked out a brooch at Tiffany's. Iseult didn't like most jewellery, or anything that offered itself easily. This piece was twenty-two-karat gold, filigreed and exquisite, set with one fiery pearl. They had shown him more magnificent things and he'd wanted to buy them, but in the end he had chosen the piece he knew she would like best. Not that she would ever choose jewellery herself. And he had bought slender wristwatches for the two girls and a pair of excellent German binoculars for Mike.

The wastrel, bearing gifts.

Presents were a form of apology, even if they didn't know where he'd been or what he'd been doing. Apology or not, the things he was bringing home would give them pleasure, he believed.

~

But something was wrong. As the taxi climbed around the steep corner from Murray Hill onto Skye Avenue, he saw that the house was almost completely dark. By the time the taxi stopped, a parlour maid—she must have seen the headlamps—was switching on lights in the downstairs hall.

As he came up the path in short, rapid steps, valise in one hand, stick in the other, the maid opened the front door and stood waiting. Alicette, from Lac-Mégantic.

"Where is everyone? *Où sont madame et les enfants?*" Joe called.

The Christmas snow had been washed away by wild rains, but everything was freezing up; the path was a curdle of ice laced with salt and ashes.

Alicette opened her mouth but nothing came out. She had very small, very brown country teeth. Iseult had met the girl at the Sainte-Cunégonde clinic when she was just in from the country, living with a sister, brother-in-law, and seven nieces and nephews in a tenement on Atwater Avenue that had once been a stable. She'd owned one dress, one pair of shoes, much mended, and no winter clothes to speak of. Now she wore a maid's uniform with starched white cap and apron.

"*Pourquoi la maison est dans les ténèbres?*" he demanded. A house in darkness was like a goddamn funeral parlour. He wanted lights blazing when he came home. He loved coming up Murray Hill in a taxi and seeing the place aglow. "*Où est madame?*"

"*À Californie,*" the girl murmured. "*Ils ont quittés pour la Californie. Voulez-vous votre souper, monsieur?*"

He stared at her, unable to absorb what she was saying. What had happened to them? Were they dead?

"Cook say, what he want for dinner, *monsieur?*" She seemed very frightened.

California?

He dropped his walking stick in the brass canister, shrugged off his overcoat, and gave it to her, along with his hat and scarf. The closest telephone was in the serving pantry, and he headed for it. He was already grasping for a plan. California?

He could hear the cook, Belfast Mary, at the kitchen stove, rattling pans. Strips of light leaked into the pantry under a pair of serving doors. The little maid had followed him into the pantry, and as he lifted the receiver off the hook he shooed her into the kitchen.

They would be somewhere in the middle of the continent, probably on a Los Angeles Limited out of Madison Street Station. He would get the timetable and wire ahead to Kansas City, Cheyenne, or Salt Lake and the wire would be delivered on board. In his head he was already composing it.

DISEMBARK IMMEDIATELY STOP WIRE PARTICULARS STOP AWAIT MY ARRIVAL

"Mr. O'Brien, sir!" Belfast Mary called from the kitchen. "I'm doing scrambled eggs on toast. Will it do for you, or is it something else you'll be wanting?"

Twice during his days in the bush, branches snapping off felled trees had clocked him on their way down. Such accidents were known as "widow-makers." For a second or two after the hot blow on his skull, he'd felt a riotous starburst of fury before it laid him out cold in the snow. That was what he felt now: stricken, leaden, uncontrolled. He must gather his thoughts before doing anything. Without making the call, he replaced the telephone receiver.

"That will do, Mary," he called. "Send a tray upstairs to the study."

The house was warm and smelled of lemon oil. Whenever the family was away, the maids tended to go mad with polishing, and when the family came back, the rooms gleamed, like rooms in the pictures Hollywood made about rich people. Iseult disliked so much shine on everything, such a glimmer of dark wood, such a burnished gleam of table silver. The fanatic neatness the French-Canadian maids imposed was inhumane, she said. "We need to feel at home, not like actors in a play. I don't want the children terrified of disturbing things. A house is to be lived in."

He too had felt the charm of their scattered toys when the children were young, but he had always secretly preferred the house the way it appeared after they had been away—usually in California—and returned. When it was briefly perfect, like English mansions or Park Avenue apartments in Hollywood pictures.

He liked things orderly, always had, though the chambermaids who'd had to clean his room at the Plaza might not buy that. Empty bottles in the wastebasket, towels on the floor, bed sheets pulled off, ashtrays overflowing. After showering long and hard he had shaved, dressed, and gotten out fast that morning, leaving the mess along with a two-dollar tip.

Tonight the shining house felt hollow and empty, like the inside of a drum. Static from woollen carpets scratched at his shoes. There was another telephone in his study. Quickly he went upstairs and found her note.

I O'B
TEN SKYE AVENUE
WESTMOUNT, P.Q.

Tues., January 18th

We depart for Calif. as I warned we would. When you read this we'll be most of the way there. It seems the best place to go. I don't want you *following us. You're no good to us. Please don't come after us. I don't seem able to help you and can't watch it anymore. Don't come after us now. Face it, whatever that requires. Don't pretend. So you always told me. You left us, remember that. <u>You</u> left <u>us</u>.—I.*

In boyhood, cold rage had given him the stomach to stand up to his stepfather and protect them all. Did she believe he'd let her get away with stealing his children?

The flow of anger was so wild and sick it made him stagger. He had to grip the edge of the desk to keep his feet under him. He sat down heavily in his chair.

Even as the fury had him, he was aware of how wrong he had been about nearly everything. But that awareness was still a weak assembly of bare thoughts, not nearly so powerful as raging feelings. Curling a fist, he smacked the desk so hard it hurt, then picked up the electric lamp and pitched it across the room, just as the little maid, carrying a tray, reached the top of the stairs at the opposite end of the hallway. The lamp broke on the floor and the study flew into darkness, but there was light in the hallway. He could see Alicette standing there frozen, holding his supper tray, another sort of helplessness scrawled across her face.

Something in the light carried him back to the old priest's house. Maybe it was the chiaroscuro effect in the hallway. Or the scent of buttered toast and tea.

Iseult had always preferred white walls, inconspicuous jewellery, rooms plain and barely furnished. He admired the simplicity, the bare energy, of her darkroom, but his tastes were baroque, if that was the word. His beloved rugs were intricate antique Persians, and the oil paintings he'd picked up in Brussels, London, and Paris were in heavy gilded frames. He enjoyed the sombre shine of such possessions, their age, their intricacy. Such qualities spoke of riches to him.

He was dark. Iseult was light, and on the lightest breeze she had left him.

The timid girl advanced down the hallway. She entered the room carefully and with a rattle of china set the supper tray on his desk. Yellow eggs on toast, a sprig of fresh parsley, a brown teapot.

"*Y a-t-il quelque chose d'autre, monsieur?*"

"No."

"Good night, *monsieur*."

"*Attends*, Alicette."

She blinked at him. Did he frighten everyone? Were his children afraid of him? He didn't like to think so, but maybe they were.

"Did Madame say anything? Before she left? *Tu comprends? Madame n'a dit rien à toi avant son départ?*"

The maid shook her head. She looked about ready to cry.

"That is all," he said. "Good night."

He ate quickly, shovelling in the food, then telephoned his brother. "Do you know anything about it, Grattan?"

"Iseult said naught to me. Not a word. Hang on."

He could hear Grattan speaking to someone else, Elise no doubt. Then he came back on the line. "Elise doesn't know anything. We didn't know you were away either, Joe. Was it New York?"

"New York, yes." He'd often wondered if Iseult had told Elise about his sprees. How many had there been in fifteen years—maybe half a dozen? He and Grattan had never discussed New York themselves.

"Grattan, are you there?"

"Right here, brother."

"Can I get a mail plane from here to New York, do you suppose?"

"I believe there's a Ford Tri-Motor that leaves Saint-Hubert at the crack of dawn and stops in Albany, then New York."

"From New York I can get a plane to California, can't I?"

"National has a run out to Chicago and the coast."

"That's what I'll do, then." Closing his eyes, he saw himself floating in the night sky between Montreal and Glendale Airport in L.A. "Listen, Grattan, you know all the pilots out there at Saint-Hubert, don't you?"

"Some of them. The veterans. My era, not the young birds."

"Can you call up someone tonight and get me a seat on that mail plane in the morning?"

"I could try, I suppose."

"What time does it leave? Can you drive me across the river?"

"Let me find out and I'll call you back, Joe."

"Get me on that mail ride. I want to be standing on the platform when they arrive in L.A. Call me back as soon as you can. I'll pay whatever it takes. My love to Elise. Don't worry, everything will come out all right."

Grattan started to say something but Joe hung up the phone. He was going to get them back, there was no question. Positive steps had to be taken. A man in command of his own affairs couldn't let things just take their course. Boldness was required.

~

He couldn't feel the house around him. Usually he could, but not tonight. After swallowing two cups of tea, he removed his suit coat, loosened his collar, and lay down on the horsehair sofa, waiting for the telephone to ring.

Without Iseult and the children it really was no house at all. A stack of bricks and timbers, enclosing nothing. If he couldn't get them back he would burn it down. Push the rubble up into a pile and burn it down again and again, until there was nothing left but a cupful of fine grey ash, and he'd stir that into a glass of water and swallow it.

He got up, went downstairs. The servants had retired and the rooms were dark, moonlight slanting in. The front door was locked and bolted. Peering out through leaded windows in the downstairs drawing room, he saw the air humming blue with frost and moonlight. The window glass was cold to the touch. Arctic air had dropped over Montreal in the past couple of hours, the normal pattern after a January thaw, the North reasserting itself. There were wolves in the outer suburbs when the rivers froze.

He could feel the furnace chugging. The furnace man would be coming at dawn to stoke it, but he decided to go down himself and check the fire. Flicking on the electric light, he went down varnished stairs into the playroom. The children were too old to spend any time there now. Maybe they were embarrassed by the boxes of their old toys and the faded animal pictures on the walls.

Off the playroom and along a corridor leading to the garage were box rooms, a laundry room, and a couple of servants' bedrooms, unoccupied. Passing all these he entered the furnace room, where the boiler sat heavy and round as an elephant. The fire made a seething chatter and the steam pipes were clanking like a stomach digesting food.

He found a dirty, oily pair of leather gauntlets. Pulling them on, he opened the burner and peered at the glowing red hearth. The fire was adequate now but would be weak by morning. He took up a long-handled shovel and started feeding coal, taking care to distribute the chunks properly, raking them smooth and waiting for gases to burn off in dancing blue flames before adding another layer. There was a way to stoke a furnace so the coal's energy released in a reliable flow, keeping just enough steam up in the boiler to pack the pipes and pressure the radiators throughout the house. If the fire burned too hot it could explode a pipe. If it wasn't hot enough, lumps of anthracite fused into clinkers that choked the grate, and then the fire had to be allowed to die out completely so the grate could be removed and cleaned.

He had always been a master of fires, lighting them, feeding them, smooring the red-hot coals so they'd light up easily in the morning. Fire had an appetite, fire was a wild child, no good at regulating itself. Fire was the heart of a house. Not once in the years after their father abandoned them had he let the fire in their old kitchen range go out.

Once he saw that the fresh coal was burning smoothly, he shook it down so that ashes fell through the grate and into the pan. He gave them a minute to settle, then slid out the pan and dumped the ashes into a pail, which he carried out into the narrow lane between the cellar and garage. He emptied the pail into an ashcan glazed with yellow ice. He was in shirtsleeves, perspiring, and the cold was pointed and subtle, like a honed knife; if he stayed out much longer it would start to stun him. When they were cold, men gradually lost the sense to take care of themselves: he'd known station men to perish after a few hours of heavy rain. Tramps riding boxcars would die of cold tonight, and children in tenements.

The trees creaked and snapped. He had always made sure to keep the house warm for his family. They could not fault him on that score. Through the gaunt spider-work of a maple he peered at the moon and wondered where they were now, and was that moon shining on them?

He took a long shower, keeping the bathroom door open so he could hear the telephone. In his silk dressing gown, wiping steam from the mirror, he heard the doorbell instead. He raced downstairs, half expecting to see Iseult at the door, but it was Grattan standing there, the collar of his cashmere overcoat turned up against the cold.

"Jesus, it's bitter tonight, Joe! Hell to get the car started. The road was slippery as the devil while I was coming up the hill."

Joe felt his expression settle into the sternness he couldn't seem to avoid around his brother, though for the past few years Grattan had been enjoying a run of good luck. He had been one of the first to take up the new sport of skiing and had bought an old hill farm in the Laurentians for practically nothing. After fixing up the farmhouse he'd cleared ski runs, installed a rope tow powered by an old Model T Ford, and turned the place into a skiers' inn called the Auberge.

The Laurentian hills with their birches and balsam reminded Joe of poverty, but he had to admit his brother had made a go of it. A ski train ran up north every weekend. Grattan hired local farmers to meet it at the Piedmont station with horse-drawn calèches and bring his guests to the Auberge. The inn had been written up in magazines and had become very popular with vacationing Americans, and Iseult and the children always enjoyed their skiing holidays there. Grattan had named the ski runs after battles the Canadian Corps had fought: Hill Seventy, Hill Sixty-Nine, Mount Sorrel. He spent his autumns up north blazing trails and cutting firewood. Elise stayed in town—she still had her studio on Mountain Street—and spent weekends at the Auberge. Grattan stayed up north most of the winter, except the first half of January, when it was usually too cold for skiing.

He was well-dressed, as usual, in a grey flannel suit. Joe was barefoot in pyjamas and dressing gown, his hair damp and dishevelled from the shower.

"Let's go up to my office."

He followed Grattan up the stairs, and while his brother headed for the study he ducked into the bathroom, seized a brush, and began slicking back his damp hair. His face in the mirror looked pouchy and grey, but at least he was clean and had eaten something and the house was in order. He would fix things so that his family was stronger than ever, the way bones could heal stronger after a break. He could manage everything, put it all to rights.

～

Grattan was sitting in the leather club chair, legs elegantly crossed. He had lit a fire, and the little blaze was snapping cheerfully.

"Well, Joe, I read Iseult's letter."

"Have you got me a seat on the plane? You could have telephoned, you know. You didn't have to come over."

"I don't think you should go. Now, hear me out, Joe. Elise doesn't think so either. From the looks of that letter, Iseult is running to get some room. If you want her back, brother, you'll proceed with caution."

Shutting his eyes, Joe could still see himself floating in those three thousand miles of cold sky between Montreal and Los Angeles.

Grattan said, "Do you remember Levasseur and Tourbot, the French aviators? If they hadn't crashed, you know, they'd have gone straight back to France when the war started and been killed anyway. That bunch—when the war started, they were all done for in a few weeks. Crashes, mostly; I saw hulks from nineteen fourteen and fifteen on every field I flew out of. They didn't know what the machines were capable of, and they weren't capable of much. No one had given any thought to tactics either. That all came later."

Joe had often thought of the Frenchmen and the aerodrome in the San Fernando Valley, because that was the dusty, crackling afternoon he had told Iseult she must marry him, just before she'd gone up. He had been afraid she would be killed but she had gone up anyway.

Uncrossing his legs, Grattan leaned forward. "What were you up to in New York, Joe? One of your spells? Holing up?"

Joe nodded.

"Remember when I was gunning for Buck, the night runs through Connecticut? You said if I kept that up it would cost me my family, that Elise would pack up and leave. And you were right. A woman can't live with a man who's tearing himself to pieces. A woman can't live with a man who's lost his sense. Elise was ready to go; she and Virginia were going to catch a train and lose themselves in Brooklyn and I would never find them.

"It was good advice, Joe. Now I have some for you. If you fly out to California you'll not achieve what you want to. These trips, these sprees, the holing up—you think they don't matter, but they do."

"Everything's under control. The children don't know."

"I wouldn't be so sure."

He had never taken a drink in this house but he wanted one right now. Wanted the heft of the bottle in his hand.

"Give them the winter in California. You stay here. You know and I know where we come from. You're no Mick Heaney. Pull yourself together, brother. When I got back from France, there was nothing behind me but dead men and one balls-up after another, but we're family men: we have to stay around, no running away. They'd shoot a man in the war, Joe, for running away. Write Iseult a clear letter; ask her what she wants and tell her you will do whatever's best for her and the children. But no wild goose chase to L.A."

"I've lost everything, haven't I, Grattan."

"Maybe."

Joe groaned.

"It sure is a beautiful home you've made here, brother," Grattan said.

"It's a grave without them."

"You can't bend other people to the way you want them to be. I guess Iseult has had about enough."

"If I had a jug of coal oil I'd burn this place down."

"When you've had time to think, write her a letter."

His head ached. He still wanted to be on that plane and in that night sky.

Grattan sat with legs elegantly crossed, tie perfectly knotted, and collar crisp, though it was nearly one o'clock in the morning. Grattan's clarity and calm, set against his own confusion, was upsetting the lifelong pattern of their relationship.

His brother stood up, took the brass poker in his hand, and began to work the fireplace logs, pushing and airing them, kicking up more of a blaze. They had all of them been damn good at laying a fire. Growing up in the wild, in the bush, had taught them some things they would never forget.

Gases released from the wood were snapping, groaning, and in that sound he could hear wagon wheels creaking and grinding, the hired wagon hauling them out of childhood so long ago. There were lessons he'd learned, but he hadn't learned them all. He was plunging into his own dark water, like Grattan, drowning.

Sea and Seawall

HIS MOTHER HAD BEEN vague and lethargic since Chicago, keeping to her bedroom on the Los Angeles Limited, not touching any food. At Cheyenne he noticed her breathing was rougher, and by the time they had reached Los Angeles there were dark circles under her eyes. She seemed to Mike to have lost any sense of purpose or strength of will, though when he asked if she wanted to see a doctor in Los Angeles and get an adrenaline shot, she refused strenuously, insisting they board the next train for Santa Barbara.

It was a musty local that stopped at Glendale, Encino, Ventura, and Summerland, taking four hours to reach Santa Barbara. He organized the luggage and hired a pair of taxis to take them out to the house at Butterfly Beach, which had been closed since August. It was a sparkling southern California winter day, and the house, even after being shut up for five months, smelled cleanly of polished wood, cool stone, pungent eucalyptus. Iseult took off her shoes and stockings and wandered around the lawn and the flowerbeds, perfectly maintained by the Japanese gardeners, while Frankie and Margo raced around reclaiming bedrooms and rediscovering clothes they had left in the closets.

When Iseult finally came inside, she said she needed a bath more than anything in the world. Would he go down into the cellar, check the furnace, and turn on the boiler?

While she bathed, Mike and Margo shook out sheets and blankets in the fresh air.

"I know why we're here," Margo said. "She wants to stow us here so she can go to Reno and get a divorce."

At the sound of the word *Reno* he felt dismayed but tried not to show it. He knew Reno was a town, in Nevada. Was it the state capital?

"We'll probably all be excommunicated." His sister was clipping one corner of a sheet to the line with a wooden clothes peg.

"Ah, stuff it, Margo."

"Don't talk to me like that. Who do you think you are? Just because mother's sick you think you can boss everyone."

"No, but somebody has to take charge."

"Doesn't have to be you."

"Right. I can just let everything go to hell and see how you like it."

"Oh, shut up."

Together they shook out the rest of the sheets. He regretted his tone—he and Margo were usually allies, usually understood each other. He kept trying to get *Reno* out of his head but it kept coming back. It made him think of fire.

Margo was heading inside with a bundle of sheets when he touched her elbow.

"Don't touch me," she said sharply.

"Look, I'm sorry, Margo."

"We're never going to see our friends again. We'll stay out here for good. We'll never see Daddy again. He's a drunk and she'll be a divorcée."

"You shouldn't say that."

"Why not? It's the truth."

He didn't say anything. They were all very tired. If they started arguing, Margo would lose her temper. Then their mother would overhear, and she'd want to start talking about things none of them were in any shape to discuss.

His mother was still in her bath, so he helped Margo make up the bed. She opened their mother's trunk and shook out a nightdress.

"It is the truth," she finally said. She was near tears.

Mike began building a fire in the fireplace. His sister watched for a moment, then took the nightdress into the bathroom, and a couple of minutes later their mother came out and slipped into her bed.

"Do you want me to go into town and send a telegram to say we've arrived?" he asked her.

"No, I don't want you doing anything of the sort. Open the window, please, Mike, so I can hear the ocean."

They left her with her window open and a fire blazing. Going outside, he walked to the bottom of the garden and took the concrete steps down to the beach. A seawall fronted their property for fifty yards. It was at least thirty years old, and every year new cracks and fissures were patched and repaired. He rubbed his hand along its cement face. The wall was warped and bulging and sooner or later would have to be replaced. He remembered his father talking about getting the work done, but nothing had been accomplished so far. The old wall was practically rubble.

For lunch Margo heated a tin of tomato soup and the three of them ate it in the kitchen, with stale pilot crackers and evaporated milk. Margo took a bowl upstairs and reported back that their mother was still asleep. "Getting a little spooky," she said. "I feel like an orphan."

"What do you mean?" said Frankie.

"Nothing," said Mike. "It's a joke. Finish your soup."

After lunch he let Frankie help him light fires in all the fireplaces, using chunks of oak that had been stacked in the coach house for as long as he could remember. Then they all went to their rooms for naps, and when he stretched out on his bed he thought he could hear the ocean licking at the base of the cement seawall, which signified a high tide. Winter was the season for Pacific storms.

His sheets were still flapping out on the line. He lay on mattress ticking, hands clasped under his head, and imagined a winter storm, the waves breaking over the seawall and crashing onto the lawn. He'd often found shell fragments and knots of dried kelp on the lawn in summer, left over from the lashing winter storms. If a storm pounded hard enough it would crack the old seawall. Backfill, clay, sand, and topsoil would gully out and sluice into the surf, destroying the lawn and eventually exposing the foundations of the house itself, which must sooner or later start to crumble. He could always see to the end of things, and it was always the same: nothing held together all that long, nothing was permanent.

An hour later he awoke and felt the swaying of the train as if he were still aboard, steel wheels rumbling beneath the floor—then realized it was only the electric washing machine, which his sister had started up in the laundry room. Struggling out of bed, he tied his shoes and brushed his hair, then went to have another look at the seawall. It was definitely not in good shape.

The next morning Margo telephoned the doctor, who came out to Butterfly Beach and gave Iseult an adrenaline shot. While Mike and the girls were eating lunch—more pilot crackers, with sardines, and more evaporated milk—the Mexican woman who'd been their housekeeper the previous summer appeared at the kitchen door. Mike told her she was hired and sent her off with the girls to put in a grocery order at the Montecito village store. Then he resurrected his old bike in the coach house, oiled the hubs and sprocket, and set off for downtown Santa Barbara.

The Western Union office was on State Street near the station, but first he went into the chop suey café next door and ordered a cup of coffee. Sitting at the counter, scribbling on a paper napkin, he composed a telegram.

```
WU SANTABARBARA CNCPMONTREAL
3089883-14232 CNCP
11 JANUARY 1931
TO: MR. J. O'BRIEN
O'BRIEN CAPITAL CONSTRUCTION LTD
CANADA CEMENT BUILDING PHILLIPS SQ MONTREAL CANADA
CABLE: WILDERNESS

SAFE AND SOUND ALL FINE I'LL LOOK AFTER THINGS
UNTIL YOU GET HERE LOVE MIKE
```

When he knocked on her door the next morning and entered her room, his mother was sitting up in bed reading the *Los Angeles Times*. The headline was

KWANTUNG JAP ARMY IN MANCHURIA

When he told her the seawall would not last much longer, she looked at him over the top of the newspaper. "What do you think ought to be done?"

He said he could hire all the men he needed at the labourers' shape-up on Nopal Street. The job would have to be completed during a period of neap tides between the new moon and a full moon. He figured five to six days for the job as long as there were no winter storms. All she would need to do was sign the cheques.

She was looking at him but he couldn't tell if she was really listening or understanding what he was saying. He was still a few days short of his seventeenth birthday. He had never built anything bigger than a radio set, but if they didn't do something, and quickly, the wall, the gardens, the house—everything sheltering them could easily be destroyed.

"My estimate came in at five hundred and nineteen dollars. That's materials and labour—everything."

"How much will you pay the men?"

"Three dollars a day for labourers. Four dollars for a finisher and a carpenter."

"Not very much."

"It's the going rate."

"All right," she said. "Go ahead. Build us a wall." She went back behind the newspaper, the Kwantung, the Japanese army, Manchuria.

He left her room feeling slightly delirious with responsibility and struggling for calm. Engineers ought to be precise and clear, and everything—everything—had to be worked out mathematically, with careful planning. It was just a goddamn wall after all, he told himself. It was no big thing.

Their summer car, an old Ford station wagon with a wooden body, was up on blocks in the coach house. After changing the oil and spark plugs, filling the radiator and tires, and charging the battery, he drove to the shape-up yard at the bottom of Nopal Street, where he hired two Mexican day labourers and a concrete finisher. Bringing the men back to the house, he set them to work demolishing the old seawall while he started drafting his plan for the new one.

The weather stayed clear and dry. The new wall was fifty yards long and seven feet high. The men he'd hired—Miguel Prieto, Guillermo Hernandez, Ruben Betancourt—worked hard day after day, and he hired a Mexican carpenter to supervise the building of the forms. They carefully laid planks across the lawn so the concrete mixer could back right up to the site without scarring the turf, and the pour took two days. The concrete was reinforced with steel rods and there were pipes and holes for drainage. The wall was thirty inches thick at the base, tapering to twenty-four inches, and incorporated a set of steps leading up from the beach. The steps were tied in and supported by sleepers, backfilled and buried on the leeward side.

While the concrete was still setting up he took a sharp stick and carefully inscribed the workmen's initials and his own on the top of the wall, and the date, *17th Feb 1931*. It felt good to make his first real mark on the world, to build something solid and useful. No matter the weather, the seawall would protect them all.

~

Mr. Spaulding, the lawyer, drove up from Pasadena to make arrangements for the two girls to attend Marymount School and Mike to enrol at Santa Barbara High. Spaulding wore a thick tweed suit and plusfours. Frankie called him "Monkey Face." After his wife died he had grown a long white beard, and his face was small, seamed, and brown from the sun. His daughters were married and living back east. He had resigned from the Pasadena Theosophical Society when it split into warring factions.

After spending an hour upstairs with Iseult, Spaulding joined Mike and the girls on the porch for lunch. He even ate like a monkey, snatching rolls from the basket with little wizened hands, tearing the bread to pieces. He took quick sips of his lemonade, chomped a stick of celery, and didn't say very much. Halfway through the meal Frankie got a bad case of the giggles, then Margo began to choke and snort. Finally both his sisters excused themselves and disappeared inside. He could hear them laughing, but Mr. Spaulding didn't seem to notice.

"I should like to have a look at this wall of yours, Michael."

They walked to the bottom of the garden. Spaulding sat on the grass, took off his brogues and thick woollen stockings, and followed him down the concrete steps to the beach. The tide was out. A flight of brown pelicans was skimming over the ocean.

"You have your father's talent for translating an idea into the material realm. Making it concrete, so to speak."

They stood looking at the wall, surf fizzing around their ankles.

"It came in at just under five hundred dollars," Mike told him. "Just about my estimate."

"Your father would be proud."

"My father probably would have done it for under four."

Mike looked at Spaulding. With his white beard, bright eyes, and hairy tweed suit, the little lawyer resembled George Bernard Shaw in a photograph Mike had seen in *Time*. He wanted to ask the lawyer if Iseult had said anything about a Reno divorce, but he was afraid that once it was mentioned it would seem inevitable.

"I'm taking your mother up to Ojai this afternoon, Michael. There's a remarkable man I'd like her to meet."

"A doctor?"

Spaulding looked at him with curiosity. "Why do you say 'a doctor'?"

"Isn't she sick?"

"His name is Krishnamurti—he's an Indian, a young man, a great teacher, a great soul. I've suggested that she photograph him; an image is needed to further his work." The old man slapped the wall. "Lovely work here. Steadfast. Your father will be proud. And your dear mother and I had better get started."

Spaulding drove Iseult up to Ojai that afternoon in his old Lincoln convertible, and it was late, near midnight, when Mike heard them return. The next morning the lawyer rode the train back to Pasadena and left the Lincoln for her use.

During their Santa Barbara summers she always spent a couple of afternoons a week at the free-milk clinic on Milpas Street, and with a couple of other Montecito women she collected produce from farms in Summerland and the Goleta Valley and distributed it at transient camps or gave it out to poor mothers at the clinic. On Wednesday evenings she visited women in the city police lock-up on De La Vina Street or at the County Jail, bringing them clothes and writing letters for them—but this year she wasn't doing any of that.

After that first trip, she started driving up to Ojai in the old Lincoln three or four days a week, and usually came home wearing wildflowers in the buttonhole of her blouse. She said the dry, scented heat of the Ojai Valley made it easier to breathe. She took her cameras up there and told them she was photographing Krishnamurti at Arya Vihara, his house in Ojai, as well as the people who came from all over the world to take lessons from him.

"What sort of lessons?" Margo asked.

"Dancing lessons?" asked Frankie.

"They want to learn to see things clearly, that's all," their mother said.

"Are they learning the hootchy-koo?" asked Frankie.

"Why must you go all the way up there so often?" Margo said.

"The truth is a pathless land," their mother said. Those words didn't sound like her. What could she mean? Why did she have to speak to them using someone else's words?

She'd married their father when he was building a railway through the mountains. Did she really not believe in him anymore?

```
WU SANTABARBARA CNCPMONTREAL
3089883-14232 CNCP
20 FEBRUARY 1931
TO: MR. J. O'BRIEN
O'BRIEN CAPITAL CONSTRUCTION LTD
CANADA CEMENT BLDG PHILLIPS SQUARE
MONTREAL CANADA
CABLE: WILDERNESS

SEAWALL $261.33 MATERIAL, $230 LABOUR, TOTAL $491.33. IT
WILL STAND. LOVE MIKE
```

~

S.B. High was much bigger than Lower Canada College. Mike had never before sat in a classroom with girls. The teachers were easygoing compared to the brittle young Oxford and Cambridge men who'd taught him at LCC, with their ferocious sulks and rages. Lessons in unfamiliar subjects—Civics, U.S. history—consisted mostly of childish fables, like tales from a storybook. Students slept in class. Sometimes teachers nodded off as well; everyone at S.B. High seemed willing to tolerate a lot of boredom. Perhaps the sleepiness was caused by the mild, sunny weather. Everyone assumed Santa Barbara to be the best place in the world.

Anxiety pressed at his chest when he awoke in the mornings, but he finally had a routine: gathering his books, eating breakfast, starting the station wagon, driving into town. After dropping his sisters off at Marymount, he drove himself to school. On Saturdays he went for solitary drives up the coast or over San Marcos Pass into the Santa Ynez Valley, past cowtowns, ranches, and oilfields stuttered with steel derricks, pumps, and storage tanks. Sometimes he stopped for dusty hitchhikers—roustabouts, Mexican ranch hands, standing by the side of the road—but he really preferred being alone, driving fast with all windows down and the wind tearing in.

Whenever Iseult was up at Arya Vihara, he lay awake worrying about her breaking down in the mountains or having an accident. She drove too fast and recklessly for the mountain roads. The old Lincoln was an ungainly car and she never bothered checking the tires or oil pressure or seeing whether the radiator was full.

The truth is a pathless land.

No. Truth was a car that could be relied upon to get over Casitas Pass without boiling over or breaking down. Truth was concrete reinforced with steel, tied down with sleepers, backfilled, and strong enough to withstand the storms and waves, probably for all their lifetimes.

There was a quiet knock on his door. When he opened it, Margo was standing there with two bottles of the 3.2 beer that Lidia, their housekeeper, kept cool in the cellar.

"Mother's not home yet," Margo said.

"I know."

"Got any cigs? Let's go out on the porch. Don't wake up Frankie."

Out on the porch he used his jackknife blade to open the beer bottles. Margo took a sip. "Do you miss Daddy? He's a crazy old bard, but I miss him. I miss my pals. She's in love with the swami. I hate her, I really do."

"Don't say that."

"All her talk about the truth—that's how people talk when they're doing something bad. It's creepy."

"He's a teacher."

"You can believe that if you want to," Margo said.

They had been at Butterfly Beach almost three months by then but he felt more unhoused than ever. The night air was scented and chilly, smelling of flowers and brine.

"Don't you worry about Daddy?" Margo asked. "Where is he right now? Once she gets her stupid divorce Frankie and I will get tossed out of Marymount—she hasn't thought that one through. They'd never let us back at Sacred Heart either. And the St. Mary's Ball, forget it. My debutante season is shot. Tasch and Mary Cohen will be having fun all year and I won't know any boys."

They finished the beer and flipped the red embers of their cigarettes down into the gravel driveway. After he went back to his room the stubborn moonlight slashing through the window still wouldn't let him sleep.

He had looked up divorce in reference books at the Santa Barbara Library. The only way to obtain a divorce in the province of Quebec was to petition for a private bill to be passed by the federal Parliament in Ottawa, and the only grounds were adultery. A Reno divorce was much simpler and took just six weeks' residence in the state of Nevada. There were divorce ranches where people stayed. Such a divorce would not be recognized in Montreal, but would that matter if she never went back there?

He rolled out of bed once more, pulled on dungarees and a sweatshirt. Their mother still wasn't home. Margo's light was off. The house was asleep. He quietly found his way downstairs. There was a flashlight in one of the kitchen drawers, but with the full moon he didn't need it. He went barefoot across the lawn and started down the concrete steps to the beach. The tide was high. A wave broke on the seawall and the spray splashed his legs. Rolling up his dungarees, he stepped down onto the soft, permeated sand as the surf was running out. Another roller exploding against the concrete wall drenched him thoroughly. As the water raced off the beach he ran out with it and dove in.

The ocean felt warm. A smaller wave rolled past, and almost without thinking he started swimming out to sea. The danger would be a wave strong enough to throw him back against the seawall. He saw the top of a big one approaching and ducked underneath. When he surfaced, he was thirty yards offshore. He saw the next wave coming, phosphorescent at its crest, and again he ducked under, swam through, and came up on the other side. He could feel the riptide, and knew he ought to swim back to the beach before it sucked him out any farther. Another roller was coming in. He was in a machinery of waves, each bigger than the last, or maybe it was just that he was getting tired of fighting them. Moonlight spread carelessly across the water. He would have to duck the next wave, then swim hard for shore to reach the steps before another wave slammed him into the wall.

He felt the next wave pass over like something passing through his body, a dangerously seductive pull that took willpower to resist. He started swimming against the backwash spilling off the canted beach.

He got his feet planted in loose, wet sand and struggled out against the fizzing rush. He was halfway up the concrete staircase when the next wave pulverized against the wall, lashing him with spray, but he made it to the top and stepped onto the grass.

Back in his room, his limbs felt heavy. The sea had neutralized enough of his anxiety. For sleep the trick now was to focus on simple thoughts. Nothing emotional, just images of light in various rooms, in various patterns. Sunlight falling into rooms in their old Pine Avenue house. Chilly evening light in what could have been his nursery in the railway camp. Such memories were weightless, but his mind had retained them, or an impression of them, and by concentrating on them and letting go of everything else he could sleep.

~

On the first of April they all went up to Arya Vihara for a picnic. The Lincoln had a cracked oil pan and was in the garage getting repaired, so they took the old station wagon. Mike drove. They started along Foothills Road, past fields of flowers at Carpinteria. Climbing Casitas Pass, he kept the station wagon in second gear, worried that the frail old engine might throw a rod. When they finally pulled into the driveway at Arya Vihara, he saw a dark young man in white clothes sitting on the porch of the cottage, reading a newspaper. The porch was deep and shady, with bougainvillea spilling over the rails, potted geraniums on the steps. The young man put aside the paper and stood waiting to greet them. He did not smile as she introduced them, merely nodding at the mention of their names.

"And what have you brought?" he said, peering at the picnic basket Margo was carrying. "What goods are there, what treats have we to share?"

"Krishnaji," said their mother. "I'm so happy. I so wanted you to meet the children."

Krishnamurti didn't seem happy or unhappy to meet them. His face looked as though it had at one time been punched or beaten. His nose was like putty someone had pushed and bent. His teeth were white and his handshake delicate. He wore sandals; his feet were large and the toes had a heavy, taloned look. The sleeves of his cotton shirt were rolled up and his forearms were the colour of mahogany. Pages of a newspaper were scattered all over the porch as though it had been torn apart by voracious reading.

"I've promised the children a swim," their mother was saying. "We'll go to the pond, then lunch at the cottage. We're so happy to be here, all together. Does that sound like fun?"

Mike could hear something in her breathing: the rasp that started when she was tired or something was provoking her asthma. She kept saying she was happy; maybe she wanted to sound happy.

"Oh, very much so," said Krishnamurti.

"Well, children, let's head for the pond."

"Where do we change?" said Margo.

Just then another slender Indian man and two white women came out of the cottage. The women were a mother and her middle-aged daughter and both were dark from the sun. Iseult took the girls inside to change in a bedroom while Mike changed in a bathroom.

Had she told Krishnamurti she was planning to get a Reno divorce?

Once upon a time his father had driven two hundred miles of railway grade through a sea of mountains. Where was he now? Maybe he was relieved they were gone. Maybe it was easier for him to be alone. Maybe all he wanted was to slide down the neck of a whisky bottle and disappear. Mike tried to imagine his father in a hotel room in New York City, voltage surging from a bottle and blowing all his circuits. What was wrong with him? Nothing. What was wrong with him? Everything.

In single file they walked across a meadow flaming with orange poppies, his mother in the lead, Krishnaji following her, then Mike and his sisters and the two white women and the other Indian man. Orange butterflies twitched over the grass. When they came to the sycamore woods at the edge of the meadow, the two women and the young Indian man disagreed about which was the best way to approach the pond without going near poison oak. Krishnamurti and their mother did not intervene, passively waiting for the matter to be sorted out. The other three could not agree and finally the man set off on his own. Krishnamurti and their mother followed the two women, the mother and daughter. The daughter was about Iseult's age.

"The truth is a pathless land," Margo muttered as they traipsed through the fragrant, sun-heated woods. The pond when they reached it was fed by a stream that scrambled noisily over pebbles before deepening into a pool shaded by manzanita, cottonwoods, oaks, and sycamores.

Who would go in first? No one seemed eager. It was hard to judge how deep it was.

"I guess I will," Margo said finally. "I'll go in with Frankie."

Their mother unwrapped cucumber-and-tomato sandwiches and handed one each to Krishnamurti and the other young man, who had turned up at last. The two women refused the sandwiches she offered them.

"You eat too much, Iseult," said the older woman. "It may not show on you because of your rapid metabolism, but it's not always good for the spirit, do you think?"

"Perhaps you're right," he heard his mother say.

Margo and Frankie took off their tennis shoes and slipped into the water as quietly as deer. While they swam across the pond, then started duck-diving to see who could stay down longest, Mike lay on his back soaking up the hot sun and half listening to the women talking.

"We really must return to India within the year," the older woman said. "If you want to come along, Iseult, you must help us organize the resources for our trip, or it simply won't happen."

"I think what Iseult needs," said the younger woman, "is to spend more time alone and develop a simpler consciousness. I always feel that you're scattered when you come up here. The aura is roiled, if you don't mind my saying so."

"Krishnaji hates to think you see him as simply another cause, like your poor Mexicans," said the older woman.

He saw his mother throw a glance at Krishnamurti, but he and the other man were eating their sandwiches and ignoring the women.

"We're not a charity case," said the younger woman.

"Krishnaji," his mother said, "do you think it wise to travel so much?"

"It does not matter," Krishnamurti said. "Are there any pickles?"

"He enjoys travel, Iseult," said the daughter. "Travel refreshes him."

"Wouldn't it be better if people came to him instead?"

"You really mustn't interfere, Iseult," the older woman said in a sharp voice.

"Stop it!" said Krishnaji. "Your hectoring makes me ill."

"But we are concerned for you, Krishnaji," the older woman said.

"There is nothing wrong in her questions. She is an honest woman," Krishnamurti said. "More than you, somehow."

The other young man gave a snort of muffled laughter. The two white women remained silent and Mike could sense their fury. They didn't like her, she must have figured that out. Why did she come up here anyway? Was she in love with this Krishnaji, so self-possessed and gloomy, with his taloned feet and brown arms?

The older woman stood up and her daughter got up too. "If you decide to stay for tiffin," said the older woman, "do let us know, Iseult. We'll need some things from the village."

The two women headed back through the sycamore woods. The girls were still splashing in the water. No one spoke. Minutes passed. Krishnaji and the other man lay on their backs on the dry, husky grass, hands clasped behind their heads; they were dozing. Iseult sat there. She wore a white linen dress and she wasn't wearing stockings; she had slipped off her shoes and her feet were bare. He couldn't really see her face under her sun hat, but she seemed to be watching the girls. She was very thin, he realized. Bony at her shoulders. Her calves and wrists were stringy and narrow. Frail. He'd never thought of her as frail before. He had supposed that all the weakness in the family was his father's, but now she was weakening too.

Dusty yellow shafts of sunlight dropped down into the pond. The girls came out of the water noisily, and Mike decided to go in. He wasn't eager for a swim but he wanted to escape.

The water felt cold at first after the hot sunshine, but really it was tepid. After swimming a few lengths he folded his body and dove straight down towards the bottom, where it really was cold, the light murky and golden. He could feel the pressure on his head as he touched bottom. It was peaceful. He wished he could stay down there, but his lungs were already hungry for air. He drove himself back to the surface, swam to the shore, and waded out.

Margo and Frankie were lying on their stomachs on their towels. Their legs were golden. Krishnaji looked up at him and smiled slightly. His mother smiled at him.

"I never had asthma after I met your father," she used to say. "He cured me. He taught me to breathe." It wasn't really true—she'd had a few asthma attacks over the years. Not many, though. Now he thought he could hear that slight strained rasp behind her breath: the sycamore woods had stirred up her allergies. The pond was calm and he could see a skim of grey pollen dust on the surface.

Instead of lying down in the sun, he began drying himself with his towel. They'd left their clothes back at the cottage. He could feel the two Indian men watching him as if they knew he was going to try something and they were curious to see what it was and whether he would succeed or fail.

"Mother?"

When she looked up from under her hat, he saw dark circles around her eyes. Now they could all hear her troubled breathing, and Frankie and Margo were sitting up on their towels. It was presuming a lot to take charge of things, but someone had to. He would drive them home, over the pass and down to the sea, away from the heat and dust of the narrow valley.

"It's time, then. We'd better go," he said.

His mother looked at him for a long moment and then nodded.

The truth might be a pathless land, but the way home was clear, and he was determined to get them there.

The other man stayed at the pond but Krishnaji walked back through the woods with them and waited by the car while Mike and the girls went into Arya Vihara to change. When Mike came out, Krishnamurti was standing with his foot on the running board. As Mike approached, Krishnamurti reached out and put his hand on Iseult's forehead as though to see if she had a fever, and in this gesture there was a certain grace Mike had never seen before: gentleness rather than tenderness. The gesture implied distance somehow, removal, rather than closeness or intimacy. Krishnaji was being kind but impersonal—a doctor's hand reaching out, cool and dry, not a lover's, not a husband's.

Mike got behind the wheel and his sisters clambered into the back seat, their wet bathing suits wrapped in towels. As he fired the motor he overheard his mother saying, "Goodbye, goodbye," to Krishnamurti.

Mike pumped the clutch and meshed the gears as smoothly as they would go. He didn't look at Krishnamurti but was aware of him stepping back from the car. "Goodbye! Goodbye!" the girls were calling as Mike shoved in the choke, dabbed the accelerator, and steered them out of there.

~

Margo wanted to summon the doctor for an adrenaline booster but their mother insisted she didn't need anything and said they should all go straight to bed, and it was true that her breathing had started sounding better as soon as they had left the Ojai Valley and came up over the pass, where they could see the ocean glinting and a purple mass of fog offshore.

The next morning was Sunday, cool and white with fog. Mike pulled on his swim trunks and went downstairs before anyone else was awake. He ate an orange in the kitchen. Then he went outside and walked across the lawn to stand at the top of his wall, looking out to sea. The air was clammy but it was just a fog, not the dreaded white marine layer. Fog would burn off in a few minutes, and it was going to be a hot day. He ran down the steps and plunged into the ocean and swam. When he came out, he was surprised to see his mother sitting on top of the wall. She had on one of his father's thick old Irish sweaters over her linen skirt and she wore the little Leica on a strap around her neck.

"What are you doing?" he said.

"What are *you* doing?"

"Swimming."

"Well, I'm thinking," she said.

"What are you thinking about?" He picked up his towel and started rubbing himself down.

For weeks she had seemed agitated, not herself, but she didn't seem that anymore. He climbed the cement stairs from the beach and sat down on his wall a few feet from where she was sitting, his legs dangling over.

"Do you know how beautiful you are, Michael?"

"Oh jeez."

She picked up the camera, cranked film, aimed at him, and started shooting. *Snap, snap, snap.* He was so accustomed to being photographed—they all were—he did not consider asking her to stop.

"Are you getting a Reno divorce?" he said, squinting at the lens.

She lowered the camera and looked straight back at him. The full white light was behind her and he couldn't tell if she was shocked, unsurprised, dismayed, or just tired. Then she raised the little Leica again and he heard the shutter click.

~

Did she summon him or had he come out on his own steam? They never knew.

She certainly never warned them. Maybe it was all his idea. Maybe she had known but wasn't convinced he'd actually make it all the way. Maybe she thought the chances were good he'd disembark somewhere along the route and she'd get a wire or phone call from the assistant manager of some fine hotel in Chicago, Denver, or Salt Lake, news that she would do her best to conceal from the children.

They were asleep when the taxi arrived. Lidia was in the kitchen sipping beer and playing cards with her husband when she heard the car, saw Mr. O'Brien getting out, and raced upstairs to warn Iseult.

Unwilling to wait for the morning local, he had taken a cab all the way from the Los Angeles train station.

Awakened by footsteps and by Lidia's and his mother's voices, Mike came downstairs, saw his father's suitcase in the hall, and found his parents sitting in the dark living room. His father was on the sofa, his mother in an armchair.

"Your father's arrived," she said calmly. Then she stood up and switched on a table lamp.

What had they been doing there sitting in the dark? Had they been talking at all or just sitting there, looking at each other? His father smelled of sweat and tobacco. His mother was wearing a summer nightgown, nothing else, no wrapper. Her feet were bare. He couldn't tell if she was pleased to see the old man or not. Maybe that meant she wasn't. How thin she had gotten, Mike realized. Her body nothing but wire and tension.

"I just walked that wall of yours, Mike." His father stood up. His blue suit was rumpled and he needed a shave. He was pale, his eyes their usual clandestine blue. "I'd like to look it over in the morning. You tied in some sleepers, did you?"

"Sure I did."

"How have you been?"

"All right, I guess."

"Good."

They stood looking at each other, and Mike didn't know what to say. While working on his seawall he'd sometimes felt closer to the men he'd hired—Miguel, Guillermo, Ruben—than he had ever felt to his father.

Not knowing what else to do, Mike stepped forward and stuck out his hand. He and his father shook, but Mike knew his father was disappointed because he had been hoping for something more, even if he didn't know what it was.

~

The girls didn't see him until breakfast. By then he had thoroughly inspected the seawall and taken a dip in the ocean. He appeared at the breakfast table showered and shaved and spruce in a seersucker suit, a rose from the garden in his buttonhole, holding a *Los Angeles Times* he'd picked up in the driveway.

After kissing Margo and Frankie on their foreheads he sat down and started eating his grapefruit while examining the *Times*. Mike and his sisters looked at each other across the table. Frankie stifled a giggle.

It isn't just me, Mike decided. *He really doesn't know how to talk to any of us.*

As his father turned the front page, Mike glimpsed the headline.

AUSTRIAN KREDITANSTALT COLLAPSE
FOUR MILLION UNEMPLOYED IN GERMANY

"Well, Daddy, you look awfully snappy in that ice-cream suit," Margo said.

Without looking up from the newspaper he said, "I'll take that as a compliment."

~

The next day he bought them a fourteen-foot gaff-rigged catboat, a Sea Mew built at Santa Barbara. Margo named her *Girl Guide* and they started going out sailing nearly every day. Their mother was the only one who knew anything about sailing, which she had done in Maine as a girl. She taught them to tack around the harbour, then the bay, and after a week they began venturing out into the thirty-mile-wide channel separating Santa Barbara and the islands. Their father became a handy sailor very quickly, with a sharp instinct for reading tides and wind, and by taking turns at the helm, Margo and Mike learned to handle the boat and sail efficiently. Frankie was the only one who didn't enjoy sailing. She hated the fog and distrusted the wind, and when land fell out of sight she panicked. She spent most afternoons at the pony club or swimming at the beach club with her pals.

Their father did not say anything about returning to Montreal— maybe he didn't intend to. There was a depression on, after all, and business had pretty much dried up everywhere according to the newspapers. Nothing was being built. Maybe they were staying in California for another winter.

Mike was surprised Margo didn't raise the subject, since she was usually so outspoken and had a vigorous sense of her own social needs. But mixed up with the question of where they'd spend the coming year was the question of their parents' marriage, or perhaps their divorce. He knew that Margo, desperate as she was to return to her friends, especially the Taschereaus, was as wary as he was of raising that subject for discussion.

Every Wednesday evening there were barbecues at the beach club, and on the first Saturday night in July a boy escorted Margo to her first club dance. Iseult still went up to Ojai two or three afternoons a week in the old Lincoln, which had been repaired. Their father had offered to buy her a new Ford coupe but she wouldn't allow him to.

One afternoon, instead of sailing, Joe drove up to Arya Vihara in the Lincoln with her. When they got back to Butterfly Beach that night, they were sunburnt and tired, but she was holding on to his arm and both of them were smiling. They said they'd stopped on the way home at the Montecito Inn, where the food was excellent and Charlie Chaplin had been sitting at the next table with a bunch of Hollywood people.

The next day Iseult came out sailing with them and Frankie was persuaded to come as well. Their father had the helm as they left the harbour. When they had cleared the breakwater and it was time to tack, Mike saw his mother touch his father's wrist very lightly. Was this a signal that affection was renewed despite all his flaws and mistakes? Or was she just signalling him to start the tack and come about?

He knew that his parents believed their strongest and deepest emotions ought never be displayed. Showing their feelings was, for them, being false somehow.

The swell was gentle that afternoon, the sea was warm, and the offshore breeze came up after three o'clock. They sailed as a family. With Iseult at the helm, Margo on the mainsheet, Frankie on the jib, and Mike and their father holding off with boathooks, they even managed to heave to alongside a fishing boat. Between them all they had enough loose change in their pockets to buy crab and striped bass, which they took home in a bucket of ice and grilled for their dinner.

Returning

S HE WENT OUT to the garden every evening to cut flowers for the dinner table, and one evening she noticed him sitting on Mike's seawall, his back to her, gazing out to sea. Since he had been in California they had been sleeping in the same bed, but he never reached for her and she didn't know how she would respond if he did. It was difficult to talk to Joe about things that mattered, and she sensed they were both trying to avoid being alone together. She was still in love with Krishnaji.

But something, some need, had led her to the end of the garden to sit with Joe on the seawall, though not quite beside him. A few feet away.

"I am thinking we ought to sell this house, Iseult," he told her.

He had lost his city pallor by then and was quite dark. A man who'd go to any lengths—he'd always somehow given that impression. The horsepower in his hands, forearms, shoulders, and neck.

The Pacific was its usual easygoing blue, the Channel islands barely visible through a sheen of mist.

"California's awfully far, and as the children get older it'll be harder to persuade them away from their friends. Our life is in the East now. I've been doing some work in Portland, Maine. Maine is much closer to Montreal. There's a house at Kennebunk that would suit us, I think. We can drive there in six hours from Montreal. We'll get a bigger sailboat. What do you say?"

"I don't say anything for now."

Every morning he had been plunging diabolically into the surf, even when the beach was battened with fog and riptides were streaming.

"You haven't asked but I'll tell you anyway, Iseult. I've not taken a drink since you left. Just to get that on the record." He patted the cement wall with his palm. "This is a first-class piece of work. The boy knows how to put through a job. After university he can kick me out and run the firm the way it ought to be run." This was how he expressed his love for them: by organizing them into his plans and rhythms, his own needs. "I want to get away, Iseult. The two of us. I was thinking we might go back up to those mountains. We left some happiness up there, Iseult, did we not?"

She felt something clutch at her throat like a pair of hands, but then it released and she could breathe again. She couldn't speak, afraid of what might come out of her mouth. There was no point reaching into the past trying to find something alive. Picking up the cut flowers, she went back into the house.

But the next day, when he mentioned it again, she agreed to go. Things had to be dealt with one way or another, but not in front of the children. Distance might help her see things more clearly, distract her from the swarm of longings infesting her skull every moment.

He booked a bedroom on the West Coast train to Seattle. On the platform at Los Angeles he offered her a blue velvet box. Opening it, she found a gold brooch set with a pearl, a delicate thing, old-fashioned. She put it on because she knew he'd be hurt if she didn't, and she didn't intend to hurt him unnecessarily.

They shared a double bed on that train, his body heat provoking a mash of feelings in her, mostly anger, resentment. He was trying to annihilate her. Putting on a wrapper, she spent the first night and most of the next in the lounge car in an armchair, reading *The Good Earth*. They took meals in the dining car and she brought the novel to the table. Joe gazed out at the long yellow agricultural valleys of Oregon and Washington, where he owned land. Every now and then she looked up from the book and their eyes met. The sight of middle-aged couples with nothing to say to one another had always depressed her horribly, and that was what they had become. Her thoughts, furious and confused, circled Krishnaji like birds fluttering around a perch.

She finished the novel in the Seattle train station. Joe picked up a *Seattle Post-Intelligencer*, and on the way up to Vancouver she read about Japanese soldiers rampaging in Manchuria. Four hours later, as the train slid through the Vancouver yards, she saw strings of boxcars sitting idly on sidings, tramps in every open doorway, legs dangling, and dozens of men and boys with bedrolls and haversacks slung over their shoulders, tramping along shining tracks in silver rain.

The last time they had been in Vancouver was in 1914, on their way up to the contract. In those days she and Joe O'Brien had shared a seamless will and one set of longings, but it wasn't like that anymore.

After checking into the Hotel Vancouver they ate a late supper in the Timber Club and retired to their room. The Continental Limited was due to leave at nine o'clock the next morning. While Joe undressed she took out her nightgown and drew a bath. When she came out of the bathroom, he was asleep. He wanted her back, that was clear; that was why he'd wanted to take her into the mountains. Joe could not live without her. Krishnamurti certainly could; there was nothing he needed from anyone. She would have liked to be that way herself. Instead she'd ended up wanting him: a humiliating situation.

They had been sitting on the porch glider at Arya Vihara with the two women—his sister-in-law and her mother—bustling in and out of the cottage like riled bees. Iseult was lost both in her marriage and outside it, living but not living. She blamed Joe, the furtive drinking sprees. She had never been able to understand such irresponsibility—where it came from and how it had survived in a character otherwise so conscientious, so determined and fixed.

The children thought Krishnaji was stealing her from them, but in fact he had refused to offer her a different story from the one she was living. "You look at me as though I am a pail of water. I am not a pail of water, madam. If you're thirsty, then go inside the house. Take a glass for yourself, drink."

$\sim$

The next morning the Continental Limited quit Pacific Station and went steaming across the Fraser Delta in slapping rain. Flat cropland looked lush after the tawny valleys of California and Washington. As the train began snaking up the Fraser Canyon, she and Joe sat in the lounge car facing each other. She was reading another newspaper story about the Japanese rampage in China. She could sense Joe watching her.

The endless train ride from California, the violent mountains, all they did not know about each other: the trip was a facsimile of the first days of their marriage—probably what he had been aiming for—only minus the yearning, perhaps, minus the belief.

At Hell's Gate, where the river pinched and the right-of-way clung to the steepest side of the canyon, she stared down into the cauldron of waters hundreds of feet below. She might have put aside her newspaper then and stood up. Walked to the end of the car, stepped out into the vestibule, and quietly pitched herself off the train.

She put down the newspaper, but instead of standing up, she shut her eyes and touched the velvet nap of the seat cushion with her finger-tips. She remained very still. She was going to resist the logic of death; her father had not, but she would. Her children would not come of age abandoned, wrecked, disinformed, without a mother. She might be ungrounded, but she would not give herself up.

She could feel steel wheels rumbling, hear couplers squealing and grabbing. In that roughness, in that sensation, a kind of life force. Rude and heedless, rushing on. She opened her eyes and saw that Joe was still watching her.

For the rest of her life, whenever she thought of that passage over Hell's Gate, she felt a renewed sense of wonder and terror. The memory gradually became a source of strength. Near to drowning in confusion and despair, she hadn't succumbed. She had resisted, she had survived.

Gathering Soldiers

JOHNNY TASCHEREAU was waiting for her in the lobby of the Mount Royal. Margo saw him glance impatiently at his wristwatch and knew right away that something had changed. She was only a few minutes late, and usually Johnny behaved as though there were all the time in the world.

Catching sight of her, he smiled. He was, as usual, almost too well-dressed: the chalk-stripe Savile Row suit that she loved, cut narrow on the leg. She had on a green summer frock and her black straw with the floppy brim.

Johnny kissed her on both cheeks. "There's a rumour we're going to be mobilized," he said.

She felt a sudden weight, like someone putting a sandbag on her shoulders. "What does it mean, Johnny?"

"*Qui sait?*" He took her arm and they crossed the lobby, heading for the bar. "I doubt they'll dispatch the Régiment de Maisonneuve to confront the panzers immediately. For one thing, we have no bullets. On the other hand, given the general stupidity so far, who knows?"

They had never before taken a room at the Mount Royal—it was risky. Plenty of people who knew them lunched at the hotel; the Mount Royal was a crossroads of Montreal social life. For years the city's biggest bookmaker had operated from a suite on the ninth floor, and the Normandie Roof on the twelfth was Johnny's favourite nightclub. Her father's office in the Sun Life Building was only a few blocks away, and he or Mike sometimes took clients to lunch at the Mount Royal. But she and Johnny were running out of decent hotels. She never wanted to use the same *endroit* twice. They'd taken rooms at the Ritz-Carlton, the Windsor, the Queen's, the Berkeley. Good hotels were expensive. Johnny's father paid him very little, but his Philadelphia grandmother had left him some money. In August they had spent two foggy, rainy afternoons in a tourist cabin a couple of miles inland from Kennebunk Beach, and one night in a cabin in the White Mountains.

Johnny always registered under the name Constant Papineau, a cousin killed in the first war. Margo wore a ring she kept in her purse. Necessary rituals, but she couldn't believe they were fooling the desk clerks, elevator operators, and glum proprietors of tourist cabins, who surely understood perfectly well what she and Johnny had come for.

The lobby bar was cool and dim and they were shown to a banquette. It was not a large room. It was dark but not sombre; the atmosphere felt intimate. The air smelled of ice and of polished wood and polished glasses. Johnny ordered manhattans. She took a few salted almonds from a little silver dish.

Over the summer Johnny had been drilling one night a week with the Régiment de Maisonneuve, his militia battalion. Margo had spent much of the summer in Maine; Johnny came down for weekends whenever he could get away. Both families owned cottages at Kennebunk Beach. She loved the hard light of the coast, loved seeing Johnny on the beach, his torso brown and wet. Loved standing in breaking surf, holding on to his arm.

Once his battalion mobilized it would be much harder to get together. The Maisies might be rushed overseas at a moment's notice.

Manhattans came in tumblers stuffed with ice, the glass cold and paper-thin, a kind of honed delicacy. She loved the click of ice cubes, the coppery colour of the liquor, and the bright, lascivious cherry.

They had a habit when together of not always filling the air between them with talk. They shared a gift for creating silences that felt as intimate as anything they did. When they were feeling distant, they usually brought themselves together by staying quiet for a little while. In silence their harmony never failed to re-establish itself, though they were quite different sorts of people, really. She was protected, closed; he was fearless and open. She was hard rock made millions of years ago by her family; he was molten, still changing. She was cold, he was warm. Yet beneath his beautiful suits and bon vivant air he was a more serious person than she was. He'd read hundreds of books, spent a year studying the history of European law at the Sorbonne, learned to cook, worked in the kitchen of an inn at Lyons, travelled through Germany on a motorcycle.

Sometimes they didn't say a word when they met. They went into the hotel room or the tourist cabin or whatever it was, took off their clothes in the available light, pulled the covers off the bed, lay down on the clean sheets. He would start kissing her slowly; everything developed from there, and conversation came after. In bed he insisted they speak only French. Her convent French was rusty but improving.

"*M'sieu et dame?*" A waiter in a short red jacket was poised to take their order.

She asked for a cup of lobster bisque and a Waldorf salad. Her arms were bare and still tanned from the beach. Johnny wore a striped shirt and a silk foulard tie, silk the colour of dried blood.

When they did speak, she usually found herself telling Johnny Taschereau things about herself and her family she never spoke of to anyone else, even to Johnny's sister Lulu, her best friend since boarding school. There was something fresh, strong, and unusual about Johnny's willingness to listen, and it had become a kind of drug, their intimacy.

The waiter went away and Margo took another sip of her drink, barely wetting her lips. The complex flavour of chilled liquor always made her aware of the past, reminding her that everything she'd ever experienced—a wild accumulation—had brought her to precisely this moment.

"So now, my dear," Johnny said, "we must talk of the war coming."

"Daddy hates the war."

"It has put him back in business, though."

"That's all for Mike's sake. Daddy thinks if they have a lot of war work, Mike won't be in such a hurry to go overseas. The government might not let him go."

Her father had shut the firm during the Depression, but after the storm troopers marched into Prague he had leased offices in the Sun Life Building and begun hiring engineers and office staff. Mike, with his McGill engineering degree, had returned from California, and their father made him project manager on a million-dollar contract to rebuild an old military airfield across the river, promoting him over lots of men with more experience.

She touched Johnny's hand. "I wish I could have one more week in Maine. Could you get away? It wouldn't have to be for long, Johnny."

"That's certainly something to think about."

"Just the two of us, alone at the beach."

"I'm afraid the call-up may happen anytime."

"Are you my hostage to fortune?"

He smiled and shrugged.

She caught a glimpse of Uncle Grattan in his air force uniform, out in the lobby. Was he coming into the bar? But Grattan—if it was Grattan—passed out of sight, probably headed for the restaurant, a more popular spot for lunch.

After selling his ski resort to American investors, her uncle had started writing about military matters and foreign affairs in the *Montreal Herald*. Grattan had made three trips to Germany since Hitler came to power; he wrote that the Germans were in love with the Dark Ages. After Prague his column had been syndicated, and now it appeared in newspapers across the Dominion, in Australia, and occasionally in the London *Evening Standard*.

Grattan had recently gotten himself elected mayor of Westmount, the first Roman Catholic to hold the office. It was a position with little power, according to Margo's father. An enclave surrounded by the city of Montreal, Westmount was run by a professional city manager, responsible to aldermen who happened to be some of the top businessmen in the country. Even with his gold chain of office and the official iron lamp posts planted outside his row house on Carthage Avenue, Grattan wasn't much more than a figurehead, her father said. "What does it pay? Five hundred a year? We pay the dogcatcher more."

During the royal visit earlier that summer, Grattan, in silk hat and striped pants, medals glittering, had greeted the King and Queen at Westmount City Hall, chatting with them in the royal Cadillac all the way up to Murray Park—renamed King George Park in the monarch's honour. In his tongue-tied address that afternoon, the little king even claimed to remember the ceremony at Buckingham Palace in 1918 when his father pinned the DSO on Captain Grattan O'Brien of the Royal Flying Corps.

In Murray Park that afternoon Grattan had delivered a speech criticizing the Dominion's unpreparedness for war. That was, Margo's father admitted, the truth so far as it went—the country wasn't at all prepared. But he still hated watching his brother performing like a dressed-up donkey for a bunch of bloodthirsty Englishmen. "Didn't you get enough war the last time?" he'd shouted at Grattan on Sunday, when England had already declared war and Canada was about to.

Now, in the Mount Royal bar, Johnny was saying, "I can't leave town the way things are. But maybe after a few weeks, if we're still here."

She had slipped the room key from his jacket pocket before the drinks were served. They had a well-established routine for their hotel rendezvous. She had furtiveness—and hotel rooms—in common with her father, if nothing else.

Why did she feel so close to Johnny? He was the only man she'd ever slept with. He had a gift for pleasure. He was good at making her feel good. And her body exercised some considerable power over his. Had her mother ever felt that way about her father? Had their bodies engaged in acts of love like a struggle, almost like fighting? In bed with Johnny Taschereau was the only time she felt complete.

They'd never discussed their relationship. Had either of them ever used the word *love*, in French or in English? He certainly had not. Nonetheless she was convinced that love composed the current between them. Being in love made silences intimate and magical. Being in love made her feelings almost unbearable during the lonely, powerful moments in hotel rooms and tourist cabins after he had fallen asleep. After sex he was like a dead bird, warm, glittering, but she always felt supercharged with awareness. These were the moments when she believed she was going to marry him. Otherwise, in the world outside hotel rooms, the prospect seemed less credible: frayed, a bit hopeless.

Johnny Taschereau and her father got on well. Of all the young men she had brought home he was the only one Joe had ever invited into his study.

"What do you two have to talk about?" she'd asked Johnny.

"You," Johnny replied. "And we have other interests in common. The stock market. Men in government. Your father doesn't have a lot to say, but what he says is usually quite perceptive."

Johnny was less vulnerable than her father, more supple, more cynical, more at home in the world. It was hard to imagine Johnny fleeing to Manhattan on a night train. Hard to imagine any predicament he could not face up to directly, any emotion or feeling he would not be able to articulate instantly, with wry style and pungent irony. Johnny Taschereau was built to last.

If war came, how was she to get through the days without him? Love had awakened a terrible sense of incompleteness.

~

Her parents had sold the house at Butterfly Beach in 1932 and built a cottage at Kennebunk, Maine. Every summer they went cruising in Penobscot Bay for two or three weeks in their old Friendship sloop, just the two of them, no children invited.

Three weeks after the jackboots stomped into Prague, there had been a telephone call from an assistant manager at the Pierre. Mr. O'Brien was ill; would a member of the family please come and fetch him?

As far as she knew it was the first time since California he'd gone on a squawk. She'd gone to New York with her mother to fetch him. They found him in his tower suite at the Pierre, with the windows open and gusts of wind blowing curtains and fluttering hotel stationery off the writing desk.

The male nurse had already cleaned him up and gotten him dressed. While Iseult lay down for a nap, Margo took her father to the hotel barbershop for a shave and a haircut, then to a coffee shop on Madison Avenue, where he swallowed orange juice and dishwater coffee and didn't touch his scrambled eggs, even after she asked the surly waiter to bring him Worcestershire sauce.

On the train back to Montreal, while her father snored in the lounge car and the train ran past congeries of factories around Poughkeepsie, she and her mother sat in the dining car spooning tomato soup, and her mother talked about their trip from Santa Barbara up to the Selkirks in 1931. She called it a pilgrimage. By going all that way, she said, they reminded themselves of what they had to hold on to, and it saved their marriage. It made a nice story, Margo had thought to herself, but did her mother really believe it? Especially since the other pilgrim was at that moment in a lounge chair two cars back, shined up and shaved but with a hell of a hangover.

There were only a few men her father's age in the bar of the Mount Royal, two of them in uniform. "Captains," Johnny said, glancing in their direction. "Lots of fifty-year-old captains left over from the last war. They'll all have to be weeded out."

After coffee, they mimed saying goodbye. Johnny stood up and they kissed politely, both cheeks. She left him standing in the bar. As she crossed the lobby, a herd of American businessmen just off the airport bus was milling at the front desk. People in armchairs were reading day-old London newspapers printed on airmail paper as thin as tissue.

Sometimes it was important not to think too much about what you were doing but just to do it. The room was on the seventh floor, and she didn't want to be seen waiting at the lobby elevator. Passing the news-stand, she continued down a corridor lined with shops, a florist, the hotel barbershop, a fur salon. Sexual hunger—really more like thirst— was impossible to disconnect from a mood of furtiveness. That was cer-tainly part of its pleasure.

A pair of steel doors opened to a service stairwell, brightly lit, painted white, unused. She went up two flights quickly, heels tapping on painted concrete steps, then pushed on another heavy door and stepped out into a carpeted hallway lined with room doors, numbered and painted glossy black. She found the elevator and pressed the button. Waiting, she con-sidered herself in a mirror. The summer frock was all wrong—girlish, not chic. She'd ordered it in the spring, before things got serious with Johnny, before she had come into herself. The black straw hat was more her style now. She still had her glow of tan from the beach. Long waist, long legs. She sometimes worried she was too thin, her breasts too small. Cameras liked her shoulders and the bones in her face. Aunt Elise had photographed her for a story the *Star Weekly* was running on Montreal's nightlife. Elise liked the photograph and wanted to include it in her new brochure, calling it "A Montreal Fiancée."

"But that's not fair. I'm not engaged, Elise. He hasn't said a single word about getting married."

"Look at you. You're the girl everyone wants to marry."

"Not him," she had murmured.

Would they be spending the afternoon in bed together or must he return to the office? The Taschereaus had been lawyers for generations, and Sir Louis-Philippe would have been angry and hurt if his only son had refused to join the firm. Johnny never complained, but she knew he found the work dull.

She wore her hat tipped low, a woman with something to conceal, a provocative mess of feelings, like a suitcase full of dirty clothes. Rancid and brutal and plaintive with desire. So this was what people called love. Literally it caused a weakness in the knees. Or maybe that was just two manhattans at lunch and her high-heeled dash up the service stairway.

She watched the elevator arrow move languidly around the dial. If she'd waited down in the lobby she felt certain she would have encountered her father. What would he have done? What would he say?

"He'll make a good husband if he doesn't get himself killed," he'd said, when Johnny had turned up at Skye Avenue in uniform after a church parade.

If she lost Johnny to the war would she tighten up, curl up into herself, like a shrimp dropped into a glass of gin? Or would she need to keep on living this way—sexually, wantonly—with some other man? She did not know. Here was life, her real life. Scars were being applied; she could feel them going in.

The elevator arrived, settled, doors punched open. It was packed with bellboys, luggage, and grey-flannelled American businessmen. What she wanted, what she needed—she'd have to work it all out later; there wasn't time now.

"Room for one more?" She smiled at the elevator operator.

"*Bien sûr, mademoiselle.*"

~

A couple of hours later she awoke in the mussed bed and heard Johnny speaking into the phone. The room was dark except for a crack of light a couple of inches wide where the drapes did not come together perfectly. There was enough light to see him sitting in the chair at the little writing desk, holding the telephone to his ear. He was naked.

"*Oui, oui, je comprends.*"

She felt ragged, sore. Hotel-room dreams were so steep and so heavy, though she was already losing the sense of this one. She struggled to remember if there was anywhere else she was supposed to be.

"*Tiens. À bientôt.*"

Johnny replaced the phone receiver. He had a beautiful neck and shoulders.

"Who was it?" she asked, her voice sounding furry.

He looked around. His blunt face was very French. So was the dark brown hair he wore rather long.

"Well, I decided to call Rainville, our adjutant. I thought if anyone knew what was up, he would."

Naked in bed at the Mount Royal Hotel, Peel Street, Montreal, province of Quebec, in the Dominion of Canada, coloured red on the globe, part of the British Empire and committed to joining England in war.

"Lucky I checked in. He's just received mobilization orders in a telegram delivered to his office. He's a publisher, you know. He's in a bit of a flurry. Very annoyed the orders were in English. *Mon dieu*, you are a lovely woman."

"What does it mean?"

"Well, my platoon is to mount a guard at Victoria Pier tonight. I don't know what after that. It's going to be a hell of a job rounding men up. Not many have telephones. I need to go home first and get into uniform. Can you drive me?"

"*Reviens au lit*, Johnny."

He smiled and came back and lay beside her. She rested her head on his shoulder and they were quiet for a while. Hotel rooms were so sombre and thick in the middle of the afternoon. She could smell the scented soap in the bathroom. His skin felt warm.

She sensed the excitement he was trying to conceal because it had nothing to do with her and he didn't want to hurt her feelings. He was impatient to get up, dress, head out into the next chapter of his life, but he also had very good manners.

A kind of remove had already occurred. Taking one of his well-shaped, masculine hands, she began kissing the fingertips.

"*Jolie*," he said.

She could see everything. The war unrolling like a hotel-room carpet, heavy and dark, smelling of moth powder and stealing the light. She had wanted this war, as most of her friends had, more from boredom than anything else.

"If you'll drive me around the East End I can try to track down my men. Perhaps it will all blow over. But those are my orders."

All the intimacy left the room when he spoke English. It was suddenly as though he had another woman somewhere, as if he suddenly had a wife. The pain of the situation stimulated her in a deep way. "Come into me, Johnny, just come into me."

He was hard very quickly and touching her and she was open. Then he was inside her, rocking them both, her legs locked around his hips. The encounter had a bolting, panicked quality. They were digging something deep and nervous out of each other. It was like driving very fast because they had to, because even Johnny Taschereau was scared of something. The sense of dangerously high speed, at the very limit of control. She couldn't know for certain everything he was feeling, but underneath his excitement, the fear was there.

He came into her powerfully and she held on to his shoulders, then let herself go, riding the panic, shuddering, shaking tears out of her eyes, tasting her own breath.

She wasn't wearing her diaphragm; he must have noticed but hadn't said anything.

He stayed on her another minute, neither of them saying a word. She could feel his heart. Then he kissed her, got up, and went into the bathroom. A moment later she heard the shower running. A phase of their courtship was over: something new and even more dangerous had begun.

~

A hotel garage man brought around the cream convertible and she picked up Johnny on the corner of Mansfield and Sherbrooke, two blocks from the Mount Royal. She seemed to have an instinct for subterfuge, for concealment and deception. She disliked wearing the phony ring but she had been rather good, on the whole, at sneaking around. It was another aspect of the intimacy they shared.

They drove into Westmount. Heading up Murray Hill, they passed Skye Avenue and she glanced at the house. There was no one home except the cook and the maids; her parents were always busy, and even Frankie was doing volunteer work at the clinic and hoping for a war job. Mike was across the river seven days a week building his airfield. He had been seeing a lot of her old convent pal Mary Cohen, who was back in Montreal after several years in Europe—Margo had seen them together at the Normandie Roof and Mother Martin's. People said Buck Cohen had gone to Europe after New York gangsters tried to murder him; he'd died of a heart attack on the Côte d'Azur. Mary and her Irish mother now lived on Carthage Avenue. Mary was a secretary at a Jewish law firm in the Sun Life Building.

Mike had his OTC commission in the Royal Montreal Regiment, another militia outfit, and Margo knew boys in the RMR who were expecting to be shipped overseas any day. But the Ministry of Munitions and Supply had classified Mike's work as "vital to the Imperial war effort," so he would not be summoned to active duty. She was a little surprised he had gone along with it, but building airfields was probably more important than drilling recruits in Westmount Park, and her brother had never shown much interest in soldiering.

No one was home at the Taschereaus' either, except the cook, who was asleep, and the elderly maid, Albertine. While Johnny went upstairs to change, she stiffly steered Margo into the drawing room and asked if she wanted tea.

"*Non, merci.*"

Margo knew Albertine was a distant relation of the family and came from Arthabaska County, where the Taschereaus still owned farms. She'd been Johnny's nurse until a Scottish woman replaced her. After twenty-five years in Westmount and as many summers in Maine, Albertine still would not speak English. She attended Mass at Saint-Léon-de-Westmount four or five times a week, sitting in one of the Taschereau family pews.

Margo crossed the room, feeling the kinswoman's dark, shiny little eyes watching her, and stood self-consciously before the window. She could see a bit of the playing field in Murray Park—no one ever called it King George Park. The tennis courts had been deserted lately. Was it the news from Europe that kept people from playing games? Maybe it was just summer closing down. She didn't want to let go of summer, not yet.

But layers of cloud were moving in over the park, where a couple of boys were tossing a football back and forth—another sign of autumn.

The day was losing its abundant light. The sky was shades of grey now, with black thunderheads. It looked like rain. Maybe an electrical storm.

Johnny had never taken his part-time soldiering very seriously. He insisted that his CO, Colonel Rivard, though he hated *les boches*, would rather be fighting the English in Ontario. Most of the Maisies' energies were focused on hockey and softball games. The junior officers were OTC from Laval University, except for a few Loyola men like Johnny. The captains and majors were all trench veterans, average age forty-six.

Johnny was still upstairs. Margo couldn't hear him. If it weren't for Albertine watching her with beady eyes, she'd go upstairs herself. She'd love to see his bedroom.

At Kennebunk Beach most of the cottages would be shut for the season, boards nailed up over any windows facing the sea. There was always a big September storm, with wild green waves and buckets of warm rain. But Kennebunk was three hundred miles away, and people said if the war lasted there would be rationing of gasoline and tires. It was already getting difficult to exchange Canadian money for American. She wondered when she would see the ocean again.

She had always admired the Taschereaus' drawing room. The sleek furniture was more modern than anything she was used to. She liked the pale grey rug and the Japanese lamps. Mme Taschereau was from a Philadelphia family and collected art by Canadian painters. Landscapes of the northern wilderness, *pays sauvage*, were hung on the walls along with more abstract works by the same Montreal painters Margo's mother admired: Borduas, Alexander Bercovitch, Jack Humphrey.

Conscious of Albertine still watching, Margo went to the grand piano, where Aunt Elise's portrait of Johnny, taken before he left for his European year, stood in a silver frame. Johnny at twenty-one didn't look particularly happy, but not sad either. Elise had located a wariness in him that most people never noticed, since it was camouflaged so well by his bon vivant style. She had chosen to photograph Johnny outside, *en plein air*, unusual for her. Johnny told her they'd walked all around downtown before Elise chose a spot in front of an old maple tree at the top of Peel Street, on the edge of Mount Royal Park.

"What did you talk about while you were walking around?"

"The light."

"Did she talk about our family?"

"Not really."

"People used to say Uncle Grattan was crazy."

"Well, they don't anymore."

In the photograph Johnny's hair was rough and windblown and he seemed to be looking at something far away. *The war*, Margo thought. *Was it the war he saw coming?*

But the picture had been taken in 1935 or '36. No one had been thinking about a war in those days. He could have been looking at a squirrel, or a bus wheezing along Pine Avenue. Elise had taken him up there for the raised light. Margo had worked with enough photographers to know they would go anywhere for the right sort of light.

"Alors."

She looked around. Albertine had disappeared and Johnny stood in the doorway in his new khaki battledress, haversack slung over his shoulder.

"On y va."

She watched him scribble a note to his parents. He went out to the kitchen and she heard him saying goodbye to the cook and Albertine, who came out with him, held open the front door, and stood watching them walk out to the car. Johnny turned and waved, but the little woman in the black dress and starched maid's apron stayed perfectly still in the doorway, like a French-Canadian folk sculpture crudely carved in pine.

The first of his goodbyes. The thought struck her like a blow on the cheek, and it was all she could do to keep walking, heels click-clacking on the slate path. If he hadn't had such a steely, military grip on her arm she would have fallen down on the grass on hands and knees and wept and spat and howled.

~

It started to rain as they were driving over the mountain. Johnny had the address of every man in his platoon listed in a black notebook. Only four had telephone numbers, and the adjutant would be trying to reach them. Johnny was supposed to collect as many of the others as he could find and report to the Craig Street Armoury by eight p.m.

The rain came on sweeps of warm wind. The road over the mountain was already littered with branches and green leaves, and they passed a dozen cars pulled over on the shoulder. The windshield was foggy and the wipers weren't much good on the uphill. As she drove over the crest, Margo could feel the car being pushed and swayed by the wind. Rain drummed the canvas roof. Johnny reached across to wipe the glass with his handkerchief but it was still difficult to see out the windshield. Shifting down to second, she switched on her headlights. It was like driving through a violent cloud, but on the downhill grade at least the wipers were going a little faster.

Johnny lit a cigarette and handed it to her. They had fallen into another of their silences.

Back in August, when everyone else had returned to Montreal, Margo and Frankie had stayed on alone at the O'Brien summer cottage, and Johnny at the Taschereaus'. They'd made plans to leave together, but at the last minute Frankie received an invitation to stay with friends at Ogunquit, so Margo and Johnny were able to set off for home alone. Their families were not expecting them. They stopped at a tourist court at Franconia, bought groceries and beer at a country store, built a fire in their cabin, and spent the night together. The next morning, driving down into the St. Lawrence Valley past lush meadows of sweet-smelling hay, Margo had felt clean, powerful, safe.

Johnny now switched on the news in French. The Poles were pleading with London and Paris to send troops. Hurricane winds had derailed a train north of Boston, and Montreal could expect the same storm, which had started in the Caribbean. A boy and girl playing on the street in St. Henry had been electrocuted by a downed power line. The radio announcer did not mention any troop mobilizations.

"We're a military secret," Johnny remarked. "Nobody knows about us—not even us. Germany, beware."

She was steering down Mount Royal Boulevard into the heart of the French-speaking city. Johnny studied his list.

"Gingras, Jean-Louis, Private. 3412 Boulevard Saint-Joseph. Let's take a right here. Go to Boulevard Saint-Joseph, then take a left."

Rain thrummed on the roof. The storm was a harbinger. Summer was being lost, and her world was changing fast.

They found Private Gingras sitting on the balcony of his family's third-floor flat, watching the downpour. Johnny called up to him from the sidewalk and the boy hurried inside to change into uniform. While Margo waited behind the wheel, Johnny rang two more doorbells on the same block. One of the soldiers, a corporal, was at work at the big bakery on Marie-Anne Street, but the other was at home, and he came out wearing battledress and climbed into the back seat alongside Private Gingras. With the two young soldiers aboard, they headed for the bakery, where Johnny located his corporal, told him to go home and get into uniform, and gave him money to take a streetcar to Craig Street. They gathered the rest of the platoon from flats and tenements on a dozen streets east of Boulevard Saint-Denis. The district was unfamiliar to Margo; it seemed buttoned up, grey. There were hardly any shops. Johnny kept flagging down taxis, filling them with young soldiers, then dispatching the taxis to the armoury. The streets were empty of people, probably on account of the violence of the storm, and few cars were on the road. They kept passing by enormous grey stone parish churches.

After two hours Johnny had filled three more taxis and dispatched them to Craig Street, and four young men in battledress were sitting practically on top of one another in the back seat of Margo's car. They sounded excited and happy. It was dark. Rain was still crashing down, and Johnny kept leaning forward to wipe the steamy windshield.

As she steered along Park Avenue Margo saw a streetcar stalled on its track in the middle of the road. The road was flooded and the streetcar was shorting out, white bolts of electricity lashing from its cable and connector. Something about it terrified her. She wanted to pull over, jump out of the car, start running. She dabbed the brake pedal, but then a cold calm came over her, numbing, maybe instinctive, as though she were a bird in a great migrating flock, about to give herself up to an almost endless journey. Her grip tightened on the wheel. Instead of braking she punched the accelerator and swerved neatly around the streetcar and its fiery connection, her tires slashing through the black water.

Johnny, holding a flashlight and studying his black book, hardly noticed. He had been checking names off the list, and now he resumed giving her extraordinarily precise directions, guiding them from street to street, tenement to tenement. Margo tried to let go of everything else— every speck of self-pity, of terror—and just follow the directions and keep going.

MONTREAL,
OCTOBER 1939

Violence

M ONDAY WAS FRANKIE'S day off so she headed downtown to shop for shoes. People said there were bound to be all sorts of shortages coming, and good shoes were one thing she could not imagine doing without.

She and Margo rode the streetcar together as far as Phillips Square. Margo was going to Craig Street to see Johnny Taschereau and discuss their wedding plans, which were being slapped together in a hurry, since his regiment expected to receive overseas orders any day.

Frankie knew how trivial, how frivolous her own mission was. She had seen boys drilling in Westmount Park and watched the newsreels from Poland showing refugee children and white horses dead on the road, machine-gunned by Nazi planes. And her sister was marrying a man who might very soon be sent into battle. But no new shoes for the duration—how terrible, how strange.

There was nothing interesting in any of the department stores, but as she walked into Holt Renfrew she suddenly knew she would find exactly what she wanted there. She rode the elevator up to the third floor, got out, and immediately saw a gorgeous pair of Italian pumps. Pale yellow. Kid lining. Her size exactly.

It had happened before, often, knowing what was going to happen just before it did. It was why she loved playing cards, and why people were always telling her she was lucky. Of course, yellow was a summer colour and summer was long gone, but she could wear the shoes on warm days and they would be nice to have for spring. The toes pinched a little but the leather would stretch.

She came out of Holt's carrying her new shoes in a shopping bag, feeling gifted and lucky. The October morning was fine, stuffed with light, and she didn't feel like going inside again now that she'd accomplished her mission. It had been sultry for weeks, the city stinking of gunpowder, it had seemed to her, though she knew it wasn't that, not really. Now the atmosphere was clear; the strongest scent was autumn leaves and earth.

She wondered if Margo might be willing to drive down to Maine with her for one last holiday. October light was gorgeous at the beach and they could have a nice time at the cottage, just the two of them. She could probably wangle a few days off from the clinic on Notre-Dame Street where she was volunteering four days a week—when the war started it hadn't felt right not to have some job. Her mother wanted her to go off to college the way American girls did, but after eleven years at the convent she wasn't interested in more studying.

She'd have preferred modelling clothes at Holt's to handing out vitamins and delousing little boys, but her mother had insisted she go down to the slums and do something useful. She didn't know how useful she was, but some of the medical students at the clinic were charming. Others seemed to despise her but she believed she'd win them over eventually. She wouldn't wear her new shoes to work, though. Yellow pumps, however comely, were not going to win the hearts of Catholic socialists.

As she strolled along Sherbrooke Street then turned down Peel, the only signs of the war were bold black headlines slathered across the newsstands. She decided she would stop by the Sun Life Building to pick up her tennis racquet, which her father had had restrung at a sports store on St. Catherine Street. When the war started, no one played tennis for a couple of weeks, but it was too sweet a pleasure to give up for the duration. There were still two or three weeks of playable weather left and she liked how she looked in a tennis dress. There was even the possibility of a match that afternoon, with a twenty-one-year-old captain in the RMR, if he could swing a couple of hours' leave. Meanwhile, her brother might be persuaded to take her out to lunch.

A shiny green army truck with an artillery piece in tow was parked on Mansfield Street. She read the hand-painted sign attached to the truck:

5th (Westmount) Field Battery
Royal Canadian Artillery
RECRUITS WANTED
Radio operators—Mechanics—Surveyors
Apply this truck or the Craig St. Drill Hall

One of the recruiting sergeants was speaking earnestly to a telegraph boy astride a bicycle. Another soldier, leaning on the truck, was picking his teeth when he noticed Frankie and winked at her. She tried not to smile as she ran up the granite steps, entered through bronze doors, and crossed the lobby towards the elevator bank.

The moment she stepped out on the twenty-second floor she heard her father yelling. The people she passed in the hallway ignored her or smiled quickly, keeping their heads down, bombarded by the angry noises from his corner office. She started wishing she'd made other plans for lunch, but she couldn't retreat now and leave them thinking she was scared of her papa, even at his most ogreish.

"What's going on?" she asked the pert little receptionist. "Has the sky fallen?"

"M'sieu Mike is with your papa." The girl was afraid to say more.

Clutching her purse and Holt's shopping bag, Frankie went up to his door and rapped sharply—*shave-and-a-haircut, two-bits*. He'd taught her that knock when she was little, and she always used it with him: their private signal. "Blessed Frankie of the Knock," Mike used to call her.

"Not now!" her father shouted.

But she was already opening the door. "Only me," she said, slipping inside and shutting it softly behind her.

Mike was leaning on a corner of their father's desk, lighting a cigarette from a silver lighter shaped like a pineapple. Their father paced in front of windows that looked across the city and the St. Lawrence River to the purple mountains of New York State on the horizon. The windows on the other side of the room overlooked Dominion Square, with its trees and flowerbeds and ugly statues.

"Mike, how about taking me to lunch?"

Mike smiled at her. Their father drew on his cigarette and looked at her through narrowed eyes. All summer he'd been distracted and in a

foul mood. In July he had left their cook behind at a filling station in the
White Mountains when she had gone to use the bathroom. Listening to
the news from Europe on his car radio, he'd forgotten all about the poor
woman and driven away.

Frankie watched him place his smouldering cigarette on the edge of
his desk, which was already scored with burn marks, and pick up a hardcover notebook, something like a ledger.

"Most of the estimates for the new airport job are in there," Mike
said. "Wing Commander Blades says the field at St. Hubert, no matter
how we stretch it, is never going to be big enough to handle the new
bombers, so they're going to want a brand-new field somewhere else,
probably Dorval. The squeeze is on with materials and labour and everything's up fifteen percent in the past two weeks, so you'll have to keep
an eye on prices. But Blades says the main thing is to bid low enough to
be sure you're in, even if it looks like losing money at first. They're going
to be building a lot more big fields after that one. Gander's really going
to get the build-up, maybe the Azores, and they are planning a bunch of
new fields out on the prairies to train aircrew from all over."

"Your numbers don't add up," their father said. "I'd lose my fucking shirt." He started ripping out a page from the notebook, so slowly
Frankie could hear every inch of the tear. Mike stared as their father
slowly crumpled the page in his fist, then started tearing out more
pages, crumpling them, dropping them on the floor. Finally he dumped
the entire book into the wastebasket, sat down in his desk chair, and
started spinning around slowly, like a little kid, the tips of his handmade
shoes hardly touching the carpet. He dressed well, but next to Mike he'd
always look like a tree stump in an expensive suit. The only noise was
the *squeak squeak squeak* from the chair.

"Mike," Frankie said. "Lunch?"

"Yeah, sure." Mike was gazing at their father as if he could not
believe how the old man was behaving.

"Where'll we go?"

"I have a lunch date with Mary Cohen but you're welcome to come
along."

"Okay."

"Aerodromes, weather stations, aircraft plants—it'll be an air war,

Dad," Mike said. "Somebody's going to get their foot in that door. Might as well be us."

"What the fuck do you mean 'us'?"

Mike shrugged. "I'm sorry."

Their father stopped spinning and reached for another cigarette.

"Going to grab my hat, Frankie," Mike told her. "Meet you by the elevators."

"Okey-doke."

Mike left the room without shutting the door. Their father lit his cigarette, then slowly spun in his chair.

They'd always gotten along, Frankie and her father. Most of the time she was able to feel what he was feeling. They were both Black Irish, with the same dark hair and blue eyes. She knew him, Frankie thought, the way she knew herself.

He stopped spinning. "Know what?" he said softly.

"No, Daddy, what?"

"That wing commander, that Englishman your mother had to lunch last Sunday, that Blades—he's cooked it up. They're shipping your brother to England with a bunch of college boys from McGill to make fighter pilots out of them. I said, 'If you want to win the war, do your job here. You don't need to prove anything. Do the work here—there's plenty. After you build that airfield there'll be another.'"

"Daddy, you know Mike. You're not going to be able to stop him."

He looked up at her.

"Of course Mike has to go. He isn't the only one, after all," she added. Maybe it wasn't the right thing to say. She wished she could help her father, get him thinking instead of just feeling. She could see that underneath the soft voice and the stillness he was terribly upset. He could always see things coming; they both could. That was the Black Irish: they knew things and didn't know how they knew them, and it scared them sometimes.

"Daddy, why don't you go home for the afternoon? You ought to talk to Mother."

"Why? He's already told her. Your uncle too. They think it's great. They're all for it. They wanted this goddamn war."

That was unfair. No one had really wanted the war. People were excited, that was all.

Or, to be honest, maybe some people—people her age—had wanted the war. To be perfectly honest, she'd wanted the war, the same way she sometimes wanted to kick a can down the middle of a dark street when coming home from a party, walking through the sleeping neighbourhood with her date. Just to make a noise. To show—to know—that she was alive.

Her father had forgotten his cigarette burning on the ashtray; he was lighting another. She watched his hands trembling as he held the heavy desk lighter and touched its flame to his fresh cigarette, which looked so small between his thick fingers.

Frankie had never before felt stronger than her father, calmer and wiser. Maybe Margo had felt that way when she went to New York to fetch him. It was a strange feeling.

"Why don't you go home and rest, Daddy?"

He turned in his chair and looked at her. There weren't any thoughts scribed on his face, none that she could read, anyhow. She realized he wasn't even seeing her.

Who would go to New York to fetch him next time? If Mike was joining the air force and Margo getting married, maybe it would be Frankie's turn. And she wanted to go. In a strange way she wanted to see her father broken down, not because she was angry with him or despised him, but because she loved him and needed to feel closer to him. She needed to see what her sister had seen, the hotel suite, the overflowing ashtray, the whisky bottles, him lying there like an animal hit by a car. She wanted to see him exactly as he was.

"Frankie! Let's go." Her brother was threading his way between desks and drafting tables in the outer office, carrying his hat. Their father stood up and went to the windows looking down on the square. For a second she thought, *He's going to jump.* Instead he reached down and picked up her tennis racquet in its heavy press from where it was leaning against the wall.

"Frankie! Coming or not? Mary's meeting us in the lobby."

Her father went to the doorway, hefting the racquet in hand. "That kike," he said, "that little moll of yours—don't think you'll ever bring her home."

Frankie could see her brother out in the main office. Mike stopped, turned around, and was facing their father. She could hear the ceiling fan creaking. Somewhere a phone jangled. It was lunch hour, so most people were away from their desks, but a couple of secretaries and perhaps a dozen men—engineers, draftsmen, purchasing agents—were working or unwrapping their sandwiches. Some of them were even smiling, as though Frankie's father had cracked a joke that wasn't funny but required them to smile because he was the boss. Maybe if one of them had started laughing they all would have.

Mike stood in an aisle between drafting tables, hat in one hand, suit coat unbuttoned. "You know what, Dad?" He didn't sound angry; he sounded tired. "That's a terrible thing to say. Why don't you go back to the bush? That's where you belong."

Their father started towards him, gripping the tennis racquet in his right hand. Frankie wanted to get out of there, run for the elevator, escape the building, but there wasn't time, and anyway, she couldn't move. No one seemed able to move except her father, picking his way between desks and drafting tables, men and girls watching him as if this were the circus and here was the elephant. Not even Mike moved a muscle.

And when their father raised the tennis racquet, maybe Frankie's brother still did not believe what was happening. Or maybe some part of him thought he deserved it—that he ought to take his licking—because he didn't try to duck or protect himself in any way. He just stood there, and as their father raised the racquet there was one big sigh in the room, as though everyone who was holding their breath had let it out at once. Then their father hit Mike over the head with the tennis racquet in its press.

Mike said, "Jesus Christ."

Their father swung again, a two-handed backhand, but this time Mike stepped back, and the swing just missed him.

Mike said, "What the hell." Dropping his hat, he seized their father's wrists. Mike was six inches taller than the old man, but their father had the power of whatever it was—craziness, love—behind him, as always. He broke free and took another swing that caught Mike on his side.

Mike yelped in pain and struck their father in the face, knocking off his spectacles and causing him to drop the racquet. Again Mike grabbed him by the wrists, but he jerked free once more, turned away, and quickly

walked back into his office. Frankie ran out as he went in and slammed
the door shut behind him.

~

Margo married Johnny Taschereau in October 1939. Mike was best man
and Lulu Taschereau was maid of honour. Her father gave Margo away,
and she and Johnny walked out of the church under a canopy of swords.
Mike announced that he and Mary Cohen were engaged but were going
to wait until the war was over, or until he returned from overseas, before
getting married. One week later he left Montreal. Margo and Johnny,
Frankie, her mother, and Mary Cohen were all at Bonaventure to see
him off, but Frankie's father did not come to the station.

Hostage to Fortune

RAF Pembrey
1st August, 1940

Dear Mother,

If anything happens you must give Mary any help she needs and see to it she feels free and clear. I probably shouldn't have tied her up with an engagement, at the time we both felt it was what we wanted. I still intend to marry her after the war, nothing is going to change in that respect but I'm not the same character she agreed to marry. One look in the shaving mirror and I know I'm not.

If something happens nothing should get in the way of her enjoying life, no one has to live with my ghost.

2 sweeps today so far. At the billet we've use of a swimming pool of all things. Weather keeps hot and blue. All the chaps in "92" are good stuff and I'll never say another word against Englishmen. 2 other Canucks, both from Toronto, both in "A" flight. 1 So. African and 1 New Zealander.

There's no place I'd rather be than here. It all happens so fast and there's so much of it—can't think my way through it all right now, but with any luck I'll have another 40 or 50 years to do that. I don't think Dad ought to close the shop. I wish he'd think it over.

Love,
Mike

~

15th Aug., 1940
RAF Pembrey

Dear Uncle Grattan,

The Spit is a wonder. View is bad on the ground—taxiing you have to swing from side to side to see what's ahead. Can't take too long or the Merlin tends to overheat. Acceleration is something I've never experienced before. In speed, climb, and turning circle she's got the edge over every German machine including the ME 109. Drop the nose a little and you're 400 mph before you notice.

Jerry's shot her up a little bit and she just keeps at it. People buy houses, worry about what they're going to wear, what's in the bank . . . do they really? Can't imagine. I always feel the little Spit will bring me home.

When it's all over we'll have a talk won't we.

> *best regards, & love to Aunt Elise,*
> *Mike*

~

16th August, 1940
RAF Pembrey

Dear Mother,

No I don't mind killing none of us does we've seen our friends get it and no one's asked the bloody Germans to come over to England and smash and bomb the country.

I don't feel anything, it's him or me.

> *Your son,*
> *Mike*

~

RAF Biggin Hill
10th September, 1940

Dear Uncle Grattan,

We moved from Wales a few days ago. It was busy enough over Bristol but we're in the thick of it here, Jerry's highway to London is straight upstairs. 3 hostile plots today, so far, they're running their power play. We're always a man short and today they pulled their goalie, too.

Got an ME on my tail this morning. Never seen an ME thrown about like that but I had the throttle open and rolled over. The controls got very heavy, airspeed needle moved far right at 410 mph, then I was on his back. He rolled and I gave him a squirt, continued firing as he started his dive. I could see bullets entering the side of his fuselage while I followed him down. We were at 5000 and the dive became quite shallow, I could see the French coast a few miles ahead. I let him have another good squirt -- white smoke started pouring from his port radiator, a glycol coolant leak. When I broke off he was spinning violently. Billy Cruikshank, behind me, saw him dive into the sea and break up. Makes three certain MEs. Three probables and pieces of half a dozen HEs and JUs. The dawn plot is usually forgotten by afternoon, no matter what happened, there's always new business. Heinkels are fat and slow, easy pickings unless they've got enough MEs for cover. If we can break their formation we knock them down. Junkers are tougher and everyone getting through carries enough TNT to hurt London badly. Like HEs they depend on fighter screen but they're harder to knock down, better armour and a lot more gunpower.

The last two weeks feels like enough lifetime for anyone. They're throwing everything they have at us and we are clawing them down. 2 fellows lost this morning. Someone will go into their rooms, pack up, that's always tough.

> Best regards, & love to Aunt
> Elise,
> *Mike*

~

RAF Biggin Hill
15th Sept. 1940

Dear Dad,

The intensity in the southeast is something. Wales was different -- here we're catching 2 sometimes 3 hostile plots per day. They say you'll know your way

around if you can survive the first three weeks. Not
quite prepared for this intensity. Rough going.

The day starts at half past four, someone pushing at
your shoulder -- your batman, Airman Gillis, waking you.
You get up and think Oh God another dawn and wander
over to the mess. War everywhere. Hangars flat, broken
aeroplanes. You think god it's going to be a lovely day,
no breeze to ruffle the hair, or anything like that. Go
into the mess. Empty tankards, ashtrays full left over
from the night before, magazines all over the place
because it's early in the morning, the steward hasn't
cleared it. Go into the dining room and cup of tea and
toast and you're munching toast and looking around at
everybody being quiet.

Screech of brakes outside, it's the van to take you to
the Dispersal hut.

Occasionally you fall asleep. Saw a chap reading a
book and it was upside down. If you've had a heavy
night -- it isn't allowed but you take straight oxygen.
And the doc has little pills, and if he doesn't like the
look of you he gives you some.

The telephone rings. Scramble base. Sling parachute
over your shoulder and off you go across the grass
to where your Spitfire's parked. Sort of resignation
really. You notice little things. Everything quiet and
still. No birds. Dew on your feet. Light like ocean
light. Silence broken by the odd clank of the spanner.
Your rigger helps you into the 'plane, straps you in
and fusses over you and you feel better. -- All right
mate, all clear, contact -- Next thing you know twelve
Merlins singing. Once airborne, you feel part and
parcel of the aeroplane. You don't fly it you wear it.
You see there are other aeroplanes with you so you
aren't completely on your own. It gets bloody cold up
there. You do things with the aeroplane never in any
book. An ME gets on your tail & you are straight down
to the deck, 50 feet, going up over hills and round
forests down valleys and up the other side because
you're a difficult target then. That's the sort of thing
to learn if you plan to survive three weeks. Think in
those terms and think quickly. Never question your

instincts, but react. If in any doubt about anything at all -- never question, react. Never fly straight and level longer than ten seconds. Ten or twenty seconds. Never fly straight and level. And if you see anything in the sun, they come out of the sun. If you have a couple of seconds to look at the sun and something feels not quite right, just don't stay there, a lot of people get the chop like this. If there's nothing there, so what, you're alive to fight another day. Always break into the attack, never away from it. If someone's coming in here and you turn away, what's going to happen? He's on your tail just like that. So you turn and go under him. Or if not, go for him. Try and ram him. You get out of the way. Straight underneath. You go underneath. Spit can do anything. When you get home you thank the aeroplane.

> We'll see we'll see
> Stay clear of me
> Stay clear of me
> I'm heading out
> over the sea
> And where I'll be
> I'll be
> No matter you no matter me

All my love to you and Mother,
Your son
Mike

~

25th Sept. 1940
RAF Biggin Hill

Dear One,

I don't think about it. Totally resigned. Totally resigned. Accept it. You mustn't think about it either. Do not let yourself think about it.

Your knees,
Mike

~

7th October, 1940
RAF Biggin Hill

   Daddy, life is a pure strain of time and all the
important numbers have been written down already.
Nothing we can say or do alters the terms. So I
believe. You do as well? I think so. <u>Don't worry too
much about me</u> there is no point.

                         Love,
                              Mike

~

January 3rd 1941
RAF Manston

Dear One,

   Your letter came in, I read it in the pub. Went
outside & walked up the English road in the English
valley very green here in December -- no it's Jan. --
there were sheep. Walking up the English road an
officer crying tears streaming oh the poor officer.
Getting nervy.
   I tell you though I was crying for me not for you.
Last week a radio program on budgerigars going wild in
London set me off. If the NAAFI's shut, running out of
cigs will start me wailing. I hope your American navy
is made of better stuff.
   We knew each other you and me. You're a knot in the
wood I won't forget you. The way you smell, your legs,
everything. Think of me what you think of me, but
remember this: when the fire is burning down low I'll
think of you, I'll listen to you.

                    Godspeed,
                       Michael

~

January 10th, 1941
RAF Manston

Dear Margo,

Six months old and I don't know what Madeleine looks
like. Send me a photo of my niece please. It's too bad
Johnny missed her. That's the army (air force too) --
months without orders then everything in a rush all of
a sudden . . . I wonder if the Cdns go to Middle East.

The fellows you asked about are gone. Those of us
left are a bit tired. I am Senior Flight Commander
now. The general mood is -- we've done our war, let
someone else have a turn. You reach a certain point
where you are as effective as you'll ever be, that phase
lasts perhaps a month maybe two then you start making
mistakes, it's being tired mostly. A chap was killed the
other day flying into a Chance light. Good pilot too.
If it were a hockey game we'd be calling for a line
change! It's possible we will be shifted to the E. coast
(Lincolnshire) a bit of a stand-down. Also Middle East
is possible. There is a chance I will be posted as a
test pilot which would be a dream but not bloody likely.

I can't see the end of the war.

Got the shake-off the other day from MC. Nice
letter. Doesn't mean much of anything to me now.

Give your little girl a kiss from her uncle.

ton frère

Mike

~

11 NOVEMBER 1942
TO: MR. JOSEPH MICHAEL O'BRIEN
10 SKYE AVE WESTMOUNT PQ

7534 MINISTER OF NATIONAL DEFENCE REGRETS TO INFORM YOU
THAT R94274 FLYING OFFICER MICHAEL F O'BRIEN HAS OFFICIALLY
BEEN REPORTED WOUNDED IN ACTION THIRD NOVEMBER 1942 STOP
WHEN FURTHER INFORMATION BECOMES AVAILABLE IT WILL BE
FORWARDED AS SOON AS RECEIVED

DIRECTOR OF RECORDS

~

No 1 NZ General Hospital
Helwan Egypt
December 4th, 1942

Dear Mr. and Mrs. O'Brien,

   I am a nursing sister at the New Zealand Army
hospital at Helwan, Egypt and have been asked by
your son Michael to write and tell you that he is
recovering very well from his slight wounds. He asks
me to tell you that he has been "enjoying his holiday"
for the past month and that he expects to be boarded
very soon and returned to active duty with his unit.

                              Yours truly,
                              L. McEntee
                              Louise McEntee,
                              N.Z.A.N.S.

~

No 1 NZ General Hospital
Helwan Egypt
December 4th, 1942

Dear Mr. and Mrs. O'Brien,

   I feel I must write as truthfully as possible the
facts of your son's condition as the letter I wrote at
his request does not give, I feel, an entirely accurate
picture of his condition and I think it best that you
know the facts.

   He was admitted to No 1 NZ Gen Hosp in the middle
of November from an Advanced Dressing Station in
the desert. His wounds in neck and torso are due to
shrapnel and glass after his aeroplane was struck by
AA fire. He has so far had 3 surgeries to remove same.
He is making a good recovery but it is possible small
fragments of shrapnel remain in the chest cavity. He
is of course confined to bed until his wounds fully

heal and his strength has only just started coming
back, but he is quite exhausted and it is only natural
that after two years flying Spitfires in England and the
Western Desert he is mentally a bit "worn out" and his
spirits are "medium to low." Cannot for example write
his own letters, is unwilling to speak more than a few
sentences at a time, easily becomes annoyed. I am not
one to say but I think it most unlikely F/O O'Brien
will return to active service with the Desert A.F.
anytime soon, if ever.

After the battles of the last few weeks our NZ army
hospital is quite crowded but be assured F/O O'Brien
is receiving the best of care and his full recovery is
expected.

Yours truly,

Louise McEntee
Louise McEntee,
N.Z.A.N.S.

MAINE,
1943

Reprieve

COMING THROUGH the White Mountains Joe told her he was going to order a new sailboat, a thirty-nine-foot knockabout yawl, L. Francis Herreshoff design, to be built at Hodgdon's boatyard in East Boothbay as soon as the war was over. "It's the type of boat Mike and I can sail to Nova Scotia and Newfoundland, or the Bahamas, for that matter."

The Hodgdon yard was accepting civilian orders though nothing could be built until after the war. She and Joe had only begun using that phrase—*after the war*—since Mike's wounding. Why? Had the war changed when their son was hit? No. There was the German defeat at Stalingrad, Germans were on the run in North Africa, but it was still the same struggle all over the world, millions suffering, fighting, dying, being herded and slaughtered.

Had Joe changed? No. Joe had hated the war right from the start. Before they got the news about Mike she'd overheard him say to Elise, "Did it ever occur to you that war is a sickness and everyone in war is a patient?"

Through the winter they had received bright, terse letters from the nursing sister at the New Zealand Army Hospital in Egypt, documenting their son's recovery. And in March a letter in Mike's own hand, assuring them that he was one hundred percent fit. Was this possible? The war had gone after her son, damaged his beautiful body, punctured him. His body had healed in Egypt and he had been returned to active duty, in Tunisia, though not as a pilot.

I'm a staff wallah now, Tac Ops (Air). Flying a desk at 8th Army HQ
Tunis. I carry a briefcase to work. I really do.

Everyone, including Mike himself, could—must—try to pretend he
was the same. But of course he wasn't, could not possibly be.

Iseult had always felt the war had to be fought. But this war had
grown too large for that one little word, *war*. It could not be contained;
that seemed to be its essence. And ever since those scraps of steel and
Plexiglas had ruptured her son's body, broken his skin, clawed him out
of the sky, the war had found its way inside her like some poison gas acci-
dentally inhaled, or a dose of the wrong medicine, a shot of the wrong
serum. All winter, the swollen war had been making her ill and weak.

~

Joe had asked their Maine caretaker, Hiram Pinkham, to switch on the
electricity, and there was enough hot water brewed for a bath. There was
no point in opening up the whole house since it was unlikely to be used
again over the summer—they were all too busy in Montreal. Margo ran
a canteen for soldiers at Windsor Station and Frankie was at RAF Ferry
Command in the Mount Royal Hotel, flirting with pilots and booking
seats for politicians and generals flying back and forth across the Atlantic on bombers. Joe's firm was building airfields in Manitoba, Saskatchewan, and Alberta, an enormous dry dock at Halifax, and a navy fuelling
station at St. John's. Iseult spent at least two days a week at the clinics
in Sainte-Cunégonde and Maisonneuve and had agreed to spend most
of July motoring around Ontario, Quebec, and the Maritimes advising
local committees raising money to aid soldiers' families.

The Kennebunk house smelled musty when they arrived. Most of the
storm shutters were still closed, mattresses were folded on bedsprings,
and the living-room furniture was covered with bed sheets. While Joe lit
fires, Iseult opened windows in a few rooms. Fog lay on the beach and
the breakwater and she could not see the ocean.

The war wasn't over but the world had been at least partially restored.
Mike was safe. So was Johnny Taschereau, at least for now, though three
years' separation from her husband was gnawing at Margo. Johnny had
been relatively safe in England while Mike was flying in the desert. Now

Mike was safe in a staff job, but there'd be an invasion of Europe sooner or later, the Canadian army would have to play its part, and Johnny was an infantry officer.

Would Mike really care to go sailing with his father after the war? Would he stay in Montreal and take over the firm, as Joe expected? The war had changed her daughters' lives, her own, even Joe's, and it must have changed Mike even more. Impossible to predict how he would feel about things when he came home. She hoped he wouldn't be as confused and unhappy as Grattan had been after the Armistice.

Joe baked haddock and potatoes for dinner. They listened to the war news on the radio and went to bed leaving the window pushed open a few inches, enough to smell fog blowing in off the Atlantic and hear waves roaring on the beach. He reached for her and Iseult responded eagerly; the lovemaking seemed to her a celebration. It was the first time they had made love since receiving word their son had been wounded in Africa. Joe might die any day, and so might she; people in their fifties died on sidewalks, died in their sleep, had heart attacks, suffered strokes and seizures, smashed their cars, got cancer. It was odd to be thinking about death with her husband on top of her, his weight and his warmth, but since Mike's wounding she had come back to her old preoccupation with mortality. Joe's body was ageing but thick and strong. She was much too thin, her daughters insisted. Margo had been bringing home ice cream and forcing her to eat spoonful after spoonful in the kitchen, which she did dutifully, though it didn't seem to make any difference. She could not put on weight, just as certain children at the clinics never seemed to thrive no matter how much milk or how many fresh vegetables they or their mothers were given.

Joe fell asleep quickly but she lay awake for a long time. The deep rumble of the surf reminded her of Mike's seawall, and she wondered if it was still standing. She hoped neither of them would die before their son came home.

~

On that trip to British Columbia in 1931 the train had made a special stop at the hamlet of Blue River, where the stationmaster's son was waiting with an old Ford. He drove them north on gravel roads. His skinniness and shyness had reminded her of Mike's. It had been a dry summer, and dust rising from the road clogged every surface inside the car. She fell asleep in the back seat and woke only as they were arriving at the fishing camp on the North Thompson, where a woman in overalls was waiting up for them though it was almost two o'clock in the morning.

Once the road dust had settled, the night air smelled of glaciers and jack pine. Iseult could hear the black noise of the North Thompson River, just as she remembered it, a constant at all the Head-of-Steel camps.

The woman showed her into a log cabin where a lantern glowed on a plank table alongside a bouquet of tiny mountain flowers in a cut-glass vase. A blaze crackled in the fieldstone fireplace. The bed was made up with white flannel sheets, plump pillows, and a red and black Hudson's Bay blanket spread out and smoothed, with another folded across the foot of the bed. Joe and the boy carried in the luggage.

She'd felt far away from her three children then, from California and Krishnaji, and a bit closer to the young woman she had been. There was an enamel sink and a tin jug of creek water that could be heated on the nickel-plated stove for washing. Their privy was at the edge of the woods.

Joe asked the stationmaster's son to come for them at ten o'clock the next morning. The boy was going to drive them in on logging roads as far as the car could go. The woman pointed out the electric flashlight on the floor beside the bed, and warned about bears roaming the camp. Then Iseult and Joe were left alone with their bed, their fire, and the hissing of the river.

He was adding another log to the fire when he looked around at her. "I feel like I'm walking in a dream, Iseult, coming back up here."

"Oh, let's go to bed," she said. "I'm too tired to talk about all that now." How typical, she thought, that it had never occurred to him she might be in love with someone else, even after she'd introduced him to Krishnamurti.

He had taken out his pyjamas and was brushing his teeth at the little sink. She quickly unbuttoned her clothes and, while his back was to her, slipped her nightgown over her head. He was still the only man she'd ever slept with. It was all their marriage really came down to, she thought. All they were was familiar. A pair of bodies that had for some years been physically proximate.

Stepping outside, she walked a few yards from the cabin. She had no intention of stumbling all the way to the privy in the dark—she knew all about bears, and she hated privies. She squatted in the cold bunchgrass to pee.

Smoke from the chimney hung low on the ground. The sky was thick with stars, and frost gleamed on the meadow as it bent towards the road, where she could just see the last speck of the Ford's taillight disappearing. This was the country where she and Joe O'Brien had forged their bond in hard work, success, and suffering. She wondered what was to become of them.

They were the only people at breakfast the next morning. All the other guests staying at the lodge were out on the river with their fishing guides. She didn't want the flapjacks with maple syrup and elk sausage. Taking a piece of warm bannock and a cup of black coffee, she said she was going to have a look at the river.

"Do you want me to go with you?"

"No, finish your breakfast."

"Well, keep an eye out for bear. Where there's good fishing there's going to be bear."

She remembered navvies coming back from the river with salmon and stories of being treed by grizzlies. Joe had always carried a loaded rifle on their Sunday picnics along the grade, and more than once they had watched silvertips humping through the alpine meadows, rising and diving amid high grass and flowers, like salmon dashing upstream. But that morning in the sunshine on the meadow there was no aspect of danger, and the sun was already opening pungent little alpine flowers whose names she had learned long ago: bearberry, willow herb, arctic daisy.

She came to the sandy banks of the North Thompson, a milky green snake of a river thickened with melt from glaciers. The strong current and the glacial silt, sand, and gravel suspended in it were what gave the river its frictioned, slithering charge. The flow had power, even then, in late summer. Joe had tried using scows to get materials to the station men beyond Head-of-Steel, and half a dozen boats spilled and smashed before he dropped that idea.

He had occupied her life like a foreign army. But was that really true? Wasn't it just as true that they had created a life together? He had promised there would be no more sprees. He had a powerful will, and when he set out to accomplish something, he usually did.

The corner of her eye caught a shadow moving in the meadow and her blood jumped. A grizzly, come to stoke its endless appetite on fish. But it wasn't a bear—it was Joe, wearing his old soft fedora, flannel shirt, and braces. He'd always had a particular grace of movement in the woods, she remembered from picnics and little sorties from the Head-of-Steel camps in the earliest days, when he would come with her, gathering wildflowers. Softness, silence. Branches and thorns never seemed to catch him. As quiet as a mule deer. When he was a boy, he'd hunted to feed his family and learned to be quiet and patient in the woods.

"Iseult, the boy is here. We'd best get started."

Started for where? Her feelings were like the river—cold, fast, brutal—and she couldn't quite get hold of them. The river didn't know where it was heading and neither did she. What were they doing, going back seventeen years to search for a daughter who had barely existed? Were they looking for a beginning or an ending?

The boy drove and Joe sat in the front seat with his arm on the seatback, chatting about hunting and hockey—she had never heard him talk so easily with their own son. The washboard gravel road had been cut straight as possible through the bush so logging trucks could travel at high speed. The lodge woman had packed a lunch, which Joe had in a knapsack.

The boy told them he had built a small boat that he sailed on Mud Lake, and a radio set (*Just like Mike*, she thought), and was studying the principles of navigation. He intended to become an officer in the navy: every year the Royal Naval College in England took a few cadets from Canada, and he hoped to get one of the slots. He had never seen the ocean.

Riding in the back seat, her tongue tasted of dust. She started to feel nauseated by the stink of oil that had been sprinkled on the road in an attempt to keep the dust down.

It wasn't as though locating the spot where they'd left their infant daughter was going to make a difference to anything. The lives of her three children weighed more than the death of her first.

Krishnaji was like a lump in her throat. Disoriented, carsick, she leaned forward, lay her forehead on Joe's arm.

"Are you all right, Iseult? Do you want to stop?"

She heard him tell the boy to pull over. As soon as the car stopped she opened the door and climbed out. Spruce and Douglas fir had a clean, warm smell. She jumped across a ditch and started walking into the woods.

Krishnamurti's calm. His elegant hands, his sense, his coldness.

She kept heading away from the road, going deeper into the woods, stumbling through fragrant light and shadows of sweet-smelling spruce and fir. She could hear Joe following her but he wasn't trying to catch up. She jumped a little stream with mossy edges furrowing among the trees, a hint of dampness and sweetness rising from its trickle. He was keeping back, allowing her room. Could their marriage endure? Could it move forward and carry them along with it?

She knew, no matter how deep in she went, he would stay with her. He would never lose his sense of direction and always would be able to find his way back to the road. There wasn't much she knew for certain anymore, but she was sure of that.

She stopped, turned around. He stopped too.

"I thought I was in love with someone else," she said. "I believe I still am. Have you any idea what that means?"

He peered at her through dappled light and shadows. Life had hardened and ruined him a little, and there he stood: a businessman wearing old clothes and an old hat. Thickened around the middle, but dark and solid, tough.

Black silences, bouts of drinking, and hiding in Manhattan hotels: she had always been able to see everything that was coarse in him, and something else too, that gleam he had always had.

And what did he see, looking at her? She was dark from the California sun, and much too thin. Unkempt—had she even brushed her hair? At that moment she probably looked a little crazy.

She shut her eyes and remembered Krishnamurti's voice, his fine hands, his coolness and dispassion.

Joe turned and started back to the road.

She waited a minute or two, then followed. She came upon him filling canteens at the little stream. Kneeling on the soft moss, she splashed her face with cool, clear water. Neither of them said anything.

Had he known his plan was working? Had it been a plan?

She helped him pick up the canteens and they went back out to the road where the boy was waiting by the station wagon. They climbed in and followed the logging road for another hour until they came to the North Thompson again, and the CNR right-of-way. They left the station wagon and started hiking in along the railway tracks.

The steel rails were shiny and glinting, more substantial than she remembered. The timber sleepers were ballasted in gravel that had been tamped solid and perfectly graded. The sun was hot and the scent of tar oozing from the sleepers hung in the still air. The boy was carrying an old military rifle slung on his shoulder and Joe was telling him that miles of track had been torn up during the war and shipped to France.

A whistle echoed down the valley, and a bald eagle burst off the top of a spruce tree and went winging up the river between the tall spruces and Douglas firs crowding both banks. After walking a couple of miles they reached the point where the new line split off from the old right-of-way and crossed the river on a modern steel bridge.

It was easy enough to follow the old right-of-way, though rails and sleepers had been torn up and the grade was overgrown. It had always been a harsh country, but things grew at brutal speed during the short summers, ferns and saplings sprouting with manic energy, the forest concealing all its scars after a month or two.

As the old right-of-way sloped on its long, gradual ascent towards Tête Jaune and the Continental Divide, the trees became smaller; larches and aspen replaced fir and spruce. The right-of-way followed a rock face that Joe's blasters had dynamited out of the mountainside. The sky was clouding. The air smelled of rock and ice.

As they came around a bend, she saw a scree slope rising from one side of the grade: a massive pile of boulders, rock chips, and gravel worn away from the shoulder of the mountain. The slope looked barren, and a cold wind swept down on them as Joe left the grade and began climbing, heading straight up. Was this really where they had left their daughter in the autumn of 1912? If Joe's map told him it was so, it undoubtedly was; he never made a mistake reading a map or a chart. But there was nothing she could see that looked manmade. The bone-house had been swept away, probably by an avalanche.

Joe was going straight up the fall line, and it was difficult work catching up with him. There was no trail, no switchbacking. The incline was steep and the loose rock treacherous. Iseult and the boy started climbing, but Joe had outdistanced them. There was a glacier lacquered on the upper reaches of the mountain but she lost sight of it behind the ridge above them. The only plants were black and orange lichens. No human trace could have lasted long on such a scoured terrain.

A mountain squirrel—a pika—leapt on top of a boulder, chattered angrily at her, then dashed for cover. There was nothing of their little girl left in that place. Not a morsel for anyone to attach emotion to.

She could hear Joe grunting and puffing. Her lungs were clear—she'd never suffered asthma in these mountains. Her eyes were leaking tears, but that was on account of the sharp wind. Certainly not for their infant, who was a candle blown out, who was everywhere, but nowhere here.

Joe had halted and was standing against the steep incline, one knee bent for balance, leaning into the slope. She could hear the boy's boots clinking and scraping on the loose scree below her. Had Joe told him what they were doing, what they were looking for? Had Joe known himself? As she came up he was mopping his face with his handkerchief and wheezing from the climb.

"There's nothing here, is there, Iseult?"

Her faith in him, his faith in the power of himself—all of it had sustained considerable damage over the years. But he had brought them here to pay tribute to something besides the memory of their infant daughter, and she had to admire his courage. This place represented their marriage and its foundation days of boldness and suffering.

"We've made the trip," she told him. "That's what counts." And it was true, somehow.

"Don't know what I was thinking of," he puffed. "Crazy idea."

"No. This is a powerful place for us."

He peered at her. They were a little wrecked, a little ruined, but they were still the same people after all, and would lay their hands on what they needed in order to go on.

"I'm glad we've come," she said. "Thank you."

"Bear," the boy said sharply. "Across the river. Female and two cubs. Griz."

She looked around. On the avalanche slope that rose on the other side of the old right-of-way a grizzly was balanced on hind legs, her head dipping from side to side.

"Getting our scent," the boy had said, slipping the rifle off his shoulder.

"She won't trouble with us, will she?" She felt fear knotting in her throat. Her voice was weak. "Once she knows we're here, she'll stay away, won't she?"

"She might," said the boy, working the rifle bolt.

"Soon see," Joe said.

The bear began descending the avalanche slope, moving easily among grey smashed trees, her cubs gambolling ahead of her.

"Got a couple of stoppers in here," the boy said, patting the breech of his rifle.

She and Joe and the boy stood very close, arms and elbows touching. Fear fluted through her body and she could smell gun oil and the spruce gum the boy was cracking between his teeth.

The she-bear halted again, rose on hind legs, and waved her nose in the air.

Don't cross the river, Iseult pleaded silently. *Don't shoot. No orphans. Let us all walk to the rest of our lives from here.*

The grizzly dipped her snout and headed for the river. She began following the bank, her lithe, swaying walk almost as fluid as if she were swimming. She was heading in the opposite direction from where they had left the station wagon. The cubs splashed in and out of the water, trailing her.

"That's it, mama, keep going," the boy said.

~

The Maine morning was a surprise: clear and warm, a breeze out of the southwest. The plan was not to trouble with their neglected house or overgrown garden, but just go sailing. The old Friendship sloop had been launched and rigged and was waiting for them on her mooring at Cape Porpoise. Iseult rowed them out in the dinghy. Joe wore old grey flannel trousers with a sail tie for a belt, a white shirt with a frayed collar, tennis shoes, and an old soft hat. She wore a skirt and an old college sweater of Mike's.

The sloop had been freshly painted. While Joe attached the jib, she unfurled, loosed sheets, and began raising the mainsail. They had owned the Friendship for twelve summers and there was nothing luxurious about her: she was more barebones fishing sloop than yacht.

The cruises she had taken with Joe over the years, up and down the Maine coast, were as intimate as any time she had ever spent with him. They anchored in quiet coves and swam naked in the mornings. She always brought along binoculars and spotted for cormorants, fish hawks, puffins, porpoises, seals, while Joe logged every sighting. They would take turns at the helm, jig for mackerel, buy haddock and lobsters off the boats. After dinner she always went forward to smoke a cigarette while he washed the dishes. After covering the hatches with mosquito netting, they played blackjack by lantern light in the galley. He slept in the forward V-berth and, because he snored, she usually plugged her ears with wax, then lay in one of the galley berths and read a novel by flashlight, and after a while she slept. She never had trouble sleeping aboard. The lilting ocean was a reservoir, absorbing all her fears.

Now he let go the mooring pendant and stood in the bow, backing the jib. She held the tiller. As the sloop began falling off the wind, Joe released the jib. She sheeted it, then quickly sheeted the main. They were sailing.

Once they had rounded Goat Island and cleared the lobster pots crowded at the narrow mouth of the harbour, Joe stretched out on the foredeck, hands clasped under his head, as he often did at the beginning of a sail. She had always felt confident handling the sloop herself. Maybe on a larger boat she wouldn't be strong enough. Maybe he wouldn't either—they were both getting older. But now, on a broad reach with a clean wind and nothing in the way, she would not waste these clear blue hours worrying what was going to become of them.

Displaced Person, Part I

Sicily
11ième août 43

Margo ma chère,

 This letter is to be the wings of a dove and somehow fly between us but it's no bird, this letter. My pen is almost dry so is my mouth I can't speak. Haven't had a decent thought in days.

 I'm trying to shake myself out like the sheets we stripped from the bed that morning in Maine. Shook them, left in a bundle for the charwoman to wash and wring and hang where the sun and the clean breeze would cure them.

 You'll never get me clean, Margo, I'm afraid.

 The sun here is the same sun as in Maine or Canada. I would not believe it, but know it's true.

 There is a rifleman in Lt. Trudeau's platoon, Pvt. Blais, a farmer— no, a farmer's son. From Arthabaska.

 I'll tell you about him later.

 Planes overhead. Our planes always. The Germans possess none, apparently.

 They say we own the sky.

 The people from Brigade say that we have beaten the Germans only they do not know they are beaten, and therefore we, the infantry, will have to walk to Germany and remind them again every mile, every farm, every village, on each street corner.

 What clothes do you wear? Do your fingers touch this paper? Does the ink speak to you? How are we connected exactly, Margo? I feel more of a connection to certain bullets than to you.

I'm thinking of your wrists now.

I once knew my wife, down to her bones.

Do you have a sweet tan this summer? Comme une huronne?

Whatever sense I once had, whatever solidity I inherited from my Norman ancestors, has been beaten out of me, I think, in this growling ground. This month of things bursting.

Let me dispose of my adjectives, please. In your arms, please let me release them.

bloody,

silly,

fecal,

loud,

beaten,

red,

terror.

You see I have slipped into nouns, so let me deliver a few more. You don't have to unwrap these, Margo. Just sign for them, then you can put them away.

Child,

children,

machinegun,

antitank,

.303,

88,

tree-burst,

counterattack,

head wound,

prisoner,

neck wound,

aorta,

femoral artery

battle

And men of good cheer are singing now. In this our "rest area" the men of the Régiment 22ième are being fed hamburgers et fèves au lard puis un bouteil le chacun de Black Horse Ale. P'tit Canada dans une olivaie sicilienne.

Are your thighs still your thighs?

I'm sorry. I apologize.

O ma femme.

Is the little girl . . . no, I shall not think of her. No. I don't want her appearing in this place.

Your cunt.

I'm sorry. I apologize. Je t'en prie.

Me, I want you on your back.

I want your belly sweet and warm like sugar pie.

Anti-tank.

Howitzer.

To lose your head out here, c'est tellement facile. The 88s come cracking through olive groves at dawn, high velocity, very flat trajectory, dismembering trees. What kills is often not the shell itself but bits of riflemen, and splinters of rocks, trees. The thing comes at you like a girl you want, like a cunt, so sweet and so indirect. Soldiers in rifle companies are killed by pieces of other soldiers in rifle companies. Arms, boots, knees. I tell my platoon leaders, it's another reason to keep from bunching up which is what the boys will always do at first, like cattle, no matter their training, our battle drill.

Think of your pals, I tell them, as shrapnel, dangerous. Watch out for those flying steel helmets. A splinter of leg bone can do astonishing damage.

My Sergeant Major, on the road approaching Catania.

There.

I want you to cover me.

Three young German boys in a staff car on a road through the mountains. As little Lieutenant Duclos reported, he fully intended to offer them a chance of surrender. Only Corporal Dextraxe offered them a lively talk from his tommy gun instead. And the young lieutenant, the jesuitical prig straight out of Brébeuf, was quite cool delivering his report. He'll lose no sleep over dead Boches. It was the corporal, one of our best, a rugged forester from Megantic, who was trembling and cursing.

Their Company Commander, this is who I am. I am not your husband anymore, Margo. I don't belong to anyone but the tree bursts and right now the greasy air floating from the hamburger tent where survivors gorge.

Replacements are due up tomorrow: for my company, seventeen fresh men.

Everyone is tired.

The riflemen assure me there are beautiful, famished girls alive in the cellars of Messina who will do it with vigor for a piece of cheese. And afterwards offer you a bottle of marsala for one lousy Sweet Caps cigarette.

That Blais, the rifleman I mentioned. The imbecile got his girl pregnant last year just before going overseas. Her old man put her off to the Grey Nuns in Montreal where she had the child and was forced to give it up and is now a slavey, scrubbing floors for the Sisters, and very miserable. Her letter, which he showed me, is pathetic—do they send girls in the country to school? This one hardly makes herself understood. In any case. Will you go to the convent and see the Mother Superior to determine what can be done, you may use the name of my uncle, the bishop. The girl is Lucie something or other, from Tingwick, fifteen or sixteen years of age. Blais is a good chap and insists they will marry if he survives. Perhaps you can find her a maid's position. With the wages they're paying at the factories these days I expect in Westmount you are short of slaves.

Oh my dear. I am shook up and no one but you knows it.

Forgive. I give you my blood, my heart, my kisses for our girl.

Jean

Prodigal

THE DOORBELL RANG just as Frankie and her parents were sitting down to dinner. She exchanged glances with her mother—they weren't expecting visitors. Ever since Mike, then Johnny Taschereau, had gone overseas, a doorbell ringing unexpectedly had been enough to spook them at Skye Avenue. Mike had what sounded like a safe desk job in Africa, but everyone knew the Canadians were fighting in Sicily, and Johnny could be one of them. Margo had been having trouble sleeping. She was drinking too much lately, Frankie thought, and was often short-tempered and snappish with Madeleine, her three-year-old.

Doorbell dread was like a sliver of ice entering the intestinal tract. Her father sat at the head of the table, and even she couldn't tell what he was feeling: nerves or gloom or wonder.

Her mother nodded at Helen, the new West Indian maid, who set the salad bowl down on the sideboard with a crash and hurried to answer the door. It seemed to Frankie that her mother had become old the day the war started. She had not bought any new clothes in years. She still ran the free-milk clinic in Sainte-Cunégonde and travelled a lot and gave speeches to raise money for soldiers' families. But she never took a camera with her anymore and hadn't spent any time in her darkroom since just after Madeleine was born. When Iseult was at home, she usually stayed in bed all morning, reading stacks of mail and writing letters that Frankie typed up on the machine at her office downtown.

Without moving from her chair, Frankie glanced out the window, caught a glimpse of a taxi driving away, and felt relieved. Had her brother-in-law or brother been wounded or killed, word would have come by telegram, not by taxi.

She heard a male voice in the hall, and a moment later a gaunt brown figure in tropical uniform strolled into the dining room.

"What's for dessert?" Mike said. "Chocolate cake, I hope. All hail the returning hero."

~

When Mike went overseas, their father had blamed their mother and Uncle Grattan, which was ridiculous, Frankie thought, because Mike would have gone no matter what anyone said or thought or wrote in a newspaper column. When their father had tried to shut down his firm, a friend of Uncle Grattan's—a federal cabinet minister—told him he had to keep it going, not just to stay out of jail but also for Mike's sake. Abandoning important wartime contracts would embarrass and disgrace Mike, who would certainly feel responsible; how could he not? And hadn't Joe planned on handing the firm over to his son one day?

So her father kept the firm going, and they'd been building war things for almost three years now. Whether it was making him richer than ever, Frankie couldn't say. She only knew that during the long winter weeks after they heard Mike was wounded, when it had been so difficult getting any information about his condition, her father and mother had been kind and gentle with each other.

Even the United States was in the war by then. Maps of England, North Africa, Russia, and Italy had long since replaced the Canadian railway maps on the walls of her father's study, with red and blue pins marking every place where his son and son-in-law had been stationed.

And now Mike was home. She hardly recognized him, but he was home. Hugging him, she could feel his bones through the frayed khaki tunic he wore.

"Awfully chic, being killed," Lulu Taschereau had remarked at the Normandie Roof one evening, a few weeks before her fiancé was killed at Dieppe. Everyone at the table, including Frankie, had smiled. What life had been like before 1939, she barely remembered.

Her two serious romances so far had been with soldiers, a lieutenant with the Loyal Edmontons and an anti-tank captain in the RCA. Both might now be in Sicily, and Johnny Taschereau, who had left the Maisies to take over a company in another French-Canadian infantry battalion, the 22ième, might be fighting in Sicily too, though no one knew his whereabouts for certain. Or even if he was still alive.

Her father had not risen from his chair; he watched silently while Frankie and her mother made a female fuss over Mike. Her brother was telling them about hitching a ride on a B-17 out of Prestwick, Scotland, flying at a hundred feet across the North Atlantic. She could tell from the blue rings on his sleeve that he was now Flight Lieutenant O'Brien, equivalent to the army rank of captain. For the past year she had been booking transatlantic flights on bombers for VIP passengers. It was a glamour job and all her pals envied her, but she'd never heard of an officer below the rank of major general or air commodore rating a seat on such a flight. No soldier, no airman ever arrived home in the middle of a campaign, unannounced, without there being some piece of trouble attached. From her father's silence, from the set of his mouth, she guessed that he too sensed trouble: all kinds of suffering, sorrow, the crash of dreams.

Her brother was exotic, strange. His speech had a clipped edge now, very English. *Frightfully cold. Bloody awful.*

He'd lost weight and his teeth were blazing white in his mahogany face. He had a glow. He'd been in the desert at least a year: of course it had marked him. He had always loved the sun. What was Tunisia like in summer—dusty olive groves, or did it rain there? The brother she had known would have found the most beautiful, most deserted beach and stripped down to take a long, solitary swim in the Mediterranean.

His face was built differently somehow. He smiled in a way she didn't remember. The bones were bold in his face, giving him a ferocious look. Around his blue eyes the skin was stretched, withered. He'd had a haircut recently, shorn at the sides and neck, thicker on top.

She felt dizzy. It was the shock of seeing him. And she'd had a long day, with hardly anything to eat.

The West Indian maid was trying to put down three little plates of salad. "Set a fourth place, Helen, please," Iseult said. Just back from a fund-raising trip through the Maritimes, she looked thinner than ever.

She had spent a few days in Maine back in June and it had done her good, but now she was very pale for the middle of summer.

The chandelier twinkled in the mirror over the sideboard. It was like having a male stranger in the house. Her brother might be called handsome, but his youth was gone. He was parched, spare. War had desiccated him. His uniform was sizes too large. His face, wrists, hands were nearly as black as Helen's.

If he weren't her brother she might have fallen for him. He looked extraordinary. Damaged, too. His glow had an animal ferocity. He was no longer who he had been.

He was nodding vaguely without responding to their mother's questions: Was he on leave? How long would he stay? Frankie kept reminding herself to go and telephone Margo, but she couldn't move somehow.

As Mike approached the end of the table where their father was sitting, Joe reached out his hand, almost reluctantly. Mike's wrists thrust out from the threadbare cuffs of his uniform like polished sticks of wood. *It must be what the desert does*, Frankie told herself. The desert had polished him down to the bone. Frankie watched him grasp their father's hand and, bending over, bring it to his lips and kiss it.

For a few seconds the air was still. She heard plates clatter in the kitchen, bits of a radio program in French. The dining-room aroma of crystal, salt, lemon oil.

"Are you on leave or aren't you?" their father demanded.

Letting go his hand, Mike pulled out a chair and sat down, and Frankie started breathing again. "My orders say report to Rockcliffe Station, but I figured I was due a little unofficial leave."

Rockcliffe was the big airbase at Ottawa, and from the thrust of his jaw Frankie knew their father didn't like the sound of "unofficial leave." Light from the chandelier blinked in his spectacles like Morse code; she knew what he was thinking: *the war doesn't send home good news, ever.* A boy she remembered from kindergarten had drowned when his destroyer sank in the Strait of Belle Isle. The twins across the street had both died at Dieppe—she had heard their mother's screams. Montreal held only the sickly and the lame and the most devout French-Canadian nationalists, along with resplendently uniformed middle-aged businessmen and plenty of zoot-suiters and black marketeers. The best men were in bombers over Germany; in convoys on the North Atlantic; in England, training and waiting; or in Sicily, fighting.

Helen lay a place setting in front of Mike. Helen's fiancé was a corporal in the RMR. Their previous maid, also West Indian, had quit to follow her boyfriend, a quartermaster corporal in the Lincs and Wellands, to a training camp in Ontario. Men were moving further and further out of sight.

Where was Johnny Taschereau at that moment, while the daughter he'd never seen slept upstairs? Frankie pushed back her chair. "I'm going to call Margo." Her sister was on duty at the canteen she ran in Windsor Station. Before he went overseas Johnny had rented a flat for them on Northcliffe Avenue, but Margo had moved back to Skye Avenue when Maddie was born.

She decided to use the telephone in her father's study.

"What news of Johnny?" Mike was asking as she left the room.

~

Their father's study was stifling and dim. Canvas awnings folded the light of the summer evening in half. His ticker-tape machine had long since been extracted. He had a radio so he could listen to the war news while fussing over stocks and bonds and bank accounts and Iseult's committee accounts and ledgers.

Mike's letters had all ended up in a green metal filing cabinet, in folders meticulously arranged by date. Joe had wanted to file Johnny's letters as well but Margo insisted on keeping those in her room. His walls were covered with survey maps of southeast England, the Middle East, North Africa, and Sicily, red pins marking where Johnny Taschereau had been stationed, blue pins for Mike. Along another wall, three charts fitted together showed the coast between the mouth of the Kennebunk River and Cape Breton, Nova Scotia. Pencilled lines and pinpricks marked the courses Joe had sailed along the Maine coast, the bearings he had taken.

She knew the telephone number of Margo's canteen by heart. A troop train was coming through tonight, three battalions of a western brigade on their way to Halifax and England. Or possibly Sicily. The soldiers would want their free doughnuts and coffee, and Frankie had promised her sister she would go down and lend a hand—there were never enough volunteers for night duty. Sometimes the men were rowdy, especially if they had been on the train for days, but usually they were shy, and grateful for the coffee and doughnuts. They might have been heading off to work on the wheat harvest, or up north to the mines or the logging camps. Swagger had gone out of style, perhaps never had been the style in the towns and farmlands much of the Canadian army seemed to be from.

The phone rang and rang and she was about to hang up when one of the volunteers answered.

"No, you can't, she's busy," the girl replied, when Frankie asked to speak to Margo. "Try later. We're just getting a whole brigade in."

"This is her sister. I need to talk to her. It's important."

There was a pause. "Oh, jeepers," the girl said. "Not bad news, is it? Not about Johnny?"

"No. Can I speak to her, please?"

"Hang on a sec."

While she waited she rummaged in a desk drawer and found a pack of her father's cigarettes. She shook one out and lit it. Everyone smoked now: it was the signature of the war.

What she needed was a man her own age, someone to take her to the Normandie Roof for supper and dancing, and Ruby Foo's afterwards for jazz and Brandy Alexanders and scrambled eggs. Scanning casualty lists for names she recognized was no fun. There weren't many Montreal boys in Sicily but there were some. She needed a man present and available, not four thousand miles away fighting Germans.

"Frankie, what's wrong?" Margo sounded tense.

"Mike's home."

"What? No. He can't be, he's in North Africa."

"He came over in a bomber."

"Does he have news about Johnny? Was he in England? Have they sent him with news about Johnny?"

"What?"

"Frankie, is this some trick to get me home?"

"No, no, he doesn't know anything about Johnny. He's just come home, that's all." Frankie could hear her sister breathing.

"If there ever is bad news, you tell me right away," Margo said urgently. "Don't ever wait. Tell me right away, promise?"

"Sure."

Another pause. She listened to Margo exhale.

"I put Maddie down at six," Frankie said. "Hasn't been a peep."

"Oh, Frankie, I'm shaking. Maybe the war's almost over, maybe Johnny will be coming home soon. I'll find a cab and come right away."

~

Margo had awakened Maddie and brought her downstairs, and Mike held the sleepy little girl on his lap while he told them about sailing from Sicily to Portsmouth with hundreds of wounded soldiers, on a ship that had once carried cargoes of frozen meat from Argentina to France.

"Orders came in and I had to leave so fast, most of my kit's still in Catania. I've got shaving gear and an extra shirt, that's about all."

Frankie glanced at her sister. For all anyone knew, Johnny's regiment, the 22ième—the Van Doos—was in Sicily and Johnny might already be wounded or dead, might have been for days. Sometimes it took that long to find out. She'd heard of people getting the telegram weeks later.

"Why'd they send you back to England?" their father demanded.

Mike was touching Maddie's hair, his fingers gentle but quick and nervous. His khaki uniform was shiny at the knees and frayed at the cuffs. Frankie didn't recognize most of his ribbons. The wings on his chest signified that, desk job or not, he would always be a pilot.

Frankie now wondered if there was something wrong with him after all. His dark, latigo-leather skin reminded her of the men who had come to the kitchen door before the war, asking for handouts, odd jobs. Exhaustion was built into his every word and gesture; he seemed tired the way very fat people were fat. It had accumulated steadily and was a part of him.

He kissed the top of Maddie's head and Margo reached for her. He gave her up, then turned to their father. "Who knows? On staff you get shifted around."

"Did you hear anything about the Van Doos?" Margo said. "They're still building up in England, aren't they?"

"What are you supposed to be doing in Ottawa?" their father said.

"Haven't the faintest."

"When do you report?"

"Tomorrow afternoon will be soon enough."

"I'll drive you up."

"I can take the train, Dad."

"No. I'll drive you."

Their mother took sleepy Maddie from Margo. "Let's go upstairs, Joe. Let the children talk."

Their father stood up slowly and gazed at Mike. "You're not in trouble, are you?"

"I was sick and tired of North Africa," Mike said. "I was getting sick and tired of Sicily. Otherwise I'm fine."

"Good," said their father.

~

After their parents went upstairs the three of them shifted to the living room. Margo switched on the radio, keeping the volume low. Jazz was playing from a ballroom near an army base in Manitoba. The CBC news would come on in a few minutes. Mike offered them English cigarettes, Senior Service. Frankie preferred her Camels but she took one. She crossed the room and switched on a couple of lamps, then kicked off her shoes and curled up in their father's armchair. The yellow damask silk had stripes in alternating textures, satiny and smooth. Layers of Persian carpets in maroons and golds and purples gave the living room a dark, intense glamour. "Daddy ought to have been a Turk," Margo had said once. "He ought to have a harem. Instead he's got us."

Mike stood with his back to the fireplace; it hadn't been lit in months. Margo sat on the sofa, legs tucked beneath her. "I think we could all use a drink," she said. "How about manhattans?"

"Most definitely," said Frankie. "Do we have cherries?"

"Of course," Margo said. "Mike?"

They usually had cocktails in Margo's room before dinner while the maid gave Maddie her bath. Occasionally their mother joined them. Margo kept bottles of black market Scotch, vermouth, and rye on the floor of her closet beside her shoes. Ice, mixes, and lemons were in the kitchen.

"Glass of ginger ale for me," Mike said.

Margo cocked an eyebrow. "Surely you jest."

"I'm pretty tired."

"*Comme tu veut, mon capitaine.*" Margo left the room in her stocking feet. Frankie heard her going lightly up the stairs. Mike walked over to the sofa and sat down.

It was strange that no one in her office had noticed her brother's name on a passenger list. They always had a cable manifest from Prestwick listing transatlantic passengers, because one of her duties was fixing up VIPs with connecting flights to Washington or New York or wherever they were going.

He had pulled off his brown shoes and now swung his feet up and lay back on the cushions. Jazz blew softly from the radio. She could hear Margo come downstairs and go into the kitchen to fix their drinks.

"Daddy's building a sailboat for you," Frankie said.

"Oh Christ." He wasn't looking at her. His eyes were closed. There were veins like worms at his temple.

"It won't be finished until after the war." She could hear Margo cracking ice into glasses. "So how come they flew you home? Are you a Very Important Person?"

He lay on the chintz sofa like someone who'd had all the war beaten out of him. She thought of their uncle coming back from his war, throwing himself into the Lachine Canal, if that wasn't just a story. It sounded more like something their father might have done—he who'd always been capable of actions mysterious, self-destructive, and passionate.

Margo came in with drinks on a tray. Frankie took hers and immediately plucked out the bright red cherry and ate it. Cherries soaked in rye and vermouth were a food she could live on, though a girl she knew who nursed at the army hospital in Lachine had pointed out that cocktail cherries were exactly the colour of fresh blood.

Mike sat up and took one sip of his ginger ale, then put the glass down on the floor and started pulling off his blue necktie and unbuttoning his khaki shirt. Frankie watched, fascinated, as he pulled the shirttail out of his pants. He undid the last buttons and turned to face his sisters, pulling the shirt open and exposing his chest. In the soft glow of silk lampshades Frankie could see four or five raised scars on his chest and abdomen, small thick stitchings, pale against his dark skin. Each approximately the size and shape of a cigarette.

"Oh, Mike," Margo said.

Would everyone who came home come with wounds? Why must he show Margo his scars? She'd only be imagining her husband's body torn and punctured.

"Feel this," Mike said, touching one of the scars. "Healed up pretty good. I was pretty sore but the swelling's gone down."

"But you were wounded last year," Margo said. "There's nothing wrong with you now."

"I've had trouble breathing. It gets clogged up for a while, then clears. They thought it was asthma. I finally saw a Canadian army doc in Sicily. He did X-rays and saw something in my chest, a piece of shrapnel. That's when they sent me back to England. Feel," he said. "They don't really feel so bad."

Margo stood with her drink and cigarette in one hand, her other hand cupping her elbow. She didn't move. The CBC news had started but they weren't listening. Frankie put down her drink, got up and walked over to the sofa, and knelt on the floor. Her brother took her fingers and guided them. She touched a rippled scar and the dark skin underneath, hard and firm.

"I was boarded in London. The air force docs said, get up to Scotland and hitch the first ride home you can. I hung around Prestwick three days before there was room."

Margo knelt beside Frankie, and he took Margo's fingers and guided her. "My lungs are infected. I read my file on the plane. They think I'm going to die."

Margo said, "That's crazy."

"You can read the file if you want, Margo."

"Air force doctors are quacks. Daddy'll get you a real doctor." Margo jabbed her cigarette between her lips and started buttoning up their brother's shirt. "If you're sick, Daddy can get you into a real hospital. You're tired, that's all. You're home now. We'll take good care of you."

Mike reached out and took the cigarette from Margo's mouth. Frankie could see the cork tip reddened from her sister's lipstick. Mike took a puff. "Maybe you're right," he told them. "I feel pretty good right now."

Displaced Person,
Part II

Margo O'B. Taschereau
10 Skye Avenue
Westmount, P.Q.

15th August

Dear Jean,

*Still no word from you, will you please drop a line, we're all
terribly worried.*

Are you in Sicily? We think you must be.

*Mike is home, and very ill. He flew across from Scotland and
walked in the door the night before last. Daddy is having him seen by
Wilder Penfield. He was never properly treated after being wounded
last year.*

*As I wrote in my last, Madeleine and I are very happy here at
No. 10. It suits us. But things are a bit hectic here now . . . Daddy's
arranging for Mike to be removed from the air force hospital and sent
to the Royal Vic . . .*

*I know you wanted us to keep up the Northcliffe flat but it was
just too bleak there, Jean, you really wouldn't have wanted me to stay.
We couldn't get anyone to clean the place and N.D.G. is not my cup
of tea. Never was, never will be. After the war we'll find something
much nicer. Mother and Frankie are such a help with Maddie. At this
very moment Frankie is giving her a bath, I hear her splashing. She's
a lucky little girl to have her aunt and grandparents taking care of
her while her papa is overseas. This morning at breakfast Daddy was*

feeding her scrambled eggs off his plate. Very sweet! I only wish you could have seen it.

I hope you're safe wherever you are, dearest.

Please, say a prayer for Mike . . .

The things you put in your letters . . .

I understand how hard it is for you to be separated from the people you love.

You're a passionate man.

When this is over and we're together once more I'll be able to show you that I love you.

All you expect of me, all you want—I'll try to be all those things but I don't know if I am able. If I fail your expectations, what will you do then? In some ways my life is easier now that you are so far away. Wartime. A perfectly good excuse not to bother each other.

Our girl is good and sweet. She is in love with balls, any sort— balloons, tennis balls, golf balls, baseballs, rubber bouncing balls. She saw the globe in Daddy's study and reached out shouting ba, ba, ba.

Listen Jean I'm cold without you. Whatever it is in you that throws me out of whack, I need that now. The days are the days are the days.

Mike is awfully thin and brown as a negro. Are you so thin? Oh Jean sometimes I want to scream at this letter paper, or lick it, chew it. I'd like to destroy my own weakness. I want to snap the pen in half and throw it out the window.

Will we ever travel? I want to see Rome. France. I want to see Paris with my husband, who was an officer in the War.

I hope the doctors can help Mike. Frankie read his charts, he had malaria.

You were always complaining that I was not affectionate enough, that you were made to feel unsure of my love, that my feelings for you were small and inaccessible. And I remember you saying any number of times that I did not understand myself.

As if you did, Jean.

It made me angry to hear you say those things and I was afraid you could be right. But now I know I must have you in a life of trouble. And lately I feel inside a sense of luck about everything, and an openness, Johnny, that wasn't there before.

Before you went away I felt this way only once or twice, when you were inside me. I tried to tell you but you weren't prepared to listen because you were a man going off to the war. Now it's with me almost all the time, this feeling, the very opposite of foreboding. I don't know where it comes from, Johnny. Joy. All the things the nuns said about you, most of the warnings were true, but I still don't care. I know now that you are going to survive and come home. I have seen in dreams, don't laugh, you and me and Maddie together. I'll be everything for you and we'll make more babies won't we. When the war is over and you've come home we'll go away for a good long time. We'll go down to Maine, or up north. I'll want you to tell me everything you have seen and felt. And then we'll leave the war behind us and walk into the rest of our lives.

I think you have to keep yourself within yourself and not give too much to your men and when you are feeling very low, get some sleep. Pray for my brother. Everyone here sends love,

yours xxx Marg

~

Re: R94274 O'Brien F/L M.F. R.A.F.

Nov 9 42 NZ Gen Hosp, Helwan. Adm from No.4 ADS. Multiple shrapnel wounds. 13 frags removed from chest r shoulder and neck. Post-op generalised pain, anorexia and sleeplessness 14 days. Headache, backache, slight cough. Discharged after 28 days.

March 19 43 RAF Wadi Sirru. Intermittent febrile. Patient had malaria Egypt 42, took quinine and Atabrine, which made him quite yellow and dark in colour. Treated by Aspirin at Station Sick Quarters with some relief.

May 20 43 55th Gen Hosp. Tunis. C/of chest pain and shortness of breath. No history asthma but possible pneumonia. Malaria in Egypt 42.
Discharged May 22

Aug 5 43 No. 1 Cdn Gen. Hosp. Catania Sicily. Appears wasted and cachectic. Tall, brown, sick looking. Reps. feels well when not febrile. Chest X rays indicate infected pleural effusion at nidus of foreign body in chest cavity. Needle aspirate verified fluid collection. Tentative diagnosis empyema chest cavity. Recommend imm. repatriation

August 8 43 Station Sick Quarters, 78 Wing Ashburton,
Devon. 102.5°. Pains in chest. Weight loss. Indigestion.
Loss of appetite. Reps difficulty breathing as if a
balloon in his chest. Consumed large no's of Aspirin.
This man is a very healthy-appearing man -- good
physical specimen without any complaints except
occasional fever and shortness of breath.
1. Loss of strength, duration 7 mos.
2. Loss of wt. - Dec 42 wt 193 lbs - Aug 5 /43 wt 173.

9 Aug 43 No 11 Canadian Gen Hosp, Taplow. Xrays reveal
empyema in chest cavity prob. from shrapnel wound
Nov 42 in ME. Pleural effusion with fluid collection.
Referred to RCAF Medical Board London for repat.

Aug 10 43 RCAF Med Board London. Recommend immediate
Repat. to Canada.

~

Hon. Charles Power, P.C.
Minister for Air,
Ottawa
14th August 1943

Dear Chubby,

Re: R94274 O'Brien F/L. M.F. R.A.F.

My son who left for overseas in October 1939, and has
since then spent considerable time in England, Africa
and Sicily with the R.A.F., was wounded in Egypt and
since then has been off and on between duty in various
hospitals.

For the past five weeks he has been, as near as I can
gather, a sort of specimen for all the passing doctors
to examine, and finally, about ten days ago, the
attention of the R.C.A.F. Medical Board in London was
called to his case.

They, I am glad to say, acted with promptitude and sent
him back to Canada by plane. He has at least a serious
infection in his chest, and an immediate operation

may be essential. I drove him to Rockcliffe Station on
Sunday, where he immediately went to hospital. I now
understand that he is to come to the Lachine R.C.A.F.
hospital tomorrow.

I want him placed at once in either the Royal Victoria
or the Neurological Hospitals here and I want Dr.
Wilder Penfield or an equally competent man to perform
the operation.

Sincerely,
Joe

~

Re: R94274 O'Brien F/L M.F. R.A.F.

Aug 15 43 RCAF Station Rockcliffe Hosp. F/L O'BRIEN
was x-rayed. Tall, thin, brown and looks chronically
ill. Empyema chest cavity pr shrapnel. Needle aspirate
confirmed fluid.

August 18 43 No.3 Command Medical Board Hosp., Lachine.
Foreign body in chest cavity about size of apple seed.
Bed rest, APC & C for pain.

20 August 43 - at request Dep Minister (Air) trans
to Royal Vic Hosp for consultation with Dr Penfield.
Appears not acutely ill.

August 21 43 Chest X-rays ind. nidus of foreign body in
chest cavity . . . empyema verified via needle aspirate
of fluid collection. Dr Penfield cons. Patient obviously
in terminal stages. Nothing further can be done.

Aug 23 43 Royal Victoria Hospital Montreal P.Q.
Post-exam marked by pt. running extremely low temp.
Complained first 2 days of chest pain . . . appetite did
not return. Felt miserable, short of breath, soreness.
Went downhill very rapidly, expired 9:19 pm. Permission
for autopsy could not be obtained.

Ritual, Part I

F RANKIE WAS IN the sewing room trying to occupy herself with tasks when a maroon van turned the corner from Murray Hill. Slipping under the late summer canopy of leaves, it came to a quiet stop in front of the house.

She stood by the window and watched two men wearing dark suits slide the coffin onto a trolley and start rolling it up the front walk. No one else was home except the maid, Helen, and the cook. Margo had taken Madeleine to the park and their parents were at Central Station to meet Father Tom, who was coming up from Washington to say the funeral Mass.

She didn't hear the doorbell ring. Helen must have been waiting at the front door to let them in. Frankie sat down and resumed picking thread from the seam of the dress she planned to wear. It was one of Margo's and needed to be taken in a couple of inches. They usually sent things out to be altered but there wasn't going to be enough time before the funeral.

Her parents and sister had still not returned an hour later, when she finally started downstairs. It was only her brother, she kept reminding herself. She didn't have to be afraid of him.

The house was dreadfully still and perfectly clean. The grandfather clock stood on the stairway landing like some staunch, domineering patriarch, some would-be emperor of the house, clubbing down her courage with its angry ticking. Helen and the cook were probably napping in their rooms off the kitchen. Frankie heard rain sizzling through the trees, tires seething on Murray Hill Avenue.

Bunches of hothouse lilies were in ugly vases everywhere she looked. Crossing the hall, she stopped at the entrance to the living room. The coffin was set on some sort of iron stand in front of the fireplace. A hulk of polished wood. So false, so unhappy.

She didn't want to go any nearer but she had no choice. She must not give in to livid fear of the thing. She owed her brother that much. She suddenly remembered him in California, rushing and cool, sensitive. In a white T-shirt and dark glasses, at the wheel of their old station wagon. Steering over Casitas Pass, one hand on the wheel, one slender brown arm propped at the window.

Her fingers found the edge of the lid. Testing, she tried to raise it. Only a section was designed to open, and it opened smoothly, on silent hinges. She raised it an inch, two inches. It was surprisingly easy. She raised it all the way.

The inside was lined with white satin, and there he was. Nothing living could ever be that still.

The undertakers had found him a perfect blue air force uniform. What had been done with his desert khaki? Had the hospital burned those clothes or had her father saved them?

His eyes were thoroughly closed. His expression was probably what the undertaker had meant by "peaceful," but it looked like death to her, nothing else. Like a Russian field or village the Germans had smashed through, trampled and wrecked. You couldn't call him peaceful without being dishonest.

They had done something to his face—powdered it, maybe—and his features had blurred, somehow, softened, so he didn't look as thin anymore. Had they stuffed his cheeks with something? The fierce red gold of his desert tan was gone. His skin was matte. The wild glow of strange ersatz healthiness had been extinguished. There was nothing radiant about him now.

She started whispering, *fuck cunt fuck, cunt fuck shit, cunt*—a challenge or a banshee wail or just an exhalation.

~

When Elise arrived that evening, Iseult had already gathered a dozen photographs of Mike from the volumes in Joe's study and arranged them in her bedroom. Frankie sat at her mother's dressing table brushing her hair while green summer light knocked through the layers of fat leaves on the old maple outside. Her mother and aunt lay alongside each other on the bed, holding hands.

Frankie studied the lush green canopy outside the window. It was stormy weather, oddly cold for late summer, and the leaves were flopping and flailing, showing their pale undersides. It was strange to think of the world still green and growing and smelling of mud, and her brother with no part in it.

Elise said, "I really don't know what we all bothered growing up for if war's all there is. Grattan thinks it'll last three more years at least. I wish we had stayed on the boardwalk. Do you remember the light there?"

"Do you really think the light was so different then?" said Iseult.

"Sure. There was more of it; the shadows weren't so deep, either. It was a washing light."

"Sea light. Ocean light. I remember the white light in that empty cottage on the canal."

"It was the light of the world before everything went bad."

"You don't really believe so, Elise. You're not really a romantic."

"No, I probably don't. I don't know what I believe. Maybe I never have believed in very much, or in anything at all, except that a certain ratio of time and light and optics will give you an image, and if you splash it on the right paper with the right chemicals, you can fix it. You can stop time. I believe in that, but not a heck of a lot else lately. You should have seen those prancing admirals and field marshals and whatnot at the Chateau Frontenac with their aides de camp polishing their buttons for them. Blood merchants." Elise had been in Quebec City earlier in the summer photographing Churchill and Roosevelt at their conference.

"It's no use talking like that," Iseult said. "The war had to be fought. We agreed that it did."

"I don't remember Joe agreeing," Elise said.

Iseult swung her legs off the bed, stood up, and walked to the window in her stocking feet.

"Whether he did or not, it doesn't matter," she said. "Mike would not have been Mike if he hadn't wanted to go."

Frankie had hardly seen her father since they'd returned home from the hospital the night before. He was holed up in his study. What would he do now? they were all thinking. How would he behave at the funeral, and after?

"What about Johnny?" Elise asked. "Any news?"

"No," Frankie said. Her sister hadn't had a letter in weeks. Johnny's silence was a torment and Margo couldn't sleep.

"Come and lie down now, sweetie," Elise said to Iseult. "No one can handle something like this alone."

"I wish I'd never met him," her mother said quietly. Her back was to them; she was still looking out the window. "I wish I'd never gone out to the ocean in the first place. I wish I'd stayed in Pasadena, where it was warm and dry and bright."

Her parents had better find a way of sharing their grief with each other, Frankie thought, or neither of them was going to make it.

"I wish I'd never had children," her mother said quietly. "I just can't bear it, Elise."

Frankie suddenly wanted to leave the room. Leave the house. Leave the country, leave her family behind. Be in a foreign city, even a ruined one, with bombs falling. Putting down the hairbrush, she stood up and headed for the door. Her stocking feet made no noise on the rug.

Iseult was still at the window with her back to them. Frankie couldn't tell if her mother was crying or not. Maybe she was just trying to lose herself in the thick, wet rustle of leaves and the cool air floating through the screen.

"Where's your father?" Elise asked as Frankie was opening the door to let herself out.

Frankie shrugged. "The study."

"He blames me, Elise," her mother said from the window. "He won't say it but he does, and I know just how he feels. There has to be someone to blame."

Frankie shut the door quietly and took herself back to her own room. She lay on her bed and stared at the ceiling and clenched her fists. Sometimes she felt like the centre of the world. Other times she felt like a meaningless fragment of something else, a nothing, a dust mote, a scrap of wind with no feelings, no constant direction, no purpose. That was the way she felt now. Her room was no refuge; it was just a box of green light borrowed from the trees outside. She'd never feel desirous again. Her heart was just a piece of meat. She would never get what she wanted—she'd never know what she wanted. So she'd never be satisfied, and it wouldn't matter.

~

Father Tom O'Brien, SJ, was more or less a stranger. Her father used to call him the Little Priest, which had puzzled Frankie when she was small, since Father Tom was so much taller than her father. Now the white-haired priest was a dean at Georgetown University. He was still lean and handsome and resembled Grattan much more than either of them resembled her father. It was as if Joe had taken the weight of his family onto his shoulders and it had shortened, thickened, and bent him while his brothers remained spare, elegant, erect.

During the afternoon visitations Father Tom sipped tea or vermouth and chatted amiably with their multitude of guests, but Frankie noticed that after an hour or so he always managed to slip away. On the second afternoon she followed him upstairs and watched him go down the corridor to the door of her father's study, where he stopped and knocked. There must have been some response, because a moment later he let himself in, closing the door softly behind him.

Slipping off her shoes, she had approached the study door and listened to their murmuring voices inside. If she'd knocked, would her father have let her in? Instead of returning to the gruesome party it would have been much better to lie on his horsehair sofa, the way she used to as a little girl when she'd been ill and unable to go to school and he'd let her stay there all afternoon covered with his Hudson's Bay blanket, watching him working at his desk.

But even as she stood there the doorbell was ringing and more visitors were swarming in at the front door. Her mother and sister needed her. Her loyalty to them was stronger than her need to see her father, so she turned and went back along the corridor, pausing at the top of the stairs to put her shoes back on.

~

Her father was like a summer fog bank lurking up in the Bay of Fundy, impenetrable and dangerous, no telling which direction he would blow. Since the night of Mike's death, when they all returned from the hospital together, crowded in a taxi, he had withdrawn from them completely. He would have nothing to do with greeting their visitors downstairs.

Selfish, Frankie thought. *Hard-hearted*. Her mother needed him, but he as usual was thinking of no one but himself. Frankie told her sister she was afraid he'd start drinking again and disgrace them all in public at the funeral.

"I don't know why *she* doesn't start drinking," Margo said. "I'd be knocking them back if I were her, and to hell with Daddy."

"He's not drinking," Father Tom had assured them. "He's suffering, as you all are, but I am hopeful he will start to look for the mercy of God. It is there, you know, and if he looks for it, it will find him."

Tom and her father were getting up at dawn every day to walk across the playing fields in Murray Park and down the hill to the parish church, where the Little Priest said early morning Mass. Afterwards they'd go to a greasy spoon on Victoria Avenue for breakfast.

When Frankie asked Tom if her father had anything to say, the priest told her they talked about the war and about their childhood. "We had a wicked stepfather, and to your father in memory he seems like Satan incarnate. He really was nothing more than a pathetic old drunk, but we saw him abuse our mother and our sisters, and of course that had some effect."

"Do you think he will go to New York?" Frankie asked.

"I couldn't say," Father Tom admitted. "When we were young we all looked up to him. He took care of us the best he was able. He lost his faith a long time ago, or thinks he did. I'm telling him the mysteries are incarnate, they live, but he's a hard case, your father. Sometimes he's even got me half-thinking he may be right, that there's nothing more to life than death and numbers."

~

They entertained two hundred visitors during the two days her brother's body lay at home. Every room downstairs was packed with the hateful white lilies. After Frankie or Margo greeted them at the front door, the visitors were shown into the living room to pay their respects. Whatever that meant. Standing by Mike's open coffin, most people looked uneasy. If they were Catholic, they crossed themselves. If not, they just looked solemn. Females were inclined to dab at a tear or two. Two minutes were sufficient, then the visitors stepped towards the dining room, shrugging off their gloom to join a gay crowd being regaled with salmon sandwiches and egg salad sandwiches, different sorts of cake, cheese straws from Dubois's *pâtisserie*, tea, coffee, and whisky.

On both days the last visitors didn't leave before seven o'clock. Frankie had never experienced the sort of raw tiredness she felt then. Her voice was pitched a half-tone deeper; she sounded to herself like a record playing too slowly. Margo and her mother were the same. If this was mourning, then mourning was mostly voracious tiredness, a longing for rest. But no matter how many hours Frankie lay in her bedroom, sleep was thin and fitful. She hated the garrulous visitors, but being alone in her room was worse.

Both evenings, after the last visitors left, a taxi pulled up outside and disgorged four little nuns. They were from Sacred Heart Convent, and one of them, the white-haired, pink-cheeked Soeur Saint-Nom-de-Marie, had taught Frankie geography and Margo French. When the Sisters arrived, everyone emerged from their bedrooms and trooped downstairs clutching rosary beads. They knelt on the Persian rugs while Father Tom led them through one chaplet of the rosary: the Apostles' Creed, an Our Father, and fifty Hail Marys, the family praying in English, the nuns in French.

Frankie had been saying these prayers all her life; they fit her mouth, and she could recite them without thinking. Thinking always seemed to lead in a blasphemous direction. She could accept that God existed, but why would he care if anyone prayed to him or not? How much adoration could an all-powerful deity need or want before it started to sicken him?

Then Helen brought in tea and plates of sandwiches and cookies left over from the afternoon's horde.

"*Mais ton frère a l'air si heureux!*" Soeur Saint-Nom-de-Marie squeezed Frankie's arm with her bony little hand. *"Il a trouvé la paix du Christ!"*

Really? Happy? Peace? When Frankie had looked into the coffin, she'd seen only absence, disappearance.

The dead must not be left alone—that was the custom—and the nuns would spend the night in the living room sitting with Mike's body. They had brought their sewing baskets. They were the only ones who seemed entirely comfortable, cheerful even, in the presence of death. They enjoyed leafing through the *Life* magazines and *National Geographic*s, and Frankie's mother tuned the dial to Radio-Canada so they would be able to hear the news in French. Their bright chatter sounded like a flock of small birds in the living room.

An hour later Frankie was lying in bed with the current issue of *Life* when there was a knock on her door.

"Come in."

Margo was wearing her red doeskin dressing gown and holding a drink in her hand, a short one, the ice cubes clicking as she shut the door and came over to sit down on the edge of Frankie's bed. "Frankie, tell me honestly. Is Johnny going to come home?"

Frankie put down her magazine and reached for her cigarettes from the night table.

"Just tell me," Margo said. "Yes or no."

"Yes."

For a long time Margo looked at her without saying anything. She needed Frankie to say yes, and maybe it didn't matter if Frankie really knew or not. How could she? Not for sure, not enough to put money on. If the war were a barbotte game she'd have picked up her money and quit the table.

She shook out a cigarette for her sister and one for herself and lit them both. They puffed in silence. She could smell the winey fragrance of the cocktail. Ice cubes crackled and a gust of rain dashed against the window. The trees were swaying. Summer was turning to fall, and the next day, the day of the funeral, was predicted to be cold, blustery, and wet.

The drifting smoke of their cigarettes was so thick it looked blue in the light, but Frankie didn't mind: it slowed things down. Suddenly

Margo, without saying a word, put her glass down on the floor, pulled aside the covers, and climbed into bed with her.

They hadn't shared a bed since they were children in a Pullman berth on the way home from California. Frankie let her magazine fall to the floor and reached to switch off the light. Rolling onto her side, she threw her arm over Margo's hip and pressed herself against the solid warmth of her body. In the darkness Frankie could smell their cigarette smoke and the nauseating ripeness of the lilies. Their parents were old and wounded and could no longer pretend to protect them, or even each other. At least Margo had a daughter and—if Johnny Taschereau was still alive—a husband. But Frankie was alone, definitely. She'd not realized just how alone a death could make her feel.

~

No one cried in church except a couple of Mike's old flames, girls he'd taken to dances at Victoria Hall: all married women now. Their mother did not, and Margo didn't, though she was very near.

Frankie wouldn't. Of course it was vanity. Of course it was pride. Pride was nothing to be proud of, Frankie told herself, but it could get you through certain situations.

Her mother had asked her to write Mary Cohen to let her know. "Let her know what?" Frankie had snapped. Let her know she was an idiotic bitch for dumping Mike? That he had been too good for her? Or let her know she'd been wise not to hitch her nuptial wagon to a dying, now dead, star? But Frankie had indeed written to Mary Brayton, née Cohen, wife of Commander Douglas Brayton, USNR, in San Diego, though she wouldn't have received the letter yet.

The undertaker's men had brought the coffin to the church early that morning. Now it was front and centre, just before the altar rail, wrapped in a Red Ensign, and six airmen in blue uniforms sat erect in a side pew: the honour guard. A shiny air force flatbed truck was parked outside on Sherbrooke Street. When the funeral Mass was over, the airmen would carry the coffin out and slide it onto their truck, which would haul it over the hill to Côte-des-Neiges Cemetery.

She still didn't know how her father would handle the funeral. For two days people had been congratulating her on her family's "remarkable stoicism."

"*Ça montre la force de ta foi,*" whispered Lulu Taschereau.

The power of her faith? How could she respect people, even old friends of the family like Lulu, who said things like that, who built their nests of words and wouldn't leave them? Poor Lulu had gotten awfully devout, was always after Frankie and Margo to go with her to dawn Mass at Saint-Léon-de-Westmount.

Frankie went into Mike's room, found his *Oxford Pocket Dictionary* on a bookshelf above an old radio he had built, and looked up

sto·i·cism *noun* emotional indifference, especially admirable patience
and endurance shown in the face of adversity

As she put the book back on the shelf she wondered just how much patience and endurance her father possessed.

Mike's radio was a naked collection of tubes, dials, and wires. He had built it almost by instinct: the first radio in their house. She remembered Margo teasing him, and their mother hadn't liked it either: the sour smell of solder and all the time he'd spent alone, tinkering, up in his room. Their brother had been thirsty for outside connection, was determined to send and receive. He'd never been afraid of the world.

While he was in hospital she had felt blindly impatient, even angry. How dare he fly across the ocean like a piece of evil news, knowing it would tip the fanatic balance, send their father back into his dark forest like a misguided child in a nasty German fairytale?

She had tried telling herself that once the dying was over and done with, there'd be no use moping. They would all just have to get on with their lives.

Over and done with. Get on with our lives.

Language thickened like cake mix unless you were watchful—and she was no better than anyone else. Those phrases tasted like rough straw in her mouth now. They sickened her.

Iseult would never, ever break down in public, never hand her grief around, and Frankie had made up her mind that she wouldn't either. Certainly not in the chill grey church, one of six parish churches the O'Brien Capital Construction Company had built for the archdiocese twenty years before. She was holding hands with Elise, who was crying quietly. Cousin Virginia—a University of Toronto grad with a master's degree, unmarried at thirty-one and exceedingly proud of her job as secretary to an important cabinet minister—sniffled from time to time.

Margo was doing her best to be *stoic*, though close-up, Johnny's absence and silence showed on her like a wound.

Frankie wondered if what she was feeling could be called grief. People would say it was, of course they would, but it was hard to collate her feelings into a single noun. *Grief* suggested a stately music that her feelings entirely lacked. They were as squalid and messy as dirty sheets in a room reeking of last night's cigarette smoke. Her grief was charred with resentment and tasted foul. It could be that grieving her brother was another test she'd fail. One that she ought to have passed, and would have, if she hadn't been so irresponsible and lazy.

The church smelled of wet wool and nylons and hair tonic and too many people, most of them strangers. It was damp and chilly, but when Margo had phoned ahead to ask the sacristan to turn on the furnace, he'd refused. "Still only August, miss, after all."

Frankie's knee kept scraping on a sharp corner of the Speed Graphic hanging by its strap from one of her purse hooks. If that damn camera started a run in her last pair of silk stockings, that would be the end. She'd peel them off and toss them into the grave with the coffin and let Elise, or her mother, take a picture of it. Or maybe she'd smash the Speed Graphic first and throw it in too.

She'd only noticed the bulky camera as they were leaving the house. It was her mother's but Elise was carrying it, the strap over her shoulder.

"What are you doing with that?"

Elise shrugged. "Your mother wants me to take some pictures."

"It's part of his life. I want it recorded," her mother said calmly.

"What for? It's not a wedding, it's a funeral! No one takes pictures at funerals!"

Their mother's determination to register their childhoods with almost daily photography had annoyed them all, although Frankie had figured out early that Iseult needed to capture them on film because that first baby had slipped in and out of life so fast. When she was small, her mother used to claim she remembered the baby perfectly, that in fact she had looked an awful lot like Frankie. Later Frankie learned that Margo had been told the same thing, and Margo as a youngster was blonde and chubby, whereas Frankie had always been Black Irish and bony. Probably their mother didn't remember anything about the baby they'd left in a grave that no one had been able to find again, so that it was almost as if she had never been born—which raised questions Frankie had always been willing to leave lying there unexplored, like bad neighbourhoods. It was no use getting too steep, deep, and philosophical when you were living with your parents, unmarried, uncollected, and semi-educated.

Her mother photographed them to hold on to them, so they would not disappear. And the damn snapshots had often got in the way of—been a substitute for—actual holding. Frankie had never forgotten spilling off her bicycle on Murray Hill Avenue and skinning her knees, and her mother galloping out of the house with the little Leica and stopping to snap a picture before comforting her.

And now, recruiting Elise to shoot Mike's funeral. It was too bloody much. "No, Mother! Not today. No camera! No pictures! I won't let you!"

And there on the front steps, while the undertaker's unholy limousine grumbled at the curb, Frankie let loose her one and only crying jag. Her mother burst into tears too, and her father squinted at them as though they were the front page of a newspaper he was trying to read.

Under a black silk umbrella, in cold, dripping late summer rain, Frankie wailed and shook like a sick cat, ruining her mascara, while Cousin Virginia clumsily tried to hug her. Margo lit a cigarette and finally took charge, leading Frankie back inside and upstairs, sitting her down on the toilet seat, and gently washing her face while the rest of them waited in the Packard.

"It's not so terrible," Margo soothed. "She needs to, that's all. You have to let things happen. We'll probably be glad to have the pictures when we're old."

By then Frankie was sitting on the john, smoking, while Margo powdered her face. Frankie hated to think of their brother's life receding to nothing but photographs. She didn't want to think of herself in twenty or thirty years looking at pictures of his funeral. By then he'd just be compounds of light and dark on pieces of treated paper. Just a bit of chemistry.

Her father sat in the pew like a freshly sedated casualty while the choir belted out the Dies Irae. Frankie hadn't been to many funerals, at least not where the body was present, but she had been to four memorial services for boys killed overseas, and at Catholic ceremonies the Dies Irae had always been sung. She glanced at the English translation on the specially printed Mass card:

> *Day of wrath! O day of mourning*
> *See fulfilled the prophets' warning,*
> *Heaven and earth in ashes burning*

Then she dropped the card back into the hymnal rack. Who needed more burning and ashes?

She looked at her father sitting at the other end of the pew. She and Margo had both worried he would come downstairs drunk, but he'd been perfectly sober so far, and well turned out: shoes gleaming, hair combed, suit pressed. As far as she knew the only liquor in the house was the stash of bottles in Margo's closet and what remained of two mixed cases of Scotch, rye, gin, and vermouth her mother had her buy for the visitation days and the reception after the cemetery. The day after Mike died, Frankie had gone downtown and placed the booze order with Jockey Fleming, the black market hustler who kept a newsstand at the corner of Peel and St. Catherine, one block from her office in the Mount Royal.

"Jeez, Frankie, these days that's a lot of liquor, practically a boatload," the little hustler had said. He was a Jew from Griffintown, with hands like monkey's paws. "Good stuff's getting hard to come by. For the wake, am I right?"

"That's right, Jock, and the visitation. Can you deliver?"

"I'll get the goods, by scrim or by scram. For you, Frankie. Honour of your brother."

"Thanks, Jock. And good stuff, right?"

"On my mother's grave, the best, I promise. I'll send it up tomorrow in a cab."

Over the past couple of days their visitors had gone through plenty of drink, but she calculated there was just enough left over for today's shindig. The booze was stored in the pantry in preparation for the wake or reception or party or whatever it was called. Hordes would be coming back to Skye Avenue expecting food and drink, and there'd be plenty of everything: Scotch, gin, rye, vermouth, baked hams, a salmon, plates of cocktail sandwiches, cream of mushroom soup, sausage rolls, cakes. Frankie had hired a bartender from Mother Martin's. He'd probably be pouring more Scotch than gin: people seemed to prefer dark liquor in dark weather, and the day was dark, wet, and blowy, perfect weather for death.

Her father was looking stunned, and dapper. He'd be damned if he'd let anybody pity him. He could almost pass for stoic, but how long before he caught the next train for New York? She had checked the timetables. The Delaware and Hudson's Montreal Limited was scheduled to leave at eight p.m.

It was Iseult who looked shabby and bereft in a cloth overcoat she had been wearing since the war began, a small, unappealing hat, and two runs in her stockings, which Frankie had noticed as they were getting out of the undertaker's car in front of the church.

Margo, like their father, was still trying for stoic, and maybe it was working. Or maybe she was just numb from all her brooding over Johnny. They had been married in this church. Maybe he'd fallen for a beautiful Englishwoman who lived in a castle and rode to hounds. Maybe he was fighting in Sicily. Maybe he was already wounded, captured, dead. Maybe it had occurred to Margo that the next time they put themselves through this hoopla it might be all about her husband. Numb, Frankie thought, could easily be mistaken for stoic. And vice versa.

Elise was holding their mother's hand. Elise at least was openly crying—she and her daughter, Virginia, were the only ones. Virginia was sniffling and blowing her nose in her hanky. She might be gawky and gauche but she was a good egg. Elise wasn't making noise but the tears were galloping down her cheeks. With everything she had been through during and after the last war, she had survived. Her marriage had survived; her husband had recovered. Elise was strong enough, though not stoic.

But looking at her parents and her sister squeezed in the family pew in the cold, smelly church, Frankie thought how low they seemed—defeated, almost broken. Part of her loved them all, loved them more than ever, wanted to cherish them and would do almost anything to protect them, and another part of her just wanted to get the hell out of there.

~

R.C.A.F.
No. 34 Service Flying Training School
Medicine Hat, Alta.

25th August 43

Dear Iseult and Joe,

We send them out of here trained aircrew -- they
ship overseas and the air force has statisticians that
could tell you exactly the percentage that survive for
exactly how long -- what sort of business is this? Why
do we give our boys war? God damn me, Joe. God damn me.
God damn everything.

love, sorrow oh christ
G

Ritual, Part II

THE HONOUR GUARD fired three brisk volleys. The noise hurt: Frankie had to stop herself from clapping her hands over her ears. Father Tom muttered incantations and the coffin was lowered in on a couple of dodgy-looking canvas straps. Her father was staring into the hole, raincoat unbuttoned and flapping in the wind. He looked like a bewildered bird that couldn't get off the ground because the wind was just too strong. Instead of lifting him it was dishevelling him, holding him down on earth, where he was most vulnerable.

Heading back to Skye Avenue, coming over Westmount Mountain in the undertaker's Packard, Frankie asked the driver to pull over at the Summit Lookout.

"We have to get home, Frankie, before the guests start arriving," Margo scolded.

"No, we don't," Frankie said.

"There's plenty of time," said their mother.

"Could you pull over, driver, please? Just for a moment?" Frankie asked.

He pulled into the little parking lot and Frankie scrambled out of the car and went to stand at the low concrete wall. Gradually the rest of them got out and stood there too. Margo came last.

The trees on the flank of the mountain below them hid most of the houses, even the big faux Scottish baronial mansions just below the summit. Before the war, the Lookout was where Frankie and her pals had gone to ponder the universe, smoke cigarettes, and get mildly frisky with nice boys in rattletrap cars. From the terrace they could see church spires thrusting above the treetops of Westmount, and the grey stone cluster of banks and office buildings downtown. They could see railway tracks and switching yards, the brown slums of Sainte-Cunégonde, St. Henry, Little Burgundy, the Vickers works in Verdun, even the strips of hayfield, cornfield, and fallow land across the river. They could see a lot, but not the war coming. In those days people in other cities were already being terrorized, but it had not mattered as much to her as a new pair of shoes.

Now it was September and four years into the war. Summer was nearly over. Warmth might return but the days were already shrinking. Every evening the light was failing faster and faster.

Frankie glanced at her sister. Margo had turned her back to the view and was leaning on the balustrade, smoking a cigarette. Aunt Elise was holding on to their mother's arm. The wind was tearing at them all and Iseult seemed to need anchoring. Their father stood by himself a few feet away, gabardine raincoat still flapping. Why didn't he button it up? Was he hoping the wind might blow him clean? Blow away all his dastardly thoughts? He ought to know that wouldn't happen.

Her parents were like a pair of bedraggled birds exhausted by a long migration. Why couldn't they hold on to each other? What was wrong with them?

It started to rain, and everyone quickly got back into the car.

∼

When the old Packard pulled up at Number Ten, the sky was stormy and black, lights were blazing inside the house, and Frankie felt like someone on a parachute dropping into mortal combat with a fully realized sense of hell. It was pouring as they hustled from the smelly old machine into the house, just ahead of the first brigade of hungry, thirsty mourners. Frankie scanned the dining room, checking to see that the rented silver-plated teapots and coffee urns were in place, along with the trays of dainty sandwiches and *bouchées* from Pâtisserie Dubois, and loads of strawberries. The O'Briens were from Ireland but it had been a hundred years since her great-grandfather had sailed up the St. Lawrence on a

coffin ship, and any tradition of riotous waking had evolved into a deco-
rous tea party that would develop into a slightly less well-behaved cocktail party as the afternoon lengthened. They were Canadians through
and through.

She recognized the barman, Jerry, from Mother Martin's, a watering
hole for reporters, cab drivers, Ferry Command pilots, stale debutantes,
and those who in Montreal passed for people in the know. He had set up
the drinks table in the front hall between the living room and the dining
room.

"My condolences, Frankie. Real sorry about your brother."

"Thanks, Jerry."

"Never knew him, but I guess he was quite a guy. Can I fix you a little
something, Frankie? How about a gimlet?"

She had been drinking gimlets that summer with F/O Basil Fitzgib-
bon, a car salesman and crop-duster in Western Australia before the war,
now an RAF Ferry Command pilot flying brand-new bombers from Long
Beach to England every twelve days or so. He had layovers in Montreal
when the weather over the North Atlantic was bad. Fitz had wanted to fly
low over Côte-des-Neiges Cemetery and waggle his wings. He was a sentimental man and loved florid gestures, but he'd taken off for Newfoundland and Scotland in a brand-new Liberator the day before the funeral.

"Or a Scotch?" the barman asked. "The Scotch is pretty good stuff—
don't know where you got it."

The mourners were feasting on plates crowded with ham and strawberries and sandwiches. No one had asked Jerry the barman to pour
anything yet, and he was looking bored.

"Not yet, Jerry," she said. "I'm in a holding pattern. Maybe later."

The house was filling up. Frankie, Margo, their mother, and Elise
and Virginia were all in black. Margo's little girl, thankfully, was not.
Frankie watched her sister kiss Maddie and hand her over to the nanny,
who swept her upstairs.

The only youngish mourners were Frankie's pals and Margo's, mostly
female and lonely as hell and ready for a good nourishing cry after nibbling a mushroom sandwich and downing a neat Scotch or two. Not
many had known Mike well, if at all. His cohort was mostly overseas.

The rooms smelled of butter and sugar and rain. It was brutal outside, trees swaying, cold. In the living room one of the maids hired for the day was on her knees trying to start a fire in the fireplace.

Frankie heard ice cubes rattling in a shaker, and looked back to see Jerry the barman diligently pouring what looked like a martini for Father Tom.

"Life goes on," she heard someone say.

But where does it go? she thought. *And can I go with it?*

She was overhearing conversations about how green and slow the greens were at the Royal Montreal this year. The price of Scotch, the availability of tires. And she had once thought the world was going to be *nice*.

With the possible exception of her brother-in-law, all the people she had ever known ran around burying their feelings the way squirrels bury their nuts then forget where. And Johnny Taschereau had been gone for so long he had become a wartime fantasy, a pin-up poster, a stand-in for all the boys she'd never met who were wasting their youth as ball-turret gunners or in anti-tanks or on destroyers.

As she stood in the living room without any food or drink, trying to get warm near the paltry fire, longing for a cigarette, stately people she didn't recognize kept coming up and squeezing her arm and launching conversations at her. She nodded, smiled, and murmured back at them, but she couldn't seem to get her brain or voice organized into a proper response. It was as if she had been aspirated from her body and become part of something else: a piece of pattern in the Tabriz carpet. A cocktail sandwich. A shaft of light.

The day after Mike came home their father had swung into action, threatening deputy ministers, rearranging schedules of eminent surgeons, demanding and getting the useless best of everything for his dying boy. A thrilling, nauseating, futile ten days it had been, all culminating in today's funeral Mass, the burial service with banging guns, the cold drizzle, and this morbid party. It was all giving her a headache and she was ready to ditch the festivities and disappear. There was a little balcony off her bedroom, and if it wasn't raining too hard she could smoke a cigarette out there in peace. She was about to make a run for it when Helen tapped her on the shoulder, saying, "Tel-lay-phone for you, miss."

The only caller she could imagine was Fitz; everyone else was at the party. But Fitz was supposed to be at Gander by now, or somewhere between Newfoundland and Scotland. Poor Fitz, with his red hair, seedy moustache, bogus public-school accent, and taste for low nightclubs. He didn't know it, but he was of a type familiar to Montreal: the hinterlands-of-Empire cad and bounder, lacking even the modest allowance that would have made him a remittance man. He did have bottomless good humour and a salary, and he was not a bad dancer. Mother Martin's was near the top of his nightclub range; he preferred nameless blind pigs on de Bullion Street. He was at least twelve years older than Frankie and had never mentioned his wife and daughter back in Perth, though an Aussie air force nurse had spilled those beans in the ladies' room at the Normandie Roof, the one time Frankie had persuaded Fitz to take her there. But he had never actually claimed he *wasn't* married. Maybe neither of them had been interested enough in the subject to raise it. She had never slept with Fitz but thought one day she might, though he didn't seem to care one way or the other. People didn't need to fall in love to shack up at the motel out on Pine Beach where the Ferry Command pilots stayed. Affection or loneliness or curiosity or boredom would do the trick.

It had to be Fitz on the phone, but when she went into the pantry and picked up the receiver and a man's voice said, "Uh, is this Miss O'Brien?," it wasn't.

"Who's this?"

"I'm one of the fellows that was in the church today. The honour guard."

Oh Lord, she thought.

"Are you there, Miss O'Brien? Listen, I realize I've no right to be calling you. I understand that. I'm very sorry about your brother. I didn't know him, but I'm very sorry."

"Where are you calling from?"

"Hell, I'm in this club on—what do you call it?—St. Antoine Street. The Green Lantern. Wonderful joint, lot of class."

"Why are you calling me?"

There was silence for a few moments.

"I don't know," he said. "I saw you in the church. I thought you were beautiful. I don't mean disrespect to your brother. I just thought maybe you'd like to have some fun, a couple of drinks."

"Sorry, chum, I'm not quite ready to kick up my heels."

All around her the noise of mourners talking, voices roaring, teacups clinking on saucers like screams, like tiny bones being snapped.

"If someone dies, maybe it's not such a bad idea to get out."

"Which one were you?" she said.

"The one who kept staring at you."

"I didn't notice."

"My name's Vic McCracken."

"Vick? As in the cough drops?"

"Minus the K. Short for Victor."

"Have you been victorious lately?"

"Well, I just earned my wings out in Manitoba."

"You're a pilot?"

"Halifaxes and Lancs. The fellows in the church today were my crew. We're headed overseas. They gave us forty-eight hours' leave at Montreal, then rounded us up this morning for an honour guard. I hope we did all right."

She didn't say anything.

"We're on our way tomorrow," he said. "Eleven hundred hours, train to Halifax or New York and a ship overseas. I've never even seen the ocean. You look like a girl who likes to dance."

"You didn't know my brother."

"No, sorry."

She heard him pull on his cigarette. She knew she ought to hang up, but she had always been fascinated by people behaving badly, usually felt closer to them than to those behaving well.

"May I call you Frances?"

"No, Frankie."

"Say again?"

"No one calls me Frances. It's Frankie."

There was a pause and she could almost hear him thinking, or whatever lonely, randy men do that passes for thinking. Calculating. Reckoning odds, measuring appetites. Brutal and simple. She tried recalling the faces of the honour guard but couldn't.

"Listen to me, Frankie. If you're worried about anything, you'll be safe with me. Your brother—hell, if we'd known each other we probably would've been pals. I was going to be a schoolteacher in Alberta until the war came along. I think you ought to get in a taxi and come down here and let me buy you one little drink. Then if you want to go home, go home. But you should come down and give it a try. Life is better than death." He had a hard western voice and had probably spent long blue afternoons playing hockey on some frozen slough, chasing the puck into a headwind screaming out of nowhere. "What do you say, Frankie?"

"The Green Lantern's a dive, strictly a clip joint. Everyone knows that. It's pathetic that you can't tell the difference."

She hung up and went back to the party, feeling hard and bleak. In the front hall mourners were discussing golf, car repairs, and gasoline coupons.

"Jerry, pour me a swift one, will you please," she said to the barman.

"What's your poison, Frankie?"

"Got any cherries? Can you mix me a manhattan?"

"Sure thing."

She took a sip of her drink and wandered out through the living room, dodging the sympathetic, awful smiles people kept throwing her way. Her sister was in a corner surrounded by a coterie of former convent girls—Margo's bridge club called itself the Ex-Cons—all wives and mothers now, many with husbands overseas.

Elise and Cousin Virginia were standing near the fire chatting to Father Tom. He had gone out west with Elise earlier in the summer to visit Grattan at his Commonwealth Air Training field on the high plains south of Calgary. Grattan was getting awfully tired, Elise had said. She intended to move out to Alberta to be with him if the war lasted much longer.

Virginia saw Frankie and blew her a kiss. Frankie went out to the conservatory, where geraniums bloomed explosively, stinking of earth and bone and wire. She sipped her manhattan as rain hammered on the glass roof. Women in hideous hats were drinking tea and boasting to one another of their victory gardens, though it was their West Indian maids who did all the work. She almost regretted having hung up on the boy from Saskatchewan, or Alberta. The brand-new pilot. Maybe she ought to have called a cab and sped straight the hell down to St. Antoine Street, or wherever the kid was doing his lonesome drinking.

Daylight even in the conservatory was dead yellow and brown, not summer light at all. She went back through the living room, avoiding all contact, across the front hall, and up the stairs. She had not seen her father since they'd come back from the cemetery. He had scampered straight upstairs.

She knocked gently on the door of the study.

"Go away." His rumble sounded like a transmission in low gear.

She waited a whole minute before she knocked again. *Tap-tap-tap-tap-tap, tap-tap. Shave-and-a-haircut, two-bits.* Blessed Frankie of the Knock.

She heard the squeal of casters from his desk chair, and the door unlocking. He sat down again at his desk as she walked in. He wore a silk smoking jacket her mother had given him and was holding a Mass card. A photograph of Mike on the balcony of the New Zealand army hospital in Egypt, looking tanned and healthy—*Merry Xmas to you all*—was in a silver frame, right next to a bottle of Seagram's VO. She had never actually seen her father take a drink, not in the house, not anywhere.

He slit open a fresh pack of cigarettes, took one out, and stuck it between his lips, lighting it with his desk lighter. "Want a snort?" he said.

Frankie shook her head. She sat down on the horsehair sofa. French doors led out to the little balcony where in summer the swallows nested under the eaves. "I'll take a cigarette though."

He raised one eyebrow, then tossed the pack to her so abruptly she nearly missed it.

When she was small she used to go on drives around the city with her father, he never saying a word if he could help it. She'd play with her dolls in the back seat while he drove through districts that no one else she knew had ever visited, or even heard of. Sainte-Marie Ward, Ahuntsic, Goose Village. Nether regions, poor and ramshackle. Horses pulling junk wagons. People sitting on balconies drinking beer from brown quart bottles. Kids everywhere. Long, strange streets unreeling.

He hadn't been driving to get anywhere or see anyone. Maybe in the beginning he might have told himself he was scouting for property, finding his feet in the city, getting to know the island of Montreal, but the drives she remembered were really a kind of floating loose, a detachment.

She'd never expected a destination or a clear purpose. He was not on any errand. He almost always kept going past where the city stopped, where the grid of broken streets and tenements petered out. He drove until there was nothing flanking whichever boulevard they were on but ragged fields, ancient farmhouses, and cold glimpses of the river. He kept on going. When he'd gone far enough, he'd slow down, swing the car around, and start to find his way back. When she was little, Frankie had wondered how he did it, how he found his way home without dropping breadcrumbs in the forest like Hansel and Gretel.

"When are you going to get married?" He spoke suddenly, peering at her through a blue cloud of cigarette smoke.

"I'm not getting married, Daddy."

"You will."

"Is that what you're worrying about?"

He didn't say anything. He was gazing at Mike's picture.

"What will you do, Daddy, when I do get married? Will you get plastered at my wedding? Will you go on a spree?" She had never talked to him this way before, but any house, any family would be changed by a corpse's being laid out in its living room. It excited her to suddenly feel capable of saying something.

"I'm not getting married anyway. Why should I want to do that? But I am moving out, Daddy. I'm going to get a place of my own downtown." She had never given much thought to moving out, but the moment she said it she believed that she would. "I've a good job. Plenty of girls live downtown. I could get a little flat. Margo and I might share one together."

Smoke dribbled from the cigarette between his fingers. He was studying the photograph of her brother. "I don't believe I can face it," he said. "I don't believe so. I am going to wrap it up and go away."

She rose from the sofa, stubbed her cigarette in the ashtray on his desk, and took hold of the whisky bottle. "You don't need this, do you."

"It's supposed to be pretty good stuff."

"You ought to come downstairs, Daddy. Mother needs all the help she can get."

He was looking at his hands; he wasn't listening.

"Next summer you'll go cruising," Frankie said. "Get on the boat and sail. Daddy, that will seem as real as this. You just have to get there."

"Why did they have to take my boy?" he demanded.

The only answer she knew was silence.

"Jesus Christ, do you know what I was hearing today? The fiddle Mick Heaney used to play—our stepfather, the son of a bitch that married our mother. 'Road to Boston,' 'Cheticamp,' 'Angel Death No Mercy'—by God, they'd hire that bastard for all the weddings and wakes; he knew all the jigs, all the reels. He'd never stop once he started; he'd saw away all night. I used to think he was the devil. We should have had him down at the church today."

She lifted the bottle from his desk. It was unopened and had an excise seal, so it wasn't from their black market supply. One of Margo's. "Daddy, I don't think this is going to help."

"What would you know about it?" he said sharply.

"Not much." Bending over, she kissed the top of his head. When he could be strong and when he couldn't was something no one had ever been able to predict. His love had always been tenacious and without limits. It had sometimes felt like being hated. Still, they were a family.

"Did your mother send you up here?"

"No."

"Don't tell her, then."

"I won't. Won't you come downstairs, Daddy?"

"And join the party?" he said. "Don't know if I've got the stomach for it. But if I can keep straight, maybe I'll figure it out. Maybe I'll come down and show you all how it's done."

Like most people he was a mystery walking through his own land, and when she thought she understood him, it was only in the way she understood certain tones, notes, and chords when a prodigy such as Oscar Peterson happened to be playing at Ruby Foo's, the roadhouse out on Decarie Boulevard that she loved because it was poised on the edge of the city and the edge of nothing, almost nowhere. Late at night, or very early in the morning, horns and bass dropping into the background while the young Negro's piano—sometimes sad but never gloomy—whispered secrets, fed her scraps of knowledge about the completeness, roundness, and implacability of the world.

"I'm going back downstairs," she said. "Will you be coming down?"

"Maybe in a little while."

She left his door open and, carrying the bottle, went down the hall

and into Margo's room. She fetched the vermouth and gin from her sister's closet and took all three downstairs. The tea party had perked up,
shaken its tail. Important men with important wartime jobs who had
not been able to show up for a midday funeral were putting in appear-
ances now, keeping Jerry the barman busy and keeping one eye cocked
for Frankie's father, who was no longer important but might still, for all
they knew, be dangerous. Some of the middle-aged were in uniform but
they all looked like businessmen. It was starting to feel like a hundred
cocktail parties she had been to since the war began.

Iseult was busy organizing sandwiches and coffee for the army drivers and chauffeurs who were waiting out in the cold and wet. Frankie
knew her mother had seen her slinking downstairs with the bottles in
her arms, but she hadn't said anything. If her father was determined to
flee to New York City, her mother wouldn't try to stop him. Maybe she'd
go to fetch him afterwards, maybe she wouldn't. Maybe this time he'd
have to bring himself home or not come back at all.

Jerry gave Frankie a nod as she set down the bottles on the bar. He
was mixing up a crystal shaker of martinis.

"Reinforcements," she said. "Looks like you might need them."

He smiled. The crackling, slushing sound of ice in the shaker reminded
Frankie of the world outside the house. Suddenly she wanted to go there,
and someone to take her. This party was no good, not what her soul
needed, and if she retreated upstairs to her maidenly boudoir or walked
down Murray Hill to sit brooding and decorously weeping on a bench in
the lilac park, she'd only feel nastier and more wicked.

"Jerry, I'm going to the Green Lantern to meet a few friends."

Jerry raised his eyebrows. He was busy filling glasses. She watched
him start handing out the martinis.

"Do you think that's terrible?" she said.

"I'm not the one that just buried my brother, Frankie. If you want to
duck out, who's to say you can't?"

"Can you do me a favour?"

"Probably."

"I don't want to disturb Mother but I don't want her getting worried
when she sees I'm gone. Will you tell her I've gone out to meet some pals?
Tell her I won't be late but not to wait up for me either."

"Sure thing, Frankie."

"You don't have to say the Green Lantern. You can just say you don't know where."

"*Comme vous voulez.*"

In the pantry she picked up the wall phone. Maids galloped by with trays of cocktail sandwiches and clean glasses while she dialled for a cab. She gave the dispatcher the address, then changed her mind. "Tell your driver not to come to the house," she said. "He should meet me at the corner: Skye Avenue and Murray Hill."

Feeling a pang of guilt over abandoning her mother and Margo, she went back to the party and worked the crowd for a few minutes. Father Tom was on his second or third martini. People were stuffing themselves on sandwiches and *bouchées* and getting plastered, all in honour of Mike. Keeping an eye on her wristwatch, she was working her way towards the stairs when Iseult came out of the kitchen looking crazily distinguished in her old black dress, so removed from the edges of her own feelings, so scared.

Frankie stood waiting on the stairs while her mother made her way towards her through the jolly, vibrant crowd, ignoring any mourners who tried to speak to her. "I have to see your father," she told Frankie.

So Frankie grabbed her hand and they went upstairs together, treading on the Persian runner—purple, blue, scarlet, and gold—that Joe had bought years before from an Armenian in—Atlanta? Tampa? Havana? Somewhere down south.

The door of the study was shut. "Joe," her mother said. Iseult wasn't pleading, wasn't even summoning him. She said his name as if it was the name of a place, an island, a country where they'd all lived once.

Frankie heard the squeal of casters and him getting to his feet. She waited for him to open the door, but he didn't. She jiggled the knob. The door was locked. Still holding her mother by the hand, she rapped on the wood panels.

"Go away," he murmured.

"Daddy, it's Mother. Mother's here. You have to let her in, Daddy." Frankie didn't dare look at Iseult. There were no sounds from the other side of the door. They all just stood there.

Everything's coming apart, Frankie thought. *Nothing is left, nothing that will hold.*

"Joe." Her mother's voice was a weak scrape of sound. Hardly any air made it out of her throat.

No response from him.

She would take her mother with her in the cab and run away somewhere, just the two of them. Or Margo too, if she wanted to come, and Maddie. Maybe to a hotel. It was just about impossible to get a decent hotel room on short notice in wartime, but she had pull at the Mount Royal, thanks to her job; she could probably get them the Vice-regal Suite. Or maybe they'd go down to Maine.

The bolt slid back, the door opened, and her father stood there in his silk smoking jacket, a cigarette curdling between his fingers. She could see one of the volumes of her mother's photographs open on the desk. Ignoring Frankie, he reached out and took Iseult by the hand. As he drew her into the room she almost tripped over the doorsill, but he caught and held her. She was crying.

Frankie turned and walked away. She knew she was deserting her parents, or maybe she was just saving herself. When she was halfway down the hall, she heard her father's door shut, and she glanced back. They were inside together. She hoped they'd stay there for the duration.

She hurried to her room, kicking off her shoes and quickly exchanging the black dress for her favourite red one. Sitting down at her dressing table, she lit a cigarette, gave her hair a good, fierce brushing, and put on fresh lipstick. Then she grabbed her pocketbook and ran down the back stairs.

Cars were parked up and down the street. The black rain had let up. All the chauffeurs and army drivers had gathered around one big Packard, where they were eating the sandwiches and drinking the coffee Iseult had sent out. Frankie greeted a couple of boys she recognized from the craps game that always seemed to be running on one floor or another at the Mount Royal Hotel. She was at the corner when the old Dodge taxi made the turn from Westmount Avenue and came chugging and clanking up the hill. She recognized the driver from the stand of cabs outside the Mount Royal. Part of her job was putting important people into taxis.

"Sorry about your brother, Frankie," the cabby said, as she settled into the front seat. "Nice guy, I heard. Too bad."

She could have been in a bomber lifting off: that was how it felt leaving behind the house on Skye Avenue with all the people and the feelings it contained. She was light-headed from having gotten away so quickly.

"Where for?" the cabby asked.

"The Green Lantern." It would be flashy and noisy, jammed with zoots and black marketeers and sailors and airmen.

The cabby made a face. "They water their booze."

"Everywhere does," she snapped. "It's wartime."

That closed the conversation, which was just fine with her. She was glad to be in the old car, to be moving. She had that giddy feeling she got in cars sometimes: that nothing could touch her. Would her parents survive? It was up to them, she told herself, as the cab swung around in the street and started down the hill. The only person she could handle was herself.

Home

JOHNNY WAS IN the office when his father-in-law came by to sign some papers. It was nearly five o'clock, and when Joe offered him a lift home, he accepted. He found his mother-in-law waiting in the Chrysler and climbed into the back seat. The car was pretty worn out. New cars were still hard to come by—you had to be on a list. He was still a little surprised that Margo's old man, with all his contacts, wasn't higher on the list. His own father had just taken delivery of a brand-new Cadillac, a 1941 model, though the dealer was calling it a '46.

Louis-Philippe had told him that Joe O'Brien had made a lot of enemies in Ottawa when he tried to shut down his firm with a dozen important military contracts already in hand. "They thought he was trying to—how would you say?—put the squeeze on them. Very nearly he went to jail. Only my excellent counsel and impressive stickhandling saved him from a prison sentence. He paid considerable fines, however, not to mention legal fees. All for the sake of—what, exactly? *Je ne lui comprends pas.* I never have. *Ces irlandais—illogiques.*"

To Margo it was simple. "Daddy hated the war. After Mike left, he didn't want anything to do with it, but he had to do what they wanted. Anyway, he could never bear to break a contract."

They were almost in Westmount when the old man announced he wanted to detour by Notre-Dame-des-Neiges Cemetery to inspect the arborvitae shrubs the O'Briens' gardener was supposed to have planted on each side of the family headstone.

"You don't mind, do you?" Joe said, glancing over his shoulder.

"Joe," said Iseult, "why now? Johnny just wants to go home."

It was true. He had been looking forward to getting home, seeing his wife and daughter, sitting down in the living room with the newspaper and a glass of Scotch. But what the hell. "By all means, let's go."

He'd demobbed in November '45, one of the first to get home. His daughter, Maddie, had seemed like any other kid to him: nothing special. He'd found his father amazingly old, his sister Lulu a Sacred Heart nun, and his wife a cold, brittle stranger.

Margo had wanted to stay on at her parents' house for a while longer but he had insisted they find a place of their own immediately. She hated the first apartment he found for them on Victoria Avenue. He had to break the lease, forfeiting a month's rent. Now they were in a flat on Carthage Avenue in Lower Westmount.

A couple of months after getting home he had started an affair with a girl he met on the 105 streetcar. She reminded him of girls he had known in England. He took her to the same hotels he'd gone to with Margo, but he felt trapped, compressed. Waking up, he had to force himself to get out of bed. He'd held on to his service sidearm, an American Colt .45, and sometimes he imagined taking the pistol down from its shelf in the hall closet, oiling it, loading it, walking into the woods in Murray Park with the gun heavy in his pocket, sitting down at the base of one of the big elms or maples, and shooting himself in the head.

His father-in-law turned off Côte-des-Neiges Road, passed through the iron gates of the cemetery, and drove along the winding road. Johnny had never visited Notre-Dame-des-Neiges before; all the Taschereaus were buried in Arthabaska. Here the trees weren't yet in leaf. There were fresh beds of daffodils, tulips. The grass was green. Robins hopped between the tombs. Everything smelled of damp ground.

There had been one awful afternoon at a cemetery in Italy—where? Ortona. SS fanatics, children, armed with machine guns and a couple of 88s, had dug themselves in among the headstones and knocked out a pair of Trois-Rivières tanks.

Notre-Dame was a big, sprawling field of death, but Margo's father knew exactly where he was going. He pulled over onto the grass shoulder and they all got out of the car, which hissed and ticked and smelled of burnt oil.

"Don't come here that often," the old man said. "Hardly at all over the winter. Snow up to my ass. Came out with Elise and Frankie a couple of weeks ago, at Easter."

"Margo comes out sometimes," Johnny told him.

"Yes, she does."

The ground was soft, a little muddy. Johnny thought of the bodies of SS children laid out in a row and his sergeant—Bellechasse, from Témiscamingue—executing two of the very badly wounded. The battalion had lost four men killed in that cemetery, four badly wounded.

Things were terribly green at Notre-Dame-des-Neiges. His mother-in-law held on to his arm as they followed the old man in the watery April sunshine, shoes slurring in the thick grass. Margo's father wore an overcoat and homburg and was carrying a walking stick; he was headed down a grassy row between gravestones. Some were quite elaborate: marble angels and granite lambs, plaster statues of saints in glass-fronted cases. Brown bedraggled palm leaves and lilies, leftovers from Easter week, were scattered on the ground.

When they reached the O'Brien family plot, Johnny and his mother-in-law stood together and watched the old man peer at the gravestones as though seeing them for the first time. The headstone marking the O'Brien plot was a polished granite slab. There were two smaller, standard military-issue headstones: Margo's brother and her uncle. Grattan had died in a plane crash in Alberta a few days before the war in Europe ended.

"Well, these aren't bad. Not bad at all." The old man bent over and patted one of the new arborvitae, as yet only a couple of feet high. "Iseult thinks in twenty years they'll be too big and bushy and we won't be able to see the stones. But it won't be my problem. I'll let you and Margo and Madeleine and Frankie worry about that."

"Sure. We'll chop 'em down."

"Just get someone out here in October with pruning shears. October—that's when you want to clip these back."

Margo had said that her parents slipped away after Mike's funeral. For three weeks she hadn't heard a word and couldn't call, as there was no phone at the Kennebunk house. She'd felt abandoned, she said, and it had nearly driven her crazy being left alone in the house with Madeleine, with Mike dead and Johnny at war and Frankie head-over-heels for some flyer. Finally she'd made Frankie borrow a car from one of the pilots she knew and they had driven to Kennebunk and found their parents living quietly, sailing their old sloop and working in their garden. After a week together they had all returned to the city and had remained in Montreal for the duration.

Before Mike's death the old man had never written to his son-in-law, but in the last eighteen months of the war Johnny had received a letter from him every few weeks, always neatly typed on business stationery. Joe reported Madeleine's progress at ice-skating and her reactions to various animals at the Lafontaine Park zoo. He outlined his techniques for raising pumpkins, cucumbers, and potatoes in garden plots he dug into the lawn at Skye Avenue. At the bottom of each letter he transcribed without comment one or two clever things Madeleine had said. His letters had been far easier to read than Margo's outpourings. In one of her last letters just before the war ended, she had confessed an urge to give up Madeleine, to leave her at the door of an orphanage and flee to New York or Los Angeles and start her life over.

"Really, Joe, we ought to get going," Iseult said. "Johnny wants to get home, I'm sure."

The old man tapped the metal end of his walking stick on his son's stone, then on Grattan's. "Some people thought Grattan plowed his plane into the ground," he said, without looking up. "Deliberately. No accident. He was the CO of a base; they were training aircrew from all over. Poles, Australians. He wasn't in good shape, was what I heard. Been drinking."

"You can't say that," Iseult said. "You don't know for sure."

"It was Tom who said so, but you're right, who knows? I'm glad you made it home safe, Johnny. You have your life back, so hold on to it, hold on to what you have."

Johnny suddenly felt as exposed as any of the hundreds of wounded he'd seen in Italy: men, women, infantrymen, children, their clothes blown to rags, their bodies torn apart or smeared with garish bruises. He was shivering, but his in-laws didn't seem to notice. They were gazing at the stones. Maybe they were praying, but he didn't think so.

At some point it had started to rain, soft, lissome springtime rain, not the hard-driving winter rain of Italy. Rain like smoke.

"Joe," Iseult said softly.

The old man turned to have another look at his arborvitae shrubs. Then he started back to the car, which Johnny could see at the end of a row of stone urns and angels. The wet gave a powerful gleam to the grey Chrysler. The moisture had thickened the grass, and when he and Iseult started after the old man, their footsteps made sibilant brushing sounds.

"There's nothing really to say," Iseult said. "That's the truth of it, Jean. There is absolutely nothing to say."

And for the first time since coming back from the war he almost felt at home, which was strange, since it was a bloody cemetery, after all, and who the hell wanted to feel at home there.

Lost and Found

THE SQUEAKING HIGHS and catches of the tune came flying through the fog and dark like birds—swallows, small and quick. They liked to play a fiddle in that town.

Aboard the yawl *Sea Son* Joe was restless in his berth. After retiring early he had been unable to find sleep. It was densely foggy, but *Son* was safe on her mooring in Baddeck harbour, and God knows he was weary enough.

They had picked up the mooring that morning. What he had seen of Cape Breton so far, sailing up from St. Peter's, reminded him as much as any place had of the Pontiac country, though they didn't have any white pine. Even the local speech was familiar: scraps of French he'd overheard from truck drivers on the government wharf, and two old women at MacIsaac's store gabbling in what sounded like Ottawa Valley Irish. Albert MacIsaac had said firmly, "No, not Irish. The Gaelic. Scotch Gaelic."

"Speak it yourself?" Joe asked.

"No, no. Hardly!"

The small, nearly bald storekeeper had a way of seeming busy and impatient even when standing still. There was no one else in the IGA but the old women and some Coast Guard men who were doing maintenance on the lighthouse across the harbour. The fishery in the lakes was lobster, oysters, herring, and winter flounder. The store itself was tiny, dim, not particularly clean, with thin stocks of tinned food, crackers, and candy on the shelves. Along the back wall, racks of wellington boots and Stanfields long johns—red or grey, take your pick.

He had lost track of the calendar, as he always did on a cruise. Picking up a copy of the *Cape Breton Post*, he checked the date—Saturday, July 30, 1960—and read that John Kennedy, the Democratic nominee for president, intended to strengthen the armed forces of the United States.

~

Almost three weeks earlier he had left the Kennebunk River with Iseult. They'd spent six days cruising the southern Maine coast in clear light with favourable winds. They'd rowed ashore and dug for clams at Peaks Island and Bustins. At Little Spruce Head they had taken off their clothes on a scrape of white beach scented with balsam. Iseult was thin. Her long legs were beautifully shaped and she moved lightly, like a deer, approaching the green water. It had been stinging cold. He went in with a yell and a crash, the way he always did, and she'd slipped in as she always did, quietly, swimming out quickly beyond the lap of tiny waves, her long form slipping like a knife through the water.

Iseult had disembarked at Camden, Maine, where their granddaughter Madeleine was waiting with the car that Iseult would drive back to Montreal while Maddie joined him aboard the *Son*. From Camden he and Maddie had sailed Penobscot Bay in bright weather, taking it slowly, dropping the hook at familiar anchorages. They encountered their first Fundy fog in Jericho Bay and lingered at Bar Harbor, waiting for another spell of clear weather before striking out across the Gulf of Maine for Nova Scotia.

~

His daughters had pretty much talked him out of a Cape Breton cruise when Maddie had surprised everyone by saying she wanted to come along. Her mother was fiercely opposed to the idea, but Maddie was a stubborn mule. She had that from him, he figured.

His goal had always been to sail north as far as he could reasonably go. Which meant, after he'd studied the east coast littoral, Cape Breton.

The Gaspé Peninsula, Anticosti Island, and Newfoundland were farther but not reasonable—at least not for an old man in a thirty-six-foot
yawl. On his first try, during the war, sailing the old Friendship sloop,
he'd been stopped by the Coast Guard and ordered back to Kennebunk.
That was the luckiest thing that could have happened to him: he hadn't
enough experience in those days to realize how little he knew about sailing small boats on the open ocean.

But in his old age he was a fairly accomplished sailor. Since the war
he'd sailed the yawl east as far as Grand Manan more times than he
could count, and twice he had crossed the Gulf of Maine alone, dropping his hook at Yarmouth but not venturing any farther. He hadn't
fixed Cape Breton in his sights again until this year, when he'd made up
his mind to do it, alone if necessary. Figuring he didn't have that many
seasons left—a case of now or never.

"What's wrong with Casco Bay?" Frankie wanted to know. "Bustins, Harraseeket, Harpswell—haven't you always loved cruising there?
Where you already know all the best anchorages? Why go so far from
home? And Vic says"—Frankie's husband, Vic McCracken, was a Trans-
Canada Airlines pilot—"the airlines have learned that almost all men
over fifty-five, no matter how experienced, just can't react fast enough in
any sort of crisis. It's a scientifically proven fact."

"Don't tell Joe what he can't do," Aunt Elise warned. "Not him."

Elise had been spending July with them. Her portrait business was as
hectic as ever, but for the past few years she had taken the summers off
and come down to Maine with them or visited Virginia in Europe. Her
daughter was a diplomat at the Canadian embassy in Brussels and married to a Dutchman.

Elise and Iseult had been driving up the coast every Sunday to photograph people at the Old Orchard Pier. Over the course of a month
they had visited most of the agricultural fairs in southern Maine and
coastal New Hampshire, from Fryeburg to Windsor, taking pictures of
fairgoers, farmers, and carnies. They planned to assemble their Venice
and Old Orchard photographs into a book. Elise had brought folders
of old prints to Maine with her, and so had Iseult; the women spent the
afternoons sorting through images from their days on the Venice pier
and boardwalk.

"Daddy, Johnny and I are just not going to let Maddie go," Margo said. "And I have a much better idea, something that would really give you a bit of fun this summer. Don't you think it's time you applied to join the Cape Arundel? The membership committee would love to have you."

Margo and her husband, Johnny—as of early summer, the Honourable Mr. Justice Taschereau of the Quebec Court of Appeal—were keen golfers.

"I don't play golf, have you noticed?"

"Daddy, that's the wonderful thing about golf. It's never too late to start."

They had him surrounded, and by the time Iseult stepped out on the porch to summon them to lunch, she probably saw that he was close to folding.

Margo smiled at her and said, "Mother, tell Daddy he has to be sensible for once."

"Joe, be sensible for once," Iseult said mildly. "And lunch is ready."

"Tell him he's seventy-three—"

"Joe, you're seventy-three."

"I'm not arguing with you," he said.

She smiled.

"Mother, this isn't funny," Margo insisted. "If he were going alone that would be one thing, but he can't go alone, and I'm not letting Maddie go. So he'd better just give up the idea. Just give the golf club a try, Daddy, please. It's not at all what you might suppose."

"All right, girls, you've told him what you think. Your father's no fool. He knows what he can do and what he can't."

"Well, she's my daughter!"

"Of course she is, dear."

"And I'm not letting him take her!"

"Mother, you're not agreeing with him, are you?" said Frankie.

"You're right, dear, she's your daughter. It's your decision."

"And I'm not going to let her go. It's ridiculous. He's seventy-three."

He knew damn well how old he was, and also what he was still capable of. What Margo was saying could not really be argued against. He understood and respected—not his daughter's unfathomable desire to see him on a golf course, but her reluctance to let her daughter go, because it was herself she'd be letting go of.

Maddie was the eldest of his six grandchildren. She had two brothers, Michel and Jacques. Frankie and Vic had Lizzie, Iseult, and William. All the kids had grown up around boats and were much better sailors than their mothers were. During the past two Augusts he'd handed the *Son* over to Maddie for two weeks. She'd cruised Penobscot Bay with two girlfriends as her crew.

He would not take her unless Margo agreed to let her go, and he would not try to persuade Margo. After working it through carefully he had come to the cold conclusion that Cape Breton was more than he could undertake single-handed. He had no wish to end his sailing days with a disastrous, humiliating failure, so he had quietly put the plan on the shelf. There it remained until the bright, cool morning when his daughter caught up with him on the beach and told him that she and Johnny had changed their minds and were giving the cruise their blessing.

Margo admitted that Johnny had been for it from the start. "He says she was in more danger riding on that boy's motorcycle in Rome last year than she'd ever be with you on the *Son*."

"I don't know about that," Joe said. "It is a real voyage, I won't deny it. I guess it seems a lot to take on. I certainly believe we can do it, though."

They stopped walking. The tide was out, the sand was hard, and they were both barefoot, an inch of clear surf lapping lazily around their toes.

"She is a young woman, not a baby," Margo said, firmly. She was still trying to convince herself. "Johnny says we can't stop her trying to accomplish things."

"And what do you say?"

"Don't you dare come back without her," his daughter whispered. "Don't you dare."

She was right, of course, and he knew that he wouldn't.

~

From Bar Harbor they'd planned a straight run of thirty hours, in four-hour watches, rounding the hull of Nova Scotia and aiming for Shelburne.

His granddaughter was *aware*, the way a good sailor needed to be. Her eye and her mind logged details. She picked up signs other people missed. She had a sailor's sensitivity to changing weather. All his life he'd been around people who missed clues, with no eye for detail, no sense of the world around them. Sailors with no nose for weather, bankers with no feel for the meaning of the numbers. Maddie could take in a chart with one look and remember every ledge, every rock, every sounding. She had shown him her sketchbooks filled with seabirds, island profiles, boats, many of them rendered with a single flowing line. His favourite was a beautifully detailed drawing she'd made of a winch.

His mother—her great-grandmother—had paid a woman on the other side of the Ottawa River to look into a blue bottle and see the future. *Ashling*, they called it, whatever was revealed: a dream, a vision.

He had always had a suspicion there was a rough justice in the world, that most things happened for a reason. You didn't always know the reason but it didn't mean the future was uninvolved with the past. The opposite, in fact.

One afternoon on the Gulf of Maine, halfway across to Nova Scotia, blue sky, blue water, they were munching pilot crackers and cheese when all of a sudden Maddie said, "There's a big fish out there."

"A whale? You see a spout?"

"Not sure. But he's out there. Fetch the binocs, Granddaddy, please."

She had the helm. It was blowing maybe fifteen knots east-southeast and they were on broad reach, making good time. After going below for the binoculars, he sat down beside her, and a few minutes later the whale spouted: a jet of water straight as a spear, so close that the moisture flecked over them and they could smell the fish-rank stink.

A minute later the whale breached twenty yards off their port quarter, flying out of the water like a dolphin and crashing down onto the surface, the biggest animal he'd ever seen, bigger than the *Son*. He didn't need binoculars to catch the silvery white pattern on its back and the massive dorsal fin before the whale sounded again, disappearing possibly directly under the boat. They waited, tense, scanning the waters all around, neither of them saying a word.

Another hiss, and they saw the spout maybe twenty yards off the starboard beam. Then nothing, silence. Slight creaking of rigging as the *Son* sped along. They kept scanning. Suddenly the whale breached again, flying across the surface before smashing back into the sea. Seventy or eighty feet in length, twice the length of the *Son*. This time the whale flapped its flukes as it sounded.

"What do you think it was?" Maddie asked.

"Don't know." He'd seen plenty of humpbacks and minkes, but never a whale that size.

She handed over the helm and went below, returning with a fat paperback, *Moby-Dick*, that she'd been reading since Camden. Flipping through it until she found what she was looking for, she read in silence while he kept a lookout. The whale sighting had shaken him. Not fear, exactly, but the way he sometimes felt when he woke from a dream. Rattled. There was something powerful out there moving below the surface, and he had been ignoring it only because he did not understand it.

Most of the time he was able to sustain a sense of himself as complete, a finished man. A comforting sense that his life story had been filled out for better or for worse. The truth was, he was still empty. So much remained beyond his grasp, things he would never feel or answer or know.

His granddaughter was lost in *Moby-Dick*. "Find anything?" he said.

"I think so. Listen to this." She began reading aloud. "Finback whale, *Balaenoptera physalus*."

Under this head I reckon a monster which, by the various names of Fin-Back, Tall-Spout, and Long-John has been seen almost in every sea and is commonly the whale whose distant jet is so often descried by passengers crossing the Atlantic. . . . His grand distinguishing feature, the fin . . . some three or four feet long, growing vertically from the hinder part of the back, of an angular shape, and with a very sharp pointed end. . . . The Fin-Back is not gregarious. He seems a whale-hater, as some men are man-haters. Very shy; always going solitary; unexpectedly rising to the surface in the remotest and most sullen waters; his straight and single lofty jet rising like a tall misanthropic spear upon a barren plain; gifted with such wondrous power and velocity in swimming, as to defy all present pursuit from man. This leviathan seems the banished and unconquerable Cain of his race, bearing for his mark that style upon his back . . .

"I guess he's referring to the pattern, Granddaddy. Did you see it on his back?"

"I did."

"'Banished . . . unconquerable . . . the mark of Cain . . . ' I suppose
Melville means that fin whales are loners. The whalers saw only one at a
time, like us. Have you ever seen one before?"

"No, never."

"Thanks for arranging it."

"You're welcome."

Certain young people, like Maddie, had thinner skins. It wasn't that
they were delicate so much as *not insulated*. Iseult had never been insulated; neither had he. They had damaged each other, damaged themselves. She'd hated and blamed him for the death of their first baby, and
in his worst moments he'd blamed her for Mike's death. But they had
collected themselves, kept the family together, sustained. She hadn't left
him for the swami after all. And he had eventually pulled himself out of
the neck of a bottle. Suffering had brought them together, though at the
time it seemed it would tear them apart. Their marriage had been there
to save them from drowning.

~

At Shelburne, Nova Scotia, they bent a set of smaller, heavier sails before
continuing on for Cape Breton. It was a week of four-hour watches,
rugged ocean sailing, easterly winds and fog and never being quite sure
where they were on account of a powerful offshore tidal set. Navigating
with a compass and a taffrail log, they dropped their hook at Liverpool,
Chester, Halifax, Sheet Harbour, and Canso. The RDF picked up weak
Morse signals from lighthouses, which they tried to triangulate on the
little chart table above the icebox.

Fog did not frighten Maddie the way it did some people. Three or
four times while she had the helm they'd caught sudden blowdown gusts,
maybe forty-five knots, the *Son* heeling violently, burying her rail in the
drink. Maddie had deftly eased the main sheet while keeping one hand
on the wheel, face glowing, perfectly calm.

Finally they had slipped through the locks at St. Peter's and come
into the Bras d'Or lakes. After the fierce easterlies and ocean swells it
had felt like entering a tropical lagoon. The lakes were an inland sea,

saline, estuarial, and warm. Madeleine had been diving off the boat and swimming every day since they'd passed the locks. They found easy anchorages near shore and saw no one but herring fishermen, bald eagles, and women who rowed out to offer baskets of oysters. They had come into Baddeck feeling grateful for having made the arduous trip and for its being just about over.

~

Baddeck was lonesome and isolated, a tiny little burg, prim, with its courthouse and churches and Legion Hall and Red Ensigns flapping. The only vessels in the harbour were some stubby Nova Scotia lobster boats and a couple of ancient herring trawlers. They had not met one other cruising sailboat since leaving Bar Harbor.

Mr. Albert MacIsaac seemed to own or control pretty much everything in the town. He owned the IGA and was more or less the harbourmaster. He rented Joe the mooring for fifty cents a day and arranged to have their laundry done by a woman in the village. MacIsaac knew the schedule of Sunday Masses and had quietly offered to sell Joe a quart bottle of clear liquor, apparently some sort of Nova Scotia moonshine.

Eager to stretch their legs, he and Maddie had walked the village. The houses of Baddeck were small and tidy. He felt eyes watching them from inside the little houses and sensed the existence of a larger, rougher world that began at the fringes of town, where the paved streets ran out and there were tarpaper shacks and cinder-block dwellings roofed with tarpaper—the cellars of houses that had been started then abandoned. There were chickens, silent, staring children, noisy dogs, and rotting boats. A muddy Pontiac had rocked by them, three husky young men in the front seat, heads swivelling to stare at Maddie. In her striped pedal-pushers and tiny shoes like ballet slippers she was probably the liveliest girl they'd seen in that fish town for a while.

Maddie had been hoping to find a restaurant or takeout shack, but there was nothing beyond the town but empty road and mountains, so they'd returned to MacIsaac's, picked up their grocery sacks, rowed back out to the *Son*, and made grilled cheese sandwiches for lunch. Afterwards Maddie stretched out on the pipe berth with her journal and sketchbook

and Joe went forward to take a nap in the V-berth. It was a fine afternoon for sleeping, the air soft and grey and both of them still recovering
from the rigours of ocean sailing. He felt a sense of accomplishment.

They wouldn't be sailing back to Maine, not this summer anyway.
His plan had always been to find winter storage in Nova Scotia and fly
home from Sydney or Halifax. Albert MacIsaac had offered to haul up
the *Son*, store her in his boatshed, and paint her top and bottom, all for
three hundred dollars plus the cost of whatever fancy exotic yacht paint
Joe might wish him to use, which would have to be special-ordered from
Halifax or Chester. Early next summer he would send up a crew to sail
her to Maine unless he felt like doing it himself, which he didn't suppose
he would. Once was enough.

He had fallen into a deep sleep and a dream set in the twenties, when
all the cars were black and high. A bridge was falling down. Grattan, in
uniform, was berating him, saying he'd cheated in the construction, used
rotten iron, pig iron. They were standing in waist-high grass at Windmill Point watching the bridge crumbling. The grass was whipping in
the breeze with a noise like bed sheets tearing and Grattan was about to
drive his car out into the current to save the people when a sharp knocking on the hull broke Joe out of the dream.

Sitting up, dazed, he heard voices murmuring on deck. The foredeck
hatch was above his head. He pushed it open and stuck his head out.

The fog had thickened or it was drizzling—hard to say which—and
the air was coated with wet. He could just make out the government
dock barely a hundred yards away, moving in and out of swirling layers
of grey fog. MacIsaac had mentioned that the harbour lighthouse on
Kidston Island, shown on all the charts, had been down for two days;
the Coast Guard were changing the lens. Now the island itself had disappeared. So had the lobster boats and herring trawlers.

Maddie, in a bright yellow slicker, was leaning over the aft rail, talking to someone. Joe stood up. Peering through the foggy dew, he saw a
fellow in a dory that kept bumping the *Son*'s side gently, despite the fellow's holding it off with one arm.

"Anything the matter?" Joe called. He heard a boat somewhere, the
guttural snarl of an old Ford V8 or a Buick Six, probably on one of the
lobster boats. Had MacIsaac directed them to the wrong mooring? It

wouldn't be much fun trying to pick up another one in a strange harbour in that depth of fog. Visibility about twenty-five feet, not much of a tide, zero breeze.

"Good day to you, mister," the young man called. "Is everything all right? Do you have what you need?"

"I think we're all right. Are we all right here?"

"It's a beauty of a sailboat. Beautifully clean."

"Do you need the mooring?"

"No, no, you're plenty fine here. She'll hold you nice." The boy had a big jaw, a ridiculous pile of greased hair combed back and tapering into a sort of wedge. Rubber boots, flannel shirt buttoned up at the neck. A real hick, the sort who carried a comb in his breast pocket.

"Do you like to eat lobsters, miss?" he said to Maddie.

"Sure."

"Here you are then." He was holding up a paper grocery sack. "Bit heavy now; careful."

A waft of fog crossed the bow and for a moment Joe lost sight of his granddaughter except for the yellow blare of her slicker. Then he saw that the boy had shipped his oars and was standing up in the dory and Maddie was reaching out and taking the brown paper bag. She peered inside. "Wow."

"Caught this morning," he said. "Fresh as can be."

"How much do you want?" Joe said.

"No, no, mister, there's no charge."

"Three lobsters, and they're huge! Thank you," Maddie said. "That's so nice of you."

"You know how to fix them, do you? Have a pot that'll do? Have any crackers? Pliers and a hammer'll do."

"Oh, yes."

"Well, there you are."

He sat down and deftly slipped the oars into the locks. The dory was drifting and he dabbled the oars to stay in close.

"Oh, there's something else. Yes. A dance on tonight at the parish hall. A bit of a band, couple of fellows with guitars. Perhaps you'd like to see it."

"That sounds like a blast," Madeleine said.

"You like country music?"

"I like music, period. How do I get there?"

She sounded eager. After twelve days on a thirty-six-foot yawl with her seventy-three-year-old grandfather, she'd probably swim ashore if she had to. She had been calling him Captain Ahab ever since their whale sighting.

"I'm Kenneth MacIsaac. My father's the IGA. I'll come out to fetch you, miss. Say at eight o'clock? I warn you, it will be nothing fancy."

"I'll be here."

"That's fine," the boy called, pulling on his oars, already disappearing into the fog. "I'll see you."

What the hell, Joe thought. *The young need the young.*

~

He lay awake in his berth, listening to a buoy clanging somewhere and the creaking of the hull. Maddie was at the dance. There was hardly a stir from the rigging. He liked making things fast once on a mooring: sails covered, halyards snug, tiller secured. There was no breeze in the harbour, just the morose blanket of fog. And every now and then a sharp strain of music drifting across from the village.

Grabbing a flashlight, he looked at his watch. Just after eleven, Atlantic time. He wondered when the party would end and when MacIsaac might bring her back. He was beginning to wish that she hadn't gone, that MacIsaac had never appeared all shined up in his windbreaker, sport shirt, and cowboy boots, hair artfully piled and lacquered with some kind of oil. Fish oil, maybe. No, that wasn't fair. There was nothing really wrong with the boy except that he was a hick. And his lobsters had been fresh, the meat tender and sweet. They'd missed having sweet corn for steaming, but there'd been no produce at the IGA except carrots and a few tasteless-looking apples. Maybe deeper in the countryside the people still kept kitchen gardens. Tomorrow, if he and Maddie walked farther, they might be able to buy beans and sweet corn straight out of the field. And blueberries—there had to be blueberries on Cape Breton.

Maddie, anyway, hadn't seemed too disappointed when the young man reappeared, rowing gently out of the evening fog. "Ahoy the *Sea Son*," MacIsaac had called. "All aboard for dancing."

Maddie had kissed Joe on the cheek. "Sure you won't come?"

"No, no. Not for me."

She had stepped down neatly into the stern of the dory and then sat, the boy had pushed off, and that had been that—they were away, disappearing almost instantly into the silver fog. For a while Joe had heard the oars dipping but he wasn't able to see a goddamn thing. Going below, he had cleaned up the remains of their lobster supper, burned the paper plates in the wood stove, dumped the shells overboard, and gone to bed.

He ought to have been able to sleep. All day he'd felt a little bit sore in his chest, slightly drugged and tired, which he knew was his body fighting back from the strains of the journey. If anything he had underestimated the rigours of coming up the Nova Scotia coast, the constancy of the fog and the heavy force of those easterlies that never blew clear but just packed more fog on top of fog. Bras d'Or had felt like a return to real summer, but now that the ocean fog had caught up with them he was relieved their trip was over. Tomorrow he'd phone TCA and book their tickets on a flight to Montreal. MacIsaac Senior had promised he would arrange a car to take them to the Sydney airport.

He couldn't help remembering what country dances had been like in his day—not that he'd been to all that many outside of the weddings and wakes that everyone living along the river had attended, invited or not—the brawling and beatings, the coarse behaviour. Tonight's dance was at a church, young MacIsaac had said, the Catholic church; and it was 1960 and things weren't the way they had been, even in this lonely, fog-haunted corner of the world. Or were they? The boy's father had offered to sell a bottle of whisky-blanc and it was probably everywhere, part of the life, just as it had been up the Pontiac. Even if they weren't allowed to bring liquor inside the church, the young bucks at the dance would be stepping out to their cars and sucking it back.

He began to feel afraid for his granddaughter. For days he had had no company but Madeleine, the weather, and the sea. He'd been at sea so long, out of sight of land, that he hadn't been thinking straight when he'd let her go off with the boy. Cape Breton made down east Maine seem cosmopolitan. The storekeeper with his dour personality, the boy with his piled hair—these people had a bitter edge; they resented people from away, anyone who came sailing into their little harbour from places where the weather was mostly sunny.

He'd been irresponsible, letting her just go off like that. Maddie was a stranger in this sort of backwater, an innocent. She could handle a boat but she didn't know their ways up here. Cape Breton was like a foreign country. Madeleine had been well protected all her life, unlike his sisters in the clearing, with their stepfather. Maddie had been raised in one of the safest cities in the world. Things could get out of her control before she even knew she was in danger.

What in hell had he been thinking, sending her off to dance with a bunch of howling men, and how was he going to tell Margo if her daughter was lost in the back seat of a car on a back road in Cape Breton Island after her grandfather had seen her off to a Saturday-night dance in the company of the local bootlegger's son? This wasn't Montreal, wasn't even Kennebunk. This was a primitive town, and he knew something about places at the end of the earth.

He reached for his pants and started pulling them on, lying flat on his back in the V-berth. He buckled his belt, then sat up too quickly and banged his forehead on the bulkhead, so hard he was stunned.

The clarity of pain calmed him for a few moments. *Nothing's happened, nothing's wrong*, he thought to himself. *You're overdoing it now. It's the music, that's all, the wild music. She'll be fine. There's nothing wrong.*

The moment was like a gap blown open in the fog, but then it closed in again. The music screeching and sliding across the water was like a taunt, and it was the only thing reaching him through the fog. He dragged on a shirt and sweater and hauled himself up the companionway. A sense of redness burned on his forehead, and touching the spot, he saw blood on his fingertips. It didn't matter.

The deck was slick with moisture. The lighthouse on the island was still extinguished. He couldn't see the island or the government dock or anything on the mainland. He couldn't see the herring trawlers. There was no tide, no current—nothing but fog, the beautiful *Son* wrapped in a ball of grey wool. He heard the buoy banging but wasn't sure of its location. He knew he should check the chart but there wasn't time and he was only three hundred yards offshore, and even if he got turned about and headed the wrong way he'd probably make landfall on the island. A Catholic church, a courthouse, and an RCMP detachment didn't necessarily imply civilization. There would be roads clawing up those rugged mountains and people living along them, not town people.

His granddaughter was utterly dependent on the boy. She was in his power. She had no way of getting herself back out to the *Son* except Kenneth MacIsaac and his dory. If she had to stand on the government dock and yell for her grandfather to come and get her, maybe he would hear her but maybe he wouldn't. He didn't want her stranded in the town while men with hanks of greasy hair falling on their foreheads rumbled through the dead streets in battered, muddy cars. He didn't want her that vulnerable, or anywhere near. He'd been an idiot to bring her up here. The sailing had been far rougher than he'd predicted, the seas too big, the fogs too dense, the harbours too few.

Without being entirely aware of what he was doing he'd been unwinding the dinghy's painter from its cleat, drawing the dinghy alongside, and unhooking the life rail. Before stepping off he glanced at the compass. *Sea Son*'s bow was pointed south-southwest, but not very steadily; with no breeze and no perceptible tidal current, she was drifting on the mooring, and any other boats he came across in the fog would also be pointing haphazardly in all directions. But he only needed to row three hundred yards bearing north-northwest to make the government dock, or close to.

If there were lights in the village, and there had to be, the fog had buried them. He had known fog in Maine, but only up in Fundy had he ever tasted a fog like this, warm and almost smoky, a real pea soup.

As he was stepping awkwardly into the dinghy, a high-pitched ringing started in his right ear. He felt dizzy all of a sudden and froze, clutching the *Son*'s life rail. It passed after a few seconds, and he extended his foot and touched the painted wood of the dinghy's middle seat, wet and slippery. He sat down quickly and pushed off. The oars were tucked under the seats. He was fitting the oarlocks into their holes when it occurred to him that he should have brought a horn or at least a flashlight.

And he had forgotten to put on his shoes. His feet were bare, sitting in half an inch of warm water slopping around the dinghy. He considered going back but didn't want to waste time going alongside and cleating, or at least wrapping the painter on a winch, and clambering aboard and going down the steep companionway in the dark to retrieve his shoes from the cabin. Most of all he didn't want to have to step down into the dinghy again in the darkness and wet and risk the ringing in his ears and that blast of dizziness.

It was a tiny village, and he remembered that the Catholic church was very near the government dock. It was an odd, ornate little wooden church painted white and just up from the harbour. Everything in Baddeck was just up from the harbour. He wouldn't go inside, just stand across the road, satisfy himself it was okay and she was in no danger. He was already starting to feel calmer now that he was under way. He just needed one glimpse of her. If she was enjoying herself he wasn't going to march in like some hillbilly father and drag her away. It was a parish dance, after all. There really wasn't all that much to get excited about. A parish dance. Last Saturday of every month, young MacIsaac had said. The priest collected the dollar or quarter or whatever he charged for admission, kept an eye on things, and ran the show. She wasn't likely to find herself in trouble in a Catholic church.

The rowing calmed him. Being on the water always had. The fog was disorienting, though, and he ought to have left a compass in the dinghy. How many rules of good seamanship had he broken in the past ten minutes or however long it had been? But he never got spooked in fog the way some people did. He had never minded letting go, losing his bearings for a while, being a bit lost. He'd grown up in the bush, after all. You were never really lost because there was nowhere you weren't lost. Those woods in winter, cutting firewood at four dollars a cord and clawing his way out through deep snow. Lynx he'd seen maybe twice, snow rabbits, starving moose, black bears roaming hungrily in the breakup season. If you got lost it didn't seem to make much difference. It was only panic that caused trouble, and being alone had never frightened him; plenty other things did, but not that.

He knew she was going to be okay, that nothing bad would happen; it was just that wild music that had spooked him. Maddie was a sensible girl and the boy seemed decent and polite—more than you could say for a lot of them at that age.

His head hurt, not just the wound on his forehead but the back of his head too. He tried ignoring it but it was unrelenting. Pain was pushing at the bones of his skull. One thin streak of blood had run down his nose and chin; he could feel it. With both hands gripping the oars there was nothing to do except row to the dock and tie up. He'd need to clean up somewhere. He couldn't tell if it was a scrape or a gash, but she wasn't going to be happy to see it; he had better see if he could rinse it off somewhere. He wasn't going to make a scene at the dance; they weren't even going to know he was here. The things he remembered—the wildness and brutality, Mick Heaney slapping his mother, sawing away at his fiddle—that was all fifty, sixty years ago. That world was gone, dead and buried. If he tried holding on to things that had never belonged to him in the first place, something would get twisted, something would get broken. Fear wasn't a lesson he'd ever meant to teach anyone.

Oh Jesus, he thought, *where the hell is that fucking wharf?* He ought to have made it by now. Peering over his shoulder, he could see nothing through the blankness of fog. No cars or lights. Even if he had a flashlight it wouldn't have done any good. Maybe if he had a horn, if there was someone on the dock to hear.

"Hello, hello!" he shouted. "Ahoy there, Baddeck! Looking for the dock! Ahoy there!"

Nothing. He gritted his teeth and pulled violently, and the left oar suddenly slipped out of its oarlock. For a few moments he lost control of the dinghy as it spun about. He held on to the oar and fitted its leather back into the oarlock, but he had lost his sense of direction.

"Follow the tide, follow the tide," he told himself, speaking aloud, just like an old man. He stared at the water surface, trying to get a sense of the flow, but if there was a tide it was very weak, or maybe he was moving on it. His head hurt. He shipped the right oar and touched the blood on his nose, then reached over, scooped up a handful of water, and splashed it on his face. The salt stung the gash on his forehead and dripped into his eyes. He was angry with himself. He tried recalling the harbour chart, the mooring field wedged between Kidston Island and Baddeck village on the mainland. He needed to calm down and listen for the buoy; it was probably at the mouth of the harbour. If he could reach the buoy, at worst he would just tie up to it and wait. Baddeck Bay narrowed to the northeast.

Not a single car, not one headlight. Either the town was smaller and even deader than he'd thought or the fog was thicker. There was a slight chance of missing everything and sliding out into the big lake—really an inland sea—but if he could keep to one heading there was a better than even chance he'd make a landfall very soon, somewhere. He dug in with the oars. His shoulders were starting to ache. The fog was warm but he was cold, cold inside. When you bled, your warmth leaked out: he'd read that somewhere. It occurred to him that he might be in real danger now.

"Ahoy, Baddeck!" he shouted again.

Then he heard a voice calling through the fog. "Granddaddy? Are you out there? Is that you?"

"It's me!" he shouted. "I'm in the dinghy. Where are you?"

"On the dock!" Maddie called. "We're just getting into the dory. Are you lost? Do you want us to come and find you?" The clear, bright line of her voice coming through the fog.

"I'm not lost," he said, mostly to himself.

"Ahoy, mister! Ahoy there!" He recognized the young man's voice, Kenneth MacIsaac.

"I'm putting up a good light," MacIsaac called. "Just hooking up the battery; give me a second now."

"Should we come and find you?" Maddie called.

"No, stay where you are." Gripping the oars, he started rowing towards the sound of their voices. All his life he'd needed their voices—outside himself, bright and alive, to take a bearing on, to find his way. "Keep talking! I'm coming to you. I'll see you in a moment."

AUTHOR'S NOTE

This is a work of fiction. Characters inspired by real people (what fictional characters are not?) soon asserted themselves and began feeling, thinking, and acting in ways that had nothing to do with anyone's family history or genealogy. My O'Briens live in the world of this novel, nowhere else.

A NOTE ABOUT THE AUTHOR

PETER BEHRENS is the author of the Governor General's Award–winning novel *The Law of Dreams*, published around the world to wide acclaim, and a collection of short stories, *Night Driving*. His short stories and essays have appeared in *Atlantic Monthly*, *Tin House*, *Saturday Night*, and the *National Post*. He was born in Montreal and lives on the coast of Maine with his wife and son.

A NOTE ON THE TYPE

The text of this book was set in Sabon, a typeface designed by Jan Tschichold (1902–1974), the well-known German typographer. Based loosely on the original designs by Claude Garamond (ca. 1480–1561), Sabon was named for the famous Lyons punch cutter Jacques Sabon, who is thought to have brought some of Garamond's matrices to Frankfurt.